KINGDOM
OF THE
CURSED

Also by Kerri Maniscalco

Kingdom of the Wicked
Kingdom of the Cursed

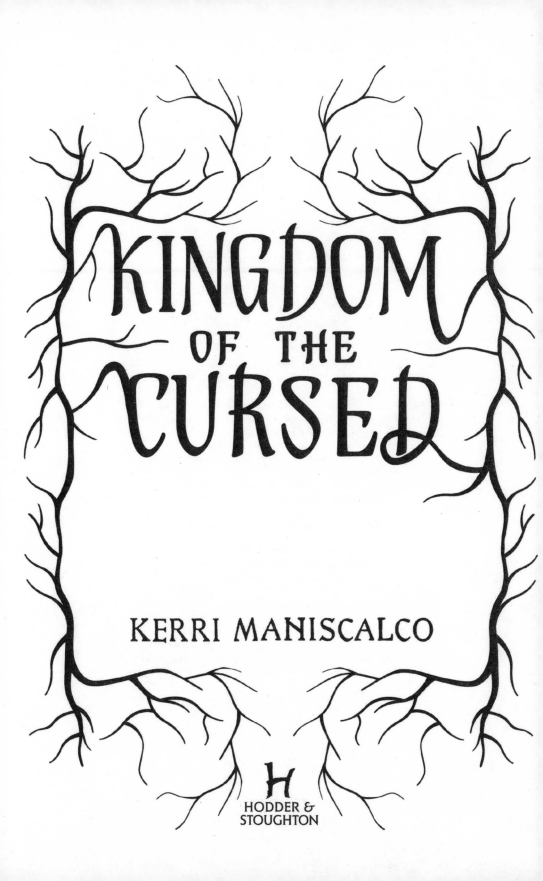

KINGDOM
OF THE
CURSED

KERRI MANISCALCO

HODDER &
STOUGHTON

First published in Great Britain in 2021 by Hodder & Stoughton
An Hachette UK company

5

Copyright © Kerri Maniscalco 2021

The right of Kerri Maniscalco to be identified as the Author of the Work has been
asserted by her in accordance with the Copyright, Designs and Patents Act 1988.

A CIP catalogue record for this title is available from the British Library

Hardback ISBN 978 1 529 35050 0
Trade Paperback ISBN 978 1 529 35052 4
eBook ISBN 978 1 529 35051 7

Printed and bound in Great Britain by Clays Ltd, Elcograf S.p.A.

Hodder & Stoughton policy is to use papers that are natural, renewable
and recyclable products and made from wood grown in sustainable
forests. The logging and manufacturing processes are expected to conform
to the environmental regulations of the country of origin.

Hodder & Stoughton Ltd
Carmelite House
50 Victoria Embankment
London EC4Y 0DZ

www.hodder.co.uk

For you, dear reader. Always.

'I come
To take you to
the other shore across,
Into eternal darkness,
there to dwell
In fierce heat
and in ice.'

Dante Alighieri, *Inferno*

On an unusually chilly summer eve, amidst a howling storm, twins arrived. It was not the start of an enchanted fairy tale, however. Those who'd been watching, waiting, recognized it for the omen it was. One would forfeit her mortal life, the other would sell her soul. Coven elders argued the hows and whys, but all agreed on one fact: the twins marked the start of dark days. Now, as one turned to fury and eyed the devil's throne, and the other lay heartless, surrounded by death, others whispered of a new prophecy—one that damned both witches and demons alike.

—Notes from the secret di Carlo grimoire

SOMETIME BEFORE

Once upon a cursed dawn, a king strode through his castle, his footsteps thundering down the corridor, sending even the shadows skittering away to avoid notice. He was in a foul mood and it was growing darker the closer he got to *her*. He sensed her vengeance long before he'd entered this wing of the castle. It swarmed like an angry mob outside the entrance to his throne room, but he paid it little mind. The witch was a plague upon this land.

One he'd eradicate at once.

Silver-tipped wings of white flame burst from between his shoulder blades as he flung open the double doors. They crashed against the wall, nearly splitting the wood in half, but the intruder didn't glance up from her indolent position sprawled across the throne. *His* throne.

Refusing to look in his direction, she caressed her leg the way an attentive lover might try with an eager partner. Her gown split up the side, revealing smooth skin from her ankle to her hip. She drew lazy circles on her calf, arching back as her fingers drifted higher. His presence did nothing to dissuade her from running her hands up, along her outer thighs.

"Get out."

The witch's attention flicked to his. "Talking with you hasn't worked. Nor logic and reasoning. Now I have a rather tempting new offer for you." Over the thin material of her gown, she slowly skimmed the peaks of her breasts, her gaze growing heavy as she boldly stared at him. "Take off your pants."

He crossed his arms, his expression forbidding. Not even his maker could bend him to his whims. And she was far from his maker.

"Get out," he repeated. "Leave before I *force* you."

"*Try.*" In one inhumanly graceful movement, she swung herself into a standing position, her long silver dress gleaming like a sword carving through the heavens. Gone was any further attempt at seduction. "Touch me, and I will destroy all you hold dear. Your majesty."

Her tone had turned mocking, as if he wasn't worthy of the title or respect.

He laughed then, the sound as menacing as the dagger now pressed against her slender throat. She wasn't the only one blessed with immortal speed.

"You seem to be mistaken," he all but growled. "There is nothing I hold dear. I want you out of this realm before nightfall. If you're not gone by then, I'll set my hellhounds loose. When they're finished, whatever's left will be tossed in the Lake of Fire."

He waited to scent her fear. Instead, she jerked forward and slashed her throat across the blade in one brutal motion. Blood spilled over her shimmering gown, splattered across the smooth marble floor, dirtied his cuffs. Jaw clenched, he wiped down the dagger.

Unfazed by her new vicious necklace, she stepped away from

him, her smile more wicked than the worst of his brothers. The wound stitched itself together.

"Are you certain about that? There isn't *anything* you yearn for?" When he didn't respond, her annoyance flared. "Maybe the rumors are true, after all. You have no heart in that armored chest of yours." She circled him, her skirts smearing a trail of blood across the once pristine floor. "Perhaps we should carve you open, take a look."

She eyed the unusual silver and white wings of flame at his back, her grin turning feral. The wings were his favorite weapons and he welcomed the fierce, white-hot heat that made his enemies flinch away in terror or fall to their knees, weeping tears of blood.

With one quick snap of her fingers, they turned the color of ash, then disappeared.

Panic seized him as he tried—and failed—to summon them.

"Here is a trick as nasty as the devil himself."

Her voice was both young and old as she spoke her spell into existence. He swore. Of course. That was why she'd spilled blood; it was an offering to one of her ruthless goddesses.

"From this day forward, a curse will sweep through this land. You will forget all but your hate. Love, kindness, every good thing in your world will cease. One day that will change. When you know true happiness, I vow to take whatever you love, too."

He'd barely heard a word the dark-haired witch said, as he strained to summon his wings to no avail. Whatever she'd done with them, his beloved weapons were well and truly missing.

His vision had nearly gone red with bloodlust, but he reined in his temper through sheer force of will. The witch would be of no use to him dead now, especially if he ever hoped to regain what was stolen.

She clicked her tongue once, as if disappointed he didn't release his inner monster to fight back, and started to turn away. He didn't bother charging after her. When he spoke, his voice was as dark and quiet as the night. "You're wrong."

She paused, tossing a glance over a delicate shoulder. "Oh?"

"The devil may be nasty, but he doesn't perform tricks." His smile was temptation incarnate. "He bargains."

For the first time the witch seemed uncertain. She'd thought herself to be the most cunning, lethal one. She'd forgotten whose throne room she stood in and how he'd clawed himself onto that cursed and wretched thing. He would take immense pleasure in reminding her.

This was the kingdom of the Wicked, and *he* ruled them all.

"Care to strike a deal?"

ONE

Hell was not what I expected.

Ignoring the traitorous Prince of Wrath at my side, I took a quiet, shuddering breath as smoke wafted around from the demon magic he'd used to transport us here. To the Seven Circles.

In the brief moments it took us to travel from the cave in Palermo to this realm, I'd concocted various visions of our arrival, each one more terrible than the last. In every nightmare, I'd pictured a cascade of fire and brimstone raining down. Flames burning hot enough to scorch my soul or melt the flesh right off my bones. Instead, I fought a sudden shiver.

Through the lingering smoke and mist I could just make out walls hewn from a strange, opaque gemstone that shot up farther than I could see. They were either deep blue or black, as if the darkest part of the sea had swelled up to an impossible height and had frozen in place.

Chills raced down my spine. I resisted the urge to breathe warmth into my hands or turn to Wrath for comfort. He was not my friend, and he certainly wasn't my protector. He was exactly what his brother Envy had claimed: the worst of the seven demon princes.

A monster among beasts.

I could never allow myself to forget what he was. One of the Wicked. The immortal beings who stole souls for the devil, and the selfish midnight creatures my grandmother warned my twin and me to hide from our whole lives. Now I willingly promised to wed their king, the Prince of Pride, to end a curse. Or so I'd led them to believe.

The metal corset my future husband had given me earlier tonight turned unbearably cold in the frigid air. Layers of my dark, glittering skirts were too light to provide any true protection or warmth, and my slippers were little more than scraps of black silk with thin leather soles.

Ice sluiced through my veins. I couldn't help but think this was yet another wicked scheme designed by my enemy to unsettle me.

Puffs of breath floated like ghosts in front of my face. Haunting, ethereal. Disturbing. Goddess above. I was really *in* Hell. If the demon princes didn't get to me first, Nonna Maria was certainly going to kill me. Especially when my grandmother discovered I'd signed my soul away to Pride. *Blood and bones.* The devil.

An image of the scroll that bound me to House Pride flashed through my mind. I couldn't believe I'd signed the contract in blood. Despite my earlier confidence in my plot to infiltrate this world and avenge my sister's murder, I felt completely unprepared now that I was standing here.

Wherever "here" was, exactly. It didn't appear as if we'd made it inside any of the seven royal demon Houses. I don't know why I thought Wrath would make this journey easy on me.

"Are we waiting for my betrothed to arrive?"

Silence.

I shifted uncomfortably.

Smoke still drifted close enough to obscure my full view, and with my demonic escort refusing to speak, my mind started to taunt me with a wide array of inventive fears. For all I knew, Pride was standing before us, waiting to claim his bride in the flesh.

I listened hard, straining to hear any sound of an approach through the smoke. Of anything. There was nothing aside from the frantic pitter-patter of my heart.

No screams of the eternally tortured and cursed. Absolute, unnerving silence surrounded us. It felt heavy—as if all hope had been abandoned a millennium ago and all that remained was the crushing quiet of despair. It would be so easy to give up, to lie down and let the darkness in. This realm was winter in all its harsh, unforgiving glory.

And we hadn't even passed through the gates yet...

Panic seized me. I wanted to be back in my city—with its sea-kissed air and summery people—so badly, my chest ached. But I'd made my choice, and I'd see it through, no matter what. Vittoria's true murderer was still out there. And I'd walk through the gates of Hell a thousand times over to find him. My location changed, but my ultimate goal did not.

I took a deep breath, my emotions settling with the action.

The smoke finally dissipated, revealing my first unobstructed glimpse of the underworld.

We were alone in a cave, similar to the one we'd left high above the sea in Palermo, the very place I'd set up my bone circle and first summoned Wrath nearly two months before, but also so different my stomach lurched at the alien landscape.

From somewhere above us a few silvery pools of moonlight trickled in. It wasn't much but offered enough illumination to see the desolate, rock-scattered ground glistening with frost.

Several meters away a towering gate stood tall and menacing, not unlike the silent prince standing beside me. Columns—carved from obsidian and depicting people being tortured and murdered in brutal fashions—bracketed two doors made entirely of skulls. Human. Animal. Demon. Some horned, others fanged. All disturbing. My focus landed on what I assumed was the handle: an elk skull with an enormous set of frost-coated antlers.

Wrath, the mighty demon of war and betrayer of my soul, shifted. A tiny spark of annoyance had me glancing his way. His penetrating gaze was already trained on me. That same cold look on his face. I wanted to claw out his heart and stomp on it to get some *hint* of an emotion. Anything would be better than the icy indifference he now wore so well.

He'd turned on me the second it suited his needs. He was a selfish creature. Just like Nonna had warned. And I'd been a fool to believe otherwise.

We stared at each other for an extended beat.

Here, in the shadows of the underworld, his dark gold eyes glinted like the ruby-tipped crown on his head. My pulse ticked faster the longer our gazes remained locked in battle. His hold on me tightened slightly, and it was only then that I realized I was clasping his hand in a white-knuckled grip. I dropped it and stepped away.

If he was annoyed or amused or even furious, I wouldn't know. His expression still hadn't changed; he was as remote as he'd been when he offered that contract with Pride a few minutes ago. If that's the way he wanted things to be between us now, fine.

I didn't need or want him. In fact, I'd say he could go straight to Hell, but we'd both accomplished that.

He watched as I reined in my thoughts. I forced myself into a frozen calm I was far from feeling. Knowing how well he could sense emotions, it was probably futile. I looked him over.

Doing my best to emulate the demon prince, I mustered up my haughtiest tone. "The infamous gates of Hell, I presume."

He arched a dark brow as if asking if *that* was the best I could come up with.

Anger replaced lingering fear. At least he was still good for something. "Is the devil too high and mighty to meet his future queen here? Or is he afraid of a dank cave?"

Wrath's answering smile was all sharp edges and wicked delight. "This isn't a cave. It's a void outside the Seven Circles."

He placed a hand on the small of my back and guided me forward. I was so shocked by the pleasant feel of him, the tender intimacy of his action, I didn't step away. Pebbles skittered beneath our feet but didn't make a sound. Aside from our voices, the lack of noise was jarring enough that I almost lost my balance. Wrath steadied me before letting go.

"It's the place stars fear to enter," he whispered near my ear, his warm breath a severe contrast against the frosty air. I shuddered. "But *never* the devil. Darkness is seduced by him. As is fear."

He ran bare knuckles down my spine, enticing more goose bumps to rise. My breath hitched. I spun around and knocked his hand away.

"Take me to see Pride. I'm tired of your company."

The ground rumbled below us. "Your pride didn't appear in that bone circle the night you spilled blood and summoned me. It was your wrath. Your fury."

"That may be true, *your highness*, but the scroll I signed said 'House Pride,' didn't it?"

I stepped closer, heart thrashing as I crowded his space. The heat of his body radiated around me like sunshine, warm and enticing. It reminded me of home. The new ache in my chest was acute, consuming. I sharpened my tongue like a blade and aimed straight for his icy heart, hoping to penetrate the wall he'd so expertly erected between us. Wrong or not, I wanted to hurt him the way his deception had gutted me.

"Therefore, I chose the devil, not you. How does that feel? Knowing I'd prefer to bed a monster for eternity rather than subject myself to *you* again, Prince Wrath."

His attention dropped to my lips and lingered. A seductive gleam entered his eyes as I returned the favor. He might not admit it, but he wanted to kiss me. My mouth curved into a vicious grin; finally, he'd lost that cold indifference. Too bad for him I was now forbidden.

He stared a moment longer, then said with lethal quiet, "You choose the devil?"

"Yes."

We stood near enough to share breath now. I refused to back away. And he did, too.

"If that's what you wish, speak it to this realm. As a matter of fact"—he yanked his dagger out from inside his suit jacket—"if you're so certain about the devil, swear a blood oath. If pride truly is your sin of choice, I imagine you won't say no."

Challenge burned in his gaze as he handed the blade to me, hilt-first. I snatched his House dagger and pressed the sharp metal to my fingertip. Wrath crossed his arms and gave me a flat look. He didn't think I'd go through with it. Maybe it *was* my cursed pride, but it also felt a little like my temper was raging as I pricked my finger and handed the serpent blade back. I'd already signed Pride's contract; there was no reason to hesitate now. What was done was done.

"I, Emilia Maria di Carlo, freely choose the devil."

A single drop of blood splattered to the ground, sealing the vow. I flicked my attention to Wrath. Something ignited in the depths of his eyes, but he turned away before I could read what it was. He shoved the dagger into his jacket and started making his way toward the gates, leaving me alone at the edge of nothingness.

I thought about running, but there was nowhere to go.

I glanced around once more and hurried after the demon, falling into step beside him. I wrapped my arms around myself, trying desperately to stop the increasing shivers, which only succeeded in making me shudder more. Wrath had taken his warmth with him, and now the metal corset top bit into my skin with renewed vigor. If we stayed out here much longer, I'd freeze to death. I conjured memories of warmth, peace.

I'd only ever felt this cold once—in northern Italy—and I'd been young and thrilled by the snow then. I'd thought it was romantic; now I saw the truth: it was beautifully dangerous.

Much like my current traveling companion.

My teeth chattered like tiny hammers, the only noise in the void. "How can we hear each other?"

"Because I will it."

Arrogant beast. I released a quivering huff. It was meant to come across as exasperated, but I feared it only gave away how cold I was. A heavy velvet cloak appeared from thin air, draping itself around my shoulders. I don't know where Wrath magicked it from and didn't care.

I pulled it tighter, grateful for its warmth. I opened my mouth to thank the demon but stopped myself with a swift internal shake. Wrath hadn't acted out of kindness or even chivalry. I imagined he did it largely to make sure I didn't die this close to accomplishing his mission.

If I recalled correctly, delivery of my soul to Pride granted him freedom from the underworld. Something he once said he prized above all else.

How exceptionally marvelous for him. His stay was over just as mine was beginning. And all he had to do was betray me to secure his heart's greatest desire.

I supposed I understood that well enough.

Wrath continued toward the gate and didn't look in my direction again. He pressed a hand to the column closest to us and whispered a word in a foreign tongue, too low for me to hear. Gold light pulsed from his palm and flowed into the black gemstone.

A moment later, the gates slowly creaked open. I couldn't see what lay beyond and my mind promptly crafted all sorts of terrible things. The demon prince offered no formal invitation; he prowled toward the opening he'd made without bothering to see if I followed.

I took a deep breath and steeled my nerves. No matter what was waiting for us, I'd do what I must to achieve my goals. I nestled into my cloak and started forward.

Wrath paused on the threshold to the underworld and finally deigned to look at me again. His expression was harsher than his tone, which halted me in my tracks.

"A word of caution."

"We're about to enter Hell," I said sardonically. "The caution speech may be a little late."

He was not amused. "In the Seven Circles there are three rules to abide by. First, don't ever reveal your true fears."

I hadn't planned to. "Why?"

"This world will turn itself inside out to torture you." I opened my mouth, but he held up a hand. "Second, control your desires or they will taunt you with illusions easily confused with reality. You had a taste of what that's like when you met Lust. Each of your desires will be magnified tenfold here, particularly when we enter the Sin Corridor."

"The Sin Corridor." I didn't pose it as a question, but Wrath answered anyway.

"New subjects of the realm are tested to see which royal House their dominant sin aligns best with. You will experience a certain...prodding...of emotions as you pass through it."

"I signed my soul to Pride. Why do I need to see where I'm best suited?"

"Live long enough to find that answer out yourself."

I swallowed my rising discomfort. Nonna always cautioned that bad news came in threes, which meant the worst was yet to come. "The third rule is..."

His attention slid to the finger I'd pricked. "Be cautious when making blood bargains with a prince of Hell. And under no circumstances should you ever make one involving the devil. What's his is his. Only a fool would fight or challenge him."

I ground my teeth together. The true games of deception had clearly begun. His warning vaguely reminded me of a note from our family grimoire, and I wondered how we'd come to hold that knowledge. I tucked those thoughts away, focusing instead on my growing anger.

He was no doubt stoking my emotions with his namesake

power. Which enraged me all the more. "Signing my soul away wasn't quite good enough. So you resorted to trickery. At least you're consistent."

"Someday you'll see it as a favor."

Unlikely. I curled my injured hand into a fist. Wrath met my gaze again, and a smile tugged at the corners of his sensuous mouth. He undoubtedly sensed my growing fury.

One day, soon enough, I would make him pay for this.

I gave him a dazzling smile, letting myself imagine how good it would feel when I finally destroyed him. His expression shuttered and he inclined his head—as if reading my every thought and emotion and silently vowed to do the same. In this hatred we were united.

Holding his intense stare, I nodded back, thankful for his treachery. It was the last time I'd fall for his lies. With any luck, though, it would be the start of him and his wicked brothers falling for mine. I'd need to play my role well, or I'd end up dead like the other witch brides.

I brushed past him and strode through the gates of Hell as if I owned them. "Take me to my new home. I'm ready to greet my dear husband."

TWO

From the darkness of the cave we exited onto a gleaming mountaintop tundra.

I blinked away the sudden stinging in my eyes and beheld this cruel, unforgiving world. Goddess curse me. This was as far away from home as I could get.

There was no sea, no warmth, no brightly burning sun. We stood in the hollow of a steep snow-covered trail, barely wide enough to walk on side by side.

A biting wind snarled through the craggy mountain pass and tore through my cloak. Behind us the gates closed with a clank that echoed loudly between the snowcapped mountains. I tensed at the unexpected clamor. It was the first noise I'd heard outside the void and it couldn't sound more foreboding if it tried.

I spun around, heart thundering, and watched demon magic spring up from the bowels of this land and slither up the gates. The same violet-blue thorn-covered vines that had bound Vittoria's diary wound through eye sockets and jawbones, twisting until the off-white skulls glowed with an icy, unearthly hue.

Cold air cut my breath short. I was trapped in the under-world, surrounded by the Malvagi, alone. I'd acted out of fear and desperation—two essential ingredients in creating a disaster. A flash of my twin's desecrated body stamped that feeling into the frozen ground.

"You told me the gates were broken." There was an impressive bite in my tone. "That demons were slipping through, ready to wage war on Earth."

"The Horn of Hades has been returned."

"Of course."

The devil's horns were needed to lock the gates. Apparently any demon prince could wield them, and I hadn't known to ask Wrath for clarification. It was another way he'd worked around the "not being able to directly lie to me" rule of my summoning.

If that part was even true.

I loosened a breath and shifted back around, staring out at the landscape. On our right a sharp drop-off was carved through the frost-coated terrain. In the distance, barely visible through either a covering of fog or a far-off storm, turrets on a castle reached up, pointing spindly fingers of accusation at the heavens.

"Is that..." I swallowed hard. "Is that where Pride lives?"

"Not so anxious to meet him now?" A smug expression ghosted across Wrath's features before he schooled his face into indifference. "The first circle is Lust's territory. Think of the lay-out like the Seven Hills of Rome. Each prince controls their own region or summit. Pride's circle cannot be seen from here. It sits toward the center, near my House."

Being so close to Lust's stronghold wasn't comforting. I hadn't forgotten how his demonic influence had made me feel. How I'd lusted after Wrath and drank too much apple-honey wine and had danced without a care in the universe while a murderer hunted witches.

I'd also never forget how hard it had been to crawl back to my senses after Lust had cruelly wrested his powers away, leaving me an empty husk. If it hadn't been for Wrath's interference, I might still be in that dark, crushing place.

I could almost feel despair trailing a sharp nail across my throat now, begging, tempting...I pretended that the growing fear was muck beneath my shoes and squashed it.

Wrath watched me closely, his gaze alight with keen interest. Perhaps he was waiting for me to drop to my knees and beg him to escort me back home. It would take far more than standing in the coldest corner of Hell for me to ever lower myself before him.

"I thought it would be warmer," I admitted, earning an amused look from the demon. "Fire and brimstone—the works."

"Mortals have peculiar cautionary tales about gods and monsters and their supposed creator, but the truth, as you can see, is very different from what you've heard."

I was distracted from further inquiry by a soft clicking. Up a dizzying incline on our left, a smattering of bare-branched trees stood, swaying in the arctic wind, their limbs lightly clacking against one another. Something about them reminded me of old crones sitting together, using bones as knitting needles. If I narrowed my eyes, I almost swore I saw the shadowy outline of their figures. I blinked and the image was gone. Almost immediately after, a low growl floated in on the wind.

I glanced at Wrath, but he didn't seem to notice the peculiar vision or hear anything worthy of note. It had been a very long, very emotionally charged day and my imagination was getting the better of me. I shook the unsettling feeling away.

"This is the Sin Corridor," Wrath continued, unknowingly interrupting my worries. "*Transvenio* magic is forbidden on this stretch of land the first time you cross into this realm, so you'll need to travel by foot."

"I have to do it alone?"

Wrath raked his attention over me. "No."

I released a slow, quiet breath. Thank the goddess for small favors. "Why is it necessary for people to pass through here?"

"It is a way for newcomers to form alliances with others who share their dominant sin."

I considered that. "If I tend toward anger, I'd be best aligned with House Wrath." The prince nodded. "And others who are best suited to other sins... would they be put off by other demon houses? Let's say a member of House Wrath consorted with House Sloth; would they be scandalized by the other in some way?"

"Not exactly scandalized, but close. Mortals align themselves with political parties and causes. It's not unlike that here, but we deal in vice."

"Are demons and humans tested the same way?"

Wrath seemed to choose his next words carefully. "Most mortals never reach the Sin Corridor, or the Seven Circles. They tend to imprison themselves on their own separate isle outside the gates, off the western shore. It's a self-inflicted punishment of sorts."

"You don't lock them away in the Prison of Damnation?"

"The isle is the prison. They live in a reality of their own making. At any point they can leave. Most never do. They live and die on their isle and begin again."

It was a hell in its own way. "Nonna said Star Witches were the guardians between realms. Why would mortals and the Wicked need guards if they never leave?"

"Maybe mortal souls—and my brothers—are not all they keep watch over."

Vague and frustrating as always. "I still don't understand why *I* need to be tested at all."

"Then I suggest you heed my earlier warning and focus on surviving."

He issued it as both a challenge and a haughty command to stop asking questions. I was too worried to verbally spar. Threat of death hung over me, low and dark like the gathering clouds. The stupid prince dragged his gaze over me again, letting it linger on my soft curves.

I wasn't wearing my amulet—he still had possession of it—so there was no confusing where his focus landed. Even covered by the cloak, I swore I felt the heat of his attention like a physical caress on my skin.

Thoughts of death vanished. "Is there a problem with my bodice?"

"Seems as if your testing has begun. I was checking your cloak."

I exhaled slowly and bit down on several colorful curses that sprang to mind.

He smirked as if my annoyance pleased him to no end. Still grinning, he swiftly moved down the steep mountain pass, his steps steady and sure despite the snow and ice.

I couldn't believe... was he packing the snow down so I could walk through it in my delicate shoes? Impeccable demon manners hard at work again.

He really would do anything to see me safely delivered to Pride.

Speaking of that particular sin…I lifted my chin, my tone and demeanor more supercilious than any mortal king or queen born to rule could ever hope to achieve. And why shouldn't I feel superior? I was about to rule the underworld. It was time Wrath showed some respect to his queen. "I am perfectly able to make my own way. You may run off now."

"I did not take you for the sort to cut off their nose to spite their face."

"If I cannot walk through snow without assistance, I might as well slit my throat now and be done with it. I do not need you or anyone else to hold my hand. In fact, I would like you to leave me alone. I'll make better time without you."

He stopped walking and glanced over his shoulder. There was no warmth or teasing in his expression now. "Fight the Sin Corridor, or I will leave you to your prideful hubris. You are more susceptible to falling under the influence of a particular sin when showing early attributes of it. That is my final warning and all the help I will give. Take it for what it is, or leave it."

I gritted my teeth and did my best to follow his trail. With each step I took deeper into the underworld, it felt like the remaining pieces of myself were slowly shedding. I couldn't help but wonder if anything familiar would be left of me by the time I returned home.

As if in answer to my circling worries, a simmering rage started to burn through me as we traveled for miles in silence. Undoubtedly, I was now being tested for wrath. It was familiar, welcome. Even though I should make sure I aligned best with pride, I tended to my anger while we picked our way down the trail, crossed over a frozen stream, and paused near a slightly wider, flatter expanse that peered over a smaller mountain range.

Clusters of evergreens that looked like the juniper and cedar sketches in Nonna's grimoire fanned out in a semicircle around the easternmost corner where we'd paused.

Above them, angry clouds raced across the sky. Lightning lashed out like a great beast's tongue, and a roar of thunder followed a heartbeat later. Unblinking, I watched as the dark mass galloped closer. I'd witnessed plenty of storms, but none that moved faster than the goddesses who sought vengeance. It was as if the very atmosphere was possessed.

Or perhaps this world resented its newest inhabitant and was making its displeasure known. It had that much in common with Wrath.

A few minutes later, we stopped our relentless march.

"This will have to do."

Wrath removed his suit jacket and draped it carefully over a low-hanging branch. I'd been wrong earlier: his dagger wasn't shoved into his jacket; he wore a leather shoulder holster over his inky shirt, and the gold hilt gleamed as he twisted around. He undid the buttons at his cuffs, quickly rolled back his sleeves, then began gathering ice-coated branches.

"What are you doing?"

"Building shelter. Unless you'd like to sleep in a storm, I suggest grabbing some evergreen branches and beating ice off them. We'll use the ones you collect to lay on."

"I'm not sleeping with you." For many reasons, the most glaring being I was betrothed to his brother and—regardless of the survival aspect—I doubted the devil would be pleased if I snuggled next to another demon prince.

KERRI MANISCALCO

Wrath cracked a branch off the nearest cedar and glanced at me. "Your choice." He swept an arm out. "But I will not nurse you back to health when you fall ill." He gave me a hard look. "If you don't want to freeze to death, I suggest moving swiftly."

Not wanting to be tested for wrath or pride—or any other sin again—I swallowed any further protestations and went searching for branches. I found some a few paces away from where Wrath worked and knocked chunks of snow and ice from them as quickly as I could. Surprisingly, I moved as fast as the demon prince. In moments, I had almost more than I could carry. Which was good since my fingers were turning red and getting stiff from the cold and wet.

Once I gathered up a heaping armful, I hauled them back to our campsite. Clouds swirled around angrily, and thunder shook the ground. We had minutes left before the first plump drops hit, if we were lucky. Wrath had already created a small circular shelter beneath one of the denser trees and was in the middle of pushing snow up and around the branches he'd driven into the ground. The exterior walls were solid snow, the roof was thatched branches, and we'd both probably have to lay curled on our sides to fit. I couldn't imagine surviving the night in a chamber made of winter's offerings, but Wrath seemed to think we'd be safe.

I looked up; the large evergreen tree towering above us would also provide an added barrier of protection. It was a smart location to choose.

Without turning, Wrath stuck his arm out. "Hand them over."

I did as he not-so-gently asked, giving him one branch at a time, all the while dreaming of whipping him upside the head with them. He laid them in a row, making sure the entire ground was covered in two layers of greens.

24

He moved swiftly and efficiently, as if he'd done this a thousand times before. And he probably had. I was not the first soul he'd stolen for the devil. But I would be his last.

Once he placed the final branch down, he started unbuttoning his shirt, careful to avoid the leather holster. That he kept on. Powerful muscles rippled as he shrugged out of the shirt, and I couldn't help but stare at the serpent tattoo that wound up and around his right arm and shoulder. It seemed grander here, more detailed and striking.

Maybe that was because his skin looked darker when contrasted against the pale backdrop of this land, and the metallic gold lines stood out more vividly.

I cleared my throat. "Why are you undressing? Are you affected by the magic here, too?"

He looked up. Sweat dampened the dark hair at his brow, making him appear mortal for a change. "Take off your corset."

"I'd rather not." I gave him an incredulous look. "What in the seven hells do you think you're doing?"

"Giving you something to wear so you don't freeze your ass off in that metal." He held his shirt out but pulled it back before I grasped it, eyes glittering with mirth. "Unless you'd prefer to sleep in the nude. Lady's choice."

My face heated. "Why can't you just magic more clothing?"

"Any use of magic during your first journey in the Sin Corridor is considered interference."

"You magicked a cloak."

"Before we crossed into the true underworld."

"What will you sleep in?"

His expression turned positively wicked as he raised a brow.

Oh.

25

I cursed this world and the devil and marched inside our chamber made of snow and ice and took the proffered shirt. I quickly removed my cloak and set it on the ground. Being a gentleman, Wrath exited the chamber—long enough to retrieve his jacket—and looked me over when he crowded back into the small space. So much for good manners.

His lips twitched as I twisted and tried turning the stupid garment around without touching him. It wouldn't budge. And neither would he. I glared at the demon as if my current predicament was all his fault. He seemed utterly delighted by my anger, the heathen.

"I need your help," I finally said. "I can't undo it myself."

The infernal prince inspected my corset with the same level of enthusiasm as if I'd asked him to recite a sonnet by light of a full moon, but he didn't deny my request. "Turn around."

"Try not to look too thrilled, or I might think you like me."

"Count your blessings. My liking you would be a dangerous thing."

I snorted. "Why? Would you ruin me for all other demon princes?"

"Something close."

He smiled and motioned for me to turn. His fingers moved deftly across the ribbons crisscrossing down my back, tugging and undoing with militaristic precision.

I held the front of my top to keep myself from spilling out as the back fell open a moment later, exposing my skin. Frost-kissed air danced over me.

I'd never gotten out of a corset that quickly before. Either his supernatural senses aided him, or he had a *lot* of practice with undressing women.

Unbidden, a flash of him bedding someone crossed my mind in strikingly vivid detail. I saw perfectly filed nails digging into his back, long, tanned legs wrapping around his hips, soft groans of pleasure escaping as he rhythmically thrusted.

A dark feeling slithered through me at the thought. I ground my teeth together, suddenly biting back a string of accusations as I spun around. If I didn't know any better, I'd think I was...

"Envious." Wrath easily detected my change in mood.

"Stop reading my emotions." I jerked my attention up to his. His expression was wiped clean. Gone was any glint of wry humor or wickedness. He stood rigidly, as if forcing himself to become an immoveable block of ice. Apparently, the idea of touching me that way was revolting.

"The corridor will continue testing you." He observed the flush staining my cheeks a deep shade of red but didn't comment on it. His attention briefly shifted to my neck before he brought it back up to my eyes. "Shut down as many of your emotions as possible. They're only going to get more intense from this point forward. Aside from fear, this world thrives on both sin and desire in equal measure."

"Isn't desire the same as lust?"

"No. You can desire riches, power, or status. Friendship or vengeance. Desires are more complex wants than mere sins. Sometimes they're good. Other times they reflect insecurities. This world is influenced by those who rule it. Over time it's come to toy with us all."

Avoiding further eye contact, he stepped away, removed his crown, and laid down on the edge of the branches, going so far as to face the opposite direction. Even still, we'd be sleeping entirely too close. There was barely a hand space between us.

Envious. About him rutting like a pig with someone else.

The notion was ridiculous, especially after his betrayal, but the lingering sense of jealousy didn't leave right away. I cursed under my breath and focused harder on getting my emotions under control. The last thing I needed was to have this realm lure me deeper into those seven ruling sins by feeding on my feelings.

I dropped the metal corset/torture device and tugged his shirt on. It was huge on my frame, but I didn't care. It was warm and smelled of the prince. Mint and summer. And something distinctly, unmistakably, male.

I looked over at Wrath. He was still shirtless despite the crispness of the air. Aside from his close-fitting trousers, he only wore the shoulder holster and dagger. It was going to be a long, miserable night. "Aren't you going to put your jacket back on?"

"Stop having filthy thoughts about me and get some rest."

"I should have killed you when I had the chance."

He rolled over to study me, his gaze slow and meandering as it traveled from my eyes, over the curve of my cheeks, and settled on my lips. After a long moment, he said, "Sleep."

I sighed, then sunk to the ground and pulled my cloak over me like a blanket. The small space quickly filled with the scent of cedar and pine. Outside the wind howled. A moment later, small ice pellets assaulted our chamber. Nothing infiltrated our shelter, though.

I lay there for a while, listening to the demon's breathing turn slow and even. Once I was sure he was asleep, I peered at him again; he slept as if he didn't have a care in the world: the deep slumber of an apex predator. I stared at the shimmering ink on his shoulders, the lines of Latin still too pale and distant to make out.

Against my better judgment, I let myself become curious

about what held enough value or importance for him to permanently mark his body with it. I wanted to crack his soul open and read him like a book, discovering the deepest secrets and stories of how he came to be.

Which was foolish.

I tried not to notice the way our matching tattoo had elegantly crawled past his elbow now as well. His double crescent moons, wildflowers, and serpents reminded me of a fairy tale scene captured in a fresco back home. Something about gods and monsters.

I desperately tried not to think about how much I wanted to trace his tattoos, first with my fingertips and then with my mouth. Tasting, exploring.

I especially didn't allow myself to think about *being* the person he'd laid out and made love to. His hard, powerful body moving on top of mine, deep inside of...

I shut that scandalously carnal thought down, shocked by the intensity of it.

Devious Sin Corridor. I was obviously being tested for lust now and, considering my bedmate, that was more dangerous than any hell beast prowling around outside, thirsting for my blood. I don't know how much time passed, but sleep eventually found me.

A while later, I stirred. The storm raged, but that wasn't what roused me. Warm breath tickled my neck in even, rhythmic strokes. Sometime during the night I must have shimmied up against the demon. And, surprisingly, neither one of us had moved.

Wrath lay behind me, one heavy arm draped possessively over my waist as if daring any intruder to steal what he'd claimed as his. I should scoot away. And not just for propriety's sake. Being this close to him was like playing with fire and I'd already felt his burn, but I didn't *want* to move. I liked his arm on my body, the weight and feel and scent of him curled around me like a python. I wanted him to claim me, almost as much as I wanted him to be *mine*.

The instant that thought came, he stopped breathing steadily.

I inched backward, pressing myself against his chest, still craving more contact.

His hold on me constricted a fraction. "Emilia..."

"Yes?"

We both stilled at the sultry tone of my voice, the longing I couldn't hide. I hardly recognized this openly desirous version of myself. Back home, women were taught that those wants were evil, wrong. Men could indulge in their baser needs and no one called them ungodly. They were rakes, rogues—scandalous but not ostracized for their behavior.

A man with a healthy sexual appetite was considered to be full of vitality, a prime catch. Experienced for his partner, should he ever decide to wed. While women were taught to remain virginal, pure. As if our wants were dirty, shameful things.

I wasn't human, nor was I a member of the nobility—who suffered more restrictions than I ever had—but I'd certainly been raised with those same notions.

I was no longer in the mortal world, though. No longer bound to play by their rules.

A frisson of surprise shot through me. I couldn't decide if it was from excitement or fear of letting myself remove those shackles here. Maybe I did know, and maybe that was the part that scared me. I wanted something I'd been warned against. And now all I had to do was reach out and welcome it. It was time to be brave, bold.

Instead of being ruled by fear, I could become fearless. Beginning now. I nestled against Wrath again, my choice made. He slowly trailed a hand down the front of my shirt, toying with the buttons. I bit my lip to keep from gasping.

"Your heart is beating very fast."

His mouth grazed the lobe of my ear and—goddess curse me—I arched into the touch, feeling just how much he liked our current position.

His arousal sent a thrill all the way to my toes. I should *not* want this. I shouldn't want *him*. But I couldn't erase the phantom image of him bedding someone else from my mind, or the way it made me feel. I wanted to be the one he took to his bed. I wanted him to desire me in that way. And *only* me. It was a primal, ancient feeling.

One my future husband might not approve of, but I didn't care. Perhaps the only approval I would seek from now on was my own. To Hell, quite literally, with all else. If I was to be queen of this realm, I would embrace each part of it—and my true self—fully.

"Tell me," he whispered, his voice sliding like silk over my flushed skin.

"What?" My own voice came out breathless.

"I am your favorite sin."

At the moment, I wasn't sure I could manage to speak in full sentences. Wrath had teased me before, kissed me furiously and passionately, even, but he'd never tried seducing me.

He undid the first button on my shirt—*his* shirt—taking both infinite care and time meandering down to the next. All rational thoughts fled; his touch reduced me to possessing only one primitive need: desire. Raw, untamed, and endless. I felt no shame or worry or trepidation.

My chest rose and fell with each quickening beat of my pulse. Another button came undone. Followed by another. The grip on my emotions soon followed. A sizzling fire slowly consumed me from my toes upward. It was a wonder the snow beneath us hadn't melted.

If he didn't touch me, skin to skin, I'd combust. The fifth button popped open, leaving only a few more. I was about to rip the cursed shirt off. Sensing my urge, or perhaps finally giving in to his own, he swiftly undid the remaining buttons and pulled it open, exposing me.

From over my shoulder, he stared down at my body, his gaze darkening as his calloused hand slid across my smooth skin.

He was so tender, so attentive while he stroked my collarbone. When he pressed his palm to my heart, feeling its beat as if it was the most magical source in his world, I thought I might toss him down and bed him right then and there. His light touch was at odds with the mighty, terrifying power that emanated from him.

"Are you nervous?"

Hardly. I was enraptured. Completely at his mercy. Although one look at his raw expression indicated the opposite might be true. I managed to shake my head.

His fingers trailed lower, learning the curve beneath my breast, exploring my stomach and pausing to toy with the serpent belt I forgot I was wearing. If I turned slightly, angled myself up more, he could easily unbuckle it. Which was why he'd stopped. He was waiting for my decision. I thought it was obvious what I wanted.

"Tell me."

I'd rather *show* him. Emboldened, I twisted around, winding one arm around his neck, and sunk my fingers into his raven hair. We might be in Hell, but he felt like Heaven.

His obstinate hands traveled upward to skim my breasts again. He gently squeezed them, the roughness of his skin creating pleasant friction.

He felt as good as I remembered. Better, even. I couldn't help but gasp as his other hand finally obeyed my unspoken desires and slid in the opposite direction. It drifted across my ribs, past my stomach, and lingered right above where I wanted him to explore.

A honeyed heat pooled low in my belly.

Wrath finally slipped his fingers beneath the band of my skirt, brushing the soft skin between my hips, his touch feather-light. *Goddess curse me.* At the moment I didn't care about his lies or betrayal. Nothing mattered except the feeling of his hands on my body.

"Please." I tugged him close. Soft lips brushed against mine. "Kiss me."

"Say it once." He gently pulled my backside to him, offering a wicked taste of what was to come. His throbbing arousal fanned the flames of my own passions. I wished he'd do that *without* our clothes on. I rubbed against the hard length of him, and whatever control he'd had vanished. He captured my mouth with his, kissing me possessively, hungrily.

One of his hands remained locked on my hip and the other went under my skirts, sliding up my ankle, past my calf, then traveled between my thighs as his kiss deepened and his tongue claimed mine. His fingers were almost to the slick, aching center.

I needed him there. I groaned his name as he finally—

"While your current illusion sounds *wildly* interesting," Wrath's silky voice came from across the small enclosure, "you might want to put your clothes on. The temperature is well below freezing now."

I jerked upright, blinking in the darkness. *What in the seven hells...*

It took a moment to steady my breaths and another to get my bearings. The shirt he'd let me borrow was discarded along with the cloak, and my bare skin puckered in the icy air. My skirts were wrested up around my waist as if I'd been tugging them off and failed.

I stared down at the cooling, empty spot beside me, confused.

"Is something wrong?" Perhaps my new association with House Pride prevented us from intimately associating with each other. "Did we break a rule?"

"I tried to warn you." I couldn't see his face but heard the satisfied, all-too-smug—and very masculine—smile enter his voice, and alarm bells started ringing. "Your longings will taunt and tease you into oblivion if you can't control them. This is a realm of sin *and* desire. It depends on your vices for its survival the same way the human world requires oxygen and water. If you lose control for a second, it will pounce. And not always in the way you believe it will. For example, if you were thinking of hatred, it might test to see if the opposite could be true."

"I—" Goddess above. My lust-addled brain finally caught up with what had happened. He'd said it was an illusion. More like a nightmare. I buried my burning face in my hands, wondering if there was a spell I could use to disappear. "That wasn't real...any of it?"

"One thing I can promise," his voice was deep and sensual in the dark, "is you won't *ever* doubt it's real when I touch you."

Frustrated, embarrassed, and furious to have submitted to desiring him for even one second, I plucked up his shirt and roughly tugged it back on before flopping onto my side. "Someone's cocky."

"Says the person rubbing up against my c—"

"Finish that sentence and I'll smother you in your cursed sleep, demon."

Wrath's low chuckle had my toes curling and my imagination flying straight back into the fiery pits of Hell. My treacherous mind replayed one little word choice over and over. He'd said *when* he touched me, not *if*. As though he planned on making that erotic fantasy a reality at some point in the future. It was a good long while before sleep found me again.

Only this time I didn't dream of being happily seduced by the forbidden prince.

I dreamed of a vicious, violent murder. And a beautiful woman with starlight eyes, screaming a curse of vengeance into the darkest of nights.

Most disturbing of all, it felt as if I knew her. And her curse had been directed at me.

THREE

Dawn fought its way into our tiny shelter. Not that I could tell for certain what time it was. This world seemed to be stuck in a permanent state of twilight. Maybe the swift approach of the next storm was to blame. So far "overcast" was the preferred state of the atmosphere here. As if proving my theory correct, wind screeched in the distance, raising the small hairs along my arms.

There was only a slight shift in the angle of the light and the way Wrath gruffly said, "Time to move," that indicated it was indeed daytime. I waited for the arrogant prince to mock what happened a few hours ago, but he gave no indication I'd been half-naked and writhing against him, taunted with a sinful illusion of our bodies tangling together.

Maybe it *was* only a dream within a dream.

That hope rallied me up from our makeshift bed. I twisted from side to side, stretching out sore muscles. It wasn't the worst night's sleep I'd ever had, but it wasn't comfortable by any means. A warm bath, a change of clothing, and a good meal were just what I needed.

At the thought of food, my stomach grumbled loud enough that Wrath turned around to look, a slight crease forming between his brows. "We don't have much farther to travel, but, due to the terrain, it will likely take until nightfall to arrive at our destination."

"I'll live."

Wrath seemed skeptical about that but kept his troublesome mouth shut.

I stared glumly at the metal corset top and started unbuttoning the demon's shirt. Might as well get the miserable garment on quickly so we could leave. While I could definitely survive without food for a while, I'd eventually get a headache if it was too much longer.

Vittoria had been the same way. Our father used to tease us, claiming our magic burned a constant stream of energy that needed replenishing, and how it was a good thing we had a restaurant. Nonna would shake her head and shoo him away before slipping us sweets.

A different kind of ache took up residence near my heart. No matter how much I tried to shut it down, thoughts of food quickly turned to thoughts of Sea & Vine, our family trattoria.

Which was a swift emotional punch that almost had me doubling over. I missed my family terribly and I'd only spent one night in the underworld. Time might move differently here, so it was possible just an hour had passed in my world, maybe less.

I hoped Nonna managed to find a safe hiding place for everyone. Losing my twin was devastating, my grief still powerful enough to drown me if I let it surface above the fury for too long. If I lost anyone else…I shoved those worries into a little trunk near my heart and focused on getting through the day. A new thought slipped in.

"Where's Antonio?" I watched Wrath carefully. Not that I would read much if he chose to shield his emotions. "You never told me where you sent him."

"Someplace safe."

He didn't elaborate and it was probably best to let it be for now. We had more important things to focus on. Like making it out of the Sin Corridor without another *prodding* of my desires, and then formally introducing me to Pride and his royal court.

There would be plenty of time in the future to speak with Antonio, the human blade one of the demon princes had influenced to kill my twin. And the young man I used to dream of marrying before I knew the truth of his hatred for witches.

In my haste to get ready, I snapped a button off my borrowed shirt and cringed at the frayed thread. Knowing how fussy my traveling companion was about clothing, I braced myself for a lecture. I glanced up, an apology on my lips, surprised when Wrath shook his head, cutting my words off before I'd given voice to them.

"Keep it." He slipped his black jacket on. I drew my brows together and he quickly noted the suspicion I didn't try to hide. "It's wrinkled and ruined. I refuse to be seen like that."

"Your thoughtfulness is overwhelming. I might swoon."

I inspected his jacket. The luxurious material pulled across his broad shoulders, accentuating the taut muscles and hard lines of his chest. Of course he would prefer to show up half-naked rather than wear a crinkled shirt in front of any demonic subjects. I almost rolled my eyes at his vanity but managed to keep my expression neutral.

I noticed something I hadn't last night: he wore both amulets now. The first licks of anger bubbled up, but I shoved the feelings down. I'd had enough testing for one day.

He fastened the button above his trousers, leaving an unobstructed visual of his sculpted torso and the barest hint of the leather holster. The demon-forged blade was not his finest weapon—one look at *him* and anyone would hesitate to raise a hand.

Wrath's eyes glinted with rakish pleasure when he saw what had caught my attention. "Would you like me to unbutton it again? Or would you prefer to do that?"

"Get over yourself. I was thinking about how conceited you are, not lusting over you."

"You wished to get under me last night. In fact, you were quite insistent."

I notched my chin up. He could sense a lie, so I didn't bother with them. "Lust does not require liking or even loving someone. It's a physical reaction, nothing more."

"I was under the impression you weren't interested in kissing someone you hate," he said coolly. "Am I to believe you'd be all right bedding them now?"

"Who knows? Maybe it's this realm and its wicked machinations."

"Lie."

"Fine. Maybe I was lonely and scared and you offered a distraction."

I tucked the shirt into my skirts. It was much warmer, and I was excited to leave the metal top behind. I bent to retrieve my serpent belt and fastened it around my waist.

Wrath tracked each of my movements, his golden eyes

39

assessing. Oddly enough, he seemed genuinely intrigued about my answer.

"Why do you care, anyway?" I asked. "It's not as if *you* will be sharing my bed."

"I'm wondering what changed."

"We're in the underworld, for one." His eyes narrowed, detecting even the smallest untruth. Interesting. "Let me clear up any confusion. You're very enjoyable to look at. And on some occasions where logic fails I may desire you, but I'll never *love* you. Enjoy last night's illusion—a fantasy is all it was and all it will ever be."

He gave me a mocking smile as he replaced his crown. "We'll see about that."

"It would be so tempting to place a wager, but I refuse to sink to your level."

His gaze smoldered, reminding me of a banked fire on the verge of igniting again. "Oh, I believe you'd enjoy every second of descending to my level. Every slip and plunge of your fall will make your pulse pound and your knees quake. Care to know why?"

"Not at all."

An annoying half-smile ghosted across his face. He leaned in close, his voice dropping impossibly low. "Love and hate are both rooted in passion." His lips whispered across my jaw as he slowly brought them to my ear. My breath caught from his nearness, his heat. He drew back enough to meet my gaze, his attention falling to my mouth. For a moment, I thought he was going to tip my face up to his, run his tongue over the seam of my lips and taste my lies. "Strange how that line becomes blurred over time."

My traitorous lips parted on a sigh. Before I registered he'd even moved, he swept out of our little shelter. A shiver slid down my spine. It wasn't the cold that unsettled me; it was the determination that flashed in his eyes. As if I'd declared war and he refused to walk away from the lure of battle. It wasn't clear if he was referring to me never loving him, or never bedding him, but provoking the general of war meant trouble either way.

As I pulled my cloak on, I recalled Nonna's warnings about the Wicked—how once someone caught a demon prince's attention he'd stop at nothing to claim them.

The way Wrath had looked at me made me think those stories were true. And despite his earlier proclamation about me being the last creature in all the realms he would want, and the fact I was now promised to his brother, something undeniably had just changed.

Goddess help us both.

Morning kicked and screamed its way toward noon as if it were a spoiled child throwing a tantrum. Snow squalls appeared, fierce and howling, and left as quickly as they'd arrived. When I thought the weather had finally turned moderate, ice pelted us.

Frozen strands of dark hair stuck to my face, and my cloak suctioned to my body like a second skin. I was cold and miserable in ways I'd never experienced at home on my warm island. Various body parts either burned or stung from the ice, and I'd long since lost sensation in my feet. I hoped I wouldn't lose a toe or three to frostbite.

Whenever I felt the first tinges of hopelessness creeping in, I gritted my teeth and pushed on, head down, as the gusting wind continued to snap at me. I refused to succumb to the elements this early on in my mission. My sister would never give up on me.

It would take far worse than ice to stop me now.

Perhaps this corridor did more than simply test for sins; perhaps battling such vicious elements was a test of grit. Of determination. And uncovering how far one was willing to go for the ones they loved. Both the demons and this realm would discover that answer soon enough.

Wrath either enacted a glamour, or the elements didn't dare to mess with his princely self. His hair was unaffected, and his clothing remained dry. If his cavalier attitude regarding the journey didn't annoy me enough already, the way the weather bent to his will was enough to irk me into an early grave. It was wholly unfair that he should look so damnably good while I looked similar to a sodden wreck that washed ashore after several long, hard months at sea.

The few times it wasn't snowing or hailing or some terrible combination of the two, a thick, chilly mist hung over us like an omen from a nasty winter god. I was starting to think there was a higher power out there who enjoyed toying with travelers.

Time stretched on and on, though the sun never quite made an appearance. There were only various shades of gray tinging the sky. Wrath and I barely spoke after our morning conversation, and I was perfectly fine with that. Soon enough I'd be at House Pride.

After what I estimated to be another hour or two into our journey, I began trembling uncontrollably. The more I tried forcing my muscles to still, the more they rebelled.

Nonna always told us to find the positive in any situation, and now that I was so emotionally and physically drained by the frosty elements, I was spared from being tested by the Sin Corridor.

My shivers quickly grew loud enough to draw Wrath's attention. He ran a calculating gaze over me, mouth tightening, and walked faster. He barked at me to keep moving. To hurry up. To lift my feet. Higher, faster, move, go, *now*. He was the mighty general of war and I could easily imagine how much his soldiers hated him for the drills he ran them through.

When painful pins and needles started pricking my body all over, I distracted myself with a new game. Perhaps it was the Sin Corridor encouraging me, but I envisioned all the ways Wrath could slip over a cliff and splatter himself on craggy rocks. I saw it all so clearly...

...I'd race after him, pulse pounding as I followed the broken branches and destruction left in his wake, his big body crashing violently into everything on its way down. Once I caught up to him, I'd drop to my knees, frantically searching for a pulse. Then I'd swirl my fingers through his warm blood, drawing little hearts and stars in the gore.

He glanced over his shoulder, brows tugged close. "What are you smirking at?"

"I'm fantasizing about painting the world with your blood."

"Explains the overly indulgent look." The twisted heathen grinned and the Sin Corridor swiftly ceased pushing me from gluttony to wrath. Before I unleashed myself, he said, casually, "Have I ever told you your anger is like my own personal aphrodisiac?"

No, he had not. But of course the demon ruling over war would be aroused by conflict. I inhaled deeply, attempting to cool my temper and the wrath I was still being prodded toward. "If you wish to keep your favorite appendage intact, I suggest not speaking."

"Once you finish thinking about my impressive appendage,

I suggest moving faster. We've got a long way to travel. And you look half-dead as it stands."

"Your talent for making a woman swoon is second only to your charm, Prince Wrath."

His nostrils flared and I did an abysmal job keeping the amusement from my face. Which only made his scowl deepen. Wrath didn't taunt me again for another few hours, but it wasn't from brooding. He was driven, tense. I had a strong suspicion he was more worried than he let on. I did my best to keep up with him, concentrating on the end goal instead of the miserable present. We worked our way down the treacherous pass, time moving in excruciatingly slower increments. I started slipping more, catching myself right before I tumbled over the edge.

Wrath glared at me, rallying my anger enough to press on if only to spite him. I wasn't sure how long it took for me to notice, but awareness tingled at the back of my muddled senses. Wrath had scouted a good distance ahead, ensuring the terrain was passable, when I'd felt the slight prickle of unease turn into a steady prodding I could no longer ignore.

I stopped walking, and the sound of snow crunching continued for a good half-beat after before falling eerily quiet. I slowly swept my gaze around. Evergreens lined this part of the pass, the branches weighted and bowed from thick snow, making it impossible to see past them into the darker section of woods. Overtaxed tree limbs creaked and groaned. More snow crunched.

I exhaled, my breath mingling with the mist. The haunted atmosphere was caused by the sound of broken branches falling. I turned back around and froze.

A giant, three-headed doglike creature gazed at me, heads tilted, and three sets of ears perked. Its fur was as white as the falling snow and its eyes were glacier blue. Those strange eyes stared into mine, its pupils dilating then contracting.

I didn't so much as breathe too deeply for fear of inciting an attack. Its fangs were twice the size of dinner knives, and they appeared just as sharp. The creature snuffed the air, its wet nose nearly touching my throat as it brought its middle head near.

I swallowed a scream as it took a step closer, those icy eyes lighting with...

Before I could cry out for help, each set of its jaws snapped open and shut as if it wanted to bite me, but changed its mind, much to its shock and mine. It shook its heads, eyes glazed, and stepped away. A predator acknowledging a larger threat. I fell into the embankment and stared, dumbstruck as it slunk backward into the woods, its gaze never leaving mine as it softly snarled.

I didn't breathe again until it disappeared from sight. So much for making a fearless impression on the underworld. "Blood and bones. What *was* that?"

"If you're finished playing with the puppy, I'd like to continue our journey."

"Puppy?"

I swiveled my head in the demon's direction. Wrath stood a few paces away, his powerful arms crossed and an annoying smirk on his face. No assistance, no offer of help. Only mockery at a situation that could have turned ugly very rapidly. Typical demon.

"That was the size of a small horse!"

"Refrain from saddling it up like one. Unlike my brothers, they don't enjoy being ridden."

"Hilarious." I pushed myself to my feet and swiped at the snow on my cloak. As if I wasn't cold and wet enough before. "I could have been mauled to death."

"There are a number of solitary lesser demons who call the woods and outlying lands home. Hellhounds are the least of your concern. If you're finished with the dramatics, let's move. We've wasted enough time."

Of course the demon would call a three-headed hellhound a puppy and say *I* was being dramatic over the encounter. I trudged past him, muttering every obscenity I could recall. His dark chuckle set my feet moving faster, lest the Sin Corridor get any more wicked ideas.

We traveled on, thankfully with no more wildlife encounters. Our biggest challenge was the relentless storm. I silently vowed I'd never fantasize about snow being romantic again.

When I thought our blustery misery was coming to an end, another towering mountain appeared from the mist. I had to lean all the way back and still couldn't see over the top of it.

I bit back a small whimper. There was no chance I could drag my frozen body up and over that behemoth. My head felt strange, a combination of dizziness and exhaustion. Or vertigo. I considered plopping down right there. Maybe a few minutes of rest would help.

Wrath strode ahead, leaving me where I stood contemplating my near-certain demise. Just like when he'd held a hand to the gates of Hell, he placed his palm against the rock face. Gold light shimmered as he quietly commanded the mountain to do his bidding.

Or maybe he was whispering a threat to a Hell god that owed him a favor.

I was too far away to hear him and I snickered at the thought of his potential demands. I full-out laughed when a section of mountain slid back like his own personal door. Of course. A mountain obeyed his every wish. Why wouldn't it?

Too bad he didn't order the storm to heel like he *should* have done with the hellhound earlier. It probably would have tucked its tail between its legs and raced in the opposite direction.

For some reason, the imagery had me doubling over, laughing so hard tears streamed down my face. A second later, I forgot what was so funny. Snow fell in heavier flakes. My pulse slowed, my heart clenched. It felt like I was dying. Or traveling to an isle of—

Wrath was before me in an instant, his strong hands wrapping around my upper arms. I didn't realize I'd been swaying on my feet until he'd steadied me. Even with his assistance, everything kept spinning wildly and I squeezed my eyes shut, which only made it worse.

I opened them again, and tried to focus on one point to ease the sensation.

Wrath's stern face swam into view.

He looked me over, frowning. If I had the ability to do so, I would have rolled my eyes at his critical assessment of whatever he found lacking. Not everyone was blessed to look like some deviously handsome deity while traipsing through Hell. His lips twitched.

I must have said that last part out loud.

"Perhaps I should carry you the rest of the way. If you're commenting on my godlike looks, you must be tremendously ill."

"No. Absolutely *not*."

I staggered toward the opening he'd made in the mountain, desperate to get out of the snow. I accomplished two steps into the dark tunnel before my legs were swept out from under me and a warm, muscular arm banded across my shoulders, holding me in place.

I squirmed, humiliated to be carried like a rag doll or child. Wrath was unfazed by my attempts to get free. As the soon-to-be

Queen of the Wicked, this was *not* the first impression I wanted to make. Half-delirious, half-frozen, and wholly reliant on a demon.

Wrath had once said power was everything here, and, even through my delirium, I knew relinquishing mine for a moment would mark me as an easy target.

"Put. Me. Down."

"I will."

My head rolled back, landing in the nook between his shoulder and neck. He was deliciously warm. "I meant now."

"I'm well aware of that."

The world swayed with each of his steps, grew darker. It was suddenly an effort to stay awake. My skin felt oddly tight. Everything was too cold. Sleep would make all of that go away. And then I could dream. Of my sister. Of my life before I'd ever summoned a demon. And of the time I'd foolishly believed love and hate were nowhere close to being the same emotion.

"I hate you." My words came out slower than they should have. "I hate you in the darkest of ways."

"I'm well aware of that, too."

"My future husband cannot see me like this."

I felt more than saw him smile. "Knowing you, I'm sure he'll see much worse."

"*Grazie.*" Jerk. I nestled against his warmth and sighed, undermining my own demands to be set down. I'd only rest for a minute. "Do you think I'll like him?"

Wrath's steps never faltered, but he held me a little tighter. "Time will tell."

I dozed off and jerked awake what I hoped was only a moment or two later. Between the darkness of the tunnel and his steady, rhythmic stride, it was difficult to stay alert. Nonsensical thoughts and memories crowded into my head and spilled from my lips. "You said you wouldn't."

"Wouldn't what?"

The rumble of his voice vibrated in my chest. It was oddly comforting. I pressed my cheek against his heart, listening to it beat faster. Or maybe that was wishful thinking. His bare skin blazed against mine. Almost painfully so. "Take care of me. You said you wouldn't..."

He didn't respond. Not that I expected him to. He was not soft or kind. He was hard and rough and fueled by rage and fire. He understood battle and war and strategy. Friendship wasn't any of those things. Especially one involving a witch. I was a mission to him, a promise he'd made to his brother, nothing more. That I understood, even if it stung deep down. I had my own goals, my own agenda. And I wouldn't hesitate to destroy anyone who interfered with my plans.

Even him.

Sleep finally wrestled me into its embrace and I relaxed against Wrath's body. Maybe he'd surprise me by sneaking us into House Pride through a secret entrance to avoid any nosy demons. I could only hope he'd grant me some mercy.

From somewhere far away, I could have sworn he whispered, "I lied."

FOUR

"Is she dead?" It took a minute to place, but I recognized the voice. Anir. Wrath's human second in command. The demon responded with an obscenity that sounded an awful lot like *Of course not, you fucking idiot.* "Can you blame me? She looks plenty dead. Maybe you should let fate run its course. No one will blame you if her heart stops. Not even—"

"Careful. I don't recall asking your opinion."

Calloused fingers poked at my throat, grabbed my wrist. I struggled to sit up but was strapped to something rock hard and unmoving. "Your majesty, we should alert the matron. I don't think this is—"

"Get a mug of warm water and blankets. Now."

My skin felt like someone had tossed me into a fire and held me there. Drinking something warm or putting on a blanket was the last thing I wanted to do. I thrashed in my chains and one of them broke free and smoothed my hair back. Arms, not chains. Wrath still held me against his body. I tried to open my eyes but couldn't. He took a few steps and placed me carefully on a mattress. At least I hoped that's what it was.

Which meant...my heart thundered. We must be at the devil's castle now. Panic had me clawing at his arms as he tried to pull away. Despite my earlier bravado, I did not want to be alone with the king of demons. At least not like this. "N-no...no..."

"Don't move too much, or your heart might stop."

I sucked in a sharp, ragged breath. "Y-your bedside m-manner—"

"Is abominable? There's a reason I'm not a healer. Complain later. You've got a mild case of hypothermia." He gently disentangled himself from my death grip and drew back. I could have sworn he brushed his lips across my burning forehead before his weight fully lifted from the bed. When he spoke, his tone was hard enough to make me question if the kiss had been real. "Lay still."

Fabric ripped. My eyes flew open as shock rippled through me. Wrath leaned over my body, tearing my frozen clothing down the center like it was no more substantial than a piece of parchment. Skirts, shirts, belt. A few more tugs and cool air blew across my scorched skin.

I almost groaned with pleasure as he pulled my damp clothes out from under me and tossed them away. I didn't even care that I was naked in front of the demon. Again.

I wanted to claw my flesh off and submerge my body in a tub of ice. Which was odd considering I'd been freezing not long ago. My eyes drifted shut and no matter how hard I fought, I couldn't reopen them. Odd images played across my mind. Memories blurred and broken flitted through a thick mist, a possible result of a dying brain. Or maybe it was visions of a future I'd never know, taunting me. Statues and flowers. Fire. Hearts in jars, a wall of skulls.

Nothing made sense.

"Emilia . . . stay with me."

Wrath picked up my hand and gently massaged warmth into each of my fingers. If he was trying to keep me awake, it wasn't working. A drowsy peace fell over me, and I relaxed under his touch, the memories and strange images fading. He moved his careful ministrations from my fingers to my wrist then slowly up my arm to my elbow, before tending to my other hand.

Once he finished rubbing life back into my fingers, he shifted lower on the bed. He lifted my leg at the ankle with one hand, and used the other to work the feeling into my toes much the same way he had with my fingers. The pads of his thumbs slipped to the arch of my foot, and I softly groaned as he used *just* the right amount of pressure to heal the ache there.

Someone rapped at the door and Wrath ordered them to leave everything outside. Footsteps thundered across the room, a door swung open and slammed shut, then he was back, gently covering my body with the softest fabric I'd ever felt.

I choked on a scream. It felt as if he'd poured kerosene over me and lit a match. I kicked the blanket off and earned a frustrated growl from the demon.

"Stop." He pressed me down and folded me into the blanket again. A heaviness settled beside me a breath later. Two large arms wound around my body, tugging me closer, his chin resting on my head. He looped a leg over my hip, securing our connection.

He felt like fire. And I was already burning. I tried to roll out from under him, aiming for the ground. I wanted to crawl under the floorboards and bury myself in the earth like an animal deep in hibernation. Wrath's grip never faltered; I was trapped against his body. And, with his supernatural strength, no amount of struggling would break his grasp if he chose to hold on. Survival kicked in—I became a feral cat clawing at the one trying to cage me.

Wrath's arms were twin bands of steel.

"Get *off* me."

"No."

"Didn't your maker teach you proper ways of treating women?"

"Live through the night and I'll respect your wishes then," he snapped.

"You don't understand..." I was mad with fury and wild with the need to move. His arms tightened around me, but never painfully so. "I need to be in the earth. I have to go below ground now."

"That's a common symptom of hypothermia. The feeling will pass when you're stable again." He slid an arm behind my shoulders and angled me up. "Sip this. *Now*."

His tone indicated that he'd pinch my nose and force it down my throat if I didn't listen. Coddling nursemaid he was not. I took a tentative sip of warm liquid and held in a scream. Everything was too hot. Wrath lowered me back onto a pillow and slowly pulled another blanket on me. It was featherlight but hurt tremendously. Pain intensified until it was all I knew.

I clamped my teeth together, trying to force the chattering to stop. Blessedly, mere moments after drinking the liquid, I drifted in and out of various degrees of consciousness. I wondered what he'd put in the drink to make me drowsy but couldn't muster enough energy to feel threatened. If he wanted me dead, he would have let nature handle that deed.

Movement drew me out of my fevered battle with lucidity sometime later. I forgot where I was. Who I was with. Warm light gilded a large silhouette.

I squinted, wondering who had sent an angel. Then I remembered. If the heavenly being staring down at me had ever been an angel, he was something *other* now. Something to be feared and avoided. Something that made hearts pound and knees quake.

He was as forbidden as the fruit offered to Eve, but somehow even more tempting.

In a dreamlike state, I watched Wrath perform the most peculiar tasks. Refilling a mug of warm liquid. Helping me sip it until a honeyed heat slowly spread through me. Peaceful and calming, a direct contrast from the inferno I'd felt earlier. He fussed with more blankets. Stoked wood in a massive fireplace across from a bed made of midnight. The sheets were the white and silver of shooting stars. They were strangely familiar, though I'd never seen them.

At one point I rolled over to face him and stared at a sheen of sweat glistening on his bare skin. Sometime during the night he'd removed the two amulets. He was tucked into the blankets, too, arms wrapped around me in a comfortable embrace, his body heat fueling mine. He was extraordinary. And it had nothing to do with his physical appearance.

I dragged my attention up to his eyes. Black flecks dotted his gold irises like tiny stars circling his pupils. He watched me inspect his features, his focus scanning my face in the same intent way. I wondered what he saw when he looked at me, how he felt.

"Sometimes," my voice came out scratchy and soft, "sometimes I think I want to be your friend. Despite the past. Maybe aligning ourselves, our separate Houses, is something to consider."

His jaw tightened, as if the mere idea of friendship or an alliance was appalling. "Rest."

Fire now blazed in the room and my lids closed as if he'd commanded them to obey. The world grew foggy. "Wrath..." I wanted to say "thank you" but my words were stolen by sleep.

He spoke in whispers and hushed tones. Smoothed hair from my face with his big, tattooed hand. It felt like he was sharing a secret—something vital. Important in a way that would forever change my reality. I burrowed closer, straining to listen. His voice rumbled through me like a distant storm, trying to shake something awake before it went slumbering again.

I couldn't retain anything and drifted off once more.

The next time I awoke, Wrath's side of the bed was empty. Without his massive body, and constant glowering or not-so-gentle fussing, the room felt too big.

A room.

I sucked in a sharp breath, instantly alert. The worst of my delirium was gone, and reality felt like a mountain crashing down on me. Wrath had taken me to...I wasn't sure. I didn't get a good look at where I was yesterday. I wiped the remnants of sleep from my eyes and stared up at a smattering of constellations. They were wholly unexpected.

I blinked at them—the ceiling had been painted to look like a sky full of stars. Though that wasn't quite right, either. On closer inspection, the constellations were actually tiny lights glowing softly in a ceiling painted a bruised shade of dark blue.

I swept my attention around the chamber. It was enormous. Elegant.

The walls were a pure snowy white with panels of decorative molding and trim, and the massive fireplace across from the bed was edged in silver that reflected the flames in its shiny surface. A giant, ornate mirror hung above it. Silver sconces sat to either side of the mantel. Another identical set was on the wall behind the bed. I was surprised to see silver and not Wrath's signature gold, though I had a suspicion the metal was actually white gold.

A dark blue rug exactly matched the hue of the ceiling, and the bed seemed to be carved from the same gemstone that surrounded the gates of Hell. Layered on top of the dark carpet was a yellow rug woven through with gold thread.

All of the fabrics looked soft, luxurious, and smelled faintly of crisp winter air and musk.

On the far side of the room, a set of glass chairs and a matching table were tastefully placed in a nook. If not for their edges glinting in the blazing fire, my attention might have skipped over them entirely. Next to the fireplace an enormous armoire made from dark wood stood tall and imposing. Little flowers and stars and snakes were carved into its doors. Crescent moons formed the handles. They reminded me of an incomplete triple goddess symbol. Beside the wardrobe was a door that either led to another chamber or a corridor.

This was a far cry from the abandoned palace Wrath had commandeered in my city.

I twisted around. On my left another door led to a bathing room, if the splashes of water were any indication. A large canvas painting hung beside it. The frame was silver, as ornate as the mirror above the fireplace, and must have cost a small fortune.

The painting itself looked like an enchanted forest taken straight from the pages of a fairy tale. Deep green and rich brown oils brought the landscape to life. Flowers in a riot of dark colors dotted the foreground. Vines of ivy wound around massive tree trunks.

Fruit trees offered ripe treats from apples to fat pomegranates bursting with seeds, to various citruses. Mist floated above soil near the center, and frost coated the petals of the flowers on the right. The artist's palette was dark, yet muted. The scene alive, yet frozen. Summer inhabited one side and it was ice-kissed with winter on the other.

It was a seasonal garden unlike any I'd ever seen in real life. I had a sudden urge to find the artist who painted it at once, curious about the inspiration behind such a unique piece. If it was based on a real location, I wanted to visit it. But first...

I glanced down at myself. The only clothes I had had been ripped from my body in Wrath's frenzied attempt to get me warm, and discarded the goddess knew where. I sighed and yanked the sheets up, attempting to tie them into a makeshift dress.

Someone cleared their throat.

The uptick in my pulse indicated who it was before I brought my focus up to his. My heart rate spiked impossibly higher the moment our gazes connected and locked.

Wrath leaned against the doorframe, dark hair tousled and damp, new suit pressed to perfection, his expression bordering on contemplative. He scanned me slowly, his gaze sharp and clinical in its assessment. An ebony robe embroidered with wildflowers dangled from his fingertips. "You're awake."

"You're observant."

"Play nice. I'm the one with your robe."

My attention slid to the clothing in question. I was at a clear disadvantage, one I intended to remedy at once. "Where are we?"

"A bedchamber, from the looks of it."

Interminable ass. "Yours?"

He shook his head, not elaborating further. I silently counted to ten. Wrath waited, one side of his mouth tipped up, as if irking me was his most treasured diversion.

If he desired an argument, I was more than happy to oblige. Until I recalled what he'd said about anger being an aphrodisiac and bit my tongue. "Are we at Pride's royal House?"

"No. This is House Wrath."

"The contract..."

"Do you want to go there?" His tone was carefully neutral.

Something about the question felt like a trap, and I did not wish to find myself in any demon's snare so soon, if ever. I swallowed hard. "I made a blood vow."

"That doesn't answer my question."

As if he answered all of mine. I took a page from his book of secrets and lobbed a question back at him. "What does it matter? I signed it. It's done."

"Do you *want* to go there?" he repeated. Of course I did not want to go there or stay here, for that matter. I wanted to do what I came here to do and go home. The faster, the better. I pressed my lips together, unwilling to answer aloud, and forced myself to think of something pleasant. He sensed emotions and lies. And I had a theory I needed to test. His eyes narrowed as he scanned my face, searching for the truth hidden in it. "Is that a yes?"

I nodded.

A rare bout of emotion flashed in his face, but he recovered quickly and crossed the room in a few long strides. If I hadn't been studying him, I would have missed the lightning-fast reaction. Now rage flickered in his eyes. A mask to cover his hurt.

"Don't worry. When my brother rouses himself from the near-constant parties and debauchery, and when his cursed pride finally surrenders enough to allow me entry into his hateful domain, I'll hold up my end of the bargain."

I was fairly confident each of their domains were hateful in their own way but didn't bother pointing that out. "We need to be invited?"

"Unless you'd like to start a feud between our Houses, yes."

I mentally filed away the information. Feuding princes would certainly create a diversion from more seemingly innocuous pursuits, such as gossip. "If you enter his territory without his consent, it's taken as a threat? Even if you're doing his bidding?" Wrath nodded. "That makes little sense. Is it because he's the king and wants to remind you of your place?"

"Royal posturing is a favorite pastime here for some."

Which didn't exactly answer *my* questions. Prince Wrath, one of the Feared and Mighty Seven, General of War, and Master of Avoidance. A devious idea sprang to mind. I schooled my features into bland interest and locked my smile away. Wrath had plenty of masks in his arsenal. It was time to add some to my collection.

"As his bride, what if I decide to go to him alone? Am I not technically part of House Pride? If so, I don't see how that rule should apply to me. Unless he's still dedicated to his first wife, which cannot be true if he's as debauched as you claim. I'm sure he'd welcome me into our marital bed."

I doubted Wrath realized it, but the room chilled a fraction. I'd struck a nerve.

"Pride will gladly welcome you and anyone else he's fascinated by into his bed. All at once if he desires to do so, and if you permit it the nights you're with him. Though I suggest pretending he is the supreme lover, else you'll injure his namesake sin and find yourself alone."

I was so stunned, I forgot the seeds of discord I'd been trying to plant. "You cannot be serious. Pride would desire another in our bed? With me? I don't understand."

Wrath hesitated a minute. "On occasion, my brother enjoys multiple lovers."

"At the same time?" I felt my face flame as he slowly nodded.

"Sex isn't viewed as shameful or sinful here, Emilia. Attraction and desire are part of the natural order of life. Mortals put restrictions on such things. Princes of Hell do not."

"But Lust...his influence. It's considered a sin, even here."

"My brother mostly toyed with your happiness, things that bring all manner of pleasure and joy, not just carnal urges. Being tested or prompted toward one particular emotion usually means it's something this realm senses you struggle with." He canted his head. "If you are interested in sex but fear passion or intimacy, you may experience a higher rate of sexual desire until you work through your personal issues regarding it. Which one intimidates you?"

I swallowed hard, uncomfortable with the topic of pleasure while I was alone with Wrath, and naked beneath my silken sheets. "Neither. And it's hardly your concern. Discussing what I may or may not do with my husband is inappropriate. Especially with you."

Wrath tossed the robe next to me on the mattress, his expression cold. "You're welcome for keeping you alive. By my count that's twice. And not a lick of gratitude for either."

His tone made my blood boil. I wondered if he knew his magic was leaking out, affecting me so potently. Maybe being inside his

House of Sin exacerbated my fury, along with the realization that I was woefully inexperienced in certain areas. I hadn't thought about bedding Pride, or considered any other wifely duties I might be required to complete. I felt trapped. My bubbling anger needed an outlet, and Wrath seemed game.

"Do you always require profuse thanks for doing the decent thing? I'm starting to think your sin is actually pride, not wrath. Your ego's definitely fragile enough. Maybe I should grovel at your feet or throw a parade in your honor. Will that satisfy you?"

"Careful, witch."

"Or what? You'll sell my soul to the highest bidder?" I scoffed. "Too late. Let's not forget if it wasn't for you and your deception, I wouldn't even be here, nearly freezing to death, or having to worry about bedding your brother and whoever else he invites between our sheets!"

"*You* chose House Pride."

"Why are you even still here? I thought you'd leave the second you gained your freedom. Have you not tormented me enough? Or is your duty not completely fulfilled until my marriage is consummated? If that's what you're waiting for, I'm sure Pride will invite you into the room to bear witness, ensuring I lay back and take it like a good little queen."

If hatred could be captured with one look, he'd mastered it. "There are clothes for you in the wardrobe. Wear whatever you like. Do whatever you like. Go wherever you like in this castle. If you decide to leave House Wrath, good luck. I'll return when Pride sends a summons. Until then, good evening, *my lady*."

He stormed out of the room, his footsteps echoing into another chamber before a door opened and shut and I heard him thunder down the hall. I blew out a frustrated breath.

That demon stoked my anger like no other.

Miserable beast. How dare he demand truth when he didn't offer any in return. I waited for my pulse to calm itself. I *was* thankful for everything he'd done last night. And if he'd given me an opportunity, I would have told him his efforts were appreciated. He didn't need to rub the arches of my feet. That had nothing to do with frostbite and everything to do with tenderness.

"Goddess curse us both." I sighed. I hadn't meant to get so furious or to snap about the cave, but the feelings had been festering. Best to lance that wound and be done with it.

Despite the tense escalation of our argument, my little experiment was a partial success; Wrath could only detect a lie *for certain* when I spoke. It was a trick to add to my mental journal.

I glanced at the door and considered chasing him to wring his neck or kiss him senseless but shut those urges down. To find out what really happened to Vittoria, I'd have to disentangle myself from him eventually. And I might as well start now. I didn't know all of the rules and etiquette of the demon realm, but at least I now knew the princes didn't infringe on one another's royal domain. Once I left for House Pride, Wrath and I would not see each other again. At least not for a while.

My lady.

What nonsense that was.

My attention settled on the robe and a strange feeling had my heart racing. I didn't notice while the demon held it across the room, but the flowers embroidered on it matched our tattoos.

The pale lavender ink symbolized a betrothal I'd accidentally forced between us when I'd first summoned him. He knew within moments what I'd done and hadn't bothered telling me the truth.

I'd found out weeks later from Anir, the night we'd stumbled across another murdered witch in an alleyway. Wrath swore he was going to tell me, that he'd been waiting until our trust was built to reveal our impending marriage, but I doubted it.

Everything he did was calculated. Every move, strategic. There were games he was still playing and secret agendas he had that I hadn't begun to figure out yet. Maybe they related to my sister's murder, and maybe they didn't. No matter how tightly he guarded his secrets, one way or another I'd find out what he was truly after. If I'd learned anything about him at all, it was the endless lengths he'd travel to get what he desired.

I looked down at my inked arm. I'd thought the matching tattoos would vanish when I'd cast a spell of un-making to end the betrothal that same night. They didn't.

Despite the broken magic, they kept growing like seeds that had been planted and tended. Bits of each of us fed the design: his serpents, my flowers, the twin crescent moons within a ring of stars. They were a constant reminder of my inexperience and his lies of omission.

I traced the delicate stems and petals replicated on the robe, the fabric silky and cool. It was so beautiful, the exact thing I'd choose for myself if given enough resources to have such a fine garment made. He knew that. Knew me.

Maybe more than I gave him credit for. And yet, *he* still remained a mystery to me.

I gathered up the robe, swung myself out of bed, and stood naked before the crackling fire. Hours ago I was near death, my skin burning from ice, not fire. He'd stayed the whole night, cradling me against his body. A body that was not ice-cold as Nonna used to claim in her stories of the Wicked. He could have summoned a royal healer to do the task.

He also could have let me die like Anir suggested. But he didn't.

I held the fabric to my face, breathed in Wrath's lingering scent, then tossed it straight into the flames.

FIVE

"Death by wardrobe" was destined to be the epitaph on my gravestone, thanks to Wrath's obsession with fine clothing and exquisite fabric. There were so many dresses and skirts and bodices and corsets and tunics and stockings and delicate, lacy undergarments and silk nightgowns and dressing robes, I had to close the carved doors and step back. It was too much.

At home I'd had a handful of simple corset-less dresses and frocks made of muslin. Two pairs of shoes. Sandals and lace-up boots. A few blouses and homespun skirts. Vittoria and I would often share clothing to make our meager closet appear larger than it was.

The items inside this wardrobe were unlike anything I'd seen in the mortal world. And it wasn't simply the daring styles and scandalous amount of skin I'd be showing. It was the vibrant colors, detailed embroidery, and whimsical nature of them.

I took a deep breath and opened the armoire again. Shoes ranging from slippers to small-heeled shoes to boots in a rainbow of dark colors lined the bottom of the wardrobe. Blacks, charcoals, deep maroons, golds, and even some dark purple and silver.

Ribbons, lace, leather. Gowns with exotic and fantastical patterns featuring thorns and serpents and flowers and fruits and glittering fabrics to rival the night sky. Silks, tulles, velvets, and something that was so soft and fuzzy I rubbed it against my cheek.

Cashmere. A half-forgotten memory sparked to life. A little cabin deep in a frozen wood; a plume of silver smoke snaking into the sky. Whispers and cauldrons and...and Nonna had given Vittoria and me cashmere gloves when we'd visited her friend in northern Italy once. I liked the material then and loved it now. I pulled the pale lavender-gray dress out and swallowed hard.

"Oh."

Fashion in the Seven Circles was a lot more formfitting and revealing than the clothing in my world. This dress would fit like those gloves and fall to mid-thigh. If I was lucky.

It was the obscenest piece of clothing I'd ever encountered, shorter than any nightgown designed for those who plied their trade in pleasure-houses. I wondered what it would be like, confidently owning my body and sensuality, neither apologizing nor simpering to anyone.

Suddenly, I imagined wearing the dress while I picked a fight with the demon who'd chosen it...

...his gaze would darken as it roved over me in a furiously slow way, making my blood boil. I'd shove him against the nearest hard surface, breathless as he flexed his fingers on the soft fabric at my thighs, carefully considering his next move.

Perhaps his troublesome mouth would taunt and tease while he strategized ways to wring pleasure from me. He'd whisper all sorts of filthy promises, heating me to my core instead of shocking me. I'd lean in and nip at his lower lip, a warning and a plea.

I would happily inform him that I was no longer fearful of my passions or willing to deny myself. That shame was the last thing I felt when he was in my arms.

He'd kiss me then, slow and deep. A commanding exploration of my mouth, my body. Proof of making good on his wicked promises. I'd feel his desire pushing against me, hard and warm and thrilling. My satisfaction over affecting him as much would slide into need faster than I could draw my next breath. I'd press against him, wanting to feel *more*.

It wouldn't take much for him to wrench the dress up over my hips, drop to his knees, and kiss his way up—

"Blood and bones."

I shook myself from the magically induced illusion. This realm and its nudges would take *a lot* of getting used to. It wasn't as strong as it was in the Sin Corridor, but that same darkly seductive magic was there, lingering, testing, teasing.

Another unfortunate complication. I'd have to carefully mind each of my thoughts and feelings. I quickly put the dress back and snatched a dressing robe, banishing thoughts of Wrath.

Thinking about the prince of this House of Sin while standing near my bed without a stitch of clothing was a courtship with trouble. After I slipped the robe on, I tied the silk belt around my waist and thumbed through the clothing once more.

I held up another gown that was slightly closer in style to clothing from home. Well, dresses a princess or noblewoman might own. This one had a strapless corsetlike top in an endless matte black. A sleek skirt that would hug my hips and fan out midthigh before dramatically cascading to the floor. Satiny black piping edged each line of the top and circled the waist. It was a far cry from the simple blouses and skirts I was used to wearing to work.

Pangs of homesickness hit me. All the finery in the world

couldn't replace the comfort I felt with my family. I wanted to be standing in the kitchen of Sea & Vine, listening to the symphony of sounds my mother, Nonna, and sister made as we worked on our dishes. Knives chopping, pans sizzling, spoons clattering, and all of us happily humming while we shared gossip from the marketplace. My father and uncle Nino chatting merrily with diners.

The scent of savory food wafting around... That simple, happy life was over.

Ready or not, I needed to step into this new role and own it. So I would. Both literally and figuratively. Starting at once.

I gathered up the gown and strode into the room the prince had washed up in, then halted.

"Divine goddesses above."

Every surface reflected my shocked expression back at me. Floors, ceiling, sunken tub, vanity—everything was made of either solid crystal, frosted glass, or white gold. Candles flickered from a circular chandelier. The chamber gleamed softly like I'd crossed from the underworld and stepped directly onto the surface of the moon.

The only bits of color came from an assortment of makeup in tidy piles on the vanity. Brushes for eyes and face and hair. Jeweled clips and tiaras and pins. Flower buds for my locks. Pots of multicolored inks for my lips. Crushed gold that could be dusted across my face or body, delicate perfume bottles with pale pinks and purples and hues I had no exact name for.

I set aside the gown and picked up one perfume and inhaled. Lilac and maybe almond with a hint of bergamot. Vittoria would have adored the assortment of scented riches. I swallowed the lump forming in my throat and grabbed the lilac perfume. I dabbed a bit on each wrist and rubbed them together. It was heavenly. I smelled another that reminded me of honeysuckle and birchwood and heavy whipping cream. Perhaps a tiny hint of gardenia, too. Another smelled almost exactly like hyacinth, reminding me of lush spring mornings.

I smiled a little to myself; Vittoria's passion for creating perfume aided me with singling out different notes. For a minute, I could almost close my eyes and pretend she was here now. The moment passed, a temporary shadow cast from a cloud racing past the sun.

I inspected each bottle and all of the items Wrath had supplied. Nothing surprised me as much as the fresh flowers. A crystal vase sat on the vanity beside the makeup.

Fragrant blossoms in whites and pale blues and rose-gold pinks cascaded around a smattering of ferns and eucalyptus stuck throughout the arrangement. The flowers were all lovely, almost exactly what was found in the human world, except they were coated in ice.

I breathed them in, surprised their scent penetrated the frost. My fingers trailed over the icy petals. I wondered if the flowers were Wrath's idea or if someone else had sent them.

Someone like my soon-to-be husband. I stopped wondering. It didn't matter.

My attention swept across the sunken glass tub; it took up almost the entire center of the room. I could swim from side to side and do laps in it. It was one of the grandest things I'd ever seen. Before bed I'd definitely take a swim. Now I had things to do, secrets to uncover. And seven demon courts to slowly infiltrate, starting with House Wrath.

Thus far the underworld was wildly different from what I'd heard about it from mortal religion. I had much to learn if I had hopes of sorting truth from fiction while here.

A quick bath was all I could spare time for. I removed my robe and waded in, quickly scrubbing my skin and hair with a bar of soap laid atop folded linen. The water was a perfect temperature. Not too hot or cold, but delightfully warm. Part of me reconsidered my plan to quickly bathe and instead spend the rest of the evening floating in heaven.

With a sigh, I rinsed off and pulled myself from the tub. The length of linen I found near the water's edge was big enough to towel off my whole body.

Once I was properly dry, I picked up the gown. Goddess bless me and the demon who ordered this wardrobe, the dress was designed to be put on without assistance. I shimmied it up over my hips and chest. Little hook-and-eye closures ran up the side and clasped with ease.

I went back to my bedchamber and rummaged around until I found a pair of heeled black shoes coated in a glittery charcoal dust and slipped them on. They fit perfectly, just like the gown. Wrath was nothing if not a perfectionist.

I returned to the bathing chamber, ready to address the matter of my hair. My attention slid to the makeup. Our family didn't have money for such a large assortment of luxury items.

I sat on the crystal stool and applied some kohl to my upper lash line. My fingers hovered above a beautiful set of orange blossoms sewn carefully onto hairpins. At home, I wouldn't second-guess my choice to weave them into my hair. But here...

I chose a violent, bloody shade of red and painted my lips the color of murder instead.

The wardrobe and the clothing weren't the only bits of extravagance I discovered.

Wrath had set me up in a bedroom suite fit for a queen. Not only did I have a bathing chamber that almost rivaled the entire size of my family home, there was also a sitting room, a bedroom, and another room that seemed to be designed for lounging or receiving guests or dedicated to whatever other leisurely activity I wished. There was an inviting divan that looked perfect for curling up with a good book. I was unsure what to do with so much space.

A rack of bottles that appeared to be expensive spirits filled one wall in the leisure chamber. I ran a finger over the cool glass, peering into each one. Different petals and crushed herbs infused the liquor inside. Bribery, no doubt. I left them unopened and continued my inspection. Every room was finely appointed, the furniture plush and welcoming, if not edged in elegance. It seemed that the demon prince was trying to impress me.

Or perhaps he was trying to apologize for the whole soul-stealing unpleasantries between us. Betrayal went down easier if it was served with fine demon liquor, personal suites in luxurious palaces, and expensive gifts. At least according to *him*.

Though, I suppose, he also might be showing respect to his future queen. Apparently being betrothed to Pride came with some benefits, even in a rival demon House.

I strode through the bedroom, heading for the exit I found in an antechamber. It was going to take more than decadent furnishings and pretty dresses to fix our current situation. For one, the prince might start with an apology. Then perhaps we might have an honest conversation.

I wanted to settle whatever was brewing between us before

I left for my husband's castle. I did not need any more animosity between House Wrath and myself.

I had enough to worry about as it stood.

A knock came at the door just as my hand closed around the knob. I yanked it open, ready to give Wrath hell for being such a pimpled ass.

"Oh." I blinked at Anir. "I wasn't expecting you."

"Nice to see you again, too."

Anir held a covered tray in one hand, and a bottle of what looked to be wine in the other. His long midnight hair was pulled into neat knot at the base of his neck and his scar gleamed silver against his tawny skin. The suit he wore now was much finer than the first time I'd met him in Palermo. I didn't see his deadly demon blade but knew he was likely armed.

"I didn't mean—"

"You did. And I don't mind." He winked. "Thought you might be hungry. Or want to get drunk."

My attention darted into the elegant stone corridor with arches rivaling any grand cathedral. Empty. "Did your prince send you to spy on me?"

"Have some food and wine and find out. I'm a terrible gossip when I'm deep into my cups."

I highly doubted Anir was ever impaired enough to not mind what he was saying. Wrath would never trust him if he let secrets slip after a few glasses of wine or spirits. I wrinkled my nose at the bottle. "Isn't it a bit early for drinking?"

"It's well into evening. You slept most of the day."

I swept my arm in welcome and closed the door behind him. Anir set the tray and bottle on the glass table in the corner and tugged the lid off with a grand flourish. Fruits, cured meats, hard cheese, marinated olives, and crostini were laid out with expert care.

I stared emotionlessly at the spread.

"Wrath acted like human food wasn't something he was exposed to. Another lie?"

"No." Anir pulled two glasses from a little mirrored cabinet near the table and poured us each a generous amount of wine. "I stock up on supplies from the human world whenever I can. Mostly hard cheese and cured meat and various nuts and wheats and rice. Things that can be easily stored or dried." He handed over my glass of wine. "His highness made sure I brought these items back. He thought you might want something that reminded you of home tonight. Now that you're not near death and can enjoy it."

I accepted the glass and sniffed it. "Red wine, or demon wine?"

"Regular, human red." He clinked his glass against mine. "You'll spot the difference when you see demon wine. It's unmistakable."

Letting that ominous-sounding information go, I took a sip. It had a smooth, sweet undertone to it. I drank more. "So. Human food and wine. Are you supposed to be lowering my inhibitions and gaining my trust? I imagine you're going to pretend to be drunk, offer some innocuous information predetermined by your prince, and see what secrets I spill in return."

"Are you always this cynical?"

"If there's one thing I've learned recently, it's to question anyone connected to the demon realm. Everyone has their own agenda. Their own game. If I ask enough questions, eventually I'll catch someone in their well-constructed lie. Though, according to the princes, they are incapable of directly telling an untruth. Another fabrication, I'm sure. Or maybe that's why you're here. *You* can lie for Wrath."

I plucked an olive from a tiny dish and popped it into my mouth. The briny flavor was a nice counterpoint to the wine. I sampled a bit of cheese and meat and bread. Anir watched me, his expression contemplative, if not a bit sad.

"I just haven't quite worked out what else he could possibly want from me now. He won."

Anir swirled his wine. "What, exactly, do you think he's won?"

"His freedom. His grand deception. Making me look like a fool for trusting him when he said we'd work together." I finished off my glass and poured a second. Before I took a sip, I ate another olive. "Why don't you explain demon politics to me so I can figure out what else he's gained by signing my soul to the devil."

"Is that what he told you?"

"I..." I thought back to the night we'd kissed, when I'd repeated what I'd heard from Envy. I couldn't recall what Wrath said, exactly, but... "He didn't deny the accusation. If he wasn't worried about being caught in a lie, why wouldn't he tell me otherwise?"

"*Acta non verba.*" Anir grinned. "He lives by that principle."

Actions, not words. I clamped my mouth shut. Wrath brought me to the underworld. He came bearing a contract with Pride. It was a fairly large, undeniable action. He didn't have to say a thing. I got his message, and it was as loud and clear as a cloudless summer sky. Wrath had no qualms about using me for his gain. He'd once said he'd lie, cheat, steal, or murder to procure his freedom. I was lucky he'd only deceived me, though that was hardly a consolation.

"What do you know about Pride's consort? How was she murdered?"

"Interesting, if not an aggressive, subject change." Anir put some cheese on a slice of crostini and topped it off with prosciutto. "My unsolicited advice? Take a subtler approach with information-gathering here. The royal Houses are ancient and antiquated in their ways. They won't give you anything if you demand it or openly ask about it. It's considered rude and uncouth. Plus, they do not believe in giving without gain. You ask for something, you better be prepared to pay a price."

I worried my lower lip between my teeth, thinking. Anir offered truth and advice freely. If I had to gamble on any friendship here, perhaps I should bet on him, regardless of his close connection with Wrath. I set my glass down.

"I'm not sure how to bring that up in a more casual or innocuous way. If I'm being truthful, I'm a bit overwhelmed."

"Understandable. A lot is changing and quickly. I imagine it's hard... processing so many emotions."

It was an odd turn of phrase. "You must have traveled through the Sin Corridor. I doubt you have to stretch your imagination very far to understand how it feels."

"True enough." He took a sip of his wine, gaze searching. "You'll need to gain the princes' trust, become their friend. Let them conspire with you, seek you out. If you play into their egos and the sins they represent, they'll offer up bits of useful information. Always be prepared to give up a secret or make a bargain. Pick things you won't mind sharing or having used against you. Define the terms before you agree, or else they'll bend things to their advantage."

I exhaled. "I was hoping for a faster solution."

"You're involved in something spanning decades and realms. There is no such thing as fast or easy. This goes beyond the bloodshed on your isle. But if you start there, perhaps you'll learn more.

Narrow your list. Concentrate on who you think has the answers you seek. What information do you need most? What will be the most beneficial to your overall goal?"

"I don't have an agenda. I'm simply curious. If Pride's wife was murdered, and each of his next potential brides were, too, I want to avoid that same fate."

"If that was completely true, you wouldn't have come here at all."

"I'm here to ensure demons don't slip through the gates. I'm here to protect my family."

Anir didn't respond. We both knew that was only partially true. If I wanted answers about Pride's consort and details of her life and death, I needed to go to Pride. Except he was locked in a childish battle of male ego with Wrath and I needed an invitation.

I hadn't gotten anywhere with Envy, and his role in my sister's murder was still murky. Discovering who killed the first consort might be the most helpful route to take with solving *my* mystery. And I hadn't fully lied; knowing what happened to her *would* help me. It sounded like Anir knew more, but the way he'd phrased his statement brooked no room for entertaining that line of questioning. At least it was a subtle clue.

"Why did you choose to become a member of House Wrath?"

Anir didn't answer right away, and I immediately regretted asking something that was likely personal. He heaved a sigh.

"After my parents were murdered, anger and wrath were my biggest comforts. He sensed that, saw the path I was on, and offered me a productive outlet for that fury."

We weren't dissimilar. "How long have you been here?"

"Hmm. Time is peculiar here. A mortal hour might be a week. A month, a decade. All I know is it's been a while." Anir took a generous pull of his wine, eyes narrowed. "Your turn. What did you do to him?"

"I'm not sure I follow your meaning. What happened?"

"He went out and brought down an entire mountain on the western edge of the Undying Lands. We've got letters pouring in from House Lust and House Gluttony so far. They believe the end days are here and want to know if we're preparing for war."

"Why is it whenever a man throws a tantrum a woman is blamed for his poor behavior? If Wrath acted like an idiot, he accomplished that all on his own. I don't see why his temper is so shocking. He *is* the living embodiment of wrath. I'm sure you've seen him angry."

Anir smirked over his glass. "You're certain he was mad?"

"What else would he be?"

"Pick another emotion."

"Does being a prideful bastard count?"

"Your room, your rules. But I don't think he was angry or prideful." His dark eyes twinkled. "You know, in all the years I've known him, he's never personally escorted anyone into the City of Ice." Whatever question he saw in my face, he clarified, "It's what House Wrath is known as within the Seven Circles. The more powerful the House, the colder the circle."

Explained all the frosty glass and crystal décor in my bathing chamber.

"I wouldn't read too much into his supposed good deed. He had to escort me because of the contract. He needed my soul to settle his debt."

"That was accomplished the instant you crossed into the underworld. He could have left you alone in the Sin Corridor. He *should* have." Anir abruptly stood and headed for the door in the antechamber. He tapped his fingers on its frame and glanced back at me. "He's on the seventh-floor balcony now. In case you wanted to fight some more. I think it's good for him. Being challenged. You certainly get under his skin."

Like a poisoned splinter straight to the heart, no doubt. It was tempting, and I might have done just that, if I hadn't noticed an object placed on the edge of the bed.

Something that didn't belong and hadn't been there a few moments before. I bid Anir good night and pressed myself against the closed door, silently counting the increased beats of my heart as I stared into the other room.

Fear. This realm thrived on it. And I would deprive it in every way I could.

I exhaled slowly, counted to ten.

Then I stood up straight, pulled my shoulders back, and marched over to the human skull.

SIX

"Angelus mortis lives," the skull crooned the moment I got within inches of it, its voice eerily similar to my twin's. Fine hairs rose along my arms. It was as if Vittoria crossed the barrier between life and death to send a message, except it was slightly off, wrong. *"Fury. Almost free. Maiden, Mother, Crone. Past, present, future, find."*

"Vittoria?" The fleshless jaws went slack, and whatever dark magic had fueled the skull vanished. I swallowed hard, unable to take my eyes off the cursed messenger. "Goddess above."

How someone had snuck an enchanted skull in without Anir or me noticing was almost as troubling as the magic used to power it. I'd never heard of a spell that commanded the bones of the dead. Sure, there was necromancy, but that's *not* what powered the skull. This wasn't even *il Proibito*. This was something other, something more terrifying than the Forbidden.

I left the skull where it was, plopped onto the glass chair, and took a healthy sip of wine, my mind racing. I thought about Nonna's lessons on dark magic, specifically spells using objects touched by death—how both should be avoided at all costs. Never, not once, did she ever tell us a story about a witch who could manipulate life into something long dead. If that was even what happened. It had to be demon magic. Which meant the sender was likely a prince of Hell.

The question was which one and why.

I replayed the message in my mind. The angel of death lives. *Fury. Almost free. Maiden, Mother, Crone. Past, present, future, find.*

To simplify, and to keep from panicking over the macabre messenger, I decided to pick it apart line by line, starting with the angel of death.

Claudia, my best friend and a witch whose family openly practiced the dark arts, used a black mirror and human bones in her last scrying session, and her mind had been taunted with the voices of the dead. She'd also mentioned something about the angel of death.

I did not believe in coincidences.

I got up and paced around the room, struggling to recall more from Claudia's scrying. That night was filled with terror, and the details were fuzzy. I'd found her on her knees in the courtyard outside the monastery, her nails broken to the quick, as she recited nonsensical messages from the cursed and the damned. She told me to run, but there was no way I'd leave her with the superstitious holy brotherhood. She'd said something about a cunning thief stealing the stars and drinking them dry. That he was coming and going.

That it should have been impossible...

I knew at least four demon princes who were roaming Sicily at that time. Wrath, Envy, Greed, and Lust. One of them had to be the angel of death. Maybe not in the literal sense, but it could certainly be a nickname. I stopped dead in my tracks, heart pounding.

Only one demon fit that description. I'd even called him Samael one night—the angel of death and prince of Rome—thinking it a clever description of him. He'd given me a bemused look, right before he'd warned me to never call him that again. Wrath.

He didn't hide the fact that he was the general of war. He excelled in violence. If he was Death, maybe he hadn't been *chosen* to solve the murders; perhaps he was furious someone sullied his title and involved him without the devil's consent. That would explain why Pride didn't want to invite him into his circle. The devil was punishing Wrath for disobedience.

Which, if true, threw into question every last bit of information I'd wrung from him. If Wrath omitted basic truths about his involvement, there was no telling how far his deception stretched.

I rubbed my temples. Wrath was my top suspect for both the angel of death and the fury portion of the riddle. Next came the Maiden, Mother, and Crone. That part was harder to connect to the murders. According to our history, the Maiden, the Mother, and the Crone were three goddesses who ruled the heavens, the earth, and the underworld.

Old witch legends claimed they'd given birth to the goddesses we prayed to, and one of them—the goddess of the heavens and sun—was La Prima Strega's mother. The Maiden, Mother, and Crone were to our goddesses what Titans were to the gods in mortal mythologies.

If she was real and not a fable, the goddess of the underworld—or any of the goddesses birthed to her realm—would likely possess the kind of magic that animated bones, but *why* she'd send a cryptic message to me remained a mystery. Goddesses had never shown interest in involving themselves with witches before. I doubted they'd start now.

However the Maiden, Mother, and Crone fit, it wasn't through a legend I'd been taught. It wasn't a stretch to think demons had their own stories and histories about them.

Answers weren't going to present themselves by staying locked away in my chamber.

I removed a scarf from the wardrobe and picked up the skull, careful to avoid touching it without cloth. If Vittoria were here, she'd have plucked it up and danced it across the room without a moment's hesitation, fueling Nonna's worry about her affinity with the dead. A smile almost tugged at my lips before I banished it. I glanced around, searching for a hiding place, then knelt down and shoved the skull deep inside the wardrobe and shut its doors.

Situation resolved, I dusted off my hands and went to search House Wrath.

I stopped counting how many stone staircases I'd descended some-where around a dozen. Each magnificent landing ended on a floor that spanned what seemed like thousands of meters. Which must have been deception magic—Wrath's castle couldn't be *that* large.

On the next landing, I stopped to look out a trio of arched win-dows. A large body of merlot-colored water pooled at the bottom of a valley, smoke rising in lazy tendrils from its surface. A branch from a nearby tree fell into the water, immediately bursting into flames.

I made a mental note to never get near the cursed lake unless

I wanted my flesh to burn off my bones. I left the windows and wandered down the corridor.

The castle was mostly built from pale stone, similar to limestone, and there were some wings that had been richly fitted with large, colorful tapestries. This particular wing had an image of angels in battle with monstrous creatures.

It reminded me of art created during the Renaissance; the colors deep and dark against the pale walls and columns. Doors carved from bone opened to ballrooms, and unused bedrooms, and sitting rooms. I stopped outside a towering set of double doors and traced the delicate carving. A tangle of vines with flowers and stars crawled up the edges and top, while the same vines twisted into roots that plunged into the bowels of the earth at the bottom of the doors.

Skeletons and skulls and things left to rot and ruin adorned the lower portion.

I pushed the door open and swallowed a gasp. Inside was a library unlike anything I'd ever dreamed of. Excitement rushed through me as I stepped into the room and stared at rows and rows of glass shelves. They went on for an eternity.

My face split into a wide grin. The goddesses must have been smiling down on me; this was the *perfect* place to research magic and myths. I marveled at the jewel-toned vellum spines of thousands of books. Someone had arranged them by color, their bindings ranging from the most brilliant shades of yellow to the palest butter creams and pure snow-whites. Reds, purples, blues, greens, and oranges; it was a rainbow of beauty set against a backdrop of ice.

I couldn't picture Wrath being serene enough for a quiet night of reading, and if he did, I never would have guessed he'd do it with a riot of color surrounding him. Maybe ebonies and gold—dark gleaming wood and leather. Masculine elegance at its finest. This was...

"Haven. Close to Heaven but not quite as boring."

I spun around, a hand pressed against my pounding heart. "Sneaking up on people is rude. I thought demon princes were supposed to have impeccable manners."

"We do. Mostly." Wrath's gaze traveled unapologetically over my strapless gown, and I became excruciatingly aware of each place the silky fabric slid across my skin. I suspected his perusal had more to do with ensuring I'd dressed the part of future queen, and would not embarrass myself in front of any members of his court, rather than anything else. "My personal library is one level down."

"Let me guess... Hell? Blacks, leathers, gold?"

"Lots of fire and chains and torture devices, too." His smile was a quick flash of teeth. Dangerous, disarming. A different sort of weapon he'd honed to perfection. Possibly the most perilous in his arsenal. Especially here. "When you're feeling brave enough, I'll show you."

My stomach did a tiny flip at the thought of chains and dark spaces and Wrath. "Naming your libraries Haven and Hell is dramatic enough to suit you, I suppose." I walked down an aisle filled with various shades of blue books, the demon trailing me. I needed to stop looking at that smile, or this realm would pounce. "Have you heard from any of your brothers?"

"Envy, Lust, and Greed have all shown interest in hosting you. We received their House cards earlier." His tone remained light, almost suspiciously so. "They've specifically requested your presence at their Feast of the Wolf celebrations. I imagine Sloth and Gluttony will eventually stop overindulging enough to send invitations, too."

Lupercalia was a pre-Roman holiday that roughly meant "Feast of the Wolf," where humans sacrificed goats, then anointed foreheads of the wealthy in the spilled blood. Some cut pieces from the creatures then ran naked through the streets, smacking bystanders with the flesh. If the demon celebration was anything similar, I'd prefer to avoid it.

Without turning around, I said, "Will you be hosting a feast?"

He appeared before me, leaning casually against a shelf. Supernatural speed on full display. I couldn't help but run my gaze over him. His suit was the deep charcoal of shadows. It made me think of nighttime and silken sheets and secret rendezvous and things I shouldn't.

"No. I'm waiting to see what Pride does."

"Has he sent a summons yet?"

"No."

"Why are you waiting to see what he does?"

"It's one of the few times all seven princes are invited into the same royal domain. Then it's three days of pomp and circumstance—dinners, hunts, a masked ball, then the feast. We decide where it will be held based on two factors. Where the guest of honor chooses to go, and which prince with the highest rank decides to host."

"Aren't you all of equal power?" Wrath shook his head, not elaborating. I locked my frustration away. "What if the guest of honor doesn't pick the prince with the highest rank?"

"They always do. And if they don't, they're strongly encouraged to from whichever House they're from. Refusing is a grave insult and has caused more than a few bloodbaths over the centuries." For a fleeting moment, he looked hungry for battle. Then his expression turned contemplative. "Princes all suffer from surges of other sins, it seems."

Our gazes locked. I understood what he really meant. Wrath was apologizing for our argument earlier. This information was an olive branch laid at my feet. I could kick it aside and continue our fight, or I could accept it and move on.

I resumed my slow procession down the aisle, looking for a particular subject matter, but projecting nonchalance to avoid suspicion.

"Why do you celebrate a pre-Roman tradition, anyway?"

"How very mortal of you to believe *they* weren't inspired by *our* rites and rituals," he scoffed. "They didn't even have the decency to keep the correct dates or practices."

I stopped my perusal of titles and studied him closely. "Why are you really telling me this? Do each of the princes of Hell turn into giant wolves and howl under a full moon? Perhaps I should be worried about you panting at my bedroom door before the feast."

"We do wear wolf masks, but there will be no panting from me. Unless you ask nicely."

I swallowed hard, forcing my thoughts away from where this realm—and this troublesome prince—was tugging them. "You didn't answer my first question. Why are you telling me about this now?"

"You've been nominated for the guest of honor." The remaining humor left his face. "The vote takes place next month. I have little doubt you're going to be chosen. Your arrival is the talk of the Seven Circles. I doubt anyone else will be half as intriguing this Blood Season."

Wonderful. "Will I be forced to kill the goat?"

Nonna didn't admit to knowing about either right away when I'd confronted her.

Which made me wonder how many other things she hadn't been forthcoming about. We learned the bare minimum of earth magic; how to cast simple spells aided with herbs and objects of intent. Charms of protection. Sleep spells and harmless spells that manipulated the dew on a glass to slide it across a surface. Things that hardly required much skill.

A Latin phrase or word here, a pinch of this there and a spell was cast, aided with our magical blood. What else was there about the curse that I didn't know?

Or our magic, for that matter.

I walked in an agitated circle. Now that I was questioning things, I couldn't stop finding more gaps in our lives. Nonna spent so much time teaching us the ways of demons, only to stunt our education regarding our own abilities. I couldn't help but wonder if there was a reason for that. Nonna was much too smart to have forgotten valuable lessons.

Surely offensive magic was just as important as our defensive spells of protection. But she never taught us those kinds of bold spells. In fact, she seemed determined to keep that magic from us at all costs. Was there something dangerous about us using it?

Vittoria and I were told to listen to her, to obey and follow the rules or suffer the consequences. I'd never wanted to anger Nonna or cause harm.

But Vittoria always pushed the limits, unafraid of the consequences.

Wrath's sharp comment carved deep, infected me. Like it was designed to do. His weaponry was not limited to steel or bullets or sly grins and heady kisses. His words were just as deadly when aimed and fired at a target. I couldn't escape the gnawing feeling that maybe he was right.

There were holes in my education I couldn't ignore.

Some spells came easily as if through body memory. Some I had to learn and almost always forgot. I couldn't recall where or how I'd discovered the truth spell, only that one day I wanted truth and out came a spell that stole away free will. Nonna had been furious when I told her. Instead of being rewarded for using that level of power, I was punished.

I marched to the end of the shelves and found a plush, over-sized chair to sit in. A thought I couldn't run from followed me there. Maybe Wrath wasn't referring only to Nonna.

My sister had found the first book of spells, used demon magic to lock her diary, and had brought Greed and the shape-shifters together for reasons I didn't fully understand, given the fact shape-shifters and demons were natural enemies.

I stared down at my finger, startled to see I still wore the olive branch ring Wrath had given me. I absently twisted the gold band around my finger. I wondered what else Vittoria might have dis-covered before her death. Was it the full truth of the devil's curse and the blood debt? Maybe that knowledge, more than anything else, was why she'd really been killed.

Something buried deep in my memory stirred, then floated away. A wisp of smoke I couldn't grasp. I had the strangest impres-sion that maybe the devil hadn't been cursed at all.

If that was true... then perhaps the witch murders had noth-ing to do with his finding a bride, and everything I thought I knew had been fabricated from deception. Nonna. Vittoria. The seven princes of Hell. At least one of them had been lying.

And I was more determined than ever to find out why.

It took a few frustrating hours, but I finally found what I'd been searching for. I pulled a grimoire on beginning magic and plopped into a chair near a darkened corner. I swept my gaze around the space; there were no sounds or indications anyone else was in the library. Not that it would seem odd if a witch was studying magic. Still, I didn't want anyone to realize how much my education lacked. I cracked the worn leather spine and began reading.

According to the witch who authored this book, our magic was similar to a muscle that needed to be exercised. If ignored too long, it atrophied. She also described it as "Source": a place within us readily available to draw from, like an endless well in our core.

The wise Spinners of Fate say our power is a gift bestowed from the goddesses and therefore has a tendency to mimic their abilities to some degree. Some bloodlines will notice an affinity for certain spells, especially those using the four elements. It is an indication of which goddess a witch should pray to in order to enhance that magic. The lesser spoken of fifth element, aether, is thought to be the rarest, but that may not be true in this context.

I stopped reading and allowed that information to sink in. And with it another emotion I'd rather not examine closely. Not quite suspicion, nor anger, but something related to both. Nonna had never explained where our power came from or how it worked. It was possible my grandmother didn't exactly know, but I couldn't quite believe that.

This was also the first time I'd ever heard of the Spinners of Fate and praying to one goddess. We'd always been taught to pray to them all. I searched my memory for any altars Nonna made for any one goddess and could think of none. Perhaps our magic wasn't closely aligned with any of the elements.

I leafed through the grimoire, searching for more information on the Spinners of Fate, but there were no further mentions. I flipped back to the beginning, concentrating on Source.

Anger at Nonna and my own lack of questioning our education distracted me.

"*Focus.*"

Skeptical of my abilities, I closed my eyes, cleared my thoughts, and tried to sense that inner source of power. At first there wasn't anything unusual, then the world quickly faded around me. It grew darker in my mind. I knew nothing, was nothing. I became nothing.

It was almost a void inside me, yawning open into endless darkness. I had the strangest impression that it had been waiting for me to tap into it, and once I acknowledged its existence, I was immediately drawn in. Now I felt *everything*. I tunneled down, down, down into my very center, near my wildly beating heart, and paused. My magic slumbered here. I wasn't sure how I knew, but I did. I brought my consciousness around the magic, trying to get a better sense of it. Something ancient and powerful and spitting mad cracked an eye, furious at being awoken.

I withdrew from that place with a gasp.

"Holy goddess above...what *was* that?"

I flipped through the pages of the grimoire, but there was no mention of a power like the one I'd just experienced. It certainly didn't fit into earth, air, fire, water, or aether. It was massive, all-knowing, powerful in a way that worried me. Its rage burned with an intensity that obliterated reason. If I could summon that force at will...I could destroy this realm.

Not that I wanted to do that. I only wanted vengeance against my twin's murderer. I took a deep breath and closed my eyes, ready to try again.

"Oh, pardon me."

I glanced up from my spell work, my education abandoned, and closed the grimoire with a loud clap. A young woman—with curly jet-black hair, rich sepia-colored eyes, and brown skin—gave me a polite curtsy. Little animal skulls were fastened in her long hair, similar to the way I pinned flowers in mine. A deep russet-copper dress hugged each of her generous curves. She held a book on arboriculture, a surprising but interesting choice.

"You must be Emilia. The whole court is vastly intrigued by you. I'm Fauna."

I gave her a tentative smile. I'd been counting on the fact that gossip would be as widely used here as it had been in the marketplace back home. "What kind of nasty rumors are circulating?"

"The usual. Your hair is made of serpents, your tongue of fire, and when you're angry, you spit flames like the mighty ice dragons of Merciless Reach." She grinned at my look of surprise. "Teasing. They're too smart to start rumors while Prince Wrath is in residence. As his personal guest, you're off limits. He's made that very clear. Lord or lady of the Royal Demon Court, if your name is on anyone's tongue, he will rip it out."

"More like he'll glare at them until they wither and die if they impede his mission."

She gave me a curious look. "Actually, he was quite literal in his threat. Lord Makaden's lucky he escaped with his intact. The prince promised the next time he speaks ill of you, his tongue will be spiked outside the throne room and stay there until it rots. Makaden's prominent standing in the court is likely the only reason he's not maimed now."

I had to mentally remind myself to keep breathing as that image took shape. "Truly? Wrath threatened to rip out someone's tongue?"

"It's no idle threat. It was a warning to be heeded. His highness is not merciful with those who challenge him. This morning he brought a mountain down on Domitius, his lieutenant general." Fauna's smile faded. "They're still searching through the rubble."

I was at a loss for words. Anir only said he'd taken a mountain down. He didn't mention anyone being crushed by it. Wrath was a prince of Hell. A general of war. One of the feared and mighty Seven. This news shouldn't be surprising. I'd seen his violence before.

Still, it served as a reminder of who I was dealing with and where I was. I would need to play my game expertly when I went to any other courts.

The fact that Wrath had harmed a high-ranking officer shouldn't have come as a shock. He'd probably taken his dark mood out on him after our fight this morning. If that was what he did after a small argument, I worried about who might feel his legendary wrath after our latest disagreement. Guilt sank its claws in deep, though logically I knew I had nothing to feel guilty about. He was solely responsible for his actions.

"Do you know why Wrath attacked him?"

"I believe Domitius suggested serving your still-beating heart to the soldiers. Though others claim he made lewd comments about your physical attributes. Something about tasting you to see if you were as sweet as your 'ripe bosom' suggested."

"And the other? What did he say?"

"Lord Makaden inquired about his highness having any other rules governing tongues and how they applied to you." She hesitated. "Neither one of them are considered to be very...

humorous. His majesty was right to act swiftly. One rotten demonberry spoils the whole bushel."

Charming. It was a delicate way of saying the demons would have acted on their statements. Or at least tried to. I might not be well versed with weapons or combat, but I did have some skill with a blade, thanks to time spent in the kitchen, breaking down carcasses. I knew vital areas to aim for and wouldn't hesitate to stick someone who meant me harm.

I'd request a weapon the next time I saw Wrath. Surely he would grant me some means of protection. I did not want to rely on him or anyone else for my safety.

"Were either of them your lover?"

"Devils, no." Fauna snorted. "You'll meet the object of my pining soon enough. Tomorrow night, in fact."

Suspicion pooled inside me along with dread. "What's happening tomorrow?"

"Nothing too scandalous or terrifying. Only dinner with the most elite House Wrath members." Her smile was full and bright. "Don't be worried. Prince Wrath forbade 'guttings at gatherings' at least a century ago. Now the only blades we arm ourselves with are our sharp glares. We stare daggers over our wine and dream of sticking our enemies in flesh. Consider it practice for the upcoming feast."

"I heard a fear is torn from the guest of honor. Can someone offer to stand in?" If so, I'd bargain with Wrath or the devil himself if I had to. "Any upper nobility, perhaps?"

"Even if it were allowed, which it may well be, no one would volunteer." Fauna gave me a pitying look. "Definitely no prince of this realm. It would give the other royals too much power." She held her book tightly. "You're staying in the Crystal Wing, correct?"

"Maybe?" I lifted a shoulder. "There's a lot of crystal in my chamber."

"Wonderful. I'll meet you before dinner and escort you down."

Before I could agree or ask questions, she hurried out of the library.

I shook my head. My first day in House Wrath had been a disaster. Arriving with hypothermia, an enchanted skull, arguments with the prince, secrets my family might be keeping about my magic, a maimed member of Wrath's army, and the new threat of the Feast of the Wolf looming above it all.

The last thing in the world I wanted was to offer up my worst fear to a realm that would torture me with it. But perhaps if I learned how to harness my power, I could solve Vittoria's murder and be back home in the mortal world well before that happened.

I collected the grimoire, pushed myself up, and retreated back to my rooms, needing to prepare for tomorrow. Given the information regarding the felled mountain, I had little doubt dinner would be its own sort of wicked battle. One I'd be lucky to escape from unscathed.

I didn't end up back in the Crystal Wing. Curiosity got the better of me and I decided to investigate Wrath's version of Hell. Know thy enemy ... and his reading habits.

I found a circular staircase near the back of the rainbow library and carefully descended into the darkness yawning below. My initial guess of ebony, gold, and leather wasn't that far off from the reality of his personal library. Dark, butter-soft worn leather chairs were placed before a fireplace that took up a wall made of stacked stone. I could easily stand upright in the opening and stretch my arms above my head and still not reach the top of it. Several rugs in various shades of charcoal and black with gold thread details were tastefully laid around the room.

Here, the shelves were obsidian gemstone, the books all bound with dark shades of leather. A circular chandelier with thin iron arms hung from exposed beams and cast an enticing glow over the room. It was the perfect place to curl up and read in front of a crackling fire. There was even a plush throw blanket tossed casually across the back of a reading chair.

In an alcove off the main reading space a set of manacled chains hung from the wall. Wrath hadn't been teasing. My mouth went dry and I quickly averted my gaze.

Torture wasn't the first thing that had sprung to mind. And I did *not* want this realm working its devious magic on any more fleeting emotions. I moved through the rest of the space, devouring as much as I could.

Books and journals on war strategy, history—both demon and human—witch rituals, grimoires, and even a few handwritten notes were placed in neat stacks on a large, imposing desk. Latin and a language I couldn't read. Nothing incriminating or useful. Nothing of goddesses or their magic, or demon fables about the Maiden, Mother, or Crone. No spells on reanimating skulls or other bones.

Just pens and pots of ink. A rough stone I imagined was used to sharpen a blade.

On a shelf behind the desk were seven volumes of journals dedicated to each demon House. Eight journals, actually, if the pattern in the dust was any indication. Perhaps one House was so prolific it had taken more than one book to get all the information down. Whatever the case, the text was missing now.

Apparently, the titles were the only things written in Latin. I thumbed through a few but couldn't read the language within. Frustration built behind my breastbone as I shoved the journals back in place. Nothing was ever easy.

A decanter partially filled with lavender liquid and a matching crystal glass caught my attention. Curious about what Wrath indulged in, I splashed some liquor into the glass and sniffed. Notes of citrus and botanicals blended together. I took a careful sip and hissed through my teeth at the burn. It was strong. Almost like human brandy but with a sweeter, vanilla undertone. If I smoothed it out with some cream and ice it would be divine.

And might help get me through tomorrow evening. I'd send for a glass before the meal.

I set the liquor aside and sat at the desk, rattling the drawers. Locked, naturally. Tucked below a copper serpent sculpture I assumed was used as a paperweight, was an envelope with elegant script. Not feeling guilty at all, I read the message.

Brother,

They have been found.
VIII

G

I read it over again, not that it helped decipher the single line. I imagined the G stood for Greed. But it could also be Gluttony.

They have been found. VIII. Envy and Greed had both been after the Horn of Hades, but Wrath never showed much interest in the amulets. Not to mention, he was now in possession of them until Pride allowed us into his territory.

"So what, then, were you searching for, dearest, secretive, Wrath?"

I picked up the serpent paperweight and rolled it between my palms. "Ouch."

I turned it over; little sharp ridges in a geometric design poked out from the bottom. It was a wax seal, not a paperweight. Or maybe it was both. I set it aside and scanned the note again. Something stood out this time. It didn't address anyone by name. Which meant there was no way to know if Wrath was the intended recipient, or if he'd intercepted it.

Maybe this message was meant for the devil—to let him know his horns had been recovered. Maybe the G symbolized Wrath's true name and he was the one sending out the correspondence. Or maybe there wasn't anything important about this at all and I was so desperate to find clues, I was inventing them.

It was also missing a date, so there was no way to know if this was recent news or ancient history. Unless that was what the *VIII* portion meant. I had no idea how the demons tabulated time. It was the late nineteenth century on earth, but it could be eight eons here. Or maybe it was indicating the missing eighth journal. I could spend eternity guessing.

I put the useless note away, commandeered a pot of ink, pen, and some parchment, retrieved the grimoire on beginning magic, and headed back to my chamber, more frustrated and lost than I'd felt before. Tomorrow, I had to hope, would bring some clarity, even if it came in the form of watching how the demons interacted and learning how they moved through court.

Given my working-class standing, I had not associated with wealthy circles back home, so tomorrow would be a test of how well I could blend in. My path to vengeance would be a slow burn, not a raging inferno. By the time I invaded House Pride, I would be well versed in proper deception.

When the demon responsible for Vittoria's death finally felt the flames of my fury, I'd hopefully have burned his House of Sin to ash.

EIGHT

Drying blood or an aged merlot, reduced in a saucepan and drizzled over a cut of peppercorn-encrusted meat. I twisted from side to side in the gilded floor-length mirror. I couldn't decide which description better captured the unique color of the gown I now wore. Nonna would call it a blood-drenched omen and offer up prayers to the goddesses.

I quite liked it.

I'd obviously never attended a royal demon dinner party before, and the note that arrived early this morning in Wrath's elegant slashes indicated I should wear something fierce and formal. This gown was both. A stiff corset bodice plunged into a deep *V* between my breasts, showing off my bronzed skin. Fine black snakeskin was embroidered onto the daring top, while the skirts remained that solid shade of dark wine. Demon finery in all its gothic glory.

Since this gown was also strapless, my shimmering tattoo was on full display. I decided to forgo gloves to show it off. I wore no jewels except for the ring Wrath had gifted me. It would make an interesting topic of discussion, no doubt.

And would hopefully serve its purpose well.

I missed the silver *cornicello* I'd worn my whole life, but had to accept my amulet was gone for good. I moved into the bathing chamber and toyed with my unbound hair. Yesterday Fauna's style had been loose and wild and lovely, so I fashioned mine in a similar manner to avoid any missteps in attire. Long dark waves cascaded down my back, and the shorter pieces framing my face fell forward as I pretended to converse with diners on either side of me.

Which wouldn't do. I didn't want to hide behind anything this evening. The lords and ladies of Hell would gaze upon me without any barriers.

No matter how afraid or nervous I was, I refused to look it.

In a vanity drawer, I discovered little bird skull clips and pulled the top portion of my hair back. I placed the bones prettily about my crown like a diadem of death and added flowers between the macabre. There. Now I looked like a princess of Hell, if not its future queen.

Although, with the bones in my hair and the familiar glint of barely leashed anger shining in my eyes, I supposed I could also pass for the goddess of death and fury.

I walked back into my bedchamber and halted halfway through it. Placed on the glass table—next to the bottle of wine left over from Anir's visit the night before—was another skull.

"Blood and bones." Almost literally.

I drew in a deep breath and moved close enough for it to deliver its message. Almost immediately, it spoke in that same, Vittoria-like voice that made goose bumps rise across my body. *"Seven stars, seven sins. As above, so below."*

"Goddess above. What does that even *mean*?"

I didn't expect a response and wasn't too disappointed when none came. I heaved a sigh. I hated riddles. Confusing, worthless things. I pulled out the inkpot, pen, and parchment I'd taken from Wrath's library and scribbled notes.

If one of Wrath's brothers was taking the time to send messages via possessed skulls, it definitely meant something. Unless one of the seven princes was simply toying with me out of boredom. Which I doubted but wouldn't rule out. Perhaps they were petty enough to do it.

> ~ *Enchanted skulls* ~
>
> Skull one: *Angelus mortis* lives. Fury. Almost free. Maiden, Mother, Crone. Past, present, future, find.
> Skull two: Seven stars, seven sins. As above, so below.

The seven sins were the easiest to decipher; clearly it meant the princes of Hell. *As above, so below* was part of the prophecy—which was less clear. No one seemed entirely sure what it meant. Nonna said it related to Vittoria and me, that we were supposed to bring peace to both realms through great sacrifice. But even she didn't have all of the answers. At least that was what she claimed. Who knew the truth anymore? The rest...the rest would take some research.

I started a new line in my notes, determined to have each

theory clearly defined so I could cross it off or add to it over time. Having something written always helped me to truly *see*.

Plus, it was what detectives in novels did, and they always solved their mystery by the end of the book. I was no expert, but I'd try my best. I jotted down as much information as I could recall about the prophecy next.

~ Prophecy ~

As above, so below

- When twin witches are born, they must wear the Horn of Hades. (Vittoria and I.)

  - Twins signal the end of the devil's curse.

- Some witches think it means the use of both light magic and dark magic.

  - Others think a prince of Hell will fall in love with a witch.

- One twin will rule in Hell, the other Heaven. (Both forced to sacrifice.)

My breath caught as I reread the second point. *Twins signal the end of the devil's curse.*

"Holy goddess above. It can't be..."

How did we all miss that earlier? My mind raced with thoughts of Claudia's scrying session once again. About how "he" roamed free and the impossibility of it. She didn't mean the angel of death. She'd been warning us about the devil. If my twin and I ended his curse, it was likely our birth that broke the magic binding him, not an action we'd taken.

Which meant he hadn't been chained in Hell like we'd believed.

And he hadn't been for nearly two decades. While I'd been investigating Vittoria's murder, he'd been free, doing the goddess knew what.

So why, then, did Pride possess the body of Antonio and send Wrath to collect me in his stead? If he was not forced to reign in Hell, he could have come for me himself. He could have come to collect *all* of his potential brides. Why delegate that duty to Wrath?

Unless my earlier suspicion was correct and he was never actually in need of a bride. And the murders were committed for another reason.

Fear slid down my spine. I glanced at the new clock on my nightstand.

I'd wished for the bedside table and clock before turning in for the night, and both had magically appeared while I slept. I didn't know if the room was magicked to my wants, or if Wrath had simply guessed I'd need them. It was likely the latter. Wrath's attention to detail was astounding. As if he had nothing better to do than send for bedside tables.

Dinner was at midnight and there was still an hour left before then. Which gave me just enough time to rush back to the demon prince's personal library. I'd planned to spend the time practicing harnessing my magic source, but that could wait. I needed to retrieve the journal on House Pride and sneak it back to my chamber. Immediately. Demon language or not, I'd find some way to read it, even if I had to bargain away another piece of my soul to accomplish it.

I managed to shove both the skull and stolen journal next to the first skull—hiding them all behind a voluminous dress—and close my wardrobe just as a knock sounded at the door. Exhaling quietly, I said a quick prayer to the goddess of lies and deception and hoped I'd not only make it through the night but that I'd come out more victorious than I dreamed.

I smoothed down the front of my bodice and crossed from my bedchamber into the sitting room that doubled as an antechamber.

With any luck, my racing heartbeat would be mistaken for nerves about dinner.

I opened the door and Fauna smiled broadly. Her happiness didn't seem forced and a knot loosened in my chest. Perhaps I could strike a bargain with her to read the journal—she was a demon; she would no doubt possess the skills needed to read the demonic language.

But I wasn't ready to hand over my trust just yet.

Unaware of my silent assessment and wandering thoughts, her gaze quickly traveled over me. "You look lovely, Emilia."

"You do, too." An understatement. She looked resplendent in a silver gown that appeared to be made of liquid metal. Images of Roman centurion breastplates crossed my mind; all she needed was the scarlet skirt or cape to complete the look. "Your gown is like armor."

"Better to shield from the murderous glances with." She winked and stepped back into the corridor, her expression turning serious. "Are you ready? We should make our way there soon. Guests are expected to arrive fashionably late, but not late enough to stoke royal ire."

My pulse pounded. I hadn't heard from—or seen—Wrath at all except for the note he sent regarding my clothing earlier. I had no idea what to expect from him tonight: how he would act in front of his subjects, if he'd ignore my presence, mock me, or seat me in a place of honor.

Maybe he wouldn't even bother to show up. Perhaps he'd throw me to the wolves and see if I was vicious enough to grow fangs and make it out on my own. After our encounter in the library, he certainly seemed to hold a grudge against my family. What better way to exact revenge on them than by leaving me alone in a room full of bloodthirsty demons?

"Will Wrath be attending?"

"Yes."

The deep, smooth voice owned my attention with just one word. My eyes snapped to his. Wrath stood in the corridor, dressed in a signature black suit, his gaze darkening at the sight of me. A crown of obsidian snakes dusted with gold sat upon his head. If a tall, menacing shadow had sprung to life—appearing both dangerous and tempting as sin—it would look just like him.

I told myself his unexpected appearance outside my bedroom suite caused the flutter in my pulse, and that it had absolutely *nothing* to do with the handsome prince or the predatory gleam in his gaze. The gaze that was trained wholly on me as if the rest of the realm could burn and he'd pay it no mind. There was something in the way he stared that...

Fauna twisted around to see who had caught my attention and immediately fell into a deep curtsy. "Your highness."

"Leave us."

With a quick look of sympathy in my direction, Fauna hurried down the corridor and disappeared from sight. Once the sound of her heeled shoes faded, Wrath stalked closer, his heavy focus sliding from the animal-bone crown I wore, to his ring on my finger, and inched all the way down to my toes before he dragged it back up. I did my best to breathe in even intervals.

I couldn't tell if it was ravenous greed, wrath, or lust glinting in his eyes. Maybe it was a combination of all three. It seemed the underworld wasn't only testing and prodding *my* desires now, it was a battle he was suddenly fighting, too.

When he finally finished his thorough inspection of my attire, his attention settled on mine. A tiny spark jolted through me as our gazes clashed and held.

It was hardly anything, a bit of static electricity one experienced after scuffling their feet and touching metal on an arid day. Except... it didn't feel like *nothing*, exactly.

It felt like the first indication a violent storm was approaching. The sort where you either stood your ground or ran for cover. It was as if the air between us grew heavy and dark with the promise of nature's fury. If I closed my eyes, I could imagine thunder rattling my teeth as winds whipped around, threatening to drag me into the swirling vortex and devour me whole. It was the kind of storm that broke cities, destroyed realms.

And Wrath controlled it all with one powerful glance.

"You look like a beautiful cataclysm."

I laughed, trying to ease the strange tension hovering between us. His choice of words made me wonder just how well he could read my emotions. Maybe none of my secrets had ever been safe from him. "It's every woman's dream to be likened to a natural disaster."

"A violent upheaval. I'd say it suits."

A smile almost made an appearance on his handsome face. Instead, he motioned for me to spin around. I slowly twisted to give him a look at the entirety of me.

The back of the gown was as scandalous as the front. A deep *V* descended all the way down, exposing me nearly to my hips. A thin gold chain linked between my shoulders and swung like a pendulum against my spine, the only other bit of adornment I wore.

It was only because I'd been straining to listen, but I heard the slightest rasp of his breath as he inhaled sharply. Something resembling satisfaction coursed through me.

I was worried I'd feel self-conscious with large swaths of skin showing between my front and back, and the way the gown clung seductively to each curve, but I felt the opposite. I felt powerful. Now I understood why Wrath chose his clothing with such care. I commanded attention without ever opening my mouth.

It was a gamble I'd taken while dressing and—judging from the points of heat at my back and what I imagined was Wrath's inability to keep his gaze from returning to me—I believe it worked. At dinner I wanted all eyes to be fastened on me when I walked in, all conversations to cease. I would not cower behind columns and slink in undetected. If Wrath's subjects were anything like him, I couldn't be seen as weak. They would scent my fear like a swarm of sharks finding a drop of blood in the sea and strike with the same predatory violence.

I went to shift around again, but Wrath stilled me with a light touch on my shoulder. His bare skin blazed against mine. "Wait."

Perhaps it was the soft way he said it, or the feeling of intimacy in his voice, but I obeyed his wish. He carefully gathered up my hair and swept it to one side, letting the strands tickle and tease as they slid across my shoulders. I bit my lip. Shoulders were more erogenous than I'd ever given them credit for. Or maybe it was just the way Wrath moved closer until I felt the heat of him against my skin, and a tiny, intrigued part of me longed to feel more.

He looped a necklace over my head, the weight of it settling just above my cleavage, and fastened it more slowly than was necessary. But I didn't complain or step away.

When he was done, he trailed one finger down my spine, following the line of the thin chain, inadvertently coaxing a small shudder. It took every ounce of stubbornness I could muster to not lean into his caress. To recall my hatred. Because surely that's what that feeling was: the all-consuming, raging fire of loathing.

I slowly turned until we faced each other again. His gaze dropped to my necklace and I finally looked down to see what he'd placed on me. I inhaled sharply as my silver *cornicello* caught the light. "Does the devil know you're giving this to me?"

Wrath didn't take his attention from the amulet. "Consider it borrowed, not given."

"Can you do that? Won't he come after you?"

He made a show of glancing down each end of the empty corridor before looking at me again. "Do you see anyone trying to stop me?" I shook my head. "Then stop worrying."

"I am most certainly not..." His mouth twisted into a troublesome grin as I trailed off, leaving the lie unspoken. I blew out a quiet breath. "It doesn't mean what you think it does. Stop smirking."

"What, exactly, do *you* think I believe it means?"

"I don't care what you think. I've simply decided to be cordial for the time being. And I am merely tolerating our current situation until I leave for House Pride."

"Are you certain?"

"Yes."

"Then tell me you hate me, that I am your worst enemy. Better yet, tell me you don't want to kiss me."

"I'm not interested in playing this game." He arched a brow, waiting, and I fought the urge to roll my eyes at his smugness. "Fine. I don't want to kiss you. Satisfied?"

A spark of understanding flared in his gaze. I realized a second too late what I'd done; what he'd known the moment the words left my traitorous lips. He stepped forward and I quickly stepped back, bumping against the wall.

He leaned in, bracing himself on either side of me, his expression smoldering enough to start a fire. "Liar."

Before I dug myself a deeper grave, his mouth slanted over mine, stealing my breath and any further denial as easily as he'd stolen my soul.

NINE

His kiss consumed and seduced me. Just as he'd meant it to. It wasn't fast or hard or fueled by hatred or fury. It was an ember, a promise of the blazing fire to come with a bit of careful tending. I almost considered it sweet—the kind of chaste embrace two courting lovers stole when their chaperone wasn't looking—until he slowly raised my arms above my head, pinning me to the wall by my wrists. He took my bottom lip between his teeth and bit down gently. Then I remembered: he was no angel. And I was suddenly all too willing to be damned.

Curse this realm and its fiendish machinations. Its need for sin. My undeniable need for *him*. Right now there was no blood oath with the devil. No betrothal or obligations to my family. There was only this moment, this wicked prince, and the heat steadily building between us.

Wrath's body molded against mine, rock hard and unyielding in all the right places. Whatever hunger I felt was equally matched by him. I wish I hated it. I wish I didn't run my tongue over his lips, or sigh as he obeyed my silent demand and deepened our kiss.

This new kiss devoured, plundered, stole. It was apology and wanting and a fierce refusal to submit to any true feelings all in one. Primal need at its most basic level. I couldn't tell if letting myself give in to this wild feeling frightened or thrilled me.

I yanked away, breathing hard. "Is this real?"

"Yes."

As if to prove the truth in his statement, his hips rolled forward and I was almost certain the whole castle quaked the second our bodies connected. There was no mistaking how much this dark prince wanted me. I grabbed the lapels on his jacket and brought his lips back to mine.

For one heart-thundering moment, I wished he'd hike my gown up right there, bury himself deep inside me and release every last one of my trapped desires. I longed to forget where I was and what I had to do. I wanted to abandon all of the hurt and pain and grief that were never far. All I desired was the sweet oblivion of touch. Wrath could easily provide that. And more.

He leashed himself and broke away from our kiss, only to begin languidly stroking the top of my bodice. Need flared through me and seemed to mirror itself in him. He dragged his hands down my sides, gripping me a little tighter to his body. "You may destroy me yet."

"Sooner rather than later if you don't stop talking and kiss me again."

"Demanding, angelic creature."

He smiled indulgently at me, then obliged. *This kiss.* It was slow and drugging and made me realize he wasn't the only one in danger of being destroyed. He tilted my face up, traced the line of my jaw, then slid his fingers down my neck, lightly brushing them across my pulse point.

Tiny bits of electricity sparked beneath his caress. I'd almost forgotten he'd Marked me, giving me a way to summon him without using his House dagger. The tiny, nearly invisible *S* tingled. Nonna said the Mark was a high honor, one that was rarely given.

She hadn't been pleased.

I immediately tunneled back into myself and forced the addictive quality of his kisses aside. I almost felt the magic of the world recede like the tide going out, its disappointment crashing in reluctant waves around us.

Wrath gently released his hold on me, sensing the emotional shift.

"Why?" I managed to get one word out, my voice still thick with desire.

"I didn't think you'd prefer an audience."

An indecent image of him taking me on the dining room table flashed across my mind. It was so vivid I swore I heard sounds of shock from guests as their prince showed me just how sinful he could be, glasses shattering and forks clattering onto the finest demon china as Wrath drove us both over the edge, heedless of anyone who looked on.

I swallowed a nervous giggle. That entrance would certainly make an impression House Wrath would not soon forget. I shoved those scandalous thoughts away.

"That's not what I meant, and you know it."

Though I *did* wonder why he decided to kiss me now.

His teeth bared in a semblance of a smile, a knowing gleam entering his eyes. Evasion admitted. I couldn't help but shake my head, my lips curling up at the edges. It was progress, small though it may be. Or maybe I was finally learning to read him better. Though I suspected—in this particular moment—he was also not trying to hide from me as much. I tried not to let wariness ruin the moment.

"I was talking about Marking me. Not whatever"—I nodded between us—"this is."

He searched my face for a strained minute, the last vestiges of heat leaving his expression. His eyes were nearly solid black now. This time there was no mistaking the rumble that shook the castle. He rolled his shoulders, as if releasing tension in them and between us.

Wrath held his arm out to me, all traces of passion wiped from his face.

Here stood the cold and unfeeling prince of Hell.

"We can't linger anymore. It's time to meet my court."

Our arrival outside the oversized bone-carved doors of the royal dining hall was a blur. I couldn't recall if Wrath had spoken to me on our seemingly endless walk here, or if he'd escorted me in complete, stoic silence. It was likely the latter; I couldn't imagine him ever engaging in something as pedestrian as inquiring about my day or the weather.

Not that I would have noticed either way.

There was an odd feeling in my chest; a slight tugging or gnawing or peculiar combination of the two. At first I thought it was panic fluttering against my ribs, fear over what had just transpired between us, but that wasn't quite right. The feeling was slowly pooling out, traveling from my heart like a meandering stream along the underside of my arm.

Wrath turned his head in my direction, a deep furrow forming in his brow.

I glanced down at what he'd been staring at. My *cornicello* glowed that pale, unearthly purple of a human's *luccicare*. It had happened twice before. Once when I'd first found Wrath standing over the corpse of my twin. And again when I'd found my amulet half-buried in a tunnel after it had been stolen. Right before the almost incorporeal Umbra demons had attacked and Envy had stuck his House dagger deep into Wrath's belly.

My hands curled into fists as I remembered the way Wrath's blood had dried on my hands, under my nails. The utter feeling of...

"Breathe." His voice was deep and calming. "We will make introductions, then leave if you do not wish to stay and dine with them."

"I'm not nervous."

And I was surprised to discover that was true. I let go of Wrath's arm and brushed my fingers over the cool metal of the amulet for comfort, an old habit I'd probably never break. The devil's horns, I reminded myself with a small shudder. Not an amulet to ward off evil. This necklace was no longer the innocent charm I'd believed it was all my life.

Upon contact, a small current passed into my skin, alarming me enough to yank my hand back. That was new. I flicked my attention to Wrath. "Did you see that?"

He nodded, not taking his gaze from the shrunken devil horn. Concern was still present in his features. "Are you able to wear it during the meal?"

"Of course," I said. "I've worn it for almost two decades."

"If you experience anything uncomfortable, tell me immediately."

Wrath seemed on the verge of saying something else but

changed his mind at the last moment. Now my heartbeat quickened. "Uncomfortable how?"

"Anything unusual. No matter how small or seemingly innocuous."

I was about to tell him of the tingling sensation, but it faded into nothing before the words could form on my tongue. Perhaps it *was* only nerves getting the better of me. I'd traveled to the underworld with one of the Wicked, made a blood bargain with the devil, and was seconds away from meeting the Prince of Wrath's scheming court of demons.

Not to mention, I'd just been thoroughly ravished by someone who was *not* my intended and my lips were probably swollen in accusation. While my emotional feelings for Wrath were much more complex, I hadn't disliked the kiss. In fact, it seemed to have unlocked a truth I didn't want to examine closely. He'd asked if I could bed someone I hated, and while my mind still churned with anger over his betrayal, my body responded to his touch.

I couldn't imagine Pride taking the news of my tryst with his brother well. Who knew if he had spies in this court, eager and ready to report back any unsavory business? While I wouldn't mind sowing seeds of discord among the two Houses, I did not want to alienate my betrothed and ruin my chance to solve Vittoria's murder. I had every right to be nervous. It would be odd if I wasn't.

Wrath leaned in and skimmed his knuckles over my neck, his voice as soft as his touch. Whatever magic fueled his summoning Mark instantly calmed me. "Ready?"

I nodded. He studied my face and must have seen I was indeed primed for my introduction to House Wrath. Without warning, he spun on his heel and kicked in the doors.

He strode through them right as they crashed against the wall, his footsteps claps of thunder in the sudden silence. My breath caught. It was not at *all* the way I'd imagined making our grand entrance. Given his penchant for fine clothing and impeccable manners, I thought he'd be more...genteel or refined. I should know better than to assume anything about him.

A wave of smartly dressed demons dropped to their knees, their heads bowed and eyes lowered as he stalked into the room. Wrath paused several paces inside the large dining hall and waited for me to make my way to him. My steps were slow and steady, unlike my pulse.

It felt like both an eternity and only a mere second had passed before I crossed the room, gown whispering over the stone, and halted near the Prince of Wrath.

When he spoke, his voice was laced with royal command. "Rise. And bid Her Highness Emilia Maria di Carlo, your future queen, welcome."

The goddesses must have been watching over me because I managed to swallow my shock without showing it. I subtly turned to Wrath, a question in my eyes. I had not been told about the "her highness" part. I imagined that would happen after the coronation, or whatever the demon equivalent was. The corner of his mouth twitched before his expression hardened again and he addressed the sea of curious demons in that cool, unforgiving tone.

"Remember what I said about respect. As a prince of Hell's intended, Lady Emilia's status has been elevated. You will only address her as 'her highness' or 'my lady.' Insult her, and you will answer to *me*."

Wrath stared at one lord in particular, and I assumed it was the one Fauna said he'd already threatened. I would not want to be on the receiving end of that look—it was cold enough to cause a shudder in surrounding nobles. And they did not seem like the kind of subjects who were easily cowed.

"Consider this my final warning."

Wrath shifted to me then, holding out his arm. I placed my hand in the crook of his arm and lifted my chin. We walked side by side to a large table set at the back of the room, and I subtly let my gaze travel across the chamber, drinking in our surroundings. A tapestry hung against the far wall, depicting a warrior angel locked in battle with demons. Severed heads rolled at his feet. Blood-splattered and milky-eyed. An interesting choice for a dining room.

I brought my attention back down from that ray of sunshine. The table we were headed to was made from a solid piece of gorgeous old wood. A garland composed of various evergreens ran down the center of its length, along with an iron candelabra with spindly arms that sat just above the greenery. Cream and gold candle tapers decorated it from end to end, giving off a comfortable flickering glow. Black earthenware plates were set before gilded chairs. And the eating utensils were also made of the same deep gold. It was pure rustic elegance. Masculine edges with unexpected bits of warmth. Perfect for a warrior prince. I liked it very much.

Wrath angled us toward the center of the table where two larger, more ornate seats were located. Not quite thrones, but close. Unlike what I'd been told of human royal courts, we would not be sitting at opposite ends of the table. We were at its center and everyone else would be fanned out around us. There were two aisles of similar yet smaller wooden tables on either side of the room, creating a path for us to walk down.

These tables didn't have gold seats; they had matching wooden benches. All of them had an abundance of candles running their length, a fiery centerpiece for the coldest circle of Hell.

Servants I hadn't noticed lingering near the wall stepped forward, gracefully pulling out our chairs as we made our way around the table. Wrath waited until I sat down before taking his seat. Glasses of dark wine were quickly poured and set before us.

Frozen berries bobbed to the surface, enchanting and tempting. My gaze turned to the prince. I was about to ask why no one else had moved to take their seats, but shut my mouth.

Wrath's attention was already fixed on me, his eyes nearly glowing in the candlelight.

Everything faded into shadows. It was as if he and I were the only two in the room, the whole realm, and I couldn't stop my thoughts from returning to their earlier, scandalous vision of him making love to me until I saw stars. Just as the rakish heroes in my favorite romance novels promised to do to the objects of their affection and lust.

Ridiculous realm and its sinful inclinations. Of all the times for it to work its devious magic, now was the absolute worst. Though I wasn't all that surprised. Wrath mentioned this realm sensing areas of struggle and bringing them to the forefront. I was certainly fighting inner emotions against physical longings.

Until I settled my internal war, I would likely be plagued by these urges.

I tore my focus from Wrath and shifted uncomfortably in my seat, looking to the wine. It would either help distract me or it would turn me into a feral creature, clawing at the prince's clothes. Thinking of his clothing was a terrible mistake; it quickly led to thoughts of him *without* a shirt. *Blood and bones,* this forbidden attraction was growing worse by the minute.

Perhaps I should excuse myself to get fresh air. I glanced around, searching for a balcony or terrace. I needed to cool down immediately. After my royal introduction, there was little doubt that everyone here knew I was promised to his brother. It would hardly seem appropriate for me to be openly lusting over this prince when I was about to marry the king of demons.

Wrath leaned in, his lips almost brushing the shell of my ear and I felt him smile. His voice was low enough so only I heard him. "One word and I'll send them away."

Temptation flared. "Do I appear that nervous?"

"I'm fairly confident what I'm sensing has nothing to do with nerves."

A flush crept up my neck. I had no idea he could sense... arousal. Goddess curse me. This realm would be the death of me yet. I forced my thoughts back to the reason I'd come to this world. It had not been seduction or wanting that made me sign my soul away. It was vengeance. Fury. And those emotions were more powerful than any sinful magic.

Or any sinfully alluring prince.

I placed my lips to his ear. "Are you sensing the knife I'm now considering stabbing you with, your highness?"

"If this is an attempt to change the topic, you're failing miserably." His hand dropped beneath the table, landing gently on my knee. There was little doubt it was a nonverbal acknowledgment of my most recent lie. "I am even more interested in where this may lead, *my lady.* You forget what sin I rule over. I am rather fond of a bit of knife-play."

"Your subjects are staring at us."

With his free hand, he picked up his wine and took a long, careful sip. He acted as if we were enjoying a drink alone together instead of being observed by the lords and ladies of Hell.

He set the goblet down and stared out at the silent, watchful crowd. "You may be seated."

I was loath to admit it, even silently, but his touch kept my nerves at bay as the royal court all took their seats. It was hard to concentrate on fear when his long fingers stroked the thin material of my gown, drawing all of my attention to that point of contact. I imagined he was attempting to soothe me, but his touch had the opposite effect. My heart raced.

The cursed prince did not appear affected at all. My attention fell to his lap.

"A pleasure to finally meet you, Lady Emilia. You look goddesslike this evening. A true enchantress for the ages."

Wrath's hand tensed on my leg, before he slowly continued dragging that finger along the outer seam of my dress. I yanked my gaze from the prince. Directly across the table, standing behind his seat, a fair-haired demon grinned. It was the royal Wrath had glared at earlier. I did not return his smile. "I'm sorry, I don't believe we've been introduced. You are?"

"Lord Baylor Makaden, my lady."

It was indeed the demon who'd made crude comments. He sat and immediately began chatting with the lords and ladies to either side of him. More pleasant nobles joined us and trays of food were promptly brought out.

Fileted meats baked in flaky pastry. Roasted root vegetables dressed in herbs. Crusty loaves of bread that smelled of intriguing spices. Serving bowls filled with dark gravy and sauces. None of the food was familiar or reminded me of home, but it wasn't as different as I'd feared. I'd been secretly harboring worries of strange multi-eyed animals and steaming, raw offal. This was truly a delight.

Wrath removed his hand from my knee only to surprise me with carving the meat and filling my plate with a bit of everything on the table. Other lords and ladies watched from lowered lashes, some bold enough to whisper. I had a feeling this was not typical behavior for the prince. He ignored them, though he no doubt felt their attention and silent speculation.

"Would you care for extra sauce, my lady?" he asked.

I flicked my attention to him, pulse thrumming. He was definitely putting on a show, but I had no idea for whose benefit. Playing along with his scheme, I shook my head. "No, thank you, your highness."

My use of his title seemed to please him, though I doubted the almost imperceptible curve of his lips was noticeable to anyone else. After he tended to my plate, he heaped generous portions onto his own, then struck up a conversation with the lord to his left.

This was the version I'd expected earlier, the prince with exemplary manners. Not the barbarian who'd kicked in doors. Though both aspects of him were intriguing. Goddess help me. I had no business finding him intriguing or attractive at all.

I politely listened to the noblewoman beside me as she complained of her lady's maid, then of her sour stomach, and of the bug-eaten tapestry in her receiving hall.

I let her talk freely about all the things that angered her while I ate. Her attention roved over my tattoo, the amulet, and rested on the ring on my finger, but she never asked about them. Thus far no one was straying to any topics of note and I doubted I'd learn much aside from idle gossip. Tonight the court would be on its best behavior.

I wasn't sure I was pleased but at least the food was worth the trouble. My meat cut like butter and tasted as rich. I did my best to concentrate on conversations and not lose myself in the flavors. Whoever cooked this meal was immensely talented. I'd love to watch them in the kitchen, taking notes. Perhaps I might tinker with my own sauce variations. Add a bit of sea salt and herbs to the flaked pastry to round out the flavors the meat had been marinated with.

Several times I felt an intruding stare and glanced up to find Lord Makaden's attention fixed on my chest. His hungry expression indicated he wasn't looking at the amulet. I ignored him as Wrath had done. Worms like him should remain beneath notice. Though that comparison was hardly fair to the poor worms.

The woman next to me, Lady Arcaline, she'd finally informed me, stopped regaling me with her wrath-filled complaints long enough to ask, "Have you met anyone from the court outside of this evening's dinner?"

"Yes, I met Lady Fauna in the library."

Lady Arcaline made a dismissive sound and turned to the demon to her other side.

With everything that had happened, I forgot about Fauna. I sipped my wine and looked around the room, surprised to see her chatting with Anir and another young demon at the end of our table. It was too bad they weren't seated closer; it would have been much more enjoyable.

Before I could reflect on feeling camaraderie with anyone in Wrath's court, Lord Makaden leaned across the table, boldly ogling my lips. It was an improvement over his not-so-subtle perusal of my cleavage. It was fortunate for him that Wrath was still engaged in a discussion with the lord to his left and hadn't noticed his crude stare. I was willing to overlook his idiocy in favor of keeping the peace tonight. Tomorrow would be a different story.

I tasted another bite of meat and a bit of the herbed vegetables. They really were divine.

"Indulge me, Lady Emilia." Makaden's grating voice drew me away from my meal. "Have you ever experienced something as pleasurable as demon fare before? With each bite, you look as though you're in the throes of ecstasy. I must admit, it's captivating. I'm envious of your fork."

The nobles seated nearest to me kept politely chatting, but I sensed their attention shift to us. It was a leading question, almost skirting the line of propriety. One detail I'd been picking up throughout dinner was that certain topics were as scandalous here as they were in the mortal world. Only the scandal seemed to involve overtly referencing other sins.

I didn't balk at answering the question.

"Tell me, Lord Makaden, are you always this preoccupied with the mouths of others? Perhaps you should reconsider what House of Sin you align best with."

He sipped his wine, then ran a finger around its rim, his attention never leaving my lips. The anger I'd been fighting to keep at a low simmer slowly began to boil the longer he stared.

I wondered what sort of impression I'd make on House Wrath if I maimed him before the next course. Given Wrath's banishment of "guttings at gatherings," I imagined it had once been a fairly regular occurrence. As the future queen, I might escape any true punishment. Facing Wrath's ire might be worth it just to wipe that repulsive look from Makaden's face.

"I've been cautioned against speaking of your tongue, my lady, so I won't comment on its sharpness. However, since you've brought mouths up, I can't help but wonder. You seem to be enjoying the meat well enough, but has that perfect little mouth of yours ever tasted cock?"

My jaw clenched so tightly, I was surprised Wrath didn't hear the grinding of my teeth. Lord Makaden was not referencing a chicken dish, though his words were clever enough he might pretend otherwise. I slowly exhaled. He was trying to get a rise out of me.

I refused to let him succeed.

"If not, we'll have to remedy that soon. Tonight, perhaps?" He dipped his finger into the wine, then slowly sucked the liquid off. The wide smile he gave me didn't reach his hate-filled eyes. I briefly fantasized about popping those beady things from his head. "I'll even prepare it for you myself. I've been told, on more than one occasion, how good mine is."

My grip tightened on my dinner knife. I wanted nothing more than to shove it into his heart. Without giving much thought to the consequences, I lifted the blade and stood, my beautiful chair scratching along the stone in shrill warning.

The room drew in a collective gasp. It was the last sound that was made before Lord Makaden's garbled screaming began. Warm liquid sprayed across my chest and face. I was so startled, I dropped the knife and wiped at my cheeks. My fingers were coated in red liquid.

A second later the metallic scent hit my throat. Blood. Blood was now splattered across the evergreen garland on the table, across *me*. My attention fell to the source of gore.

On the place set before the vile lord sat a severed, impaled tongue.

I stared down at my dinner knife, unblinking, unsure if I'd attacked him. Then I noticed Wrath's House dagger. It still vibrated from the force he'd used to shove it through the plate and then that far into the table. I let out a quiet breath, unable to look away. The lavender gemstones in the snake's eyes glowed in fury. Or maybe bloodlust.

I'd forgotten how the dagger gloried in its offerings.

"Dinner is over," the demon prince declared, his voice dangerously low. He yanked his bloodied blade free. "Get out."

TEN

Chairs and benches scraped across the stone floor at once. Anir was at my elbow a moment later, his grip firm but gentle as he escorted me out of the royal dining hall and up a flight of stairs hidden behind a vibrant garden tapestry.

I was so shocked, I didn't protest. Nor did I look to see if Wrath had followed us. Perhaps he was butchering the rest of Makaden. Skewering various organs to put on pikes outside the castle, a generous offering to whatever carrion birds circled these cursed skies. Goddess above. I still heard the faint echo of the wretched lord's howls. They chilled me to the core.

"How?" I could hardly comprehend the last sixty seconds. Wrath had moved so fast I hadn't registered the attack until it was over. And then he'd stood there, quietly commanding everyone to leave as if he hadn't just brutally divested someone of a body part...

I rubbed my arms; the stairwell felt unbearably cold all of a sudden.

"Watch your steps. The stones are uneven in this corridor."

I gathered up my skirts and focused on climbing the stairs as quickly as my shoes and gown allowed. My shock was incrementally giving way to a different emotion altogether. One that surprised me as much as the sudden burst of violence. My grip tightened almost painfully on my gown, as if I was now strangling the material.

Anir led us up flight after flight, occasionally tossing glances over his shoulder, his free hand resting on the hilt of his blade. I couldn't imagine anyone being brave or stupid enough to follow us, especially after the blood-soaked scene we escaped from.

Wrath exploded from an *insinuation*. If someone tried physical harm or assault, a swift death would be a kindness. And there had been no hint of kindness in the demon prince's face.

Only cold fury.

Which was much worse. A hot temper eventually burned out, but the ice that coated the prince's features was glacial. Centuries would pass and his anger would remain fresh.

We exited through a hidden panel at the top of the stairs and a slight tingling sensation passed over me. Anir didn't speak again until we stood outside the door to my suite.

Even there his sharp gaze swept around the empty corridor as if he expected trouble to materialize. I did not share his concern. My private rooms were near the end of this wing and there was only one other set of doors here. Regardless if Makaden had allies, furious demons driven wild with the sin of their chosen House, Wrath would eliminate them with nary a thought.

If my anger was an aphrodisiac to him, his court's anger likely nourished and fed his power in droves. Wrath thrived on fury in every sense of the word.

I glanced down the opposite end of the corridor; an ornate iron gate had dropped from the ceiling, locking out anyone who tried to enter this section. My jaw ached from how hard I now clenched it.

Being caged in didn't thrill me, but at least there was another exit in the secret panel if I wanted to leave. One that was magically warded, if the tingling sensation was any indication. Wrath had used the same magic back in my realm to protect me from his brothers.

The fact that he'd taken precautions in his own royal House wasn't comforting, but I trusted that no one would slip past his wards.

"Makaden had that coming for decades."

I pulled my attention to Anir. "I imagine he did."

"Then why..." His voice trailed off as he really looked me over. "You're angry."

Wrong. I was furious. It was a wonder steam wasn't billowing out of my ears.

If I could not handle repugnant creatures like Lord Makaden on my own, I would never gain the respect of this court or any other.

Wrath ought to count his demonic blessings he wasn't the one standing here with me now. I'd take his precious blade to his throat, tear the clothes from my person and bathe in his warm blood as I slit him ear to ear.

The unexpected pleasure I felt, thinking such a dark, wicked thing yanked me back to my senses. While the flames of my fury banked, the embers of rage remained. I was not nearly as horrified as I should have been by my almost literal bloodlust.

Anir's mouth twisted up on one side. He must have read the promise of murder flashing in my eyes and found it amusing. He was wise enough not to laugh.

"His private chambers are at the end of this hall. Give him ten minutes, I'm sure he'll be there by then."

I was too angry to show my surprise. Of course Wrath placed me close to him. He was keeping a careful watch on his brother's fiancée. Ever the dutiful soldier. Except for when he'd kissed me before dinner. I doubted *that* was part of his orders. Though, knowing him, maybe it was another twisted scheme he'd dreamed up to keep me preoccupied and not causing trouble.

I spun on my heel and slammed the door to my suite behind me.

I passed the time by removing Makaden's blood and gore from my body. I sat at the vanity in my bathing chamber, dipping a linen towel into the crystal washbasin, turning the water there a pinkish red. I dabbed at the remaining dampness while staring at the silent woman in the mirror. I couldn't find any hint of the girl I'd been before my sister's murder.

That Emilia had perished in the room with my twin, had had her heart ripped from her, too, and it didn't appear as if she'd ever return. No matter how hard I fought, who I deceived, or how much of my soul I bargained away, nothing would ever bring my sister back. Even if I succeeded in destroying those who'd hurt Vittoria, I could see no way of ever happily returning to that simple, quiet life. The one where I was most content with my books and recipes.

This new reality felt strange, but fitting. It was a life where I didn't cringe at violence, only seethed that the punishment that had been dealt was taken from my eager hands. I wondered at death, at the ones we lost and how their loss stole something vital from us in return.

A tear slid down my cheek as I set aside the bloodstained towel.

"Enough," I said, quietly, forcefully to myself as I stood. I planted my hands on the vanity top and leaned in, glaring at my reflection. *"Enough."*

There was no longer any room for sadness or grief in my world. In my heart.

I focused intently on that anger, that spark in my core close to my magic's source. It was as if a lava pit were bubbling inside me, ready to erupt. I'd never felt my power so strongly and realized it wouldn't take much to harness it. All I had to do was reach in and grab it.

I concentrated on my magic, imagined pulling it from wherever it originated and turning it into a handful of flame. Instead of fighting myself and forcing it to come, I let go.

Of my thoughts, of my fears. Of my worries.

I released everything except my wrath. That I held on to as if it were the most vital essence in my universe. Because it *was* the most vital thing in this circle of Hell. If the Prince of Wrath's anger was a glacier, mine was a raging inferno. And it would not burn out quickly.

I inhaled and exhaled, picturing myself breathing new life into the fire. If I could master my anger, focus on it without emotion, it might burn so powerfully and for so long it could even melt Wrath's impenetrable ice.

I held my palm out and whispered, *"Fiat lux."*

Let there be light.

Blasphemous to some mortals, perhaps. But not to a witch currently residing in the underworld and betrothed to the devil. A tiny ball of rose-gold flames hovered above my palm. It crackled like real fire, but did not burn me. I waited for the pain to begin, for my flesh to bubble and welt. Or char. For Wrath's ring to melt off my finger.

The fire only burned brighter, pulsed softly as if saying hello.

I stared, unfeeling as it shifted into a flaming flower. For a fraction of a second, I considered throwing it against the wall and watching my room—and all of its fine furnishings—incinerate. Tiny buds of embers catching and blooming into a garden of ash and flame.

I slowly closed my fingers around the burning flower, extinguishing it the way I should have extinguished the light in Makaden's eyes. I was still too angry to rejoice in what I'd just done. The magic I did not know I could summon. Later, there would be time to celebrate.

Now, I had other things to do. Like confront the demonic master of this house.

That same fury set my feet in motion exactly ten minutes from the time Anir had left. It propelled me out of my room, down the corridor, and made it easy to barge into Wrath's personal suite as if it were my own.

The door slammed against the wall, setting the candles flickering wildly on the mantel. Wrath was neither startled nor disturbed. He stood with his back to me, undressing. As if he knew I'd come to him, furious instead of scared.

I crossed my arms. "Well?"

The demon prince studiously ignored me. He shrugged out of his shirt and tossed it over an armchair. His trousers sat low on his hips, and with the fire blazing in the hearth, I had a very good view of the lines of ink that curved over each finely carved muscle on his back.

Without speaking or looking at me, he moved deeper into his personal space. I trailed behind, too mad to focus on any details of his rooms aside from the deep merlot walls and black furniture and fabric. It was dark and sensual. Like other parts of the castle where the prince spent most of his time.

"Look at me." My voice was low, soft. It sounded like a caress, though that was intentional. The softness was meant to distract from the underlying steel in the command.

Wrath turned with intention. There was something seductive in the way he moved; powerful and strong, yet fluid in all the ways he'd require for battle. Everything about his movements indicated he was a predator. But I was not afraid. Not even after his violent display. Wrath would never harm me. And I was almost certain it had little to do with duty.

Looking at him now, with the promise of unending punishment and not an ounce of regret in his glare, I understood what he did, *why* he did it, even if he didn't yet.

He stood before a large bed, the silky sheets like an undisturbed lake behind him. An ebony fur throw covered the bottom portion. I thought about disrobing and tossing myself onto it, causing another ripple in the smooth perfection of his world. For a split second, I almost imagined I'd done that before. I cut that thought off before any sinful magic could take hold.

Wrath's expression turned unreadable. "It's late. You should leave."

"We need to discuss what just happened."

"I issued an order, Makaden ignored it. Twice. The consequences were made clear."

I narrowed my eyes; his answer was a little too stiff and practiced. I stalked closer. "Is that all? You attacked him because of your order?"

"He chose to insinuate you should taste his cock. In front of my court." His shoulders moved with the effort he was exerting to control his breaths, to remain calm. He shouldn't have bothered. There was no quieting the storm currently raging in his eyes. "If I let his disobedience slide, I will be seen as weak."

"That was *my* fight. If you interfere whenever someone says something unflattering, no one will ever respect or fear *me*. I will not appear weak for you to maintain strength." I moved until I stood directly before him, the heat of our combined anger prickling my skin. I wonder if he felt that, too. And if it soothed him. "Was this a male pride issue? I highly doubt your hold on your court is so tenuous that one obnoxious noble could diminish your rule."

"You know pride is not my sin."

It was not the first time I'd wondered if that was the full truth, but I let it go.

"I want my own blade. Perhaps if I'm armed and can disembowel someone myself, you won't act so overbearing in front of your subjects again. Because if you do"—I allowed just enough sweetness into my tone, making his eyes narrow with suspicion—"next time I will stick my dinner knife in *you*. Consider that a vow from your future queen."

Wrath crossed his arms and stared me down. His eyes flickered with some emotion I couldn't quite place; he was no doubt calculating a hundred reasons why arming me was a bad idea. Especially after my last declaration. I waited for the argument he seemed eager to give.

"I'll see to it you have a blade of your own. And lessons."

"I don't require—"

"That is my offer. It will do no good to arm you only to have you injure yourself in a fight because you can't wield it properly. Do we have a bargain?"

"Only one reasonable demand…and you're agreeing with me? That easily?"

"It appears I am."

I looked him over. "You already considered arming me."

"I am the general of war; of course I considered it. We'll discuss other training options in the morning. If we're going to practice physical lessons, we'll add blocking magical influence, too. Do you accept the terms of our bargain?"

"Yes."

"Good. Go back to your rooms. I'm tired."

I let his poor attitude go without comment. He was still tense, his own anger not quite leashed. I considered leaving him to his own foul company, but instead I gave him a teasing half-smile. "I imagine so. Maiming is exhausting business."

He almost returned my grin, but it never quite reached his lips. "Good night, Emilia."

"Good night, my jealous, mighty tongue-slayer."

"You say such horrible things."

But the gleam of intrigue indicated he didn't mind. Quite the contrary. I waited for him to turn and walk away, but he seemed rooted in place. Indecision scrawled across his features.

Belatedly, I realized I hadn't taken myself from the room, either.

I held still as he angled my face up, his long fingers stroking the side of my neck in the lightest caress. I should have been thinking of the dagger he'd just held, of the blood that had stained his hands moments ago. Of the ruthless way he'd acted. These hands could remove a tongue without much effort, but they were also capable of tenderness. Of protection.

And, undoubtedly, pleasure.

I wet my lips, recalling our earlier kiss. "I only spoke the truth."

Wrath stared into my eyes before tearing his gaze away with obvious effort. He did not deny being jealous. Nor did he appear surprised by the emotion. I wondered if he'd already identified it and was unsure what to do with the knowledge. Not that much *could* be done if either of us entertained the thought. I was promised to his brother. And his duty to that mission would always come first. What happened earlier between us would not happen again.

His hand fell away, my skin instantly missing his heat, while my mind reeled with confusion over my conflicted feelings.

"I'll see that you have your blade and first lesson tomorrow. Good night."

This time, there was no hesitation on his part. He disappeared through a doorway covered with sheer panels, and, feeling dismissed, I finally turned and headed out the way I'd come. I paused just inside the entrance to the antechamber, my feet unwilling to carry me from the room. I knew I should leave; I'd gotten what I'd come for, but something held me back.

I drifted into the bedroom, closer to those billowing panels, and peered through them.

Wrath had escaped onto a balcony. He stood with his back to me, staring out toward the snow-covered hills and mountains jutting up in the distance, a bottle of wine perched beside him on the railing. The temperature never seemed to affect him. It certainly hadn't prevented him from sleeping outdoors during the storm. Perhaps it was another perk of immortality.

Or maybe I'd gotten it slightly wrong earlier, maybe he wasn't always cold fury. Maybe he possessed fire, too. And his ability to withstand the cold was simply the heat of his constant wrath, simmering, blazing, warming him more than the icy elements could hope to infiltrate.

My attention drifted to his drink again. Frost crept up the side of the glass, creating little spiderwebs of ice. The liquid inside the bottle was unlike anything I'd ever seen at home; similar to mer-lot or chianti, but not a deep red. It was a purple so dark it almost appeared black, but that wasn't the most unusual or beautiful part. Silver specks floated like glittery bubbles all throughout it. Wrath topped off his glass and swirled it, setting the silver glinting into a frenzy.

It looked like he'd created his own shimmering galaxy. He set the glass on the railing beside him and inclined his head. "If you're going to continue lurking in my bedchamber, you might as well drink this. It'll help you sleep."

I thought about returning to my room, but curiosity got the better of me. I moved across the balcony and examined the glass without touching it. "It won't make me jump over the railing and dive into the snow, will it?"

Instead of answering, Wrath swiped the glass away and drank deeply. He handed it back and looked at me. Challenge lit his dark gaze.

I briefly fantasized about shoving him over the railing into the snowbank below, but I imagined he'd bring me with him and something about our bodies falling together made my heart race. Not because I feared the fall or getting hurt; I knew Wrath would maneuver us so he'd hit the ground. It was where I'd land that caused the uptick in my pulse.

I settled on sipping the starlike liquid. It was . . . delicious.

"Well?" he asked. "What do you think?"

"I love it."

"I thought you might." His voice turned quiet, contemplative. As if he hadn't meant to speak aloud or admit that. I wished I pos-sessed a tiny bit of his ability to sense emotions. I was curious to know what he was feeling, why he sounded resigned.

I took another small sip and focused on the flavors. Something spicy, like fresh ginger. A bit of citrus, similar to lime. And there was a deep richness that blended the two perfectly. Not rum, but something close. I finished the rest of my glass and contemplated pouring more.

Wrath grinned. "Demonberry wine is one of the two finer offerings of this realm."

I picked up the bottle and shook it a little. The liquid glimmered like stardust. It was one of the most magnificent things I'd ever seen. "What makes it look like the night sky?"

"Those are demonberry seeds. They're small enough to look like bubbles. Or stars."

I topped off my glass and leaned against the railing. I was a little chilly, but I was far from cold. Maybe it was the wine heating me from the inside. From here I could clearly see the fiery lake that separated this stretch of territory from the ornate castle in the far distance. A bridge connected the two swaths of land, dark waters churning like a bubbling cauldron below.

For a second, I considered telling Wrath about the magic I summoned. I nodded toward the castle instead. "Which royal House is that?"

Wrath followed my gaze. "Pride's."

I took another sip of my drink. Demonberries fizzled on my tongue. It was suddenly so quiet I could hear the slight crackle as the bubbles popped in the glass. "Have you heard from him yet?"

"No."

"Does he know I'm here?"

"He does."

I sighed. I sincerely hoped Pride would get over his namesake sin soon enough and send his cursed invitation. I wanted to solve the full truth of my sister's murder and return to my family before I was old and gray. Or before *they* were old and gray. I'd likely not age much while here. That thought pierced the armor I'd erected around my heart, so I pushed it away.

We stood in companionable silence, each lost to our own thoughts while sipping our drinks. Wrath moved a little, his arm nearly touching mine, and I thought about how comfortable this was. Being here. With him. My enemy. Well, not quite.

The lines of who *we* were and how *I* felt about us were blurring. I had no idea if it was simply because he was familiar, and I was desperate to clutch at anything even remotely comfortable while here. Or if the sins and illusions were doing their hardest to confuse the matter. When we kissed earlier he'd felt nothing like an adversary.

As much as I wanted to receive Pride's invitation, I'd grown somewhat fond of spending time with Wrath. I even looked forward to verbally sparring with him. Seeing his nostrils flare with frustration was becoming oddly endearing. The thought should have disturbed me, especially after the incident at dinner. But it didn't.

I wasn't sure what it said about me, about the entity I was becoming, but there was a deep sense of primeval desire that sparked when Wrath took that blade to Makaden, defending me.

For a little while, it seemed like we were partners again. I didn't think I'd miss our time together in Palermo, and wasn't sure what it meant that I did. I felt his attention shift to me.

"What's the second offering?" I asked, meeting his gaze. He was closer than I expected, his attention briefly falling to my mouth as if it intrigued and beguiled him. My heart kicked up its beat. Wrath drew his brows together and shook his head, seeming to recall I'd asked a question. Whatever realization he'd just had had thoroughly entranced him. "You said the wine was only the first. What's the second-best thing about this realm?"

"The Crescent Shallows." He hesitated. "It's a lagoon."

That strange tension hovered between us like a spell that refused to break. I raised a brow, my lips half–turned up at the edges. "Let me guess, since this is Hell it's frozen over?"

"No, actually. It's one of the few places in the Seven Circles not touched by ice. It sits above a lava field, so the water is warmer than bathwater, regardless of the air temperature."

"Do we have to fight a three-headed dog to get there?"

"No."

"Is traveling there like going through the Sin Corridor?" Wrath shook his head but didn't elaborate. I stepped closer, eyes narrowing. He was being more tight-lipped than normal. Which meant he was *definitely* concealing something. "Where is it?"

"Forget I mentioned it." He refilled his glass and took a strong pull of wine, refusing to meet my inquisitive stare. "It's late."

"Blood and bones. It's here, isn't it? Have you been hiding a hot spring from me?"

"Not hiding. There are rules that must be followed before entering the water. I doubt you'd like them. And even if you did, I don't think it's a good idea."

"I see." Wrath straightened at my tone and slowly glanced in my direction. When his full attention settled on me, I continued. "Instead of *asking* my opinion, you decided for me. Since I am to marry the devil, that makes me your future queen, doesn't it?" He didn't answer. "I would like you to take me there. Now, please."

"Nothing made may enter the water."

"Nothing...you mean clothing?"

"Yes. You'll need to fully disrobe before entering the water, my future queen." His smile was pure wickedness. "I didn't think you'd want to bathe with me naked."

"Is that all?" I highly doubted it. He'd seen me without clothing on more than one occasion over the last few months. That would not be a deterrent. This was about self-preservation. For him. "I imagine there's something about the water you'd like to avoid."

He looked me over slowly. It was impossible to tell what he felt. "On occasion it seeks the heart of those who enter. And reflects their truth."

I held his gaze. Maybe it was the wine, or this world and its proclivity toward sin, or the way his eyes glittered with triumph, but I refused to cede this battle.

I recalled what Anir said about challenging him. If I had to give up some of my truth to gain some knowledge of him, it was a small price to pay.

I jerked my chin at the bottle and glasses. "Take those and let's visit this magical lagoon. I could use a warm, relaxing bath after tonight."

Wrath's grin vanished. "You're certain that's what you want?"

"Yes."

It was a terribly dangerous answer, made apparent by the thick layer of tension that swiftly fell between us again, but it was the truth. I did not want to go back to my chamber alone, nor did I want to part ways with this prince just yet. A night adventure to a magical hot spring sounded like the perfect distraction. I wanted a pleasant memory to cling to before bed. I did not want to replay the staked tongue incident over and over until sleep claimed me. And if I went back to my chamber alone now, that's exactly what would happen.

Instead of walking me there, Wrath took my hand in his and magicked us away. The familiar sensation of burning was replaced by a slight, warm tingle across my skin. It was far from unpleasant. I gasped as solid ground formed beneath us a moment later.

Wrath let go once he was sure I wasn't about to tumble over. "*Transvenio* magic isn't as jarring when we're traveling in this circle."

I wanted to ask him more about the magic but found all logical thought had been stolen as I took in our new location. We stood on the dark, glittering shore of a lagoon. It was shaped like an enormous crescent moon, and the water was a milky, glacier blue.

Fog drifted lazily above its surface. I managed to tear my gaze away from the sparkling pool long enough to glance at the obsidian walls that surrounded us. This lake was subterranean.

"Where are we, exactly?"

"Below House Wrath." He strolled down the shore a little way, then pointed out a stone arch. "The Lake of Fire feeds into these shallows from over there."

I looked up, expecting to see more stone, and sucked in a quiet breath. Stone did indeed cover us, but someone had painted the phases of the moon across it, along with a smattering of stars. *Breathtaking* was hardly the most accurate description. *Ethereal*, maybe, did it more justice.

I went to stick my toes in the water when the demon prince carefully hauled me back. "No cloth of any kind can taint the water. You need to remove your gown or hold the skirt up."

"Why?"

Wrath lifted a shoulder. "See those?"

I followed his gaze as it landed on a mammoth piece of

driftwood. I leaned closer and squinted. "Is that...are those bones?"

I dragged my attention away from what remained of the unfortunate creature and focused on the prince at my side. The glint of amusement in his face was almost as sinful as he was. "Still want to go for a dip?"

"What happens if you bring the wine and glasses in?"

"I wouldn't. Come," he offered his hand. "I'll take you back to your room. You can keep the wine. It will relax you just as well as the lagoon would have. You've got a large private bath of your own. That will have to suffice."

Either he was worried about the lagoon revealing a truth he wanted to keep hidden, or he was convinced I'd change my mind and go back to bed. I gave him my own taunting smile as I deftly undid the enclosures on my gown. He watched as I slipped out of the silky red material, his throat bobbing a little as my lacy undergarments hit the ground next.

I took his ring off and set it on a smooth, flat rock. Then I straightened and held his gaze.

I stood bare before him, feeling anything but shy. I raised a brow. "Are you going to get undressed so we can swim, or are you planning on watching me all night?"

ELEVEN

Wrath's clothes vanished, leaving him standing naked and proud.

Any hint of smugness I'd felt disappeared when his clothing did. Devil curse me, I tried and failed *miserably* to not feed his ego by openly admiring him.

Great artists might try to capture his likeness but would undoubtedly fail. There was a certain mastery about him that defied his true form from ever being cast in something as mundane as bronze or carved in marble.

My gaze drifted across his broad shoulders, down his sculpted chest, then slowly inched lower, over each ridge of his abdomen, across his hips and lower until I finally took in his . . .

I jerked my attention back to his face. He was *very* obviously attracted to me. Clearly the sinful magic that thrummed below the surface of this world affected him more than I'd imagined. Though given his comments at dinner and the way our kiss had turned hungry and full of primal need earlier, maybe it wasn't so simple. For either of us.

My traitorous attention dropped again. I tried not to stare too long, but his left thigh had an interesting design inked onto it. Pointing downward, a dagger spanned from his hip to his knee. The blade looked like it had a close-up of roses on its surface, while geometric patterns were etched onto its hilt. Unlike his other metallic tattoos, this one had been done in grayscale.

I pulled my focus back to his eyes and waited, heart pounding, for him to drag his attention over every inch of my exposed skin. My nerves hummed with anticipation; it was the first time I'd disrobed in front of him without it being the result of something clinical needed to revive me from near-death. Wrath's gaze remained fixed on mine as he offered me his hand, palm up. Something inside me deflated a bit.

I went to unhook the *cornicello*, but he shook his head. "That may stay. Along with the flowers and bones in your hair."

Confused, I dropped the amulet and wound my fingers through his. Technically, since they were the devil's horns, I supposed they didn't count as something made. And the bones and flowers were also organic material, so hopefully Wrath was right and all would be well.

We walked to the lagoon's edge and water lapped at my toes, warm and silky.

He watched me, waiting to see if I wanted to continue. I took another step and lavished in the way the water felt like a million tiny bubbles on my skin.

Once we were deep enough out, Wrath let go of my hand and bobbed under the water. He exploded up a moment later, whipping his head back and pelting me with droplets. His laugh was full and rich and his smile was one of the most genuine I'd ever seen from him. It made my heart stumble a bit. I dove under the water before he could see my expression.

When I broke the surface and pushed the tangle of wet hair from my face, I caught him staring. Unlike me, he didn't attempt to hide what he was feeling now. I thought about the Wicked, about their sinful games. The stories of their kisses being addictive enough for a mortal to sell their soul for the chance at another. The danger in gaining their attention. I'd undeniably gained Wrath's full attention. And the only danger I sensed was how powerful it made me feel.

Here lay a choice. Wrath, temptation incarnate, waited, as if he knew where my thoughts had drifted. I swore there was something about the forbidden that made it sweeter to taste.

Or perhaps that was just a lie I told myself. Maybe I simply liked the taste of him, against my better judgment. I waded closer and slowly reached for him. His breath caught as I turned him away from me and tentatively traced the lines of Latin tattooed across his shoulders. I'd been curious about the ink from the first moment I'd summoned him in the bone circle all those months ago. Goose bumps rose on his skin with each gentle pass of my fingertips.

"*Astra inclinant, sed non obligant.*" I bit my lower lip, trying to translate it. "The stars..."

He rotated until we faced each other again, his eyes glowing softly in the dark. "The stars incline us; they do not bind us."

"Beautiful."

I did not miss the significance of him permanently inking onto his body that he did not want to be bound by anything. I thought of our betrothal bond, of how I'd forced it on him without knowing. Then I'd bound him to the summoning circle for days, refusing to set him free. No wonder he despised me then. It was a wonder he didn't hate me now.

"I'm sorry." The words were so soft, I wasn't sure he'd heard me. "For binding you."

He reached over and tucked a wet strand behind my ear, his touch lingering before he stepped back. "Fate may deal its hand, try encouraging our path or intervene, but we are ultimately free to choose our own destiny. Never doubt that."

"I thought you were without free will."

His smile was tinged with sadness. "Choice is granted to all. But for some it comes with a price."

"Did you get that tattoo to remind yourself of your choice?"

"Yes." His gaze fastened onto mine. "I believe John Milton, a mortal poet, said it best. 'Better to reign in Hell than serve in Heaven.' I told you the power of choice, the appeal it holds for me. I would do terrible things, unforgivable things, to choose my destiny. Cursed and wretched though it may be. It is *mine*. Unless you've been without true choice, you can't understand the allure it holds."

"What of the serpent, was that another choice?"

"All of the ink on my body, with the exception of our tattoos, were my choice."

My attention fell to his lips and lingered before something a little lower caught my attention. Faintly, in silver ink, another phrase was scrawled under his left clavicle. I'd never seen it before. Without thinking, I ran my fingertips across the writing. *Acta non verba.*

I had no trouble understanding that one. Actions, not words.

"And the design on your thigh?"

Wrath went still, and it was only then that I realized I'd

drifted near enough that our bodies were almost touching. I forgot my question, forgot everything except the fire in his gaze as it slowly consumed me inch by inch. I didn't think he could see much because the water was nearly to my neck, but it certainly didn't *feel* as if that were any true barrier.

When he looked at me with the heated intensity he was now... any lingering hatred or animosity between us burned away. Perhaps that was the truth he did not want revealed by the lagoon. The world's magic took hold, encouraging my emotions until I could no longer deny my growing desire, either. His wet-slicked skin slid against mine as I closed the distance.

Maybe it was the dreamlike beauty of the celestial scene painted on the ceiling, or the sultry steam of the Crescent Shallows. Or maybe it was simply yearning made flesh, but I craved the sensation of his hands on my body. We were two consenting adults. And I wanted him to unleash all of his sensual power on me.

I thought about my earlier fantasy of him taking me against the wall or table.

Never, in all my life, had I reacted to someone in such a carnal way. I'd had crushes, dreams of kisses and more, but this was no small infatuation. This was desire in its purest form.

My longing was growing out of control. I wanted to touch him, no longer content with denying myself or my passions. All I needed to do was take that first step.

I rolled up onto my toes and brushed his damp hair back in gentle strokes.

I waited to see if he'd put distance between us. If he'd tell me I was the last creature in all the realms combined that he'd want. His expression was almost as tense as his body. I couldn't tell if he was fighting attraction, or if he was dutifully allowing an enemy to seduce him.

I leaned in and pressed my lips against the ink along his collarbone, giving him another opportunity to move. Instead of stepping aside, his hand splayed across my lower back, holding me in place. I knew, without a doubt, the mighty warrior would let me go if I decided to stop or walk away. My mouth moved to his other shoulder, kissing him there.

"Emilia." He said my name softly. It was so close to the version of him I'd conjured in the Sin Corridor, but this wasn't another fantasy. This moment was real.

"I know you won't tell me your true name." I trailed my hands down his chest. His intense gaze tracked each of my movements. "But it feels a little odd, murmuring 'Wrath' at a time like this."

I flicked my attention back up as he closed his eyes and leaned his forehead against mine. The mighty general of war was struggling with some inner battle. Perhaps he was worried this was another game of strategy, one he'd lose if he started playing by my rules.

I no longer knew if his fear was warranted. For once, we were on equal ground.

"So maybe we shouldn't worry about talking anymore," I continued. "At least not tonight." I explored the ridges of his abdomen, and he did not move away or flinch from my touch. "Maybe we can both choose to communicate a different way. Without words."

I thought about our last kiss, how savage and unrestrained it had turned. It was fueled by primal need and lust. I guided his face down to mine and brushed my lips across his. It was whisper soft, sweet. There was a question in it, one I wasn't sure he'd answer.

This time I wanted things to be different. Even if it wasn't meant to last. We could have tonight, this moment, and surrender to whatever magnetic force was pulling us together.

There was no past or future, simply the present.

This encounter did not have to mean more than what it was. We did not have to fall in love or forget our schemes. Tonight we could form a truce, one that lasted only until sunrise. For one night, we could stop pretending this wasn't what we both desired. If I faced this unfamiliar part of me now, maybe the realm would stop tormenting me with so many sensual illusions.

I broke away from our embrace. "Unless you don't want this."

For one heart-pounding second, he didn't react. I thought I'd misjudged the moment. Then Wrath answered with a tender kiss and it didn't feel like he was my enemy. Or as if he was kissing me for any reason other than the fact he *wanted* to. Down in this chamber, far from the watchful eyes of his court and the roles we were supposed to play, we could simply be.

He chose this. Just as I did. And choice was power.

His strong hands slid down my sides as he stepped closer, bringing us flush together. I was suddenly surrounded by him, his scent, his massive body. All of his power and attention. He felt like living magic—maybe even more so than our last two encounters.

Something inside me came alive.

This time, when he swept his tongue into my mouth it was all I could do to not buckle from the sheer bliss. My hands drifted to his hips, and his inched down to mine, slipping under the warm water and gliding along my back as he anchored me against him.

I arched into his touch, forgetting any notion of going slowly. I needed pleasure. And I wanted him to give it to me as much as I would give in return.

He smiled against my neck before pressing a chaste kiss below my ear. I didn't have to see his face to know he was amused by my response. "Your highness is quite demanding."

If he was trying to distract me with that summoning Mark again, it wasn't working. Each time he'd touched it before, it doused any elevated emotions. I wouldn't *allow* it to distract either of us now. The part of me that had just awoken didn't want to drift off and slumber again.

My hands dipped below the water and I slowly dragged them back up his legs before sliding them away again.

He cursed under his breath and I grinned. "No more talking, remember?"

"Keep doing that, and I'm going to damn all the deities."

I drew small circles on his thigh, moving them higher and higher until his full attention zeroed in on precisely where *he* wished I'd explore next. Let him have a taste of how wild he'd driven me at dinner. "It's terrible, isn't it? Wanting something so badly only to be teased when it's finally within reach."

Apparently, he received my message loud and clear. His hand slid between my legs and he touched his tongue to mine the precise moment he stroked against that aching part of me. I gasped into his mouth, but it was cut off as he drew me tighter to him. His arousal pressed against my body. Hard and enticing. Just like him.

"Is this better, my lady?"

Oh, goddess, yes. *Much* better.

He slowly circled that wicked finger around my apex, all the while kissing me senseless. Heat exploded in my veins with each taunting stroke. I'd made a few poor choices in my life, but taking Wrath as a lover would *not* be one of them. He'd be just as unrestrained as I'd imagined, and that primal part of me welcomed this new battle of wills.

I lifted my hips, urging him to continue his exploration as I wound my arms around his neck, pulling him in for a deeper kiss. His finger partially plunged inside and I bit down on a moan. He withdrew it, his focus entirely on my body's reaction to the motion; the slight, shuddering exhalation, the way I reflexively moved against him, and held on tighter. He was learning what gave me the most pleasure, varying it a little and repeating it.

Goddess help me. The demon of war was a strategist on all levels.

He gently rubbed against that throbbing part of me with a second finger before turning his attention back to his slow, drugging kisses. Fire. Through no magic except for the exquisite power of his touch, he was turning my body into a million tiny flames of desire.

And he knew it. All of the teasing was driving me wild.

"Will you take me to your bedchamber?" My voice was like smoke. "Now."

"Is that what you want?"

"Yes." More than anything. I managed to nod and his clever fingers rewarded me with another loving stroke. "Hurry."

He nipped at my lower lip. "Does my queen command it?"

"Yes." Oh, goddess yes.

"Am I your humble servant now?"

I drew back. There was a devilish glint in his eyes. Even if I wanted to answer, my response was obliterated with his next kiss. We both knew he was not the kind to be ordered around. So he didn't rush. The Wicked creature took his time kissing me, all the while his fingers kept exploring, teasing, wringing pleasure in ways I didn't know were possible.

He'd promised I would not mistake reality with an illusion when he touched me. He hadn't been lying. The Sin Corridor, this realm, nothing could compare to the magic of him.

The next time he touched me, I involuntarily rocked my hips forward and he finally answered my silent plea. His fingers slid all the way in, and he gently bit down on my lip to quiet my gasp. Which only succeeded in driving me wilder.

"Take your pleasure, my lady." I tentatively repeated the rocking motion. He watched me, his gaze burning. "Just like that."

He captured my moan with his next kiss and I buried my hands in his hair, needing to feel more of him. Somehow I'd leapt up and wrapped my legs around his hips. His free arm easily secured me in place. The sensation of the warm bubbling water and the friction of his calloused fingers was enough to drive me over the edge with raw need. Instinct took over.

Our bodies pressed together, our tongues and teeth and mutual hunger pumping through my veins. I realized the magic of the world wasn't creating this longing; it was enhancing what I already felt. And I felt more than I'd ever allowed myself to admit. I rolled my hips in time with each of his deep strokes. No longer timid in chasing the pleasure he was giving me.

In my fervor to experience all sensations, I slid down his body, accidentally brushing against his hardness. He moaned, the sound deep and rumbling. My grin was pure wicked delight. I repeated the motion and air hissed through his teeth. His kisses turned ravenous.

I steadily rocked up and down on his hand, against him. Heat was building to a crescendo within me, searching for release. His

KINGDOM OF THE CURSED

eyes were glazed from his own mounting lust, his fingers still buried inside me. I'd never seen him look out of control before. It only added to my pleasure.

"Emilia—" I silenced him with a kiss. Forget his room. I'd take him here. Now. My hand closed around his arousal and he groaned. "Demon blood, I need to—"

"Take me to bed. *Now.*"

The prince of Wrath, who would not be commanded by anyone, submitted to my order.

Without any more taunting or teasing, he magicked us, bodies half-tangled together, to his bedchamber.

TWELVE

Wrath's fingers were still buried between my legs as he leaned us up against the door of his chamber, his breathing coming hard and fast. He'd missed the bedroom. With good reason. My hand remained wrapped around his impressive length. I kept caressing his silky-smooth skin, marveling at the way each stroke had him coming further undone.

It felt a little wrong to feel prideful at the moment, but I certainly adored the fact *I* was the reason the tight leash he kept on himself had finally snapped.

There was no other reason I could imagine he'd transport us into the public corridor connecting our suites. At least the gate closing off this wing was still down, and no one could travel near enough to see us. Nor would they glimpse much of me with Wrath's massive body covering mine. Not that it mattered if they could see me.

I was too lost to the waves of pleasure building and cresting inside me to care where we were, or who was around. I wanted him right here. To hell with the whole Seven Circles. I was not married to Pride yet. Aside from his brief possession of Antonio, I'd never even met him. I doubted the devil would mind my taking a lover before our wicked vows were exchanged.

Ours was certainly not a love match. And if Pride did care, he certainly didn't show it. There was still no letter, no invitation, nor acknowledgment of my arrival. The Prince of Pride was content in his castle alone, and, at the moment, that was more than all right with me.

Wrath kept kissing me, kept pumping those fingers while rocking against my unwavering grip on him, and I wanted nothing more than to bring this mighty creature to his knees with unrelenting ecstasy. This untethered, wild part of him was almost as intoxicating as his touch.

I'd never experienced something like this, so powerful and right. *He* was right. And I knew, with unending certainty, we were on the precipice of discovering how good we were together. Maybe we were always meant to end up here, lost in each other's passion.

The sound of his pleasure mingling with mine was creating its own spell, and I was so close to shattering, so close to that power that was building and breaking and...

Pain erupted in violent torrents, stealing my breath. Ever in tune with my emotional shifts, Wrath stopped instantly, the euphoric spell broken. "Are you all right?"

"No." I'd never hated a word more. "There's a horrible p-pain."

"Where?" His voice was rough, thick.

"My heart." I let go of him and winced. "Blood and bones. It's bad."

"Come. I'll send for a healer at—"

"I think it's from the Horn of Hades."

Wrath had been reaching for the handle to his room but

dropped his hand. His attention shot to the amulet I still wore and he cursed the goddesses impressively.

Everything disintegrated into smoke and glittering black light. I hadn't seen him move, but one moment we were naked outside his bedchamber on the verge of mutual release, and the next we stood, partially dressed, before a scarred wooden door in a tower.

Medieval-looking torches burned brightly on either side of it. I was almost as shocked by our location as I was about the ebony nightgown I now wore. The one that still did little to hide my form. Wrath had on black trousers and nothing else. Except maybe a slight look of concern.

"Where are we?" I reached up to unhook the *cornicello*. The pain was intensifying.

"Don't remove that." It was as if the last few minutes of passion hadn't existed. Wrath was all granite edges and fury again. Except it wasn't directed toward me. He brought his fist to the wood and pounded hard enough to rattle the iron hinges, his voice pure steel. "Matron!"

The next wave of pain made my knees buckle, but I refused to let it pull me under. Even without looking at me, the demon prince missed nothing. His next knock shook a stone loose. I laid a hand on his arm and gently squeezed. "Wrath."

"If you do not open this door, I vow on my blood—"

"You're about to bring the whole tower down with that nonsense, boy." The door swung open, revealing an older woman with long silver and lavender hair. She wore a deep purple robe with a ropelike belt that reminded me of images of priestesses I'd seen in paintings and books.

Her dark gaze turned to me, assessing.

"Daughter of the Moon, welcome. I am Celestia, the Matron

of Curses and Poisons. And I've been expecting you." She stood back and pulled the door wider in welcome. "Come in before his majesty breaks the realm."

"Next time answer your door faster."

Wrath stalked into the chamber first, alert and ready for battle. Aside from tinctures, antidotes, and poisons, I wasn't sure what enemy he expected to find here, but I was in too much pain to worry. I followed him inside and paused. The circular room was composed of dark wood, cool stone, and shelves that climbed all the way up the tower. A ladder leaned against one section as if the matron had been cataloging items on the highest shelves when interrupted. An eclectic mixture of scents wafted around, mingling into something enjoyable.

I could scarcely take a deep breath and the scent, appealing as it was, was beginning to turn my stomach. Sweat beaded my brow as I forced air in and out through clenched teeth. To avoid focusing on the growing nausea, I let my gaze drift around the space.

On a long table near a lone arched window were several vials of strange liquids: some smoking, some bubbling, others tapping against the thin glass as if testing an escape route. Sentient liquid was something new to me and more than a little unnerving.

One shelf had full-grown plants and seedlings and dried petals and herbs. There were poultices and charms, cauldrons, carved figurines of creatures like chimeras and winged deities and gods. Stones, both rough and smooth, and—if the dark sap was any indication—poison-tipped blades and needles glinting in the flickering firelight.

Fat candles dripped wax onto a wooden mantel above a generous fireplace near the center of the room, and incense sticks burned in neat plumes.

It seemed as if the Matron of Curses and Poisons was stocked for any devious pursuit.

I swallowed hard as the next wave of pain lashed through me. It felt as if my body was suddenly in the midst of a brutal war with itself. Whatever was causing the pain was winning.

With a strong hand on my back, Wrath guided me to a little wooden stool and turned on the matron. "Do something. Now."

She clucked her tongue as she slowly crossed the room. "Demands and threats belong to the scared and weak. Neither trait suits you, so hush."

"Don't test me."

Celestia went to a container filled with scissors and shears. Some had gold or silver handles, others were made of gleaming gemstones or dull bones from mortals or creatures from the underworld. I didn't look too closely.

Wrath, however, loomed over her supplies. "Move faster."

"I don't interfere in your work, boy, don't intrude on mine. Now stop hovering and sit, or get out and work that anger off elsewhere." Her cold gaze turned to his. "Do it for her sake, not mine."

Wrath didn't leave, or sit, or comment further, but he did give the matron space to work. I decided I liked this fearless woman and wondered who she was to Wrath. Surely she had to know he'd just cut out a tongue. At the moment, the demon prince was especially ferocious, and she paid him no mind. I doubted very many were brave enough to turn their back on him, especially while his power was striking around like an angry viper the way it currently was.

I wasn't complaining, though. In his own boorish way, he was watching out for me.

She picked up a pair of slim gold scissors with handles shaped like bird wings, then took a pitcher full of sparkling cerulean liquid, a vial of dried herbs, and chose another jar filled with petals in shades of frosty blue and silver. She brought everything over to her worktable, pulled a wooden bowl from a cabinet followed by a mortar and pestle.

After looking everything over one last time, she turned those ancient eyes on me. "I must take a lock of your hair for the tincture."

"No." Panic overtook me, and the word was out of my mouth before I realized I'd given a fear away to a stranger. Nonna's warnings rang in my ears. We were always told to burn our hair and nail clippings, rather than allow anyone an opportunity to use the dark arts on us. "Is it necessary? The pain is already ebbing. I think his highness might have overreacted."

Her gaze softened. "You have nothing to fear from me, child. You will drink the tincture in its entirety. Then we'll burn the bowl. Nothing will remain for those who wish you harm."

I felt Wrath's attention on me like two hot pokers at the base of my neck but refused to look to him. This was my decision and mine alone. I took a deep breath and nodded. "All right."

Celestia clipped a small portion of my hair, sprinkled it over one part herbs and two part petals. She mashed everything together with the mortar and pestle until it formed a powder.

Once the consistency was to her liking, she whispered a charm in a tongue I didn't know, then added a few splashes of the sparkling blue liquid to the mixture.

She poured everything into a silver chalice etched with runes and stirred vigorously. "It won't be the most pleasant drink, but the Tears of Saylonia will help with the taste."

"Tears of Saylonia?"

"Some say she's the goddess of grief and sorrow. But there's more to her than that. The tears are gathered at a temple in the Shifting Isles."

"Where are they located? Here?"

She slid her attention to the prince as she stirred the drink in the opposite direction, the contents splashing from the sudden shift. "It's almost ready."

Wrath watched every step the matron made toward me with a dangerous gleam in his eyes. As if one wrong movement would signal the fight he'd been primed for.

I ignored his odd behavior and returned my attention to the approaching woman. "I've worn the amulet for decades, and I've never experienced pain like that before."

"You visited the Crescent Shallows, did you not?"

"Yes." My hair was damp and there was little use in lying. "How could you tell?"

"A good guess. Certain magic cannot enter those waters without grave consequences. Some say the water there once belonged to the goddesses and burns away that which doesn't belong. Others believe the Feared seek to reclaim what was taken from them. And they do not care how they succeed in restoring their power, only that they do. Vengeance is a brutal pursuit."

"The Feared?" I searched my memory for any stories or legends from childhood, but the name was unfamiliar. "Is that what you call the goddesses, or the demon princes?"

"Enough." Wrath's voice was quiet, but his tone brooked no room for argument. "Some would be wise to keep superstitions and old folktales to themselves." He folded his arms against his chest, his expression hard. "Is her tincture finished?"

I glanced down at the devil's horn charm. Wrath had told me

to leave it on. I gave him an accusing look. "You neglected to tell me about any of the dangers. Now you're concerned?"

Celestia narrowed her eyes, but didn't speak for another few moments as she continued stirring the tincture. "If he knew the effect it would have on you, I doubt he would have taken you there. It's his other secret you need to inquire about. He is fully aware of how *that* one affects you both. And yet he hasn't uttered a single word. I wonder why that is? Perhaps we've finally found your Achilles' heel, your majesty."

Wrath went preternaturally still. The temperature in the room plummeted enough for me to see my breath. Jars rattled as the shelves shook from the force of the power he was holding back, the temper he was battling. The matron had clearly struck her intended target.

Intrigued even more by his response, I studied him closely. He was almost unrecognizable. There was no outward shift in his cold features, but I sensed the immense wave of magic he drew in like the tide.

"Careful," he warned. "You're treading on dangerous ground."

"Bah." She waved her hand at him, completely unconcerned with the growing hum of anger in the air. She handed me the chalice and motioned for me to drink.

I raked my attention over Wrath, and whatever had ignited his namesake sin vanished when he met my worried stare. The temperature returned to normal. He nodded at the cup. "It's all right. Drink."

I brought the concoction to my lips and halted. The smell was not even remotely pleasant. I steeled myself before the pain returned and downed it all in one gulp, ignoring the saccharine yet bitter herb taste. My symptoms vanished.

"You're all set, child."

I gave her the chalice back and watched as she tossed the wooden bowl into the flames. It burned to ash within mere seconds. "Should I take off the amulet now?"

She looked to Wrath, one silver brow raised. I didn't swing around in time to see his reaction, but the matron pursed her lips. Her focus darted to my neck before she met my eyes again. "No. The *charm* won't trouble you anymore."

"Watch yourself, Celestia."

"Go swing a sword or toss a fist at another chunk of rock and begone. Did you not think I heard about your grand show of temper? Domitius and Makaden are fools. But only a larger fool would act as you did. Some might think new sins are stirring. You ought to be mindful, *your highness*. Others are watching. And they take particular interest in your court."

"Mind what you say." His fury whipped around like the gusting winds of a storm. She smiled, but it wasn't the kind of loving expression a grandmother would give to her grandchild. It was edged in steel. Wrath's expression was worse. "I don't take orders from you."

"Then consider it a suggestion. Regardless, it's irresponsible to not tell her."

"Yes, I should very much like to know what you're both talking about." Now that my pain was gone, I was getting annoyed. I knew Wrath was still keeping secrets. Secrets that even Celestia felt I had the right to know. And after what just happened between us in the shallows, I wouldn't tolerate them anymore. I gave Wrath a pointed look. "Someone needs to answer my question. Now."

Celestia glanced between us. "This is a conversation best carried out between you two. Alone." This time her grin was pure trouble. "Though you may want to take her to the Temple of Fury, far from where you can be overheard. I have a feeling you two will wake the entire castle."

With that she ushered us out of her chamber of tinctures and slammed the old oak door at our backs. I stared at the prince. One way or another, he would tell me the truth. I couldn't fathom how Celestia knew his secret when I didn't, and my annoyance was giving way to anger. And that emotion was not brought on by this House of Sin.

How many others in his court were privy to the information he kept from me, that pertained *to* me? It was unacceptable that I was the only one kept in the dark.

"I want the truth. No more lies. You owe me that much."

He seemed to be very much on the verge of finding a weapon to swing. Though his frustration didn't appear to be directed at me or even the matron.

Perhaps he was angry with himself. Whatever game or scheme he'd been planning was clearly over. And hadn't played out the way he'd hoped it would.

"*Fuck.*" Wrath shoved a hand through his hair and paced away from me. "I thought we'd have more time. But after tonight, it obviously can no longer wait."

Wrath brought us to his personal library and magicked the room to contain our voices within it. I stood before the giant fireplace, warming my hands. Between the cool temperature in the castle, the exhaustion that swept in following the pain, my thin night-gown, and the dampness of my hair, I was chilled to the core.

Fear was also playing a role with my shudders. Was it possible something happened to my family? If they were harmed—or worse—I wasn't sure Wrath would tell me.

He knew they were my weakness as much as my strength and I'd bargain my way back to my world and break the contract with Pride. That would certainly complicate his mission and be motive enough for his not being forthright with me.

Wrath's tense mood wasn't helping to soothe me, either. It invaded my senses until my own nerves were yanked taut enough to snap.

He paced the room like a large animal trapped in a cage. Prior to our passionate embrace in the lagoon, and then in the corridor outside his bedchamber, I'd never seen him anything but calm; even while furious he was never so...on edge. It was disconcerting, seeing him like this. His snapping at the matron was unusual, too. On occasion he could be gruff, arrogant, or brimming with masculine smugness, but he was never rude.

"Will you sit down?" I rubbed at my arms. "You're making me nervous."

He prowled over to his desk and poured two fingers of lavender liquid into his glass. He tossed it back before swiftly refilling it and offered the second drink to me. I shook my head.

Waiting was unbearable. And my stomach was already tied up in several intricate knots. I wanted to know what he had to say, and why whatever it was was affecting him this strongly. Even when he attacked Makaden earlier there had been no regret or worry on his part. Only cold efficiency. He'd carried out a sentence and was impartial to its brutality.

"Is the suspense truly necessary?" My voice was surprisingly calm. It was a complete contradiction to the frantic pounding of my heart. "Whatever you have to say can't be that bad."

I hoped.

He finally stopped moving long enough to look me in the eye. His expression was impossible to read. A cool, unnerving calm had settled over him. Trepidation slid down my spine. His demeanor reminded me of when a midwife delivered fatal news.

"Earlier this evening, you asked why I Marked you. I'm not sure you fully understand what it does. Why it is something given so rarely."

I stared at him, momentarily taken off guard by his sudden shift in topic and how the summoning Mark played a role in this. At least I understood how Celestia had known about this secret; her attention had briefly shifted to my neck. I'd mistakenly thought she was looking at my devil's horn charm.

"Well?" he prodded, drawing my attention back to him. "What do you know of it?"

"Nonna said it allows someone to summon a prince of Hell without an object that belongs to them. That it's a great honor not many are given. And that, as long as he draws breath, the demon prince must always answer the summoning. Except, of course, when I tried to summon you and you didn't show." My tone turned frosty. "I thought you were dead."

He stepped back, his focus quickly roving over me in quiet calculation.

"After being injured with Envy's House dagger, I hadn't healed enough to travel between realms. I didn't realize you were upset by my absence." I gave him a dirty look that seemed to bring out a mischievous tilt of his mouth. The look faded almost instantly. "Do you know why it's given so rarely?"

"Because princes are ornery bastards and don't like being summoned at will?"

A ghost of a smile touched his lips again before he banished it. "Because it is a magical bond that can never be broken."

"Impossible. All magic can be undone."

"Not this bond. Not even in death."

"But you are immortal."

"Imagine then, how long that bond lasts."

We stared at each other as the weight of that truth settled between us. I was struggling to absorb the information, the implications of it. Wrath didn't speak, his expression turning grim as I sorted through the shock. If the bond lasted even after death, I couldn't fathom how that worked. Our souls would forever be linked. Except I'd sold mine, and had no clue what that meant for the bond. Or for him.

"Emilia." His voice was quiet, but held a commanding edge. "Say something."

"You said to avoid speaking in absolutes. They have a tendency to *never* stick, remember?"

"Do you recall anything I said the night you were attacked by the Viperidae?"

Wrath moved nearer, watching me carefully with each of his measured steps. I imagined he sensed how close I was to bolting and was doing his best to not make any sudden movements and spook me. His attention strayed to his Mark.

Unconsciously, I reached up to touch the place on my neck where the nearly invisible symbol marred my skin. I'd been in too much pain to absorb anything he'd said that night, and then we were in the bath together and the nightmares had begun soon after.

And before I awoke he'd said...

"I told you to live long enough to hate me. And I meant it."

He reached out and traced the side of my throat, his touch feather-light. "That was the night I Marked you. But that's not all."

Panic fluttered inside my rib cage like a trapped bird.

I had a terrible feeling I knew where this was going and I wanted no part in it. I swore my betrothal tattoo started tingling, reminding me it was there. As if I'd forgotten.

I forced my feet to stay firmly planted on the ground, though a large part of me wanted to take flight and race up to my rooms, lock the door, and never emerge.

"Stop." I turned and started walking away. The new fear was growing. I didn't want to hear any more of his confession. "Take me back to my chamber."

"Not until you know the whole truth."

Wrath now stood before me, his gaze fused to mine. I really despised his supernatural speed. He didn't reach for me again, didn't bar my path or crowd me into a corner, but his expression was laced with the promise of staying close to me until I was ready to hear his full confession. I knew he'd wait for an eternity if he had to, he'd wait until the sun burned out and the last star faded from the heavens. And I didn't have that sort of time to waste.

I finally nodded, granting him permission to continue. To uproot my world once more.

"The magic I used that you'd mistaken for a rebirth spell? It was the Mark. It tethered us, flesh to flesh, in a way that allowed my powers to heal you. You only walked away from that attack because I took the venom into my body through that magical bond."

His immortal body. A body that would not be cut down or ended by poison or venom or anything else that would have killed me. I swallowed hard. Wrath bonded himself to a sworn enemy just so I would live. The gravity of what he'd done. What he'd sacrificed to save me the night I'd gone after my sister's amulet, fought the snakelike Viperidae demon, and had almost died, crashed into me. No wonder he'd been furious I'd been so cavalier about it.

His price had been steeper than I'd ever imagined. But then again, so was mine.

"The Mark was more than a way to summon me, or save you. Because of another magical bond we share, it was also part acceptance. I believe you understand where this story is headed, but would you like me to continue?"

My heart was now beating very fast at his choice of words. *Acceptance.* We weren't talking about his summoning Mark and the magic he used to take the venom anymore. We were talking about my fear, the one that kept growing even now. I couldn't bring myself to look him in the eye. "I broke the spell after that."

"You don't sound certain. Yet the truth has always been there for you to see."

I looked down at the traitorous ink on his bare arm; the magical tattoos that hadn't disappeared. I'd suspected my spell reversal hadn't worked but had pushed those worries aside. He was correct. I hadn't *wanted* to acknowledge what it meant. I still didn't.

"May I?" Wrath reached for my hand but stopped short of touching me. I nodded and he gently took my arm and rolled up the sleeve of my nightdress. He held his forearm to mine, waiting until the truth stopped fluttering around like a frightened bird and settled into me.

There was no denying they matched perfectly. And I knew why.

I dragged my attention from our tattoos up to his face. His

beautiful, cold, royal face. The face that belonged to a fallen god. And my destroyer. Anticipation prickled my skin.

"You seek the truth? Allow me to give it freely. Pride has not summoned you to his court, nor will he ever attempt to. At least not for the reason you believe."

"Because..."

I knew, oh goddess, I knew. Still, I needed him to say the words.

"You are not his intended, Emilia." The world beneath me tilted. Wrath's gaze was steady enough to keep both my knees and the realm from quaking. "You are mine."

THIRTEEN

You are mine. Everything outside of those three words faded. My shock, denial, and utter confusion were simply gone. It was as if I'd stepped from Wrath's library back into the nothingness of the void. My pulse pounded in every one of my cells. The phrase echoed softly, drummed against each of my nerves, embedded themselves into my heart.

It felt like the magic that bonded us fully came awake. Wrath's admission somehow wrenched it from its slumber and gave it permission to stretch its arms wide.

This mighty warrior prince, brimming with immortal vitality and power, death and rage made flesh...suddenly, I was drawn into a vision.

Past or future or pure illusion crafted of this sinful world, I couldn't discern. We were in Wrath's bed, hundreds of candles flickering across the glossy surface of his silken sheets, his dark colored walls, and the sheen of sweat coating his bare chest.

I was astride the demon prince, my thighs spread wide to accommodate the breadth of him. He watched me with a primal sort of possession, his half-lidded gaze drinking in every inch of my body while my hips undulated, seeking pleasure but not fully. I teased us both by not quite closing the slight distance between our bodies.

He reached for me, but I pinned him to the mattress, nipping playfully at his mouth before losing myself in his slow kisses. Soon he was no longer content with being a spectator; his hands clasped on to my sides, guiding me down onto his fierce arousal. With a whispered word of endearment and a quick upward thrust, we were joined in all ways. For eternity.

I managed to draw in a deep, ragged breath, banishing the vision. Some denial slipped back in. "*We* are still betrothed."

Wrath's eyes momentarily glazed, as if he'd been in that seductive illusion with me and still felt the tremors of pleasure rocking through him. His cool tone did not match the heat lingering in his gaze. "Yes. I am to be your husband."

"My husband. You, not Pride."

"Emilia..."

"Please."

I held up a hand to stall him. Something ancient rattled my bones. I ignored the feeling, instead focusing on the anger unfurling in fiery tendrils, replacing any lingering sense of shock or denial, and clearing my head. This could *not* be happening. It was a complication I could ill afford for several reasons; the largest being my vow to avenge my sister.

"You lied to me."

He fell silent for a few moments, then said quietly, "Despite the less-than-ideal circumstances of our union, we are well suited. Enough."

I stared at him, unblinking. With such a *wildly* romantic

declaration, who needed love or passion? If I wasn't marrying Pride to carry out my scheme, I was going to marry for love. "Well suited enough" was also grossly misrepresenting the situation. I still wished to strangle Wrath more often than I wished to kiss or bed him. I had a feeling he felt the same way. Which perhaps was an indication of being *well suited enough*. Ours would be an unholy union of fury.

"Your brother is aware of this?"

"Of course."

The demon prince seemed braced for a violent outburst; his feet were subtly planted shoulder-width apart, his body angled forward. He deserved a good slap for keeping this from me, but I could hardly wrap my mind around his confession and the strange way his words—innocuous though they were—suddenly heated my blood.

My whole body hummed with awareness, almost preternaturally. I was aware of every one of his movements, from the slight shifting of his feet to his steady breath. My new awareness of him did not alleviate my anger. If anything, it only stoked it more.

New realizations clicked into place. If I was a member of House Wrath, other royal houses—such as Pride's court—would never share gossip regarding their prince. Any hopes and plans I had of gaining information I needed about Pride's first wife were ruined.

"This is madness."

I had taken the chaos my world devolved into after Vittoria's death and had created a tiny semblance of order by coming here. And I'd only accomplished that because of my vow to her.

Now...now my life was once again spinning out of control because of the Wicked.

Wrath in particular. My fury finally exploded.

"You keep telling me I have a choice. When does that actually happen? Certainly not when it comes to which demon House I choose. Or which prince I thought I was betrothed to. Let's not forget my personal favorite, back in Palermo when I asked if you'd make me come here. To rule in Hell. You said you would never force me. Apparently *tricking* is a perfectly acceptable substitute. Congratulations." I clapped slowly. "You truly know your way around bending the truth. I must admit, I'm impressed."

He didn't look relieved, but he did relax his stance, marginally. I saw the exact moment he recalled the night I was talking about, when I thought I'd broken our betrothal with a spell of un-making. He'd sworn he wouldn't force me into a marriage or take me to the underworld. Apparently, more half-truths if not full lies.

"You still do. You do not have to complete our marriage."

I pointed a finger in accusation at the summoning Mark.

"And what about this unbreakable bond? It doesn't feel like a choice. I realize you had much to sacrifice, too, but at least you were aware of what you were deciding. Regardless, you should have told me before now. I had every right to know."

"The Mark was the best alternative I could come up with at the time. And thanks to the venom, I didn't have many other options to explore before it stopped your heart. I asked you to grant me permission to help that night. *There* was your choice. You betrothed us. I accepted."

As if I needed a reminder of that grievous error. "Alternative to what?"

"To delay certain urges the acceptance creates."

"Urges."

My mouth shut with an audible click as understanding sank in. All of my lust-filled thoughts and feelings toward Wrath had slowly been intensifying. They'd been eroding my distrust and the betrayal I had felt. I'd thought it was *only* this realm, its tendency toward desire, fueling my emotions, nudging me toward that almost primal frenzy to bed him. But it wasn't. It was also an ancient need to claim my husband. To secure our marriage.

Goddess above. *Wrath* was my intended.

I'd been fighting a battle on many fronts and hadn't even known it. No wonder resisting temptation had been so hard. I'd been battling the bond, the realm, and its nudges for me to face my fears of owning my sexual desire without guilt or shame.

If I was being honest, the conflicted feelings had started well before we came to this world. When he'd been attacked by Envy and bled out before me, something had shifted then.

And prior to that, when I'd been under Lust's spell, I'd wanted Wrath desperately. For a moment that night, he seemed to want to close the distance between us, too.

I snapped myself into the present. "Your acceptance of the betrothal creates desire?"

"Consummation, along with a traditional ceremony, complete the marriage bond." He searched my face, probably seeing if I was about to hit him now. I wanted to. Tremendously. "You look..."

"Angry?" I raised my brows and canted my head. He was wise enough to know that the silence that followed was twice as dangerous as raising a hand.

"*Create* was a poor word choice. It *encourages* the completion of the bond. At some level, you have to already possess those feelings, or else there'd be nothing for the bond to encourage."

"Has the realm ever been *encouraging* me, or is it only our bond?"

"Both."

"And your summoning Mark does what, exactly?"

"Marking you subdues the marriage urges because it's its own unbreakable link between us. If you were to think of it in terms of a body of water, it would be similar to a river that breaks into two smaller streams. Each diluting the other to an extent, until they rejoin."

Which was why he'd brushed his knuckles across the Mark whenever we kissed; he'd been trying to dilute my *urges*. He also did that while I was under Lust's influence at the bonfire. Which meant he'd been tamping it down for a while. And hadn't bothered to tell me.

I don't know why it stung so badly, but it did.

"What happens if I refuse to accept the marriage? Will I still want you in my bed?"

"The urges will remain, but they won't ever force your hand, Emilia. That's not the way the bond works. You will always have a choice. Just as you would with any other partner."

"I always have a choice," I scoffed. "Except if I want to marry the devil."

Wrath stiffened. The words were out of my mouth before I'd given much thought to them. Or how they might impact the prince. In order for him to experience those urges, too, he must possess some level of feelings for me.

And that was . . . it was too complicated to sort through.

I knew it was unfair to blame him, especially since I was the one who'd originally trapped him in a betrothal, but I couldn't help but cling to my fury. All of my plans were going up in flames. If I didn't get to House Pride, I might never discover what really happened to my twin. The only reason I'd even signed that contract was to place myself in the viper's nest and stop any more witches from being murdered.

Now I was in this realm and stuck in a situation that wouldn't further my mission. I didn't come here to find love, or to become Princess of House Wrath. I came for vengeance. I came to be Queen. I was here to destroy the demon who'd killed Vittoria and save my family and island from further danger from invading demons. And Wrath was complicating my entire world.

"Why the secrecy?" I demanded. "If you didn't want me to sign Pride's contract you could have told me about this back in the cave that night. Why not ask me to align myself with your House? It makes no sense that you'd hide this from me."

"Fiancée or not, you are free to join any House of Sin you wish. I won't ever stand in your way. And I did not tell you because I didn't want you to come here."

"Why don't you want me here?" He pressed his lips together. I wasn't about to let him get away with that non-response answer again. "Tell me. Tell me this has something to do with the curse and not with another person you love. I need to understand why you keep some secrets and give up others."

"I cannot. Be content with the answers you've gotten."

I noticed his word choice. *Cannot* and *will not* were vastly different. I looked him over, but his expression gave nothing away. I knew he'd chosen those words with care.

"Is this why I can't travel between the demon courts without an invitation? Because I am technically bound to your House?"

He nodded. "You would still need an escort through the realm since it's dangerous to travel alone, and we'd need to have a delegation from each House meet at the border of our territories, but yes. As my intended you are seen as the future co-ruler of House Wrath. Therefore, it would be an act of aggression if you were to simply show up at another court without warning or permission."

"What of the contract I signed with House Pride?"

"If we complete our marriage, it becomes void."

"And if we don't? What about the witch murders? Are they still happening?"

"No. They are not."

"How is that possible? Your entire mission revolved around finding the devil a bride. Unless it was never truly about that..."

Wrath looked as if he wanted to say more but either couldn't or wouldn't. His growing silence solidified my earlier worry about the murders having nothing to do with the devil needing a bride to break his curse. Which meant the witches were killed for some reason I'd yet to uncover. Annoyance warred with anger as I glared at the prince of secrets.

"If you choose to do nothing," he finally said, breaking the silence, "then it will eventually be sent to the Temple of Fate. A council of three will then convene on the matter. That path is ill-advised, but is your choice to make nonetheless."

"Wonderful. The council will what? Decide then if I marry you or someone else?"

"They will decide the fate of us all."

I regretted not accepting the drink he'd offered earlier. I rolled my head, trying to ease the mounting tension. There were way too many emotions fighting for dominance right now. Wrath walked over to where I stood and put the glass in my hand, then began circling the room.

"How did you know I wanted the drink? Can you sense my emotions that clearly, or is it an added bonus from our betrothal bond? Or maybe the summoning Mark. It's hard to keep all of your tricks straight."

"Your gaze darted to the glass, Emilia. I simply read your body language."

I watched him pace, my mind spinning with each of his revolutions around the room. His actions were all starting to make sense. He hadn't let me die from the elements because I was his future bride. It was also why he'd stayed with me in the Sin Corridor, though Anir said he shouldn't have. Another memory came back to me. In Palermo, Anir had mentioned completing the marriage bond and securing his House, something about gaining full power. When he'd come to collect me in the cave, I'd noticed a shift in his power. It had felt infinite. Stronger.

Wrath may have *some* feelings or physical attraction for me, but, given his nature, I wondered if he'd acted partly out of self-preservation.

"Do your subjects know?"

"Yes. The whole realm is aware."

Which was why he'd made such a public example of Lord Makaden. The noble hadn't simply disobeyed a royal command; he'd challenged Wrath and insulted his soon-to-be wife. The same was true for the officer he'd brought the mountain down on; he'd threatened to kill the princess of House Wrath. If either of them harmed me, it would in turn diminish Wrath's power to some degree. I knew precisely how much princes of Hell coveted power.

Enough to bind themselves to someone they may enjoy between their sheets on occasion, but would never truly love. For eternity.

Well suited enough.

The choice of words grated on me. He also hadn't denied there was someone else in his life. Someone he'd chosen before I destroyed his world.

"I invited you to bed tonight." My voice was low, but not meek. Wrath stopped pacing and his heavy gaze clashed with mine. My attention roved over his face. "Would you have told me any of this before we slept together?"

"No matter how tempting, I would not have consummated our marriage tonight. There are plenty of ways to give and receive pleasure that would not jeopardize your free will."

"Is that the truth? Or just what you think I wish to hear?"

He stared at me, his jaw tightening. The temperature around us chilled a few degrees. I half-expected the castle's foundation to shake. "What kind of monster do you believe me to be?"

I had no good answer. And until I did...I drew in a deep breath, thinking over my options. Wrath had mentioned a few of his brothers were interested in hosting me at their Houses. Perhaps it was time for a visit.

"I want you to escort me to House Envy in the morning. Will you send a note letting him know I accept his invitation?"

Wrath didn't react for a long moment; he looked like he wasn't sure if he'd heard me correctly. He stared so hard I started to worry he could see through flesh and bone straight into my soul. I kept my expression bland and forced thoughts of tranquility: collecting shells by the sea, laughing with my sister and Claudia, drinking wine and talking about simple things.

Anything to keep my emotions from betraying me.

He finally nodded. He wasn't pleased, that much was obvious from the way he'd tensed up at the request, but he also wasn't trying to stop or imprison me.

I was not his cosseted princess. Thus far, my choices remained my own.

"You're certain that's what you want? Even after what Envy did?"

"Yes." I thought about my next request. "I also need a mending kit."

"You don't need to sew your own clothing anymore, Emilia. A seamstress can do that."

"All the same, I'd like one for emergencies."

"Very well. I'll have one sent to your room and let my brother know tonight. Will that be all?"

"For now."

"Come." He offered his hand, his voice and expression both genial enough to make me wary as I stepped closer. I ignored the little spark that passed between us when his fingers closed around mine. If he felt it, too, he didn't let on. "I'll take you to your chamber to pack. We'll leave for House Envy at first light."

FOURTEEN

Wrath made one small, seemingly innocuous request of his own before leaving me to pack a trunk for my visit. He'd asked to have a gown sent in the morning, one in which it was appropriate to be received by a prince of Hell. Regardless of any ulterior motives, of which I was certain he had many, I'd decided there was little harm in granting his wish and quickly agreed.

I told myself my swift acceptance had *nothing* to do with the fact my *betrothed* was in my private suite, standing shirtless near my bed, looking like he was carved from the very essence of temptation itself. He kept a careful distance, almost painfully so, but there wasn't anything he could do to dampen my awareness of him. The space between us seemed to vibrate with both tension and anticipation. I wasn't sure if it was only coming from me, or if he felt it, too. He'd retreated back to the enigmatic prince who was cordial, but otherwise difficult to read.

I was not nearly as calm. My emotions were still aflutter after learning the truth, and I had every right to tuck myself safely in denial until I sorted through them. Far away from the prince.

The twinkle of mirth finally broke into his cool features as I ushered him out of my rooms and practically shut the door on his heels. I leaned my head against the wall and exhaled. An hour earlier I'd felt much differently. I couldn't get him *into* my bed fast enough.

I slammed the memory of our romantic encounter outside his rooms from my mind. Recalling the pleasant sensation of his hands stroking and exploring would do nothing to clear my head.

"What a nightmare."

I rushed into my bathing chamber to splash water on my face and caught a glimpse of myself in the mirror, immediately understanding his amused reaction. My dark eyes were wide and wild, my hair unruly from our earlier dip into trouble, and my skin was flushed as if some torturous fever had overtaken me. I was an untamed, frenzied mess on the inside and it was shining through to the outside. Certainly not the ideal reaction to matrimony to boost any male ego or confidence. Though it wasn't as if Wrath lacked in either of those areas.

My gaze snagged on my amulet, briefly wrenching me from thoughts of husbands and wives and unbreakable magical bonds. Given Envy's reaction to the Horn of Hades last time, I wanted the necklace far away from him. I refused to take any careless chances by parading it under his nose while staying in his royal House.

I took it off and placed it at the bottom of my vanity drawer. I'd let Wrath know where to find it in the morning. As I closed the drawer, I noticed something that hadn't been present earlier: a silver hand mirror and matching brush and comb were placed atop the table.

They appeared sometime after I'd cleaned up from Lord Makaden's blood and now. I admired the detailed etching, marveling at the craftsmanship. Another beautiful—and thoughtful—gift from my future husband. I sighed. If Wrath started wooing me, I wasn't sure I'd recall all the reasons we weren't a proper match. Of which there were many.

First, he was a prince of Hell, a mortal enemy to witches. Next, he was secretive and did not trust me any more than I trusted him with full disclosure. He also might feel lust around me, but that did not equal love. I wanted a true partner, an equal and confidant. Wrath would always hold his proverbial cards close, and I wasn't sure he'd ever deal me in. Given the tenuous nature of our current relationship, I might never fully include him in my plans, either.

I removed the animal skulls and flower clips from around the crown of my head, then ran the comb through my loose curls, trying desperately to slow my pulse. It was no use.

I set the comb down and returned to my bedchamber, pacing so quickly around the room I almost worked up a sweat, too wound up to attempt sleep. As appealing as shoving my feelings aside was, I needed to sort through some of the tangle before I left for Envy's House.

Wrath was a handsome, unwed prince, and he was no doubt highly sought after by all eligible ladies of the nobility. He was a bit aloof at times, and arrogant, but he was also charming and flirtatious when he wished to be. He'd once even called himself "His Royal Highness of Undeniable Desire." And, goddess curse him, I could see how that was true. If he set his attention on someone, I doubted they would resist his romantic pursuit for long.

He approached everything strategically and it would only be a matter of time before the object of his desire happily surrendered to his careful seduction. He'd certainly been a generous lover in the Crescent Shallows, focusing on my needs as if that gave him ultimate pleasure to do so. In fact, I imagined he had his pick of all-too-willing bed partners before I entered his world. Some vying for his throne and power, others solely interested in his body.

I abruptly stopped pacing as another thought occurred to me, one that pricked like the little spikes on a crab shell when we served those at our trattoria. I'd thought of it earlier, and now it seemed to taunt me with larger implications.

Wrath hadn't professed love or affection, only that we were well suited enough. While it wasn't the romantic moment of my dreams, there was truth in his statement.

I knew him enough to know he would never force me into anything or interfere with my free will, and at least I wouldn't be tied to the devil. But I couldn't stop myself from wondering if there was someone else *he'd* prefer to wed. Before I'd accidentally summoned him and betrothed us, it was possible there had been someone in his bed and his heart.

Someone he might be thinking of now. When we first met, he'd made it abundantly clear how much he hated witches. Even if his feelings for me were thawing, it might not ever be enough for him to truly love me. Would he keep a mistress if we completed our marriage bond?

I didn't like the pinch of discomfort that came with those thoughts.

No matter how hard I tried to quiet my brain, I couldn't stop thinking of our passionate encounter in the lagoon and then outside his bedchamber. His hands on my body, my back pressed against the wall, his tongue claiming mine...in those moments he *felt* right.

But that didn't mean he was. For a multitude of reasons. Passion and lust couldn't erase the lack of trust between us or the secrets we both kept. A good relationship was built on a solid foundation of honesty, and I didn't even know his true name.

Aside from the real possibility of Wrath never fully allowing himself to love me, I was unsure if I could ever fully allow myself to love him. Bed him, certainly. Marry, perhaps. But to let go of everything else and accept him as he was, with all of his secrets? I wasn't as sure.

"Goddess help me." This was disastrous.

I'd been willing to have a marriage of convenience with Pride. But only because it granted me access to his House and a better understanding of how his wife's murder might tie in with Vittoria's. Binding myself to Wrath...I was unsure how that would assist in my mission.

If anything, all I came up with were more complications.

I tossed myself across the bed and summoned Source. My magic responded almost instantly, happy to be used while I was otherwise distracted. I created a garden's worth of rose-gold burning flowers and floated them up to the ceiling, my mind returning to the two princes currently occupying the majority of my thoughts.

I didn't know the first thing about Pride, other than the fact he was the devil. Wrath I was starting to know a little better, and being near him sometimes made the ache in my chest lessen. He didn't erase memories of my twin—no one could ever do that— but when he was around, I found a perverse sense of peace arguing with him.

I released the hold on my magic, the flowers of flame slowly burning out. I watched as the petals became blackened embers that floated to the floor, extinguishing before they touched the carpet. I sighed, too distraught to be thrilled over my most impressive use of magic yet. It wasn't the marriage bond that bothered me; it was the realization that my family hadn't managed to drag me from the depths of my grief, but the demon prince had.

Some days I hated him for it, but there was a larger part of me that was grateful for his unwillingness to tolerate my fire burning out. He'd poke and prod and taunt me until I wanted nothing more than to wrap my hands around his neck and squeeze. And it was far better to be angry rather than turn into a ghost of my former self from sadness and grief.

It had been a very long, restless night and this realm did nothing to ease my way as I cycled through emotions. Twice I'd gotten up, made it to the outer door, my hand hovering above the knob, then shook sense into myself and returned to bed.

I was here to find out the truth about my twin. The more I thought of Vittoria, the easier it became to distance myself from those other *urges*. And when those thoughts weren't enough, I continued to delve into Source, creating a variety of flaming flowers in various sizes. I practiced extinguishing some flowers, while increasing the intensity of the flames on others.

When the gown arrived just before dawn, along with the olive branch ring Wrath had given me back in the mortal world, I'd been bleary-eyed opening the package, but pleased. It was solid black lace, with long fitted sleeves and a full skirt, but it wasn't entirely modest. The sides were cut out from just under the upper part of my ribs to my waist.

Those open edges were lined with shimmering gold designs that reminded me of flowering vines. Snakes also twisted through the flora.

Temptation was what the dress should have been called if garments were given names.

Now, as we stepped into the dark emerald–colored antechamber outside Envy's throne room, amidst a sea of waiting nobles clad in various shades of deep green silks and velvets, it was not lost on anyone that Wrath had chosen my clothing with greater purpose.

His perfectly tailored suit was the masculine version of my gown. Black jacket, black and gold waistcoat with that same floral and snake design, black shirt, and matching trousers. Gold rings glinted from his knuckles, looking more weaponlike than mere ornamentation. His crown was made of gold laurel leaf intertwined with glittering ebony serpents.

I wore no diadem or tiara, but Wrath had dressed me in his signature black and gold. It was his way of showing this court where I truly belonged. At *his* side.

Judging from the whispers and curious glances that kept sliding our way after the herald rushed in to prepare for our announcement, Wrath's plan had worked.

Truthfully, I'd been onto his scheme the moment I took the gown out of its dark tissue wrapping. My prince was not as subtle as he imagined. Or maybe he hadn't been aiming for subtlety at all. The last time he'd seen Envy, his brother had disemboweled him. Maybe this act of possession had more to do with whatever private feud was happening between them.

Though it was possible it was also Wrath's way of ensuring anyone of this court would think twice before striking me. He was protecting his potential power enhancement *and* irking his brother. I was certain there was also some deep sense of chivalry at play, too.

Wrath did not want harm to befall me. I knew that, more than anything else, was the real driving force behind his actions.

That was why I'd stepped into the gown that claimed me as part of his royal House as much as our magical tattoos and his royal Mark did.

He was extending his protection, and only a fool would turn that away. I may have been foolish before, but, thank the goddess, I was learning quickly.

The herald nodded at two guards stationed at the double doors, then stomped an emerald-tipped staff on the ground. The doors swung open, revealing my first glimpse inside Envy's royal court. Hunter green marble floors spanned the cathedral-like room with rows of matching columns on either side of a long aisle. Groups of finely dressed royals stood in small circles throughout the space, their attention riveted on the herald.

And the two people standing behind him, awaiting our introductions.

Wrath paid them no notice, though I suspected he'd already mapped out the exits and placement of guards. Right now the general of war was hidden beneath the cold prince. Arrogance dripped from him as if he'd expected this court's regard and was unsurprised by it.

I looked past the crowd, ignoring their stares until my attention landed on the dais. The Prince of Envy sprawled on his throne, his expression one of complete disinterest. He looked as if there were a hundred other more interesting places he'd rather be, and a hundred other people he'd rather be associating with. It had to be an act. Surely he sensed his brother. And the wave of unease rippling through the room.

After a pregnant pause to eke out the most dramatic effect, the herald's voice broke the silence, "His Royal Highness, Prince

Wrath of House Wrath, General of War and one of the Seven, and Lady Emilia di Carlo of House Wrath."

I didn't think it was possible for the room to grow any quieter, but it did. Whispers ceased. Shuffling feet froze. It was as if the whole court had turned to stone. Except for their prince. The moment we were announced, Envy straightened. That indolent expression was replaced with shrewd interest as we slowly made our way down the aisle. I studied him as closely.

He wore a velvet swallowtail jacket the color of an evergreen forest with a jeweled silver crown. His jet-black hair was different from the last time I'd seen him. It was shorter on the sides and a bit longer on top. The new style showed off the harsh lines and angles of his face, the cheekbones that were sharp enough to carve open a few hearts. His facial hair was also mostly gone, except for a slight shadow that only served to enhance his rugged appeal.

If I didn't know what sort of ruthless monster lurked beneath his skin, I'd be lured into those mesmerizing features.

I tried not to let trepidation show as his unnaturally green eyes skipped over his brother and fastened to my face. Envy had kidnapped my family and then harmed Wrath in his pursuit to get the Horn of Hades. I did not have to like or trust him while visiting.

I only needed to use him for my gain.

"Brother. I see you've brought your shadow witch." His expression was once again bored, though I swore his lips twitched slightly at the edges as Wrath tensed beside me. "I didn't think you'd wish to share. But you've certainly dressed her in the most appealing way. All that skin begs to be worshipped. It's about time I found religion, wouldn't you say?"

It was only because of my need to secure information that I held my tongue.

"Your manners seem to have disappeared along with the length of your hair." Wrath gently squeezed my hand. "Lady Emilia graciously accepted your invitation. I would have advised her to burn it and send back the ashes. Along with a steaming pile of hellhound shit."

"Yes, well, you never were one for subtlety. Leave the *lady* and get out."

"I will see her to her chamber before I depart."

"No."

A slow, threatening grin spread across Wrath's face. "That wasn't a request. I *will* escort her to her chamber. Then I will depart."

Tension descended like an army between the two brothers, poised and ready to strike. I didn't dare glance behind us, but I heard the swish of skirts moving across the floor as if members of the court were putting plenty of distance between themselves and the two royals.

I wondered how often they might fight and if they used magic or weapons or both.

Neither prince broke the other's stare and I all but rolled my eyes as they continued to glower. Another moment and they'd undo the stays on their trousers and compare lengths.

Envy finally sat back, his gloved fingers drumming the arms of his throne. His attention slid between me and his brother, and that taunting half-smirk returned.

"Very well. If it'll get you out of here faster, I'll allow it." He jerked his chin toward a silver-haired servant waiting nearby. The demon immediately stepped forward, eager to please his prince.

"Show my brother and his plaything to her private quarters. If he's not gone within a quarter of an hour, use force. My hospitality and good graces toward House Wrath only stretch so far. For every minute he stays over the time allotted, I will plot something creative to do to his precious enchantress."

I subtly watched Wrath from the corner of my eye. This time he didn't rise to Envy's bait. He offered a slight incline of his head, then turned his back on his sibling. Which I quickly realized was, quite possibly, the biggest show of blatant disregard he could offer.

His action deemed Envy unworthy of his fear. I could practically hear the Prince of Envy's molars grinding together as we walked away.

Honestly, I was surprised he hadn't put up more of a fight. Wrath had come into another demon court and no one seemed shocked by his demands. Or their prince's fairly swift acceptance of them. Maybe Wrath's reputation and role as general made them wary.

He placed my hand on his arm as we made our way back out of the throne room and followed the servant up a wide, grand staircase.

Envy's castle was mostly decorated in silvers and greens with splashes of black and white. We traveled over checkerboard tile and I smiled to myself as I took in the floor's design. His guests were merely chess pieces moving along the finely appointed corridors, meant to invoke feelings of envy. From the many shades of green to the riches on display, all played into the sin this House was governed by.

Marble statues lined each side of the gilded corridor, but I didn't give them more than a cursory glance. I did not want to inadvertently succumb to feelings of jealousy over the bounty of beautiful art. Wrath hadn't adjusted the pressure of his grip, but I sensed the tension pouring off him the farther we went into his brother's stronghold.

The next landing broke off into two wings and we were ushered to the right.

The servant stopped before a door near the end and bowed. "The lady's suite. Her trunk is already inside. Will you be needing anything else?" Wrath shook his head. The servant exhaled and turned his attention back to me. "Ring the bell if you need anything."

Before Wrath could scare the demon, I gave him a warm smile. "Thank you."

The servant froze for a moment, then nodded once and quickly disappeared down the corridor we'd just come from. Wrath watched him go before turning back to me. "The staff doesn't expect to be thanked for doing their job."

"Everyone who's working or providing service that's a comfort ought to be thanked."

Wrath looked me over, his expression inscrutable, before he swept through the chambers I'd been appointed. His attention landed on every nook, cranny, and speck of dust as if he expected some nefarious creature to spring forth and attack.

Or maybe he was put off by all of the green and silver tones.

I trailed after him, trying to keep my lips from curving upward as he peered beneath the canopy bed, then yanked back the curtains and rattled the windows. He barged into my bathing chamber, hand on the hilt of his dagger, his expression fierce. prince of Hell or personal guard. It was hard to distinguish who he was as he tended to my suite.

I bit my lip to keep from laughing as he plucked up a pitcher, shook it a little, and brought it close to his nose. I doubted Envy slipped poison into it, but Wrath was not taking any chances.

He caught my eye and turned that fierce glare on me. "Do you find me amusing?"

"At the moment? Very."

He tossed the pitcher aside and stalked toward me, his movements slow and deliberate. Here was the predator he barely kept hidden under all the fine clothing. His civilized appearance was simply a mask, a way to hide the truth of his nature. The hunter was now on full display and his new target was set firmly in his sights.

A thrill shot through me before my smile vanished and I scrambled back. He didn't stop his pursuit until the backs of my thighs brushed the bed. He paused then, giving me a chance to escape to the other side. But I didn't move. I stayed where I was.

He took one more step, then halted, offering one final choice before he erased the distance. I could either sit down, or remain standing. Sitting was trouble. Standing was worse. It put us entirely too close. I held my ground.

Wrath now stood near enough that with each of my breaths, my chest brushed against his. Truth be told, I felt anything but afraid. I wet my lips and his gaze darkened.

"What about now?" He angled his face down, his mouth hovering right above mine. "Are you still amused, my lady?"

My pulse raced faster. Judging from the smoldering look in his eyes, he knew perfectly well how I was feeling at the moment. I took a steadying breath and slowly exhaled.

"If I decide to return, do I need to send a request to your House?"

A muscle flickered in his jaw, indicating he'd picked up on my choice of words and wasn't pleased by the possibility I wouldn't return. Instead of arguing, or issuing any sort of arrogant command, Wrath stepped back and took my hand in his, carefully turning it over. He lifted my palm to his lips, pressed a chaste kiss to it, then closed my fingers around it. Heat shot up my arm, warmed my blood, and my body hummed with need. His unexpected tenderness was not helping matters between us become less murky.

"My home is your home, Emilia. You do not need an invitation. When you decide to return, I will send an escort." He motioned to the bed. "Sit. I have something to give you."

My attention shot to his mouth and I quickly wrenched it back up, fighting the realm's sinful magic, our persistent marriage bond, and Wrath's general appeal.

Now was not the time to think about kissing.

He didn't say anything, or smirk, but I almost sensed his pleasure as I worked through my emotions. Deciding he wasn't likely to ravish me here, I perched on the edge of the mattress.

Wrath slowly went to his knees, then lifted my left foot and settled it onto his taut thigh. I went to draw it back, but he held it in place. We both knew I could break his grip if I really wanted to, so I stilled.

"If we decide to consummate our marriage, it will not be in my brother's home, for mere moments. You deserve better than that." He waited for me to relax, as if that were possible after *that* statement, then began sliding my skirt up. He paused near my bare calf, his gaze locked on to mine. "Trust me."

"Says the prince of lies."

He took the insult in stride. I thought of his tattoo, how actions were more precious to him than words. Trust was something earned, but in order to gain that, I'd need to allow him a place to start. One of us had to take that first step.

I nodded for him to continue and he seemed rooted in place before breaking the spell. Wrath gripped my skirts in his fists and dragged them past my knee and paused with them mid-thigh. Not once did he take his attention from my face, nor did he allow his bare skin to brush across mine. He also made sure that only my left leg was exposed.

"Here." He jerked his chin at my skirts. "Hold them like this."

I took the material from him and watched as he pulled a leather sheath from inside his suit. He removed the slender dagger and held it up for my inspection. Wildflowers were carved into its hilt and the silver blade shined enough to reflect my awe.

"It's gorgeous."

"It will do for now." He placed the dagger back and slipped the leather strap around my thigh, securing the buckle in place. He slipped a finger beneath the strap and glanced up. "Is it too tight?"

"No, it fits perfectly."

"Stand up and walk around just to be certain." He quickly stepped back and averted his attention as I righted my skirts and pushed myself to my feet. I walked around the bedchamber, twisting and turning. "Good?"

"Yes. Thank you. How did you know I was left-handed?"

Wrath glanced down at the weapon now hidden. "You favor the left hand when cutting bread or sipping your wine." Without giving me a chance to respond, he added gruffly, "When you wish to come home, send a missive. I'll return for you."

"I…"

I wasn't sure what to say. If I went back, I didn't know if that would signal my acceptance of our marriage. There was an undeniable attraction between us, but that fire might largely be the result of the magic trying to tempt us together, to literally and figuratively become one. There was no telling if that desire would still burn as brightly if we submitted.

And I had other plans for my life. Like returning to my family. Choosing Wrath would mean the door to my old life would remain closed forever. I might be able to visit my family on occasion, but my world would fracture even more than it already had. I did not believe true love was ever supposed to steal from a person's life, only enhance it.

"I better get settled in."

The demon prince kept his expression perfectly bland, but I saw the flash of *something* he wasn't quick enough to extinguish flare in his gaze. Before I could say good-bye, he vanished in his glittering black light and smoke, leaving me to the fate I'd chosen.

And my newest scheme.

FIFTEEN

I didn't have long to sit and stew over my decision. Shortly after Wrath left, a servant came with a dress box and a note from the master of this house. In less than an hour, I'd be dining with the prince of this court in his private quarters. Apparently Envy did not want an audience for our meeting. Or perhaps he didn't wish to share his latest "curiosity," as he'd once said.

Nerves buzzed like a swarm of bees trapped in my belly. Envy was ruthless, but I was mostly confident he wouldn't harm me now. Not while I was in this realm and doing so would potentially start a war between House Wrath and House Envy. Being a member of House Wrath certainly had some political perks. I was no longer simply a witch without a royal demon court to protect me. Envy would need to think long and hard before he stuck any dagger in my back.

Logically knowing that didn't ease *all* of my worry, though.

It was hard to push aside the night he'd held my parents hostage and then commandeered our house. I still couldn't believe Nonna had banished him back to the underworld using magic I was unaware she possessed. That swirling vortex was one of the strangest things I'd ever seen.

I shoved those memories away and focused on the here and now. I recalled what Wrath had said about victors and victims. Tonight I would be victorious. I was here to get information.

And I would do everything in my power to succeed. If I had to don the attire of my enemy, so be it. It was an extremely small price to pay. I'd wear his silly dress and bat my lashes, all while counting down the moments until I got what I was truly after.

"Let's see what dress you've chosen, Prince of Jealousy."

I opened the box and rolled my eyes. The gown was gorgeous, a hunter green velvet that was dark enough to almost be mistaken for black, with long fitted sleeves, a snug bodice that plunged open almost to my navel, and flowing skirts.

A single emerald the size of a robin's egg was fastened onto a sparkling silver chain. The outrageously opulent necklace was likely a pretty weapon Envy wished for me to use against his brother. I could picture Wrath's expression shuttering when he spied the gift that belonged to House Envy glittering on my chest.

Apparently, pissing contests were not simply an idiotic mortal pastime.

I thought about staying in my current dress but figured Envy might be more amenable to sharing information if he wasn't scowling at the offensive House Wrath attire. And I also did not wish to sink to their level of ridiculous royal posturing.

After I slipped on the gown and rolled up the sleeves to show off my forearms, I dabbed some rouge across my cheekbones and lips. I picked up the necklace. The gemstone was flawless; I would no doubt become the envy of anyone who saw it.

I managed to clasp it around my neck when a servant entered my chamber.

"If you're ready, I'll show you to dinner, Lady Emilia."

I'd been hoping for a few moments alone to practice summoning my magic just in case things went very wrong, but even a few hours wouldn't feel like enough time to overcome years of training I'd missed. I smiled at the servant. "Please, lead the way."

As I moved toward the door, I caught my reflection in an oversized mirror. I looked ready to do battle in the most elegant, vicious way. I truly was turning into a princess of Hell.

Goddess help the demons.

We traveled down the opposite end of the corridor where my suite was located. Unsurprisingly, Envy had situated me in the royal wing. Better to keep one's enemies close, and one's future sister-in-law closer. I wondered if that was one of the reasons for Wrath's foul mood. The brothers clearly enjoyed digging at each other as often as possible. Though they would need to find something else to fight over. Magical bond or not, I belonged only to myself.

A stoic guard inclined his head, then stepped back and opened the door. An expansive room spread out before me, mostly dressed in darkness. It was meant to unnerve.

But there was little for me to fear in the shadows. Soon they would do *my* bidding.

I stepped inside and paused to fully evaluate the room as the door snicked shut behind me. It was not quite a study, nor was it a formal dining room. If we were in the mortal world, it would be similar to a gentleman's club often described in my favorite romance novels.

A circular table with two chairs was placed near a wall of windows, offering a bit of soft light to filter in. Tapers in an impressive silver candelabra were lit on the table, and a few sconces in the farthest corners also added hints of warm light.

Most of the chamber was cast in shadows, including the door where I stood. I glanced up. The tray ceiling was adorned with a fresco: winged beings on clouds, some bright, others stormy.

My gaze traveled around the room and stopped on the shadowy figure of the prince. Envy lounged in an oversized velvet chair near a darkened corner, a glass of amber liquid in one hand. One long leg was kicked up, his ankle resting on a knee. He couldn't look more comfortable or relaxed if he tried. Though his grip indicated he was not as at ease as he'd like me to believe.

He took a long sip of his drink, his gaze hidden from view, but I felt it travel over me all the same. "You certainly know how to stir up trouble, pet."

I remained in the shadows. "I may have claws, your highness, but I assure you I am no one's pet. Least of all yours."

Envy leaned forward into a pool of candlelight and somehow, even while seated, managed to look down his regal nose at me. His beautifully harsh features were set into an unimpressed frown. "Thank the devils for that. I don't share what's mine."

"Keeping lovers through force is nothing to boast about."

"Choice is appealing, force is not. Might does not always make right. Unless my bedmate asks nicely." His gaze raked over me, and I wondered how well he could see into the shadows. "I take it you've accepted my invitation to play with envious emotions."

"Don't you enjoy inspiring envy?"

"Coming here to make my brother jealous does nothing for *me*." He set his glass on a low table and flicked at imaginary lint on his suit. I caught sight of his emerald-tipped blade peeking out from his jacket and resisted the sudden urge to use it on him. He plucked up his drink again and finished it off. "Using someone is rude by any standards."

If that was what he believed, all the better. I stepped into the light, watching as his focus dropped to the pale lavender tattoo on my forearm. He'd been amused by it the first time he saw it. Now I knew why.

"The first night I met you, you knew about my betrothal to Wrath. You mentioned something about tangled webs. Being less cryptic would have been nice. Especially if you were looking to form an alliance with me."

"In case you haven't already noticed, I'm not *nice*. Nor do I pretend to be. And, even if I were afflicted with a conscience, I would have hated to ruin all the fun." Envy's lips pulled into a cruel slash when he noticed my necklace. "It was much more interesting to sit back and see how it played out. Some of us even wagered on the outcome. I cannot tell you how much I made off of Greed. But he is now in my debt, and I'm sure you can imagine how little he enjoys that."

I moved with purpose across the room. A sideboard with a decanter and glass sat waiting, and, without an invitation, I poured myself two knuckles of amber liquid and sat in the velvet chair beside Envy's. His eyes narrowed, but he didn't call out my rudeness. Or lack of propriety or respect for his elevated rank.

"You wanted me to join your House, even knowing about the betrothal bond I shared with your brother." I took a small sip, anticipating the burn. "It must get lonely. Playing all those games by yourself."

"Whatever you're attempting, I suggest stopping while I'm still feeling hospitable."

His tone was frosty, but he wasn't quick enough to hide the flash of hurt in his eyes. My first shot had struck a bull's-eye. I shoved any feelings of guilt aside. His temporary moment of pain was nothing compared to the finality of my twin's brutal murder.

"Imagine that." I grinned over my drink. "And here I was under the impression I hadn't yet been introduced to your manners. First, threats to me issued by your vampire lapdog, then holding my family hostage. We also can't forget that nasty little incident in the tunnels with your invisible demon army and, of course, gutting Wrath."

"For someone who is *here* instead of with her betrothed, you certainly seem angry about that. I would have thought you'd consider it a favor."

"Turning your blade on yourself would have been the ultimate favor."

Much like when Wrath was displeased, the temperature around us seemed to plummet. I'd felt the frozen horror of Envy's power and influence before, the ice-cold jealousy that eroded all sense of morality. The first licks of his power slid down my spine, but I'd been waiting.

I lifted my hand, as if brushing away a strand of hair, and subtly ran my fingers over Wrath's Mark. It broke this prince's influence before it took hold, just as I'd hoped it would.

Envy jerked back, his attention snapping to mine. A slow smile spread across his face, dousing the flicker of rage. "Aren't you full of intrigue tonight. And here I worried dinner would be boring."

I kept my expression bland, but my heart raced. If he tried to use his power again, I wasn't sure my little trick would work a second time. He seemed to sense that and was contemplating his next move. His lazy assessment reminded me of a cat that was deciding whether the bird fluttering close by was worth the effort of leaving his sunshine patch for.

Envy's gaze flicked to his House dagger.

He removed it from its sheath and ran a finger along the blade. There was little doubt in my mind he was dreaming of creative ways to use it on me. My hand inched toward my own weapon, but I did not lift my skirts to reveal it. Whatever happened next, I'd be ready.

We sat there for an uncomfortably long beat, the only sound the ticking of a clock somewhere in the room. Envy stroked the metal, and I swore the blade almost purred. Just when I was certain he was about to pounce, a knock sounded at the door, breaking the murderous tension between us. Envy replaced his dagger. At his command, servants filed in carrying emerald trays and platters of food to the circular table near the far end of the room.

The prince stood in one graceful movement and offered his arm. "Let us break bread tonight, not bones, Shadow Witch."

I pushed myself to my feet, ignoring his outstretched arm. We were not friends and I did not think he'd like for me to pretend in this instance. Everything about this evening felt like a test. Which suited me fine. I had a test of my own.

I made my way to the table and sat as a chair was pulled out for me. Envy did not appear insulted, only more amused as he took the seat across from me. I doubted many of his subjects ever attempted to irk him. Like Wrath, my refusal to simper before his almighty power might intrigue him enough to entertain me. And my questions. Until he tired of them. I must tread carefully along the line of challenging him without going too far over it.

"*In vino veritas.*" He waved the servants away and filled our goblets on his own. "In wine there's truth. Mortals occasionally impress. Though I suppose they're especially susceptible when it comes to their vices. Give man wine and he'll wax poetic of its flavors. He'll probably even liken it to a woman he bedded." His gaze slid to mine. "Or wishes to."

I held my tongue. I did not believe he wanted to bed me. And if he did, it wouldn't be for any other reason than to use it against his brother. "Why do you hate mortals?"

"Assumptions are the death of truth." He took another sip of his wine. "I do not suggest wandering down this current path." He motioned to my goblet. "Have you ever tried using your magic on food or drink?"

"No. Why in the seven hells would I do such a thing?"

"Eight. And I ask because you can spell the wine to give you truth. Just as you would with a truth spell. Whoever drinks it will be under its thrall."

"I'm supposed to believe you're telling me this out of the goodness of your heart?"

"Don't be daft. I can assure you, the closest I get to moral fiber is from ingesting whatever fiber is found in demonberry wine. You want truth and so do I. Why not ensure we both get what we desire? No games."

I narrowed my eyes. "You must want something terribly bad if you're willing to sacrifice that information to your enemy."

"We can be friends tonight." He grimaced at the word *friend* as if pained by the idea. I arched a brow and he feigned ignorance. "Or lovers."

I waited to sense it, the magic of this world seducing me with thoughts of beds and bodies and passion. Just as it had done nearly every time the idea of spending the night with Wrath entered my mind. Envy was handsome, his body lithe but hard with muscle. I

imagined he'd be attentive to any lover, even one he didn't particularly find interest in. If only to drive them wild with envy when
he moved on to other partners.

There were no romantic feelings aside from the overwhelming desire I felt to kick him.

"If I said yes, you would truly take me to bed."

"There are always sacrifices in war, love. I would do whatever
I must. Though it would hardly be a sacrifice. Pillow talk is quite
enjoyable. There are many secrets one reveals after such intimate
affairs." Envy gazed at his wine, his expression far away. "Now be
a dear and spell our wine."

I hesitated. I wanted honest answers to my questions, but I
was not sure I was ready to give him the same in return. He could
ask anything and I'd be forced to lose *my* mask.

Some risks were worth taking. And others were simply
foolish.

Envy's head tipped to the side as he looked at me. "Is holding
on to your truth worth more than learning mine? Perhaps it's fear
that's holding you back. Maybe I ought to seduce you instead."

"You can't goad me into doing your bidding, your highness.
It's prudent to consider all angles before subjecting myself to your
interrogation."

"I could force you to tell me what I want, you know." His voice
was light, casual. Threats rolled off his tongue with the same ease
one remarked on the weather. I ran my fingers across the Mark
again, drawing his attention to my neck. "Through violence,
my lady. Alexei isn't the only fanged member of my house. Lose
enough blood and I find that the effects are rather similar to truth
wine. With less detriment to me, naturally."

Of course. He'd resort to gifting me to his vampires. I thought again about my twin. Vittoria must have made some difficult bargains, too.

I pushed back from the table and someone rushed over to pull out my chair. It would take some time getting used to being doted on as if I were a pampered royal.

I walked to Envy's side and took his goblet. I whispered a truth spell over it, then repeated the process with the spare bottles, and my glass.

Envy's grin was positively disturbing as I retook my seat. He lifted his glass. "Cheers to a night of truth amongst enemies. May our hearts only bleed at the loss of our dignity and not because of a dagger in our backs."

He downed his entire glass in one go. I raised my brows. "Is that necessary?"

"Not at all." He refilled his goblet and took another large gulp. "But it doesn't hurt."

I took a tentative sip of the wine. It didn't taste different. If I hadn't uttered the spell over it myself, I'd never know there was anything suspect about it. I frowned into my drink.

Envy's sudden bark of laughter broke me from my thoughts. "The witches who raised you kept many secrets, I see. It's utterly delightful."

"What is?"

"Watching as your perfect world crumbles."

"You're an awful person."

"My dear, you keep forgetting. I've never been afflicted with humanity." He lifted a shoulder and drank more. "Besides, I meant it in a good way. A phoenix rises from the ashes for a reason. Your world must be destroyed for you to rise anew. And rise you shall. Just as they always feared you would."

"How long before the truth spell works?"

He finished off his glass and promptly poured another. "It's already active."

"Do you like me?"

"I find you tolerable. Should you meet a violent ending, I wouldn't shed a tear. Nor would I rejoice. I would go on as if you never were."

I snorted in the most unladylike manner and took another sip of my drink. "The night my nonna attacked you . . . you seemed to know her. How?"

"Curses are curious things." He downed another glass and splashed more into his empty cup. "Sometimes they're like trees. They stay rooted to the spot they're planted. Other times they're like wildflowers. Their seeds float along with the bees and fly with the birds. They tangle and grow and thrive outside of that original patch they were sprinkled upon. Kind of like keys. Not all keys fit in locks. Some keys are much more cunning."

I waited for his nonsensical ramblings to revert to a coherent answer. He simply gazed back at me. "That's not even remotely close to what I asked. Are you drunk?"

"Quite." His smile was the first real one he'd given me. A dimple appeared in his right cheek. It softened the harshness he wore like armor. "But what I said is true. There are things I cannot say, no matter the spell used on our wine, because there are greater powers involved still. I know your grandmother. Though I know many other interesting secrets."

I wanted to know how he knew Nonna, but there was little use trying to pry information he clearly either couldn't or wouldn't give. "Tell me about the curse, then."

"It's a tale so old its origins are known only to a few. And even their memories have become copperlike with the age and patina that's formed over them, dulling their shine until the shadow of what was is all that remains."

"What are you talking about?"

"The story of curses and stolen memories. And the unraveling of many lies." He abruptly leaned back, nearly tipping his chair over. "My brother will never force you to marry him. It goes against all that he stands for."

"I didn't ask about your brother."

"No, but I imagine you're curious. Has he indicated he wishes for you to complete the bond?"

I didn't want to answer, but the truth spell enticed the words from my lips. "He's told me about it, but he hasn't indicated which he prefers."

"I won't ask if you've considered it. Especially since we know the manner in which it's accepted. At least in part." I tried to not show relief, but Envy must have seen the slight flash of it in my face. His smile was cruel delight. "He may not force you to wed, but he will not meekly wait in the background. That is not his way, either. He will make his presence and intentions known to each royal House. As he did today."

I took another sip of the truth wine. "Why do you do that?"

"Pardon?"

"You always sow seeds of distrust between your brother and me." I did not need to drink my wine to ask my next question. "Are you that envious of him? Or do you simply covet anything that isn't yours?"

"I am not always plagued by envious thoughts." His green eyes flared with an emotion that wasn't based in sneering or his namesake. "My brother's temper caused something important to be taken from me. I hope to one day return the favor. It is not envy I am motivated by. It is retribution. Something I imagine you and I share in common, though I doubt you'll admit it, even with the truth wine."

He hadn't phrased it as a question, so the spell didn't compel me to answer. "I would do anything to have my sister back. You ought to forgive whatever sins have come between you and Wrath. Happiness should be the only thing that matters."

"I don't give a devil's damn about his happiness." He glared at his wine, but left it untouched. "It's obvious you do care, though. More than you're probably comfortable sharing. Are you in love with him?"

I clamped my teeth together, and gripped my glass. It was no use. The words bubbled up. I clutched on to the phrasing Envy used and allowed the truth to pour from my lips. "No. I am not in love with him. But I do not deny there's an attraction. He brought me to this realm, sold my soul to his brother, and lied about being my potential husband."

"The lady doth protest too much."

"Shakespeare." I all but rolled my eyes. "How pompous and unsurprising that you'd quote him. Should I be envious over your education now?"

He watched me over the rim of his glass, his gaze sharp. "Odd, isn't it, that a peasant from Sicily would have such refined taste in books. Or reading anything at all, for that matter."

I prickled at his insinuation. "We may not have had money and servants, your highness, but we know how to read and write."

"I assume you'll tell me your proficiency is because of the spells your grandmother taught you. Or the recipes from your little food shack, or some other such drivel."

"What are you getting at?"

"It's simply curious, is all. And you do know how much I enjoy curiosities."

I grinned. It was the perfect segue into my next line of questioning. "Why are you so interested in collecting objects?"

"I'm mostly interested in divine objects. Well, that's not entirely true." He laughed, as if he couldn't believe the truth was still pouring so freely from him. "I'm only interested in one fully divine object now: the Triple Moon Mirror."

"What is that?"

He snapped his fingers and a servant appeared. He whispered something too low for me to hear and the attendant dashed away. A moment later, he returned, holding an etched glass case. It was plain, unassuming. I immediately leaned across the table, hoping for a better view.

"It's a mirror of the gods. *Goddesses*, I should say." He ran his pointer finger along the glass case, then rubbed it against his thumb as if checking for dust. "It is said it has been embedded with the Maiden, Mother, and Crone's magic, and can show you the past, present, and future upon request. It used to reside in this case, or so I've been told."

Past, present, future, find. Chills raced along my spine. It was almost exactly what the enchanted skull had said, even down to the Maiden, Mother, Crone aspect.

Envy flipped the lid back, showing a deep lavender crushed velvet bed, indented where a hand mirror once sat. I did my best to not react. But my heart was thrashing wildly in my chest. If there was a divine object that could show me the past, it would solve my sister's murder.

Excitement coursed through me. This *had* to be what the skull wanted me to find. I was certain of it. If I had the mirror, I no longer needed to worry about marrying Pride or Wrath and choosing my place in their House of Sins.

"It sounds like a children's legend."

"All legends contain fragments of truth." For a second, his gaze was far off again. "Anyway, it is said one needs the Crone's book of spells, the Temptation Key, and the mirror in order to activate the goddess magic."

"Let me guess," I dropped my voice into a conspiratorial whisper, "you've collected all but the mirror."

"My dear, I believe it's time you viewed my curiosities yourself." Envy stood. "Shall we?"

SIXTEEN

Envy pushed open the ornate doors with exaggerated show-manship and stepped back, suddenly the gentleman, and allowed me to cross the threshold into his curiosities chamber first.

Dubious about his true intentions, I hesitated for a moment. I doubted he'd led me into a vampire nest, though anything was possible when it came to him.

Remembering the dagger at my thigh, I walked in and halted at the sight.

It wasn't vampires waiting, but tall, shadowy giants, standing in place. The chamber was eerily close to a mental image I'd had when I'd first met Envy in the mortal world. Back then, I'd pictured humans posed and frozen on a macabre checkerboard. The floor we stood on now was not part of a game; it was simply made of black and white marble tiles. And the frozen beings were works of art, not mortals trapped by a sadistic prince of Hell.

Sculptures stood in silent welcome, some cast in bronze, others carved from marble. They were haunting, beautiful, so lifelike I had to reach out to be sure they were not made of flesh. I'd never been to a museum, but I'd seen illustrations in books and could not believe the size of his curiosities collection.

"Are you stunned into silence, or is the wine sloshing around your insides?"

I blinked, realizing I still stood rooted in place. "I had a strange sense of déjà vu."

Envy's attention flicked over my features, but he only lifted a shoulder and dropped it. "Many mortal museums and collections are fashioned after it. It's unsurprising that it's familiar."

"I've never been to a museum."

Which was enough of the truth to satisfy the truth spell. But I couldn't shake the uncomfortable feeling of how I'd seen the flash of it all those months ago. I'd never been to this realm, or this royal demon House. Perhaps I had a latent seer talent that was starting to emerge.

According to Nonna, it wasn't uncommon for magic to continue developing throughout a witch's lifetime. It would also make sense that my newfound use of Source unlocked other magic. Latent talent or not, it wasn't important. I shook myself back into the now.

The room was cavernous, enough for our steps to echo as we quietly moved to the foot of the first sculpture. A man wearing a winged helmet, bandolier, and not a stitch of clothing stood with one hand extended, holding the severed head of Medusa. A sword was gripped tightly in his other hand. Something about it made me sad.

Envy strolled over to the scene, his expression softening. "Perseus and Medusa. There are similar pieces in the mortal land, but nothing as exquisite as this. The sculptor captured his downcast eyes, his refusal to be turned to stone and cursed."

"It's stunning craftsmanship, but horrid."

"Not all stories end happily, Emilia."

I knew that. My life had taken unexpected twists, most of which weren't ideal or for the better. We all had bones, if not full skeletons of heartache, in our closets. It hit me suddenly. I subtly looked at the demon prince. Envy was deeply hurt. I wondered who or what had broken his heart so thoroughly. He caught my eye and gave me a hard look. Questions about his heartbreak would not be welcome. For some reason, I allowed the opportunity to interrogate him while he was compelled to answer truthfully slide. Not all secrets were meant to be shared.

We moved in silence to the next statue. This one was magnificent. My favorite by far. An angel—with a powerful body sculpted from war—arched back, his wings extended, arms tossed behind his head, as if he'd been shoved from a great height and was cursing the one who'd taken him down. The feathers were so detailed, I couldn't stop myself from reaching over and stroking one finger along them.

"The Fallen." Envy's tone was quiet, reverent. "Another fine piece."

I studied the great warrior angel. His body was similar to Wrath's. I wouldn't be surprised if the artist had been inspired by him. "Is it meant to symbolize Wrath or Lucifer?"

"It's my interpretation of my cursed brother." Envy's lips twisted into a grin. "Right before the devil lost his precious wings. And we all followed suit shortly after."

"Why would you have such a moment memorialized?"

"To always remember." His voice was suddenly as hard as the marble statue. He shook his head, his expression once again indifferent, as if he'd replaced a mask that had accidentally slipped. "Come. There's another room filled with objects you might find more interesting."

We were halfway through the next chamber, decorated with

paintings and sketches and mirrors in various ornate frames, when I noticed the bookstands.

I drifted over, drawn to one in particular. A strange, familiar humming started in my center. I knew that feeling. Recognized it. Though it was not quite as I recalled. There were no whispers or fevered voices rising and falling in a cacophony of sounds. Only that subtle hum. I'd experienced it in the monastery the night I'd found my twin. And then again when I'd confronted Antonio. Back then I hadn't known what it was or what it wanted.

I paused at the open grimoire. A glass case enclosed it, but I knew, without seeing its cover, what it was. It was the first book of spells. La Prima's personal spell book.

"How did you get this?" My voice was too loud in the smaller room. "It was with me the night I—"

"The night you nearly killed the human sycophant?"

I spun on my heel, glaring. "It disappeared that night. I thought...an Umbra demon." I inhaled deeply. "You sent one to spy on me, didn't you?"

"*Spy* is a nasty word. Not to mention, it was watching the monastery. You happened along. Wrong place, wrong time." He stuck his hands in his pockets and strolled over to the next stand. Another open book. "What you call the first book of spells is not a complete manuscript. It's one third of a grander, more elaborate text." He nodded at the book. "The Mother and the Crone are in my possession; the Maiden has gone missing. Goddesses are tricky beings with even trickier magic. And to cross one..." He whistled. "That's inadvisable."

"The first book of spells belonged to the First Witch, not the goddesses."

"My dear, I don't know what the witches who raised you claimed, or why, but these books were written by the goddesses.

Your so-called First Witch stole the book of the dead, the Crone's book of underworld magic. I can tell you the Crone was not amused."

He spoke as if he knew the goddesses. "Where is the Crone now? Perhaps I should speak with her myself."

"By all means, if you find her, please send my regards."

I blew out a frustrated breath. Something wasn't quite right with this story. Envy not only had a book of spells that could enchant skulls, he'd practically used the phrase one had uttered verbatim. He *had* to be the mysterious sender, but for whatever reason, he wasn't admitting to it.

"Are there spells on necromancy?"

"The Crone is the goddess of the underworld. Her spells reflect the moon, the night, and the dead. Amongst other things, like darker, more violent emotions." He watched me closely. "Blood-wood Forest is a spectacular sight. It lies between my land and Greed's. No demon house may claim it; therefore, you don't need an invitation to travel there. The trick, however, is gaining passage through the territories that border it."

I pulled my attention away from the book of spells. "Why are you telling me about it?"

"Why shouldn't I?"

If we were being friendly, I might as well push that to my advantage. "You mentioned something called the Temptation Key earlier. Is it part of your collection?"

"I'm afraid not. Though not from a lack of trying to acquire it on my part." He started walking away but called over his shoulder, "Before you retire for the evening, you may want to read the plaque of this painting. I find it to be quite informative."

"Where are you going?"

Envy did not answer.

Apparently our time together was over for tonight. I stared in the direction of the demon prince long after he'd left the room, mulling over all I'd learned. Envy was after the Triple Moon Mirror and the Temptation Key. Two objects I was now very interested in obtaining myself.

When I was sure he wasn't returning, I strode over to the painting he'd pointed out. It was an unusual tree. Large with gnarled wood and ebony-and-silver-veined leaves. There was something about the painting that reminded me of the artist who'd captured the seasonal garden in my bedroom suite in House Wrath.

The shadows and care with which the artist had shown each piece of bark or falling leaf was remarkable; it looked as if I could reach into the painting and pull a leaf from the tree.

I ran my fingers over the silver plaque and read the inscription.

CURSE TREE FABLE
Deep in the heart of the Bloodwood Forest lies a tree planted by the Crone herself. It is said, among other favors, the tree will consider hexing a sworn enemy if the desire to curse them is true. To request the Crone's Curse: Carve their true name in the tree, write your wish on a leaf plucked from its branches, then offer the tree a drop of blood. Take the leaf home and place it beneath your pillow. If it is gone when you arise, the Crone accepted your offer and has granted your wish. She is the mother of the underworld— beware of her blessing.

I reread the fable, unsure why Envy had pointed it out among the fifty or so other paintings lining the walls in this room. Nothing a prince of Hell did was by accident. I had a feeling I'd been unwittingly brought into one of his schemes, but I'd twist his deceit to my favor.

I tucked the knowledge away and slowly made my way through the rest of the gallery, pausing at a map of the Seven Circles. Each demon House sat upon a mountain peak, towering above their territory. I spied the gates of Hell, the Sin Corridor.

A place between House Lust and House Gluttony was marked VIOLENT WINDS. I wondered if that was the howling sound we'd heard in the Sin Corridor.

I continued to study the sketch, committing as much of it as I could to memory. To the southeast, Bloodwood Forest sat between House Greed and House Envy. The Black River carved through the western Houses of Sin, dividing Wrath's castle from both Greed and Pride's territories. It forked off into a smaller tributary that ran behind Greed's castle, winded through the lower portion of House Pride, and up along Envy's northern border. I followed the main portion of the river until it ended in the Lake of Fire. Across from the largest section of the lake was the devil's castle; House Pride sat slightly northwest of House Envy.

Once I felt confident in my ability to recall most landmarks and the general lay of this realm, I left the map and wandered back through the gallery. A liveried member of Envy's staff was waiting for me in the room with the sculptures.

"His highness sends his apologies, but he's left the premises. He said you are welcome to stay as long as you desire, but he will be gone for quite some time." The servant hesitated, cleared his throat, as if uncomfortable with delivering the rest of the message.

"Was there more?"

"His highness also said if you wish to make Prince Wrath jealous, you may sleep in his highness's bed tonight. He suggests doing so in the nude. And ... I quote, 'think filthy thoughts regarding the most well-endowed prince in this realm,' while tending to yourself. There is a life-sized painting of Prince Envy on the ceiling, should you require a stimulating visual."

I mentally counted until the urge to hunt Envy passed. "I'd like to send word to House Wrath. Tell them I'll be home tomorrow at first light."

"Straight away, my lady." He bowed. "Would you like an escort back to your chambers?"

"I believe I can find my way. I'd like to admire the statues once more."

"Very well. I'll send the missive to House Wrath now."

I waited until he left before turning back to the gallery room. Annoyance at Envy quickly gave way to elation. I *knew* I'd have use of the mending kit.

And it had absolutely nothing to do with sewing tears in pretty dresses.

My heart thudded in time with the horses' hoofs as the carriage rolled away from House Envy. Wrath didn't show up to escort me home himself after all; he sent an emissary and *a* royal carriage. The emissary was only too pleased to point out it wasn't the prince's *personal* carriage or steeds. Just whatever he'd had in the stables.

As if that information was of great importance. I wasn't sure how I felt about her sneer or the fact that the prince sent someone in his stead. The emissary sat primly on her side of the coach, pointedly avoiding eye contact and therefore any conversation with me.

I was at a loss regarding her obvious contempt.

I studied the demon from under lowered lashes, feigning sleep. Her deep red hair was coiled into intricate knots around the crown of her head, while the lower portion was a set of long, perfectly styled curls. A muscle in her jaw feathered, as if she was entirely aware of my scrutiny and was biting back a string of admonishments. Maybe her simmering anger was simply a marker of the House of Sin she belonged to and I was reading too much into it.

I shifted my attention to the window. For some reason, she'd pulled the drapery shut before we set off. I moved it back and she glared. "Keep it closed."

I drew in a deep breath through my nose, centering my growing annoyance at her curt attitude. Arguing with her would serve no purpose. And I did not need one more enemy to watch out for. "What's your name?"

"You need only address me by my title."

Though I noticed she refused to call me by the title Wrath had demanded his court use. It didn't bother me one bit. I was no noblewoman. "Very well, Emissary. Where is Wrath?"

Her cool gaze slid to mine. "His highness is occupied."

There was no mistaking the edge in her tone, or the warning that more questions would not be tolerated. I laid my head against the plush carriage wall. We steadily moved down a mountain and I tensed to keep myself pressed against my seat and not slide forward. In what felt like eons, we finally began climbing again before eventually clamoring to a stop. Heedless of her ire, I drew the drapery aside and swallowed a gasp.

I'd never seen the front exterior of House Wrath. When I'd first arrived, it had been delirious in Wrath's arms, and we'd entered through a mountain. His castle was massive, with a gate house, turrets, towers, and an enormous wall that spanned the entire perimeter. Pale stone with black tiled roofing. It was a magnificent study in contrasts.

Vines, frozen solid, clung to the walls.

We passed through the gates and rolled to a stop in a half-circular drive. The emissary waited for a footman to open the coach and then accepted his assistance out. She left without a backward glance, her duty to collect the wayward fiancée done.

I stared after her, wondering why she'd been so cold and if I'd done something to offend her. I knew I hadn't. Aside from my surprise at seeing her instead of Wrath, I'd been friendly.

An uncomfortable suspicion slithered in about her relationship with Wrath, but I shoved it aside. I refused to let it matter.

The footman handed me down and I took my time walking up the stone stairs to the front door. To my right, tucked near the wall, was a garden hidden within a hedge. I made a mental note to visit it once the weather warmed.

If the weather ever warmed. As if on cue, snow began lightly falling, dusting the castle in a fine layer of shimmering flakes.

I hurried inside and brushed off my traveling cloak. Aside from the footman, who was seeing to my trunk, there were no servants waiting to tend to me, for which I was relieved.

I made it back to my bedroom suite without running into anyone. No servants cleaning the castle or its many rooms. No Fauna or Anir or Wrath. I was immensely grateful I didn't see any of the other noble occupants, like the now tongueless Lord Makaden or overly talkative Lady Arcaline.

As the afternoon wore on, I grew restless, though. I was not used to having so much idle time. Back home I was always in the trattoria, or working on my craft in our home kitchen, or reading when I wasn't falling into bed, bone tired from a hard day's work. I was also rarely alone—my family was always there, laughing and talking and warm. Other nights I'd comb the beach with my sister and Claudia, sharing secrets and our hopes and dreams.

Until my twin was murdered. Then my world irrevocably changed.

Unable to bear the morbid twist of my thoughts, I marched down to Wrath's suite and knocked. No answer. I considered testing to see if the door was locked but refrained. When I'd intruded on him after his violent outburst at dinner I'd had a valid excuse.

I trudged back to my room and decided to work on finding Source again. I closed my eyes, concentrating on the inner well of magic. A few seconds later, I tunneled down into my center, then crashed. It felt as if I'd collided with a brick wall.

I tried to muster up the energy to locate it again, but I was more exhausted than I'd thought. I'd spent the better part of last night awake in bed, fearful of Envy returning in a rage. And the previous night I'd barely slept because of Wrath's confession. I imagined to harness Source I needed to be well rested. And I was anything but.

I pulled out the journal on House Pride I'd *borrowed* from Wrath's library and slowly flipped through each page in hopes of something being written in a language I knew.

My efforts were wasted. There weren't even drawings or

illustrations for me to decipher. It was just page after page of small, handwritten notes in what might be demon script. My attention kept straying to my trunk, to the object I'd smuggled from Envy inside it.

I didn't want to remove it from its hiding place just yet. I had a feeling someone might come looking for it soon enough. I couldn't believe it had been so easy to snatch. Too easy, really. Part of me expected alarms to sound and Umbra demons and vampires to swarm in the moment I'd lifted the spell book from its case. Nothing happened. I'd simply walked to my room, sewn it into the inside of my trunk, and waited for a reckoning that never came.

I turned back to the here and now, flipping through the next few pages. I refocused on Pride's House journal, the squiggly lines blurring together.

I woke up several hours later, my face pressed against the open journal.

It was not my kind of book, obviously. A romance novel would have kept me up into the wee hours of the morning, never quite turning the pages fast enough while also trying desperately to savor each tension-filled interaction between the hero and heroine.

I adored how they more often than not despised each other, and how that spark of disdain flamed into something else entirely.

Real life certainly wasn't anything close to a romance novel, but there was still a small part of the old me left that hoped for a happy ending. There was no denying a spark existed between me and Wrath—along with plenty of disdain—but the likelihood of it turning into love was the true fantasy.

I combed my hair and went to check Wrath's rooms again. The demon was still out. Or he wasn't bothering to answer his door. I stood there, hand falling to my side. It was possible he was upset by my dismissal of him at Envy's. But something about that didn't feel right.

He'd been by my side for months in the human world, and then for nearly two weeks here. If he did have a lover, he might have stolen away to visit her. I doubted he would have expected me to return so quickly. I ought to rejoice in the solitude. I had no one looking over my shoulder, no lust-fueled urges toward completing a marriage bond. No distractions. And yet... and yet I didn't want to think about why I was gripped with unease.

I called for dinner and ate in my rooms, thinking about Envy's conversation and all I'd learned. Specifically, the truth spell used on wine and what it might mean for the rest of my mission. The magic worked on a prince of Hell. And while *I* hadn't noticed anything different about our beverage, it didn't mean a prince wouldn't sense the *otherness*. Envy had known what was coming, so I couldn't use him as any means of judging.

What I wanted was to test a theory. And I needed Wrath. If I could spell his wine without him knowing, I might find it to be a useful skill to employ at the Feast of the Wolf. All of the princes would be in attendance. I could whisper the spell over our toast and find out who was responsible for Vittoria's death without any-one being the wiser.

If Wrath couldn't sense the spell. That plan only worked if the test was successful.

I told myself that was the main reason I'd been pacing the cor-ridor outside his rooms the next morning. Listening for any sign of his return. Surely it had nothing to do with missing him. Or growing suspicions of where he'd gone, and who he might be with. Which was nonsense that belonged to House Envy. Maybe those were simply residual jealous emotions left over from my visit to that House of Sin. If such things even occurred.

Two more days passed and still no word from the prince of the House. I had tried a few more times to summon the source of my magic but was met with that same resistance. There was no information on it in the grimoire, so I had to wait it out. Eventually I'd master dipping into that well. I spent my time in the library, searching for new fables. I was interested in learning more about the Curse Tree, especially the line that claimed it granted *more* than wishes.

I also searched for any books on the Temptation Key or the Triple Moon Mirror. Thus far my efforts were *all* in vain. Finally, when I thought I'd go mad, a knock sounded at my door.

"Hello, Lady Em." Anir grinned. "I'm here to bring you on an adventure."

"Lady Em?" I crinkled my nose. "No one has ever called me Em. I'm not sure I like it."

"That's because you never had a clandestine meeting. Come on. Put on a tunic and trousers, then meet me out here. We're late."

"Where are we going?"

He flashed another smile. This one made my stomach twist up with nerves. "You'll see."

Deciding whatever he'd planned had to be better than sitting alone in my room, or roaming the library and not finding anything useful, I quickly rushed into my bedchamber and changed into the clothes he'd suggested.

Once I tugged on some flat shoes, I followed him into the corridor. We went up one flight of stairs and stopped near the end of a long hallway.

"May I present..." Anir shoved the door open. "The weapons room."

"Goddesses above." I sucked in a sharp breath, though I shouldn't have been surprised at the grandeur, given Wrath's role as general of war. Here was the pearl of House Wrath. "It's impressive."

"I hear that a lot," Anir teased. "Go in."

I stepped over the threshold. My focus darted around the cavernous room that seemed to go on and on. Columns broke the space into smaller, interconnected chambers. If Envy's gallery was the most telling part of his personality, here was Wrath's soul laid bare.

Beautiful. Elegant. Deadly. Honed to brutal perfection and unapologetic about glorying in violence. I stood there, cataloging everything.

The glass ceiling allowed light to filter in and illuminate what would otherwise be a darkened space. The walls and floor were black marble with gold veining. In the main room we'd entered, there was an occult design—featuring the phases of the moon on one side, a smattering of stars on the other, and a serpent swallowing its tail in a circular shape—inlaid in gold on the floor. From what I could see, each corner of that section of the floor featured one of the four elements. Part of the design was covered by a large mat placed directly in the center.

Gold serpents coiled around the ebony marble columns, making them the most fantastical and gorgeous columns I'd ever seen.

Swords, daggers, shields, bows and arrows, and an assortment of knives gleamed in black and gold from their meticulously spaced positions on the walls.

I spun in place, taking in the splendor of it all. In the very back of the room there was a mosaic of a serpent. Unlike the ouroboros inlaid on the floor, this snake's body coiled into an intricate knot. It reminded me of something, but I couldn't place it.

Against the far wall was a bale of hay with a giant target painted on its center. A small table lay to the left with daggers lined up in a perfect row. I stared at them, my fingers itching to grip their hilts and toss them through the air.

"Our first lesson will be on your stance." Anir moved to the center of the weapons room and pointed to the space on the mat in front of him. I stopped gawking and stood where he'd indicated. "Your feet should always be planted firmly on the ground, giving you steady leverage to lunge, strike, or dodge swiftly in any direction without losing balance."

I shifted so I mirrored his position. His feet were slightly wider than his hips, with one a step forward and the other planted back. There was something almost familiar about the pose, but I'd never fought or had reason to have lessons such as this.

"You'll want your weight distributed evenly. Make sure your knees follow the direction your feet are pointed."

I wobbled a little, then adjusted myself. I'd barely glanced up when Anir rushed forward, forearm thrust out like a battering ram, and made contact with my solar plexus, sending me flying backward. My arms windmilled before I landed ungracefully on my rear.

I glared up at my teacher. "You, *signore*, are terrible."

"I am. And you, *signorina*, just learned your first lesson," he lobbed back at me. He held out a hand and helped me to my feet. "Never take your attention off your opponent."

"I thought this lesson was on stance."

"It is." He winked. "Looking down doesn't do you any favors

with balance. If you have to glance down, use your eyes, not your entire upper body. Self-awareness is key."

We repeated the routine with varying degrees of my being knocked on my bottom. Even with the padded mat on the floor, I'd be sore in the morning. With each strike, I grew a little more secure in my stance, wobbled less. Sweat beaded my brow as we sparred again and again.

It felt good, working my body, emptying my mind.

Sometime later, Anir called for a break and blotted at the perspiration on his neck and face with a length of linen. I was still ready to go but stepped back, bouncing on the balls of my feet. I felt alive, my muscles shaking but hungry for more use.

He bent at the waist. "Take five."

I followed him to a side table set up with a pitcher of water and glasses.

"Where is Wrath?" I don't know why I blurted it out, but it seemed odd that the demon of war was nowhere to be found while we were in his glorious weapons chamber.

Anir glanced sideways at me as he poured himself a glass and downed it by half. "I didn't think you'd mind his absence."

"I don't. I'm just curious." When he didn't respond, I found my ridiculous mouth filling the silence. "He seemed uneasy about my choosing to visit House Envy. I would have thought he'd wish to see me when I returned."

"Do you ask after me when I'm away?"

"No."

"Ouch."

Blood and bones. I immediately kicked myself as Anir's grin widened. I poured myself some water and took a sip. "I just meant..."

"No offense taken." His eyes glinted with amusement. "Lie to yourself all you want, but you'll have to do better around me."

"Fine. The truth is the emissary got under my skin."

"Lady Sundra?" Anir snorted. "I imagine so. Her father's a duke, and she's never let anyone forget that elevated rank. She always believed she'd make an advantageous marriage match with a prince."

"Ah. That's why she became emissary. It put her in close proximity to all of the royals."

"Look at you, Lady Em. You're thinking like a cunning noble now. Most of the princes have no designs of being caught in a marriage snare, though. No matter how many schemes noble families like hers attempt, the princes are content as they are. Her natural state runs angry; it's nothing personal against you."

"So, the higher the rank, the more the demons exhibit the sin they've aligned with."

"From what I've gathered in my time here, yeah. Though no one can ever gain enough power to overthrow a prince. They are something else entirely. It's like the difference between a lion and tiger. Both are large, predatory cats, but they are not the same."

"And the lesser demons? They're different from the nobles."

"Indeed. And it's why they often choose to live on the outskirts of their circles."

"If Lady Sundra is best aligned with House Wrath, how would she marry a prince who represented a different sin?"

"It would be rare, but not unheard of for her to shift sin alignment."

I propped myself against the table's edge and set my glass down. "You knew Wrath had initiated his acceptance of the marriage bond the night the Viperidae attacked me."

"All hail the queen of changing topics." He offered a dramatic bow. "Is there a question in there, or are you looking for confirmation?"

"I know I'm not his first choice in a wife," I hedged, still thinking of the duke's daughter, "but I'd like to know if there was someone he was interested in before...everything."

The teasing light left Anir's face. "It's not my business or my place to share his story."

"I'm not asking you to. I only want to know if there was someone else."

"Would it change anything if there was?"

I thought about it. My curiosity was at play, for certain, but it *would* change matters. I would refuse the bond and have our fate decided by the council of three Wrath had mentioned.

If he loved someone, well, that would both make me uncomfortable and also clear my way to pursuing Pride. Which was still the surest path to achieving my goal of vengeance.

Unless, of course, I beat Envy to finding the Temptation Key and Triple Moon Mirror. And if a demon prince couldn't sense the spelled wine or food, I might be able to garner truth that way. But I'd need to practice on a prince of Hell, and one was still notably absent, curse him.

I returned to the matter at hand. I would not want to be tied together in a loveless marriage with Wrath if he would always be pining for someone else.

"Yes. It would. It would change a lot."

"Careful." A low voice drawled from behind me. "Or I might think you'd actually *like* to marry me."

SEVENTEEN

I closed my eyes and silently swore before glowering at Anir. "You are truly the worst."

"I bet seven devil coins you feel different after your next lesson." The traitor shot me a devious grin. "Don't forget your purse tomorrow, Lady Em."

"Lock the door on your way out."

Wrath's voice was much too close. I felt his breath near the base of my neck, and I briefly considered rushing to the door or inventing a spell to have the floor swallow me whole. Instead, I squared my shoulders and slowly turned around. His focus was entirely on the human. Anir lost a bit of his playful swagger, replacing it with a seriousness I hadn't seen in him since the night Lord Makaden lost his tongue.

"No one is to enter this room until I give the signal that our training is over. Is that understood?"

"Yes, your majesty."

Anir offered me a polite bow and quickly made for the exit. Coward. I smiled to myself. Speaking of cowards, pretending the demon prince wasn't there, and hadn't overheard something I never meant him to hear, would not serve *my* bid for being fearless, either.

I forced myself to meet Wrath's imposing stare and hid my surprise as I assessed my newest opponent. He wasn't dressed entirely in black today; he wore a brilliant white shirt and tailcoat. I took in his huge frame, the cold set to his features, and swallowed hard. He was not in a pleasant mood. I decided now was not the time for bravery. A clever schemer understood the art of retreat. Wrath was up to no good and I wanted no part in discovering how bad he could be.

"I don't think your training is necessary. Anir was doing an exceptional job."

A smile spread across the prince's face, though there was no hint of mirth to be found in it. The look confirmed that remaining around for this training was a terrible idea. I took a step back and something dangerous sparked in Wrath's eyes.

"He doesn't possess the skills needed for this lesson."

"Oh, well, I have a prior engagement. We'll have to re-schedule."

"Is that so?"

"Yes, as a matter of fact, it is."

"Do you recall the bargain we struck in my bedchamber?"

I went to nod when an immense wave of lethargy washed over me, and I suddenly found my head too heavy to move. Wrath's intense focus homed in on my emotional and physical shift. There was no concern present in his expression, only a hard edge that should have worried me.

And it would have, if I wasn't in such a horrid state of lassitude.

I couldn't bring myself to care, or stand, apparently. My legs folded of their own volition and I sank to the ground, crashing in a heap of tangled limbs. My cheek pressed into the thick mat, the fibers scratching and uncomfortable. Still, I didn't so much as roll over to get comfortable. I didn't even blink. To my horror, a dribble of saliva worked its way out of the corner of my mouth. I couldn't care less.

In fact, I found I *really* didn't much care for anything. Not even the gleam of victory flashing in Wrath's eyes as he towered over me.

He strolled around my prone form. "Look at me, Emilia."

I wanted to, almost more than anything, but energy was too hard to come by. I had nothing left in my reserves to spare. My eyelids drifted shut instead. Despite my undignified position, laying sprawled on the floor, drooling, I couldn't muster the resolve to—

The slothful feeling snapped, as if it had never been. Anger, all-consuming and red-hot, brought me to my feet a breath later. Rage had my body trembling. Or perhaps it was wrath.

I flung myself at the demon. "I'm going to kill you!"

"Kill? I'm sure you mean kiss."

Wrath chuckled at my sudden change in temper, then, before I could touch him, the atmosphere once again abruptly shifted. Suddenly, I was no longer trying to get my hands around his throat; I was clawing him closer, wrapping my legs and arms around his body. I wanted him.

Goddess curse me. The need to bed him was overwhelming, the ache unbearable.

I thought I knew desire before in the Crescent Shallows. Nothing came close to this. I could think of nothing else except his hands on me. My hands on him.

In the back of my mind I knew something was terribly wrong. This was exactly what Lust had done to me that night on the beach, but I was unable to focus on anything but my desire.

Our mutual fury would have a perfect outlet in passion, granting us both release as we fought to undress, to out-caress, to make the other come undone. I dragged Wrath's face close to mine, his eyes flaring with that same desire as I slowly took his bottom lip between my teeth.

"Kiss me." I left his mouth only to run my tongue and teeth over the side of his neck, tasting and suckling his skin as I brought my lips close to his ear. "I need you."

"Want, but never need, my lady." He did not return my pursuit, but his grin was positively sinful as he stepped away from my touch. "In the Sin Corridor, you were tested for envy. I'm curious what got you so incensed. Do you recall what illusion spurred that on?"

My desire evaporated. An image of Wrath engaged in bedding a woman who wasn't me resurfaced. Once again I saw her legs wrapped around his body, his hips rolling forward with each deep thrust inside her. Instead of her moans, I could now hear his.

A possessive, dark emotion bubbled inside me. I was so jealous of them, I wanted to kill. My blood turned as cold as my tone. "Yes."

"Tell me what you saw."

"You and another woman. In bed."

There was a moment of silence. As if he hadn't expected that to be the reason. "And how did that make you feel?"

I exhaled, the sound more akin to a growl. "Murderous."

Wrath slowly began circling me again, his voice quiet, but

taunting. "Was that before or after you saw the pleasure she'd given me? The pure ecstasy I felt buried inside her warmth."

A tear slid down my cheek. I was not sad or even furious. I was now fully consumed by jealousy. Not of the other woman, but of the night of intimacy they'd shared. I wanted that. Wanted Wrath with an intensity that razed all reason from my mind. And that level of envy was almost as overwhelming as the night I first met the prince who ruled over that sin.

Envy had used his influence on me and I'd never forget the iciness of—

Understanding descended in a burst of anger, breaking the spell. "You monstrous beast. You're using your powers on me!"

"And how easily you succumbed to them." Wrath's fury rose to meet mine. "Do you want my brothers to manipulate you? Maybe you wish to become an object for their amusement. Perhaps you will start by being *mine*. Remove your clothing and dance for my pleasure."

"You're a pig."

"I am much worse than that. But a bargain is a bargain."

"I did not consent to this bullshit."

"Lie. *You* asked *me* to arm you. Demanded, if I recall correctly. I countered with training you against physical and magical threats. Did you not agree to that?"

"Yes, but—"

"Remove your clothing."

There was a strange echo of power in his voice. I tried to shove it away, tried fighting it, but felt the pressure building and caving in. I desperately tried to erect an emotional barrier between us, but Wrath would have none of it. Before I could touch the summoning

Mark on my neck, his voice rang out clear and strong and filled with dominating power.

"Now."

The dam broke, and so did my will. My fingers swiftly loosened the buttons and stays of my trousers. I shimmied out of them, allowing the material to pool at my feet. My tunic was gone next. Wrath slid his attention from the top of my head to my toes, and pulled it up as slowly. There was no lust or warmth or appreciation in his gaze. Only anger.

And he wasn't alone in that feeling. I hated that he'd compelled me to disrobe. Choosing to do so in the Crescent Shallows was powerful, freeing. This was neither of those things. I would make him pay for this. As quickly as my need for revenge flared, it vanished with the next wave of his will.

I went to remove my undergarments, but his voice cut through my haze. "Leave those on. Sway your hips."

I focused on the single ember of fury that hadn't been tamped down by Wrath's magical command. Trying with all of my might to ignite that kernel of emotion that still belonged to me, and use it to swat his magic away. *I* would be the one to decide when to undress before him or anyone else. *I* would be the master of my own will. And I would keep fighting for myself, no matter how dire or desperate or futile the situation became.

Sensing my resolve, Wrath unleashed more of his power.

"I said, *sway your hips.*"

Sentient thought, emotion, and free will were locked deep inside me. All I knew was the sound of his voice, his desire. His will pumped through my veins, dominated me in every sense of the word. Became one with my heart.

I did as he commanded. I became sin and vice. I was lustful. And I adored it.

Swaying suggestively, I kept my attention on him. I wished he'd ask me to remove my undergarments. Then I wished he'd remove his.

Wrath moved closer, his expression a study of cold fury. I could not understand why he was displeased. I erased the remaining distance between us and danced against him, pressing up against his tense body. Something about our position reminded me of another time, another dance. And the same anger that coursed through him at that bonfire.

He was a difficult creature then, and doubly so now.

"Is this not what you desire?"

"Not at all." He took a large step away, placing a hateful distance between us. "You will address me as master from now on. Drop to your knees."

"I will *never*—" Anger flared, then extinguished as quickly. I went to the ground, head bowed. "Does this please you, master?"

"Remove my right boot."

I undid the laces of his boot, then pulled it off, waiting for his next direction.

"Slide your hands up my to calf." I reached for his leg and he yanked it back. "Start from the ankle."

Without hesitation, I dragged my hands up his body, and over the muscle of his calf. My fingers brushed against something hard. I glanced up. "Have I pleased you now, master?"

Wrath reached down to lift my chin, his focus roaming across my face. He was searching for something, but the deep frown indicated he hadn't found it.

"Learn to protect yourself. *That* will give me ultimate pleasure."

With him, I somehow understood the very essence of pleasure. That I could do. I let go of his calf and reached for the band of his trousers. "Let me please you now, master."

The temperature around us plummeted several degrees.

"If I wanted you on your knees, bare before me, without a thought of your own in your head, I would will it. If I desired to fuck you into our marriage, you'd do exactly as I said. And you'd beg for more. Neither attracts, nor pleases me. I long for an *equal*. Grab the dagger hidden on my leg. Get up."

I slid the blade from the leather sheath and pushed myself to my feet, heart sinking at his harsh tone and dismissal of my advances. I reached for his hand, hoping to entice him to take what I was offering. "I—"

Fury, untamed, overwhelming, and all-consuming burned away the lust I'd felt. I gripped the dagger so hard my hand ached. Wrath did not take his attention from mine as he slowly undid the first few buttons of his pristine shirt. "Press the blade to my heart."

I closed the distance between us, the tip of the dagger pricking his skin. I was now wrathful. I was fury in the flesh. And I would take what was owed to me and mine.

Beginning now. With this hateful prince.

Wrath leaned in, his voice low and seductive. "This is what you dream of. Blood and revenge. Take your vengeance, *witch*. Recall what I just made you do. How you fell to your knees, begging to please me. Let hatred and your favorite sin consume you."

"Shut up."

"Perhaps you liked it when I made you strip. When I bent you to my will."

"I said *shut up*!"

"Maybe I should show you how very wicked I can be."

I stared at his chest, at the blade piercing his skin. A slight trickle of blood rolled down his body. Through the wrath and fury overwhelming my senses, I remembered. I'd taken a blade to his heart before. In the monastery. He'd sworn it would take much more than a dagger to his chest to end him. I'd wanted to test the truth in those words then. He was offering me the chance to do so now. I swallowed hard, my throat bobbing. Unshed tears burned my eyes.

My hand shook, the blade digging in harder as I strained against it.

"*Take. Your. Vengeance.*"

His demonic influence battled my will. And won.

A tear slipped free as I leaned into the blade, using my upper body weight to shove through muscle and bone. I watched with blazing fury as it slid into his chest. Blood poured from the wound, stained his shirt, made my fingers slick. I didn't pull it out. I twisted the dagger, gritting my teeth before I screamed loud enough to summon Satan himself.

The demon prince watched impassively as I yanked the blade free and stabbed him again.

And again.

And again.

EIGHTEEN

Wrath removed all influence over me at once.

I stared at the blade sticking out of the demon's chest, my whole body violently trembling in the aftermath. Nausea coursed through me in place of the rage I'd just felt. I let go of the weapon and jerked back, unable to look away. There was so much blood. Wrath's blood.

It bloomed obscenely across his white shirt like a flower of death. And if it had been anyone else, they would be dead. I would have killed them. I dragged in breath after breath, the weight of what could have been, of what I did, nearly crushing me.

Wrath wrenched the dagger from his chest and tossed it away. I flinched as it clattered against the far wall, the only sound in the chamber now aside from my ragged breaths. He'd made me stab him. In the heart. I . . . I couldn't stop looking at the place I'd shoved the dagger in. Couldn't stop hearing the sickening crunch of bone as I pierced his chest. I fought to keep my hands at my sides, to not cover my ears and scream until that wretched sound ceased in my head.

The wound was already healed, but his shirt was damp with blood. Memories of another chest, another heart, flooded my senses. My twin. All I could envision was her brutalized body. How easily it could have been her under my blade. Fighting back had been useless.

I turned my hands over, sticky, bloodstained palms up, and cried, "How dare you? How dare you subject me to that depravity?"

"Yes, how dare I teach my wife to protect herself against her enemies."

"I am not your wife yet. And if this is your idea of proving why we ought to marry, you're mad. You are the most despicable creature I've ever had the misfortune to know."

"If that were true, I would have left you as Lust had when I released you from my thrall."

The demon thrust a dressing gown at me. I hadn't seen him holding it before, but I hadn't noticed much of anything aside from the sins he'd wanted me to experience.

I was seeing plenty now.

His expression was the closest thing to murder I'd ever witnessed. As if his little power display infuriated him more than it had me. As if that were even possible.

I'd pierced his heart with a dagger. I'd never been so upset in my life. And I'd felt *a lot* of angry emotions since my twin's murder.

I snatched the dressing robe and shoved my arms through it, hating him for knowing I would need it. I also understood with vivid clarity why he wore white. His preparation for the training made me seethe all the more. It indicated he knew exactly what sins he'd use, what he'd influence me to do, and he'd thought ahead to what I'd need after his little power display.

I was tempted to stride back to my bedroom suite in my underwear, or strip down to nothing. Let his court see me in all my glory.

"Be my guest." He no doubt discerned my thoughts from my body language. He swung an arm out. "If you'd prefer to walk around without the robe, I certainly won't object."

"You really should quit speaking now."

"Make me."

"Don't tempt me, demon."

"Do it." He moved until he towered over me. "Use your power. Fight back."

Childish taunt. I dipped into my source of magic, trying to wrench a bit of power up to knock him on his smart ass. A wall of nothing greeted me again. I was so frustrated, I wanted to scream. Wrath's eyes narrowed, missing nothing.

"We will train every day until the Feast of the Wolf. You will learn to protect yourself from my brothers. Or you will suffer greater indignities than the ones I have demonstrated today. Be thankful, *fiancée*, that I do not wish to harm your person. Only your ego and pride. Both, if I am not mistaken, can be repaired."

"You made me stab you."

"I heal fast."

Too bad the emotional impact of today's little lesson wouldn't heal as quickly. I cinched the belt at my waist. "I despise you."

"I can live with your hate." A muscle in his jaw flickered. "Far better to use it to your advantage, rather than adore me and succumb to the depravity of this world."

"Why violence?" My voice was quiet. "You did not need to unleash my wrath that way."

"I offered you an outlet. Vengeance is poison, a slow death of self. Seek justice. Seek truth. But if you choose revenge over all else, you will lose more than your soul."

"You cannot seriously be claiming to care about my soul."

"Your grief cannot be extinguished through hatred. Tell me, do you feel as you imagined? Did spilling my blood heal your wounds? Have those scales of justice finally tipped into balance, or did you slip a little further into something you don't recognize?"

I set my jaw and glared. We both knew I did not feel better. If anything, I felt worse.

"I didn't think so." He turned on his heel and strode toward the door. "I will meet you here tomorrow evening."

"I never agreed to multiple training sessions."

"Nor did you set parameters during our bargain. I suggest you come prepared to do battle, or you will find yourself once again in your underthings, on your hands and knees before me, begging. Or stabbing. Or both."

I reined in my emotions. Wrath was currently a giant ass, but he was never impulsive. "Does the timing of this first lesson have to do with my visiting House Envy?"

"No." Wrath did not turn back, but he paused before opening the door. "Votes to choose the guest of honor for the Feast of the Wolf were cast yesterday."

And there it was. He must have hoped someone more interesting would have emerged to take my place. "You still believe I'll be chosen."

"Of that I have little doubt."

"Your plan tonight was to what? Show me how heartless you truly are, how powerful?"

"My brothers will be more than happy to show you how sinful they can be in front of a large, eager audience." He took a deep breath. "If you thought Makaden was bad, his behavior is nothing compared to a gathering hosted by my family. They will take until they're bored. Then they'll discard the broken pieces. And," he added quietly, "if you are so appalled by what just happened here, in front of only me, you truly have no idea what you're in for."

"You should have warned me we'd begin training tonight."

"My brothers will not ask. Nor will they give any warning."

"I am not betrothed to your brothers. If you want an equal, I suggest treating me like one. We may have made a bargain, but that does not mean I couldn't be forewarned."

"The point of this lesson was to show how vulnerable you are, not shame you."

I stared at the tense lines of his back. The white-knuckled grip he had on the door handle.

"I am not a hero, Emilia. Nor am I a villain. You ought to know that by now."

"Leave me. I've heard enough excuses tonight."

He didn't move for a beat, and I braced myself for whatever he seemed to be struggling with saying. Without another word, he slipped from the room, the door quietly shutting behind him. I stared at the door for a few moments, gathering myself.

I imagined this training was as much for his benefit as it was for mine. If anyone succeeded in having me half-naked and writhing during the feast—or worse—the general of war might remind his family how he'd come by that military honor. And I didn't think the path to that particular title had been cleared without a good deal of bloodshed on Wrath's part.

I glanced at the dagger I'd used to stab him, the blade coated in his drying blood. I couldn't quite identify the exact emotion raging through me in place of the fear, but I no longer felt nauseated.

I felt like I could breathe fire. And with my ability to summon it, I might be able to do just that with a bit of practice. Goddess help the demon princes now.

I stormed into my bedroom suite and slammed the door with enough force to shake the large painting hanging near the bathing chamber. Of all the arrogant, spiteful, nasty tricks to pull. Yes, I'd agreed to the cursed bargain, but I hadn't known it was a binding contract.

My cheeks flared with fury. Losing my sense of control rattled me more than any of his demonic tricks. When he walked into that training room, he had a plan and executed it flawlessly. And I'd been at his mercy. *That.* That was the core of my anger.

" 'You will address me as master from now on.' " I mocked, using my best impression of his voice. "Hateful monster."

I charged into my bathing chamber and began scrubbing the blood from my hands, all the while seething at Wrath. Even though he didn't appear particularly pleased or smug by his efforts, it did not change the fact he'd unleashed himself on me.

I dried myself off and marched in an angry circle around my room. I was mad with him for proving his point, but even more upset that I'd been rendered nearly helpless.

Taking all that aside, I had to admit it was far better to be subjected to Wrath's influence, wretched though it may be, because at least I knew he wouldn't carry things too far. He might make me strip and beg, or take a blade to *his* heart, but he'd never take true advantage or cause me to hurt anyone else.

I stared down at my now-clean hands. A troubling thought

entered my mind. If a demon prince willed it, I would murder someone at their command. Wrath proved that tonight. Part of me wanted
to stab him, but I never would've crossed that line on my own.

I thought of Antonio, how he'd been clearly under *some* influence. If Wrath could wield other sins with ease and strength, it
stood to reason that his brothers also possessed the talent.

Which meant any one of them could have been manipulat-
ing Antonio into killing the witches. His hatred was already there
because of how his beloved mother died. It would not have taken
much for that emotion to be drawn out, used against him.

Shoving thoughts and worries from my mind about my sister's murderer and the Feast of the Wolf vote, I went to my wardrobe and donned a simple black dress.

I glanced down as a flash of off-white peeked out from the
darkness. One of the enchanted skulls had slipped from its covering when I'd removed my dress.

I expelled a breath. I still needed to sort through the skull puzzle and figure out if Envy had been the one who'd sent them. Doubt
crept in regarding his involvement. It made little sense for him to
secretly send the skulls only to openly share information with me.

I bent to replace the scarf when the outer door creaked open.

"Emilia, I wanted to—" Wrath's attention fell on the
enchanted skull. Whatever he'd been about to say was immediately forgotten as he crossed the room in a whirl of black, gold,
and fury. He wrenched the skull from my wardrobe and spun
around, staring as if he hardly knew me. "What the—"

"Unless you wish to be slapped with an unpleasant spell, I
suggest you rethink your tone. We are no longer in your training
ring. I won't tolerate rudeness outside of our lessons."

He inhaled deeply. Then exhaled. He repeated both actions.

Twice. With each inhalation and exhalation, I swore the atmosphere grew charged. Storm clouds were gathering.

"If you would be so kind, my lady, to please explain *how* this came to be in your possession, I'd very much like to know."

I noticed a vein in his throat throbbing. After what he made me do to him, it gave me a perverse sense of glee to see him so mad. "Why are you here?"

"To apologize. Answer me. Please."

"Someone left it. Along with a second skull."

"Second skull?" He spoke through his teeth, as if forcing polite manners against the incredulity playing out across his features. "Where, pray tell, is it now?"

"My wardrobe. Behind that ridiculous gown with the big skirts."

Without uttering another word, Wrath calmly ducked inside my wardrobe and retrieved the object in question. It appeared to take Herculean effort on his part to remain calm. "Might I ask when the first skull arrived?"

"The night Anir brought food and wine."

"The first night you were here?" His volume went up a notch. I nodded, which seemed to set his teeth on edge. "You didn't think this information was worth sharing because..."

My smile was anything but sweet. "I was unaware that I needed to report to you, *master*. Would you have answered any of my questions?"

"Emilia—"

"Which brother possesses this sort of magic? Who would want to taunt me? Someone must hate me an awful lot. They enchanted the skulls with my sister's voice. Another lovely dagger to my heart. Do you have any ideas to offer?"

I raised my brows, knowing he wouldn't say a word. His lips pressed into a firm line and I couldn't help the dark laughter that bubbled up from deep within.

"I suspected as much. Though I can promise you this, it will not be the last time I decide to keep my own counsel until I've thoroughly investigated on my own." I pointed to the door. "Please leave. I've had quite enough of you tonight."

His eyes narrowed at the dismissal. I doubted anyone ever spoke to him in such a way. It was high time he got used to it. "Regarding the training earlier—"

"I am fully capable of understanding the value in the lesson, no matter how appalling your methods. Regardless of our bargain, in the future, you will ask if I want to train." I schooled my face into indifference. "If you're not planning on sharing information with me, this interrogation ends now. Put the skulls back and get out."

"The skulls will be locked somewhere safe."

"Vagueness will not work for me. Be specific. If I permit you to take the skulls, where will they be?"

"My private suite."

"I will see them when I wish. And you will share any information you learn."

He glowered at me. "If we're making demands, then, so long as you agree to dine with me tomorrow, I will grant your request."

"I cannot give you an answer tonight."

"And if I insist?"

"Then my answer is no, your highness."

"You may beg off conversation tonight. Refuse to dine with me. But we *will* speak about everything. Soon."

"No, Wrath. We will speak about this when we're *both* ready to." I watched him absorb the statement. "I will consent to the training, and your influence, *only* in that room. Everywhere else, you will respect my wishes."

"Or else?"

I shook my head sadly. "I understand your realm is different, and your brothers are diabolical and conniving, but not every statement is a threat. At least not between us. Know this: from here on out, if you do not respect my wishes, I will not stay here. It's not to punish you, but to protect myself. I will forgive your lapse in decorum, judgment, and basic decency if you vow to learn from this mistake. You will, however, share all information you glean about the skulls, whether or not I decide to dine with you. Do we have a bargain?"

He looked me over, *really* looked, and finally nodded. "I accept your terms."

Wrath collected both skulls and paused, his attention landing on my nightstand. And the journal on House Pride. "How were you planning on reading it? Let mè guess." His voice turned suspiciously low. "You were going to strike a bargain with a demon? Offer a piece of your soul."

"I considered it."

"Allow me to save you the trouble. It's not written in a demonic language. And no bargain you strike with anyone—save me—will give you the answers you seek with *any* of those journals. All you had to do was ask and I would have given it to you."

"Perhaps. But would you have given me a way to read it?"

"I don't know."

He strode from the room, and I didn't move until I heard the click of the outer door closing. Then I slumped against the wall.

I counted off my breaths, waiting until I was sure he would not return, and then I allowed the tears to come hard and fast. I doubled over, sobs wracking my body, consuming me. In the matter of an hour I'd been subjected to multiple sins and had stabbed my potential future husband. Tonight could certainly be classified as an evening from Hell.

I abruptly stood, chest heaving with the effort to rein in my emotions.

I brushed the wetness from my cheeks and vowed once again to best my enemies. Even the ones who no longer felt like adversaries.

NINETEEN

Ice-coated flowers sparkled like crystal and branches tinkled like winter chimes above my head as I strolled through the garden.

It was cold enough that I needed fur-lined gloves and a heavy velvet cloak, but the morning itself was lovely. Peaceful. I hadn't had many of those days over the last few months, and this felt decadent. I squinted up through the latticework of boughs. On a good number of trees leaves stubbornly clung to life, frozen until either warmth or sunshine set them free.

I still hadn't seen the sun through all the snow and overcast skies, so it would probably be a good long while before a thaw happened. If ever. I recalled the way Wrath had soaked up the sun one lazy afternoon on the roof of his commandeered castle in my city. Back then I'd assumed he'd missed the fiery pits of his hellish home. Now I knew better.

Clusters of flowers—pinkish purple roses and peonies and something with petals that looked like tiny silver crescent moons—sprung up in wider sections of the maze. I slowly walked along the inner pathway, the hedges towering on either side, beautiful living walls dusted with snow. The gardens of House Wrath were another stunning example of his refined tastes.

I followed the meandering trail until I came upon a reflecting pool near the center.

A marble statue of a naked woman stood in the water, a crown of stars on her head, two curved daggers in hand, her expression one of icy fury. She looked as if she'd tear through the fabric of the universe with those nasty blades, and regret nothing of her actions.

An oversized serpent—twice the circumference of my upper arms—wound up her left ankle, slithered between her legs as it clung to the left calf and thigh, then coiled around her hips and rib cage. Its large head covered one breast while its tongue flicked out toward the other, not as if it were about to lick, but as if it were blocking it from the view of curious passersby.

I moved closer, entranced and a little horrified by it. The serpent's body actually hid most of her private anatomy. A wicked protector of sorts. Its scales were carved with expert care, almost fooling one into thinking it had been real and turned to stone.

I circled the giant statue. Her hair, long and flowing, had little crescent moon–shaped flowers carved into the unbound locks. Near the bottom of her spine, a goddess symbol had been etched horizontally. I reached over to pet the serpent when a low, keening howl grumbled up from deep below the earth. I jerked back and connected with a wall of warm flesh.

Before fear registered or I had time to react, an arm with steel-like muscle snaked around my waist, tugging me close. A sharp dagger pressed into my side. I stilled, breathing as shallowly as possible. My assailant leaned in, their breath warm against my icy skin. Hair on the back of my neck rose.

"Hello, little thief."

Envy.

I shoved my fear into the deepest part of my mind, far from where he could detect just how much he'd rattled me. "Attacking a member of House Wrath is foolish. And coming here without an invitation is doubly unwise. Even for you, your highness."

"Stealing from a prince is punishable by death." His low chuckle lacked any trace of humor. "But that's not why I'm here, Shadow Witch."

He dropped the dagger and released me so quickly I stumbled forward. I squared my shoulders and faced him, my expression cold and hard. "If you've come for the book of spells, your trip was wasted. It belongs to me."

I'd meant to say it belonged to witches, but it felt like the truth when the words escaped my lips. Envy blinked slowly.

"Bold and brazen. Perhaps you've found those claws after all." His attention slid over me and then to the statue. "Have you noticed anything odd lately? Perhaps something strange about your magic?"

"No."

He flashed a quick grin. "We all sense lies, Emilia. Allow me to be blunt. You stole from me, but I stole right back from you. Tit for tat."

"Nothing has been stolen from me."

"There was a curse on the spell book. Anyone who removed it from my collection would lose something vital to them in return."

Cold dread sluiced through my veins. I had not been able to dip into my source of magic since I'd come back from his royal house. "You're lying."

"Am I? Perhaps you ought to cast a truth spell on me."

257

He sheathed his dagger and gave me another slow once-over as he waited. Even though I suspected it would be futile, I concentrated on that well of Source, trying to dip into it and draw enough magic to wipe him—and his smug expression—from this circle.

There was nothing but an impossibly thick wall where I'd once felt that slumbering beast. He sneered, as if the sight of me disgusted him.

"I didn't think so. You, my dear, are no more than a mortal now."

He turned and started walking away.

I marched after him, fuming. "You had no right to curse me."

"And you had even less right to steal. I'd say we're even."

I thought of my plans to spell the wine at the Feast of the Wolf. I needed my powers back. That was nonnegotiable. "Fine. I'll return the book. Wait here while I go get it."

Envy stuck his hands in his pockets, considering the offer. "I find this is a much more interesting turn of events. Keep the book. I'd much rather watch your plans crumble."

"I'm willing to strike a bargain."

"Too bad you didn't think of that before. I might have been open to an agreement that would benefit us both. Now? Now I'll enjoy watching fate run its course."

I clamped my teeth together to keep from either cursing him, or begging him to reconsider. A faint wail drifted up from the bowels of the earth again. Goose bumps swiftly rose along my body. I turned to stare at the statue.

"I'd not become too curious about that, pet."

"I told you not to call me—"

I faced Envy again, only to discover he was already gone. A

wisp of glittering green and black smoke wafting around was the only indication he'd been there at all. I glanced back at the statue and listened to the cries of whatever was being tortured deep beneath it. It was mournful, hopeless. Brokenhearted. A sound that pierced through my emotional armor.

I wondered what was damned enough for Wrath to bury below his wicked House in the underworld, alone and miserable. Then I realized it must be more horrid than I could even fathom to receive that punishment. Wrath was a blade of justice, swift, unemotional, and brutal.

But he wasn't cruel. Whatever was making that terrible cry...

I did not want to encounter it alone without magic. I hurried from the garden, the sounds of suffering still ringing in my ears long after I'd slipped between my sheets that night.

The next day, Fauna excitedly danced in place outside my door. Her knocks were as fast and light as a hummingbird's wings. I opened the door and grinned. Her slippered feet moved as swiftly as she spun us around. "Invitations for the feast are arriving this week!"

My smile vanished. After Wrath's devilish training session, I did not share her excitement. Honestly, I hadn't been thrilled by the feast the first time he had told me about it, either. But now... now I found my gaze straying to the clock, jumping at every sound in the corridor. I was nowhere near being ready to withstand a demon prince's influence. Not to mention, being without my magic was another obstacle I hadn't anticipated.

Fauna seemed to think we wouldn't hear about who was hosting for a few more days, but I had other suspicions. I had no base for the fears that kept growing, so I did my best to ignore the air of foreboding that settled over me like a storm cloud.

My friend called for tea and sweets and lounged in my receiving room with a book. I tried to relax the same way but was wound too tightly. After my encounter with Envy in the garden, I'd combed through books on magic, searching for a way to break a curse or hex.

It was complex—I'd either need the one who'd cast it to release me, or figure out the intricate structure of the curse; it was described in one grimoire as being similar to a series of magical threads woven together. I'd have to locate the source knot, then snip it. If I guessed wrong or undid the wrong knot, I could end up magically snipping the thread of life. And die.

The author of the book on hexes made sure to point that out several times, as if anyone could mistake the meaning of "snipping the thread of life."

I'd briefly contemplated visiting the Matron of Curses and Poisons, but I'd still face the very real possibility of death if she didn't locate the correct thread.

It was a gamble I was unwilling to try. At least not yet.

I wished Anir would show up and start our lesson early. The physical training would help burn off the excess nerves. And I desperately needed to rid myself of jitters.

Finally, late into the evening, a servant delivered the envelope I'd been dreading. There was no royal crest, no indication of what it contained, but I *knew*. My name and title were the only bit of writing on it. Indicating it was not just a note from the prince of this royal House.

I took the envelope from the servant with the same level of enthusiasm as if it were news of my execution. I used the slim dagger Wrath had gifted me and ran it along the upper edge, neatly cutting it open at the seam.

YOU ARE CORDIALLY INVITED TO

House Gluttony

FOR THIS BLOOD SEASON'S

Feast of the Wolf.

GUEST OF HONOR:

LADY EMILIA DI CARLO,

CURRENTLY OF HOUSE WRATH

If my heart pounded any harder, it might crack a rib. I'd been told I'd have a choice, even if ultimately I'd be *encouraged* to choose the hosting House. I couldn't help but fear other rules would be tossed aside at the last minute, too.

I stared at the invitation, its elegance a severe contrast to the panic it induced. My being chosen as the guest of honor wasn't a surprise; Wrath had already made it clear I'd likely be the unlucky one, but seeing it in black and white made the whole thing terribly real.

Especially the part about my greatest fear or a secret of my heart being forcibly wrenched from me in front of the entire assembly. With Wrath's "lessons" and the mortification and horror they brought fresh in my mind, I felt as if I was going to be sick.

"What is it?" Fauna set her book aside. "Has his highness sent for you?"

"No." I blew out a breath. "It's the invitation to the Feast of the Wolf."

"So soon?" She shot up from the divan, thrusting her hand out with excitement she couldn't contain. "Who's hosting this season?" I gave her the card and her mouth formed a perfect O of surprise as she scanned it. "House Gluttony. Interesting. His parties are legendary for their debauchery. Envy and Greed must have removed their requests to host."

"I imagine the Prince of Gluttony's got quite a bit of food."

"Not only that. His House is indulgence on every level. Alcohol flows from fountains, clothing is optional in his twilight garden, and trysts are often done in glass rooms lining the ballroom. There is no such thing as clandestine in his world. All is available for consumption: flesh, food, drink, carnal desire, and any manner of vice. This should be quite an event. Did you already know he'd be hosting?"

"This is the first I've heard anything. Have you attended one of his parties?"

"No. Last time he hosted, I was too young. I've always been curious. Some of the stories have taken on a surreal, fablelike aura. It's hard to know what's real and what's pure fantasy. Especially with what that writer printed about him in her latest royal exposé."

"I imagine columnists have much inspiration."

"Oh, they do, and she does in particular. She positively *detests* him. Rumor claims he ruined her cousin's chance to marry into the nobility, which is why she took up the cursed pen. So much scandal!" She happily sighed, then drew her brows together as if a new thought suddenly rained on her sunny daydream. Her focus moved over the invitation once more. "What fear do you think will be wrenched from your heart?"

"Whatever it is, I'm sure it will be horrible."

"Maybe we can work on something that won't be too awfully bad."

"If only worrying about how to dance at a ball without stepping on toes and causing a scene was my biggest fear."

My nerves about dancing weren't exactly a lie. I'd never attended a royal ball or formal dance. We'd only danced at festivals with other people of our station. Everyone here would be watching, judging. It shouldn't matter what they thought or if they laughed at me, but when I thought of standing there, feeling raw and exposed, my stomach clenched.

"You are a genius!" My friend slowly turned to me, her face splitting into a huge grin. "We can look into a spell or potion for you to take. We will make you *the worst* dancer in all the Seven Circles, worthy of your biggest fear."

"Fauna," I warned. "I was only teasing."

"No, it could work. If you drank a potion to make that fear come to life in an out-of-proportion way, it's even more likely to be wrenched from you while at a ball."

"And if our ruse is discovered, what then?"

"We'll just have to make sure we use an expert spell or potion."

"Even so, the royals might sense treachery and lies."

"We'll simply need to practice to ensure it's perfect."

"There's no need to worry about that because we're *not* deceiving anyone, Fauna."

"We should ask the Matron if she can—" Fauna dragged her attention away from the invitation and took in my expression. "Oh, angel blood. You look like you're in need of a serious distraction. I have just the place in mind. Come. Let's go at once."

Without giving me a chance to object, she took my arm and raced us from my rooms, the invitation falling from her hand, forgotten for the moment. For her, at least.

Fear beat like a drum against my chest, the rhythm steady and unrelenting. And I suspected it would remain that way until the dreaded feast.

Fauna's idea of a distraction couldn't have been more fitting for me. She half-dragged me through the royal hallways, down several flights of stairs, into the servants' corridor, and finally burst through the doors to a bustling kitchen. I stood there, drinking in the sights and sounds.

The kitchen was bursting with life as the staff prepared tonight's dinner.

Several tables ran down the length of the room, with clusters of workers assigned to different tasks. Some were cutting vegetables, others carving meats, more kneading dough for breads and biscuits. Still more people stood over saucepans and skillets.

Tears threatened, but I choked them down. It would do no good to cry in front of the inner workings of House Wrath.

The cook ran his gaze over us, then nodded to a table near a wall of windows. They'd been thrown open, letting out warmth from the oven fires. "You may use anything you desire, Lady Emilia. If you don't see something you need, simply ask."

"Thank you."

"Thank his highness. He instructed us to secure anything you wished."

"Did he now?" Fauna barely hid her squeal as I walked deeper inside the room. "How unbelievably thoughtful. Wouldn't you agree, Lady Emilia?"

"Indeed."

I glanced around. It was nothing close to our small family restaurant—it was much larger and grand—but still, it felt like home. Against my better judgment, a wave of gratitude washed over me. Wrath had guessed I'd eventually find my way here, to the one place in this realm that would feel familiar to me unlike any other.

I turned back to the head cook. "Thank you for letting me into your kitchen."

The cook inclined his head, then marched back to bark orders at the line cooks.

Tension melted from my limbs as I opened the icebox and spied a basketful of plump berries. A tub of what suspiciously appeared to be ricotta sat beside them. My mother was the huge talent with dessert in our family, but I'd learned enough to make a rustic pie.

I gathered up all of my supplies and set up my station near the giant window. In moments I already had the pie crust dough sorted and mixed. The berries were quickly rinsed and set on a towel to dry, awaiting the sugar I'd toss them with. Perhaps I'd make custard, too.

Metal clanging on metal drew my attention up. Wrath and Anir darted back and forth outside the window, their swords and daggers clashing like thunder. I couldn't help but gawk as they charged each other, whipping their weapons through the air. Sparks literally flying upon each contact their blades made.

I gave Fauna an accusatory look. "The kitchen wasn't the only distraction you had in mind, I see."

Her grin was too wide to be innocent. She hopped up onto the window's ledge and snagged a pen and notepad, feigning interest in taking recipe notes as she peered over the pages and watched the two warriors do mock battle. They swung the swords above their heads, their powerful bodies heaving from the exertion of the heavy weapons and the training.

"I have no idea what you mean, my lady. I didn't know they'd be here."

"You're a terrible liar." I watched as she gazed at Anir, recalling the two of them chatting merrily before Makaden's tongue removal. "How long have you been in love with him?"

She jerked her attention to mine. "Why would you think I cared for the mortal?"

"You mentioned pining for someone when we first met and haven't stopped looking at him. I won't pry if you prefer to keep it a secret now, but I like Anir." I nodded to the dessert station I set up, giving her a way to evade the topic. "Don't be afraid to pick up the rolling pin and help. It doesn't have teeth."

She giggled behind her notepad. "Perhaps not, but have you seen the way the prince is looking at you? It's *his* bite you need to watch out for."

I rolled the dough for the crust with singular focus. I was doing everything in my power to *not* look at him. Of all the places in the entire castle, he simply had to choose this moment to train, in sleeveless leather armor, directly outside the kitchens.

Though I supposed Fauna was equally to blame for this so-called *unexpected* meeting.

"He's got a sweet tooth," I said, realizing she was still waiting for a response. "He's likely looking at the pie."

"Dessert isn't the only thing he looks hungry for, my lady. I wish Anir would gaze upon me with such longing."

"Pursue him."

"Trust me, if he gave any indication he'd be open to my advances, I would pounce. His highness currently seems to be experiencing the same dilemma."

My fiendish attention slid to the window. Torchlight glistened off a sheen of sweat Wrath had worked up wielding his sword. Our gazes clashed in time with the metal of Anir's blade. Fauna was right. Wrath looked like he was working off the magic of our bond. And was losing the battle. He didn't bother hiding his attention.

I promptly went back to rolling the dough, using more concentration than was required.

I could not forget the feeling of the blade sliding into his flesh. I set the rolling pin aside and started on the custard, forcing the silent crunch of bone from my thoughts.

"If I may speak freely, it's no small favor he's granted you."

"What favor?"

"Not insisting you finish the marriage bond. It's all anyone's been talking about."

I hoped the flush in my cheeks would be mistaken for the warmth of the kitchen. How fabulous. The entire court was gossiping about us bedding each other. "This realm certainly needs to learn the difference between choices and favors."

She lifted a shoulder. "Some might argue that you did make a choice, the night you started the betrothal. That he was the one without true choice."

"I find it hard to believe Wrath is tolerant of his court discussing our personal business."

"Your potential position as the princess of this circle is *everyone's* business."

"I—"

"No one blames you, my lady. It's just...having a co-ruler grants more power to the royals. It secures us from any bored princes in other Houses. Ones who like to stir up trouble on occasion. Princes are immortal, and while most demons live extremely long lives, we are not. Most in the court worry if war comes, our prince will not do all he can for the good of our realm. There are whispers that he may be weakening."

"That's ridiculous," I scoffed. "He is the most powerful prince I've met."

"His power isn't in question, only his heart. He can seduce you easily enough. Use his influence if necessary. And yet he's giving you time to decide for yourself."

"I'm sorry, but I'm having trouble understanding how that is such a foreign concept. Do people in the court really believe he should force me into our marriage? Or bed me against my will? There are laws in the mortal world about that disgusting act."

"I was not speaking of rape, my lady. That is not tolerated here without Wrath ending the life of the one who dares to take another against their will." Fauna looked me over. "Don't appear so shocked. The Seven Circles may be governed by sin, but there are some acts too depraved even for our realm. Punishment for rape is death. Dealt by Wrath's hand. Other courts favor castration. I promise, if a prince decided to seduce you, especially our prince, you would *choose* to be in his bed of your own accord."

"And the court is wondering why he isn't trying to tempt me?"

"Amongst other things." She lifted a shoulder as I stopped making the custard and stared. "Consider this. If one cuff is frayed on his suit, it sets the courts talking. They believe if a prince cannot be in control of something as simple as his clothing, there is no hope of him caring about those who live in this circle."

"They must have entirely too much idle time if they're gossiping about loose threads."

"It's never really about the clothing. It's about the underlying meaning behind *why* the prince would not pay enough attention to, or care about such small details."

I thought back to how affronted Wrath had been when I'd brought him that old shirt from the marketplace. I'd thought he was simply arrogant and unused to peasant clothing. Now I knew it ran much deeper—if anyone from this realm had seen him, they'd call his rule into question.

"A distracted ruler is dangerous, Emilia. It signals weakness. It makes the denizens aligned with that House of Sin question if they should seek new alliances."

And the princes of Hell all coveted power. Wrath must want to complete the bond very badly. But he'd give up the security of his House, the added power, the rumors in court, all so I could have the one thing he coveted above all else: choice.

"He mentioned something about a ceremony also being required. If we..." I drew in a deep breath. "If we were to—"

"—make sweet, passionate, lust-filled love?" Fauna supplied, her face innocent. "Ravage each other until the early morning hours? Scream each other's names as he bends you over and slams his—"

"—yes. That. Our marriage wouldn't be complete until the ceremony was also performed, correct?"

"Correct."

Fauna smiled as if she'd been privy to the direction my thoughts had journeyed. "Whatever may have transpired between you in the past, do not doubt him now. He must respect you enough to damn his own court. No matter how fleeting."

I noticed she hadn't said anything about him caring about or loving me. I wondered if having a husband who respected me would make up for the absence of the other two. Maybe I belonged in House Greed. I didn't think I'd settle for a marriage that did not contain all three.

More troublesome yet...I wasn't sure when I'd started considering taking Wrath as my husband. I was already in the underworld. I would soon meet each prince and have an opportunity to learn some of their secrets. I did not need to marry. And no matter what my feelings might be now, I would not give my family up for anyone. As long as I focused on that, all of my romantic notions would fade away.

Hopefully.

A note scrawled in Wrath's hand arrived later that night.

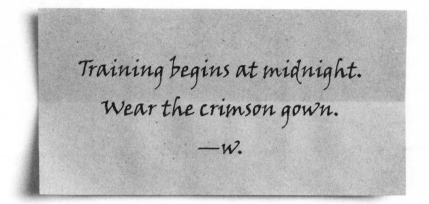

Training begins at midnight.
Wear the crimson gown.
—W.

I considered ignoring his request, or choosing a pair of trousers and blouse just to prove he neither commanded nor owned me. But acting out of spite wasn't the road I wanted to travel.

No matter how satisfying it would be to see the glimmer of incredulity on the demanding demon's face, his lessons would ultimately benefit me.

And I would take every advantage I could get my hands on now. The Feast of the Wolf was quickly approaching, and I would be ready to meet the demons on their playing field and crush them at their own game. In the most well-dressed, backstabbing way imaginable.

With a sigh, I fed the note to the flames and went to dress for my training date with Wrath.

TWENTY

"**As soon as** you start to sense the magic's caress, you must grip your own emotions in a tight fist. You naturally gravitate toward anger; use that initially, if you must."

Wrath circled me in the weapons room, a predatory gleam in his eyes as he ran his attention over the gown. The consummate hunter stalking his prey. Little did he know, he wasn't the one who'd set this particular trap. Nor would he be emerging victorious.

Tonight he was definitely more beast than man, especially in matters resembling battle.

With snug leather pants and matching sleeveless armor that buckled up the front, he seemed transformed. This was not the well-mannered prince, presiding over a court of demons. This was the creature made for fighting. And it was the first glimpse I'd had of the battle-scarred warrior outside of his training with Anir earlier tonight.

His teeth flashed in a poor imitation of a smile, furthering my suspicion that he was all animal now. And he liked it. I let my gaze travel over him. Maybe I did, too.

"It will feel like a whisper across your skin. Subtle enough to barely be noticeable. Your free will is all you need to remember. You will not succumb to anyone if you choose not to."

The atmosphere between us was charged. After he forced me to stab him we weren't quite on friendly terms, and we weren't solidly consumed by hatred anymore, either. With him looking like War and me Seduction, things were bound to become interesting during this lesson.

"So, what you're saying is to focus on my mind and will. Or imagine killing you to maintain command over my emotions. That should be easy enough." I smiled. "If I master tonight's lesson, I think you should agree to grovel before me. In fact, I'd love to see you on your knees, begging."

His attention drifted back over my bodice.

Tiny ribbons laced up the front. I harbored no illusions as to what he'd planned for such a dress, especially if our training was anything close to the last session. He would no doubt use demonic influence on me to undo each and every one of the bows. I wouldn't stop until I stood before him, clad only in the lace undergarments I wore beneath it.

Or maybe those were my own secret desires surfacing. I'd chosen those particular unmentionables with care.

"Greed is interested in wagers. I am not."

"Yet it sounds like your pride will take a blow if I win. Which is why you won't kneel before me. Perhaps you cannot stomach the idea of surrendering to anyone. Even your potential future wife."

"Make no mistake, Emilia. When I go to my knees before you, it will be to conquer, not surrender. If you harbor any doubts, I shall enjoy proving you wrong. Now unbuckle my armor."

His statement was laced with magical command.

I felt the slight tingling sensation he'd described as his demonic influence sought to take hold of my emotions, bending them to the demon prince's will. I was halfway across the weapons room before I shook myself out of the sinful grip. A tiny thrill went through me. I didn't need my magic to fight against him. Only my will.

"Unbuckle my armor, *now*. Then take your blade to my belt and cut it off."

This time, Wrath used the full strength of his power. Magic caressed me, urged me forward. His armor was undone and discarded in seconds.

I slipped my hand beneath my gown and removed the dagger hidden there in one swift motion. The blade was to his belt by the time I regained control.

Wrath's mouth pressed into a firm line. "You're distracted."

"I can't imagine why." I pretended to think on it. "Maybe it has to do with the invitation I received for the Feast of the Wolf. I've heard Gluttony's parties are legendary for their debauchery."

"Most gatherings are laden with sin and vice. It's the way of this realm, and why we're training. But that's not what you're worried about."

"I thought I was to have some small say in where the feast was thrown." I fiddled with the dagger. "I don't—I'm not looking forward to it."

"You'll be able to sense any emotional manipulation by then. And you will be equipped to break free of their influence should they behave poorly."

"It's not that, either."

He scanned my face. "It won't be pleasant, but it won't be the worst thing you'll live through."

"As always, you are exceptional with easing nerves. I..." I shook my head, then bent to replace my dagger in my thigh sheath. "It's not just the fear being ripped from me."

"My brothers will not hurt you."

"I don't know how to dance."

His brows raised. "You won't be forced to dance if you don't want to."

I didn't meet his gaze. Dancing would allow me an opportunity to spend time with each of his brothers. I imagined there would be some talking involved, and I didn't want my lack of refinement to impede my mission. Since I no longer could attempt to spell the wine, dancing and sipping a refreshment after would be perfect for conversation.

"You're probably right." I forced a smile. "It's silly to worry about."

Wrath didn't respond right away. He cocked his head to the side, eyes narrowed. "You danced at the bonfire the night you encountered Lust. You were magnificent then. I don't see why you'll have any trouble with a waltz."

I lifted a shoulder and turned my attention back to the table near us. Several strange daggers had been neatly lined up. They were solid black with one long piece cut out in the center of the hilt and the blade.

"Eight-inch throwing knives." Wrath moved to the table and plucked up a knife. "They are solid steel with a smooth handle as to not disturb your grip and are weighted in the front to make throwing more accurate. Would you like to practice?"

I ran a finger over the cool metal. "Yes."

"Take it by the bottom. We'll work on a spin technique."

I held it by the handle and aimed for the wooden target Wrath indicated at the far end of this section of the weapons rooms. It flew through the air, landing left of center, and fell to the ground. The demon prince nodded and handed me another blade. "The knife didn't stick because you're standing too close."

"How can you tell that?"

"When it spins, if the blade is angled down when it falls, it indicates you need to step back. Half of throwing knives and getting them to reach your target is all about where you're standing."

I shifted my stance, then repeated the steps. This time the hit came to the right of the red circle and stuck. A deep sense of elation went through me.

I held my hand out, waiting for the next blade, and was surprised to feel Wrath's fingers wrapping around mine instead. I twisted, confused.

"What are—"

"We're starting a new lesson." He gently pulled me closer. "Place one hand on my shoulder. And hold lightly to this one. Good." He angled our bodies, then straightened to his full height. "The movements are simple. We'll be dancing in a box shape. Step back on the ball of your right foot, and follow with your left. Keep them a foot apart as we move."

"We can't dance here."

"Of course we can."

We struck an odd pair. Without his armor, Wrath's chest was bare, his leather pants molded to his form, and I was dressed in crimson silk. He didn't seem to mind. He acted as if he were in the finest evening attire, too.

The warrior prince guided us slowly through the steps, keeping us shoulder-width apart as we swept back, to the sides and forward in a loose interpretation of a box.

I watched our feet, worried I'd step on his or get tangled up in his legs.

"Tilt your chin up so you can gaze adoringly into my eyes." He grinned down at my scowl. "I want you to focus on how handsome I am, how talented at dancing *and* killing, and forget everything else. Except for how much you want to kiss me."

I couldn't help myself; I laughed. "You're incorrigible."

"Perhaps." His voice turned low and seductive as his hand slid down to the small of my back, drawing me a little closer. "But you're waltzing like a goddess now."

The warmth of him, his praise, the hard muscle beneath my fingertips...all had me swaying nearer. Wrath placed his lips against my ear. "You're—"

"Is this a godsdamn ballroom now?" Anir propped himself against the doorjamb, arms crossed. A lazy grin spread across his face as he batted his lashes. "Will you be teaching this new technique to all of the soldiers, your highness, or just us pretty ones?"

With what appeared to be immense effort, Wrath tore his gaze from me, but didn't release us from our position. "A good fighter is skilled in weapons. A great fighter is skilled in dance. Perhaps I'll appoint you as the new dance master."

"While that sounds titillating, I do come with news from the dungeon." Anir pushed himself up from the spot where he'd casually leaned, his expression serious. "It's the mortal."

Wrath tensed. "What happened?"

Anir's attention slid to me. "He's asking for Emilia."

"Antonio?" I stepped away from Wrath, heart thundering. "He's here?"

TWENTY-ONE

I expected the dungeons of House Wrath to be subterranean. Unending darkness broken only by meager bits of torchlight set along desolate corridors. Stones damp with piss and other foul odors of the forgotten and damned permeating the very essence of the chambers. Screams of the tortured souls who were abominable enough to find themselves imprisoned in Hell. I'd convinced myself the wailing I'd heard out in the gardens originated from the cells.

Reality was much different.

We climbed a wide stone staircase in a tower, the air crisp and clean, while light poured in through a series of arched windows set high above. A lovely wooden door greeted us at the top. There were no guards stationed outside. No weapons trained on the murderer who was waiting—just beyond the pale stone walls—for his audience with the prince and possible princess of this House of Sin.

I gave Wrath an incredulous look. "You've left him unguarded?"

"The door is magicked shut. And also locks from the outside."
He placed his palm against the wood and it clicked open. "It's
spelled to open for the both of us."

I blinked slowly. I seemed to have lost the ability to speak.
Wrath either trusted me more than he let on, or he didn't consider
me a threat. It was foolish on his part to underestimate me.

I walked into the room and halted.

Antonio sat in a plush leather chair with a book and a
steaming cup of tea placed on a low table next to him. A throw
blanket was spread across his lap. He was in an alcove that over-
looked the snowcapped mountains of the realm. An ebony river
slithered through the land like a giant snake. The view was
breathtaking, and the room was far better than the dormitory
of the holy brotherhood. This prison cell was the height of cozy
comfort.

I wasn't certain I was breathing.

Antonio glanced up at our arrival, his brown eyes warm and
friendly. Gone was the previous hatred he'd gazed upon me with.
The disgust.

"Emilia. You came."

An overwhelming wave of anger washed over me at the sight
of his smile. The soft tone of his voice. Here was the human blade
who had killed my twin, lounging with a book and a warm drink.
As if he was on a lovely respite from the holy brotherhood instead
of suffering for his crimes. Wrath had been wise after all, keeping
his location secret from me.

I was halfway across the room before Wrath's arms circled my
waist and lifted me in the air. His touch did little to soothe the fire
in my veins.

I kicked out, trying to land a blow on the despicable human.

"Drop me at once! I'm going to murder him!"

Wrath held me against his body without giving any quarter. I bucked against him, wild with fury that was spiraling beyond control. In the back of my mind, I knew my reaction was extreme, but I had lost the ability to see reason.

All I could see was red.

The red of anger and the crimson of my twin's blood, puddled on the hard ground. Staining my hands as I slipped over it and lost any remaining sense of peace I'd know. Now I would take from him until he had nothing left. Until he met Vittoria's same fate. I'd rip his damned heart from his chest with my teeth if I had to.

Antonio dropped the book and pressed himself deep into the chair, his eyes wide. The only thing standing between him and a vicious attack was the demon. Irony was located in there.

"Do you recall what I said about your anger, my lady?"

The prince's low voice held a hint of teasing that doused the blazing inferno of rage. The fight left my body, only to be replaced by a different sort of tension.

Without letting me go, Wrath maneuvered us out into the corridor and kicked the door shut behind us. He carefully set me on my feet, my back against the cool stone, his arms casually placed on either side of my body.

A glimmer of amusement shone in his eyes as I leveled a glare at him.

"Master your temper, or we'll attempt this again tomorrow."

"This was a test."

"You're failing miserably."

Like he surmised I would. I inhaled deeply through my nose, then exhaled through my mouth. Just as he'd done the night we fought over the enchanted skulls. I repeated the exercise twice more before my emotions settled. "I'm calm now."

The corner of his mouth kicked up. "I find it fascinating that you continue to lie to my face, knowing full well I can sense each untruth. Rage makes for messy battle strategies. If you cannot control your fury, you risk getting hurt."

"Fine. I'm calmer. Though not for long if you keep poking at me."

"That creates quite the mental imagery."

And just as he'd intended, I was suddenly no longer thinking of murder, anger, or rage. A new pulse pounded through me that had little to do with my heart. My attention dropped to his wicked lips, noting the tantalizing curve of them. He hadn't used an ounce of magic or influence. This lust-filled emotion belonged only to me. And this realm and our provocative marriage bond.

Or maybe he wasn't the only one whose anger swiftly turned into passion.

Maybe it was an aphrodisiac for me, too. "You're wholly inappropriate."

"Lie." Wrath moved slowly, placing his body flush against mine. The physical contact was a welcome distraction from the anger still simmering inside me. I focused on the demon, on the heat not originating in fury. "I am your intended. And a living embodiment of sin, as you once called me. A certain amount of inappropriate behavior should be expected. Especially when the future princess of House Wrath is so appealing."

"You are a heathen. I just tried to murder a man."

"Precisely." He pressed his lips to my cheek. "Are you ready to try again?"

"To murder him?"

"I suggest talking, but you are free, as always, to choose your path."

"Murder, or at least a good thrashing, then."

"Try." Challenge rang in the single word. "We'll just end up out here again."

As if that was a deterrent. "You trust me?"

"It's more important for you to trust yourself." He pushed back from the wall. "Only you can decide how to move forward. What would you like to do?"

Dangerous question. I would like to open the murderer from gut to gullet and watch his stinking, steaming entrails spill across the floor. That answer wouldn't get me back inside. And, no matter how I'd felt moments before, I did not want to become someone I could no longer respect. Murdering a man, even one who'd violently killed my twin, would only put me on his level. Which was why Wrath had made me take the dagger to him the other night.

I knew how it felt, hurting someone. Blood would not stain my hands. Today.

Wrath waited silently, giving me time and space to decide my next move. His expression was perfectly bland, offering no judgment. No hint to his inner thoughts.

I rolled my shoulders, releasing the tension. "I'm ready to ask him about my sister."

"Emilia." Antonio jumped to his feet. "It's good to see you."

His tone indicated what he actually meant was "It's good to see you no longer snarling and kicking like a rabid beast trying to rip out my throat."

This meeting was young, though. There was still time for snarling and snapping. The leash I'd put on myself was already slipping. I did not return his tentative smile. Just because I'd decided against gutting him did not mean we would ever be friends again.

I moved carefully into the small tower chamber, feeling Wrath close behind. His trust only went so far, apparently. Smart demon.

"Is it? I would imagine initially it was like staring into the face of one of your victims. Only to discover they weren't dead after all."

There was a beat of silence that fell awkwardly between us.

"I cannot...words and apologies will never be enough to make up for what I did to you."

"What you did to Vittoria."

"O-of course." His throat bobbed. I almost believed the emotion was real. "I've been taking a tonic." He indicated the steaming mug on the small table. "The matron is talented with breaking enchantments."

I paused in the center of the room. Wrath was a shadow looming in my periphery. "Is that what you're claiming now? Magic was the true villain, not your hatred?"

Antonio watched me closely as he settled back onto his chair, his gaze never once straying to the demon prince behind me. He did not know I was unable to use magic, that my threats were all bark and no bite. His fear did something to me. Made me want to strike harder.

"Do you recall my trip to the village? Where they claimed a goddess was feasting with wolves in the spirit realm, and teaching them ways to protect themselves from evil?"

"Let me guess." My tone turned frosty. "You're claiming a

goddess actually descended upon that village and was the one who cursed you?"

"Emilia, my god." He looked affronted. "I didn't..."

"You expected forgiveness? Unearned mercy? You murdered my twin. You killed other innocent women. Instead of taking responsibility for your actions, you're telling me superstitious stories. Ones you were only too happy to claim as silly and unfounded, if I recall. Own your truth, admit your wrongs, and do not waste my time with old folktales or lies."

I spun on my heel and headed back to the door. I didn't trust the growing darkness of my temper. Wrath moved aside and let me pass, his expression still unreadable.

I turned at the threshold and looked at the man I'd once believed I'd loved. How young and foolish I'd been then. Antonio had devoted his life to the holy order and would never be half as honorable as the prince of Hell standing beside him.

"When you regain all of your memories, or whatever it is you're claiming the matron is helping you with, send for me then. But if you lie to me again, I will come for you. I will rip out your heart and feed it to the hellhounds. Wrath cannot stand guard and protect you forever."

Antonio pressed his lips together. "I know I must earn your forgiveness. Please, Emilia. Please visit me again soon. Let me prove I am trustworthy."

Hell was already frozen over, so I didn't point out it would take it thawing into the Garden of Eden for me to willingly seek out his friendship again.

I left Wrath in the tower and rushed back to my chambers, heading straight into the bathing room. I needed to soak away the experience of being in Antonio's filthy presence. I'd made it to the glass stool near my vanity when I heard the faint knock. "Come in."

"My lady, I'm Harlow. I'm to tend to you when you need assistance."

I glanced up from where I sat, pinning up my long hair. A young demon maid—with lavender skin and snow-colored hair—nervously stood in the doorway. I took a deep breath and released it. I refused to let my bad mood taint the rest of my evening.

"It's lovely to meet you, Harlow. You don't need to trouble yourself, though. I can manage preparing for my bath." She bit her lip, eyes darting to the sunken tub. I wondered if my refusal came across as an insult instead of an attempt at being friendly. I forced a smile. "If you could add some oils and soap to the water, that would be nice."

"Straight away." Harlow rushed into the room, her expression brightening. "I'll go fetch a length of linen and leave it on the side for you to dry off after you bathe, Lady Emilia."

"Thank you."

The maid bobbed a quick curtsy, then exited the room. I knew Wrath had said that servants didn't expect to be thanked for their jobs, but it felt strange to ignore anyone's efforts at bringing comfort. She tended to the water, laid out the linen towel, then quietly left me alone.

I slipped the silk dressing gown off my shoulders and hung it on a crystal hook near the vanity. Candles in the chandelier flickered with my movements, adding a sense of serenity to the already lovely bathing room.

After the burst of fury that had consumed all rational thought brought on by Antonio, this was exactly what I needed. Time to simply breathe and soak and let go of the anger.

I stepped down into the warm water, the perfumed oils rising up with the steam. Between the aches that crept up from my lessons with Anir and the tension that had coiled in my body from Antonio, the water felt like heaven.

I submerged myself up to my neck, leaning back against the lip of the enormous sunken tub. I was trying to empty my mind and emotions. Each time I replayed what Antonio said about the goddess and the shape-shifters, I felt that unsettling murderous rage flare up.

Once the initial fury passed, I tried to pick it apart. I didn't believe him. But perhaps he *hadn't* been influenced by a demon. It was possible a witch crossed his path and pretended to be a goddess. Or was it a matter of two mortals being influenced with demon magic? Maybe the person who came to him as the angel of death had been another victim. It would be clever of the demon to never actually be seen by Antonio. Then he'd never be able to identify them.

After my lessons with Wrath, I knew how hard it was to fight off a magical attack, but I still found forgiveness and sympathy to be out of reach. Part of me hated to admit that, even to myself. When I got that furious . . . it felt as if I left my body and all sense of humanity was replaced with elemental rage. I sunk against the tub, drained both emotionally and physically.

I must have drifted off; the sound of the door creaking open jarred me awake.

No footsteps or sounds of the maid's return rustled in the suite.

An uncomfortable feeling prickled along my skin. I was not

alone in the chamber. Someone was watching me. Someone who was not identifying themselves.

"Harlow?"

A length of linen tightened around my neck. My fingers flew to the material as my airflow ceased. I thrashed in the tub, splashing water in violent waves. A strangled sound escaped my lips, but it wasn't loud enough to alert anyone of the assassination attempt. My throat burned, white spots filtered in at the edge of my vision. Panic made me buck.

Then I remembered the one item I hadn't removed for my bath.

My hand shot below the water and emerged with the slim dagger Wrath had gifted me. With one final burst of energy, I thrust my arm back and felt vicious glee as the blade sunk into soft flesh. The intruder gasped and dropped the garrote.

In the seconds it took for me to wrench the fabric from my throat and spin around, they were gone. The only sign that anything had happened was the obscene amount of blood leading to the door. I calmly got to my feet and pulled on a dressing gown. Then I called for a servant to fetch Wrath. All the while my pulse pounded in my ears. Someone had tried to murder me. And I'd stabbed them. Someplace vital if the amount of blood on the floor was any indication.

I couldn't muster an ounce of regret. Or perhaps I was simply numb from shock.

One thing didn't escape my notice, though. Thanks to Envy's curse for stealing the book of spells, I had no magic to defend myself against the attack. No power aside from the physical blow I'd struck with the dagger.

Wrath appeared in a cloud of smoke and glittering black light, rage etched into his ice-cold features. "Are you injured?"

"No." I pointed to the blood on the tile. "But the same isn't true for the assailant."

Wrath scanned me first, his attention catching on my neck. His expression turned thunderous. I imagined a red welt was forming. The very foundation of the castle vibrated.

"Do you wish to accompany me?"

I glanced at my hands, at the dagger I still held, coated in blood. Perhaps it made me weak, but I couldn't bring myself to witness what was about to occur. I shook my head, not meeting Wrath's gaze. If there were a House Cowardice, I'd probably be queen of it.

"It takes enormous strength to acknowledge your limits, Emilia." His hand trailed from my temple to my chin, then gently lifted it so I looked at him. "A true leader delegates. Just as you're doing now. Never doubt your courage. I certainly don't."

Dropping his hand from my face, Wrath finally glanced at the blood.

He prowled toward it, an almighty predator on the hunt, and didn't utter another word before he disappeared, House dagger gripped in hand, looking like a nightmare made flesh.

And, to whoever had just attacked me in his House, I supposed that's exactly what he was. May the goddesses grant the assailant a swift death—Wrath certainly wouldn't.

TWENTY-TWO

I took a loaf of bread from a tray of freshly baked offerings and brought it to my oversized wooden cutting board. Two heads of garlic, a generous portion of basil, pecorino, pignoli, and olive oil all joined my station. The cook was just finishing up when I'd arrived and informed me that Wrath had the ingredients brought in from the mortal world for me.

Apparently, he'd also had seeds purchased and planted in the castle's greenhouse so I'd have all my familiar herbs and vegetables at my disposal. A touch of magic helped them along, according to the cook, and there was a veritable bounty awaiting me whenever I'd like to tour the indoor garden. I rooted around in the icebox and pulled out a hunk of what tasted like goat cheese, then donned an apron I'd found hanging on a peg with an army of clean linens.

Cooking relaxed me. When I was in a kitchen my problems faded away. There was only me and a dish, the scents and sounds and satisfaction of creating something nurturing and delicious overtaking all else. There were no murders. No lost loved ones. No liars or secret keepers. I knew nothing of assassination attempts or marriages brought about by a spell gone wrong. I felt joy, peace. And serenity was something I desperately needed at the moment.

I cut off the top of one head of garlic, exposing all of the cloves, drizzled olive oil over them, covered it with a tin can, then placed it in the oven to roast. I turned my attention to the basil, pine nuts, garlic, and olive oil.

Chopping, mixing, pouring all of my love and energy into the sauce, erasing the rest of the night from my thoughts. It wasn't denial, only a brief respite I sought.

I'd just finished making pesto when I felt his presence. I continued working, waiting for him to speak. I didn't know whether I was eager for him to have found my attacker, or if I suddenly wanted to pretend the night hadn't happened at all. When several moments passed, I finally glanced up. "Is there something you needed to tell me?"

Wrath leaned against the end of the table I worked at, his arms and feet crossed. The picture of casual calm. I noticed he'd changed into a new shirt and his hair was slightly damp. "There is little I need. But much I want."

"I'm not going back to that room tonight."

"I didn't ask you to." He straightened and moved to my side, nodding at the loaf of bread. "May I help?"

I peered at him from the corner of my eye. "There's not much left to do, but you can pour us some wine. Red would be nice."

"Red it is."

He left and returned a breath later, bottle and glasses in hand. He rummaged in the icebox and brought over a container of blackberries. After uncorking the bottle, he added a few berries to each glass, then set mine next to where I sliced bread.

I laid the bread slices on a baking sheet and drizzled olive oil across the tops. I set them inside the oven and adjusted the little timer before taking a sip of wine. Wrath clinked his glass against mine, his gaze content. "May we always feast after spilling the blood of our enemies."

I smiled at him over my glass. "You're a barbarian."

"You defended yourself. If being proud makes me a barbarian, so be it."

"Do you think I killed him?"

He swirled the liquid in his glass, his attention riveted to it. "Would it matter if you did?"

"Of course it matters. I don't want to be a murderer."

"Defending yourself is not the same as attacking without cause or reason."

"Which, by your refusal to answer, I'm assuming means I did."

"You do not bear the burden of that demon's death, Emilia." Wrath set his glass down and faced me, his expression hard. "I do." The smile that tipped up the edges of his mouth was not warm or friendly. It was cold, calculating. Designed to frighten, to call forth fear and seduce it. "Here I am, the very essence of evil and sin. Am I the monster you feared?"

I looked at him—really, truly looked. There was nothing overtly indicative of his emotions in his face, but there was *something* in the way he'd asked the question that made me carefully formulate my response. He did not want me to think he was a monster.

And, goddess curse me, I didn't. I met and held his gaze. "Did he suffer?"

"Not nearly enough."

"Were you able to get information from him?"

Wrath shook his head. "His tongue was recently severed. It appears to have been a choice he made, likely in case he was caught."

I don't know what madness came over me, but I put my wine down and moved to where Wrath stood rigidly, awaiting judgment. Slowly, as if approaching an animal ready to bolt, I wound my arms around his waist and laid my head against his chest.

For several long moments, he barely breathed. Then, he wrapped his arms around me and rested his chin atop my head. We stayed there, holding each other, until the little windup clock dinged. Even then I didn't let go right away. This demon, this living embodiment of sin, was so much more than the monster he was supposed to be.

I pulled back gradually, and rolled up onto my toes, pressing my lips to his cheek in a chaste kiss. "Thank you."

Without giving him an opportunity to respond, I hurried to the oven and removed the toast and roasted garlic. I placed them both on the cutting board, then added the hunk of goat cheese and the bowl of pesto. I grabbed two small dishes and stuck a butter knife near each item on the board. I smiled down at my work, pleased beyond measure with the outcome.

"You'll have to serve yourself, but it's easy." I took a slice of toast and smeared a few roasted garlic cloves across it like jam. "Next spread some goat cheese on top of the garlic. And finally"—I added a generous spoonful of pesto—"top it off with the pesto."

Wrath watched me work, then picked up a slice of toast and made his. He took a bite and his attention slid to me. "I think I like this almost more than the sweets you made."

"That's high praise indeed, coming from the cannoli king." I grinned at him. "Sometimes I'll add a poached egg if I have any leftovers from breakfast or lunch. Vittoria likes to—"

I abruptly stopped speaking and set my snack aside.

Wrath lightly touched my elbow, drawing me back to the present. "What is it?"

"I miss her."

"Your twin."

"Yes, desperately. Sometimes, for a second, I forget she's gone. Then it all comes back. Part of me feels terrible for forgetting. And the other part wants to lash out. Lately it seems like I'm at war with myself, and I can't decide which part will win."

"I have no personal experience with death, but I know that's normal for some mortals."

"I wonder, though." I looked him in the eye. "I've been consumed with rage and anger since her murder. The intensity of those emotions doesn't scare me, which *does* frighten me. I never used to be like this. Then tonight...tonight, when that demon tried to kill me, I wasn't scared. I was furious. I wanted to inflict pain. One of my first thoughts after the fact wasn't terror, it was anger that I hadn't been taught dark magic."

"Your mortal family should have taught you to protect yourself."

I inhaled deeply. I might as well lay all of my fears out. After the events of the evening, I needed to purge the dark feelings from my whole person. "Sometimes I worry that it's not the devil who's cursed. But me."

Wrath went still. "Why would you believe that?"

"My twin was murdered. My grandmother attacked. My parents were held hostage by Envy. And yet what has happened to me? Aside from tonight's assassination attempt, I mean." I searched his face for answers. "Maybe I'm cursed and everyone I love is in danger. What if I'm the villain? One who's so vicious, so terrible, I was punished to forget? What if the witches who were murdered started to remember? Maybe I am the monster and I don't even know it."

Wrath was silent for an uncomfortably long time. When I'd started to feel foolish for sharing so many fears with him, he said softly, "Or maybe they all dabbled in pursuits they shouldn't have. And you're the one picking up the pieces of their mistakes."

Demonberry wine dribbled over my chin and spilled onto my sleeveless gown, but I didn't stop guzzling it from the bottle to bother wiping the mess from my face. The magical sensation holding me in its thrall vanished. I set the bottle down, seriously contemplating throwing it across the table. Wrath gave me a smug grin.

He'd had a large, gilded table and two plush chairs brought into the weapons room. More thrones that weren't thrones. Complete with metal serpents—not quite gold or silver, but in between— making up the outer rim of the seats.

Gold platters of fruits and desserts and whipped creams and rich, savory foods covered every inch of the cloth-covered table. Some dishes towered so high they toppled over, spilling onto the floor. It was a despicable waste.

I shook my head. "This is shameful."

"The puppies will feast like royalty."

"Puppies." I snorted. "You mean those three-headed hell-hounds?"

"Need I remind you that *you* asked for us to train. Stop avoiding the lesson."

"Considering the fact I do not drink to excess, I'm not sure what I'm supposed to be learning from this little session. There must be something more useful you can teach me."

"Allow me to try harder to prove the point."

I should have known better than to assume the prince would take it easy on me during our training session the next night. He seemed to toy with lust, envy, wrath, and sloth the most, but tonight he exposed me to the sin of gluttony. Everything from my clothing, to the jewels I wore, to the rich meal we'd picked at, to the wine I drank spoke of overindulgence.

I *had* sent him a note, requesting our lessons to resume. After the assassination attempt, I was even more determined to protect myself from the demon princes. I was struggling to find the value in drinking wine to excess, and how that skill was going to aid my endeavors.

Wrath poured an enormous goblet and handed it to me. It was the third time he'd done so. And that wasn't counting the two bottles of demonberry wine I'd already consumed over the last hour or two.

It was getting harder to fight off the demonic influence, or even sense that slight tingle that indicated magic was being used on me. I inhaled deeply, breathing through the wave of dizziness. I'd only ever gotten drunk on wine once before, but I recognized the signs.

"Drink this all as quickly as you can. Then pour another and do the same."

His magic grazed the back of my senses. I gritted my teeth

and focused on how annoyed I was. He grinned over a platter of chocolate-covered berries. Then his power overwhelmed me.

I held it at bay for another strained moment, then gulped down the goblet.

My head spun and my vision doubled. I swiped at my mouth, grinning like an idiot, and poured another drink. Wine sloshed from the goblet onto the floor. My silk slippers looked like I'd been traipsing through a murder scene, but I couldn't care less.

The more he influenced me to drink, the more impossible it was becoming to concentrate on my free will. Which, through my drunken stupor, finally made sense.

His brothers could nudge me toward drinking, and in turn, a slow inebriation would make it nearly impossible to stave off their influence. The more out of control I became, the easier it would be for them to slip past my defenses. Wrath had a point after all.

He wasn't just trying to have me fight off gluttony.

I pushed out of my seat and tripped my way over to the demon's side of the table, the empty glass dangling from my fingertips. He'd had me dress in a long, extravagant silver gown made of silk. It was luxurious to the point of excess. I wore no undergarments and the material did not hide any part of my form. With the wine soaking through the front of the bodice, I might as well have been waltzing around naked. I doubted he'd planned for that.

Wrath hadn't so much as dropped his gaze below my neckline. Ever the proper gentleman. At least when he wasn't ripping out tongues or torturing would-be assassins to death.

Heavy strands of diamonds hung around my neck. There were so many in varying lengths, it felt as if I was carrying an extra five pounds around my throat. It was so excessive, even Envy would be appalled instead of jealous.

I leaned precariously over Wrath, my face close to his. I wanted to kiss him. Possibly break a bottle and stab him first. But then definitely kiss him.

"You're getting me drunk on purpose." I gave him what I thought was a saucy grin. "Naughty demon."

"Being under the influence of alcohol or other substances will greatly reduce your ability to sense a prince of Hell's magic. Especially Gluttony's. He will push you to drink little by little until you lose control and he can take over." His tone turned harsh. "You need to fight back."

I was trying to pay attention to the lesson, but I was fascinated by the shape of his lips when he spoke. I reached over and touched them. He pressed them into a firm line.

"Emilia. Focus."

"Oh, I promise I am. I am *extremely* focused at the moment. Enthralled. Or is it enchanted?" I drew my attention up. There were two of him, glowering. I blinked until only one annoyed demon remained. "Why haven't you seduced me?"

It was difficult to be sure, but I thought he removed his influence.

"If you cannot battle through the haze of alcohol, then it's best to avoid drinking anything at the feast. You may accept a toast, but only pretend to sip it."

"You worry too much." I smoothed the furrow between his brows. "Nonna says all of the steam from the kitchen will keep wrinkles away. Vittoria and I will remain ageless. Like you."

"Considering you're not human, I imagine there's truth in that."

"You never answered my question. About seduction." I swayed a little on my feet. His lap looked comfortable enough. I

297

plopped onto it. His body tensed, but he didn't lift me. I internally grinned at that small victory. "Fauna said the whole court would like to know."

"Lady Fauna talks too much. Perhaps I ought to insist she visit a distant relative."

"Don't take your foul mood out on her; she was only passing along gossip to me. And I'd like to know, too. Maybe I want you to seduce me now." I leaned on his shoulder and rested my chin in my palm, gazing at him. Belatedly, I realized I must look like a mad person, staring the way I was in our current position. "You know, some believe avoidance is a sign of cowardice."

"I'm aware of what you're doing, and it won't work." His scowl deepened. "I am not seducing you because I currently do not wish to. It's as simple as that."

If he'd stuck *me* in the heart with a knife, it might hurt less.

I twisted around and pulled the plate of chocolate-covered berries to me. I added a dollop of whipped cream to them and speared one with a fork. I missed. The fork connected with the dish. A berry catapulted across the table. Goddess-cursed things.

It was definitely their tiny, round forms, and not my current state of inebriation.

I took aim and squinted at the plate. Berries were swimming. They were no match for me. I aimed again and another berry went flying. I swore roundly.

Wrath's deep exhale tickled my bare shoulder as he reached around and took the fork from me. He stabbed a chocolate-covered berry and swirled it into the whipped cream.

He paused with the fork to my mouth.

"If you so much as breathe *one* word of this, I vow revenge, my lady."

"Very well. Though I doubt I'll even remember this extreme act of chivalry in the morning."

I leaned against his shoulder, head thrown back, and waited for him to feed me the dessert. With only a fraction of hesitation, he did. I swore the food tasted sweeter. I felt like a pampered Roman goddess as he fed me one decadent berry at a time.

"Mmm. I can hardly recall a word of what we were saying already."

"Liar." He set the fork down and brought his mouth close to my ear, suddenly taking the lobe between his teeth. Heat spread through me and my toes curled from the sensation. I wasn't sure if Wrath had done it, but any inebriation I felt vanished. "Then again, so am I. In a sense."

TWENTY-THREE

Wrath trailed a line of searing kisses down my neck, igniting my desire.

The chocolate-covered berries were forgotten. There was a new indulgence being served. And I'd gladly take my fill of this pleasant delight. I'd asked for seduction, and the prince was delivering. His hands drifted along the silhouette of my body, pausing to rest on my waist.

It didn't feel possessive as much as it seemed like he was holding himself in check. Or maybe he was contemplating clever ways to slowly torture me. He fiddled with the clasp on one of my necklaces. The excessive strands of diamonds were hardly a barrier, but I wanted them gone all the same. I wanted nothing between us.

He brought his mouth to my body again and my mind emptied of all else.

I tossed my head back, lost in ecstasy as his tongue smoothed over the sharp little nip he'd given me. He pulled me against him, his teeth now lightly scraping where my shoulder and neck connected. Chills danced over my body in the most tantalizing way.

This feeling…it was not sinful, as mortals tried teaching their daughters. It was natural. Blissful. If it was socially acceptable for Wrath to take a lover, then the same right should be afforded to me.

After all, there were two people involved in such encounters.

I arched into his touch. I owned this desire, enjoyed it. And it did not make me lustful or wanton. It made me feel human, in control of my wants. Denying my passions no longer.

I braced myself with a hand on each of his thighs, gripping him as he lavished all his attention and kisses on my neck, my shoulders. I wanted to spin around and face him, needing to explore his body as languidly. For some reason, even with my newfound conviction, I hesitated.

"Is there something you want from me, my lady?"

"You don't have to call me that when we're alone. There's no need for a show."

He smiled against my neck. "Any other requests?"

"I…"

"Assert your wants. You need not apologize for them."

"Even if I want you to stop?"

"Especially then."

"Take my diamonds off. Please."

The prince undid each strand of precious stones, letting them clink to the ground.

"I'm curious." His voice was velvet soft as he leaned in and removed the final necklace. "About the Sin Corridor. What you experienced that night you called out my name. Tell me."

There was no magical command or demonic thrall attached to his request. Only genuine curiosity. I realized the feeling of dizziness brought on by drinking was also gone. I was no longer under the influence of anything, save being drunk on my own passions, and hadn't been since before he first kissed me.

Maybe it was our current position—the fact I didn't have to see his face—that made my confession easier. Or perhaps I simply did not wish to feel guilt or shame regarding my body and the things I wanted and craved. I gathered up my courage, knowing precisely where this admission would lead. Praying for it to travel that path, really.

"You were...you were behind me, like this. Except we were laying down."

He rewarded my honesty with a gentle stroke along my arm. "And?"

"I was wearing your shirt and you were unbuttoning it. So slowly I was going mad."

"I imagine you demanded I remove it." His fingertips ghosted across my shoulder, then my clavicle, before dipping lower, teasing the skin exposed above my décolletage. My breath hitched as he paused his ministrations, one hand slipping beneath a strap of my gown. Only the thin scrap of silk stood between us. "And I obliged. Is that correct?"

"More or less."

"Would you like me to do the same now?" With only the slightest pause, I nodded. "I need to hear the words, Emilia. Do you wish for me to stop?"

"No." My grip on his thighs tightened as if I could keep him there forever. "No, I do not."

He moved my hair aside and leaned back in his chair, allowing enough space between us for him to lightly massage my shoulders. Gripping one strap in each hand, he pressed his lips to my spine, kissing me there as he slipped the top of my gown off.

Cool air blew across my flushed skin.

"What happened next?"

Fantasy and reality were colliding. My breaths quickened in anticipation. "You wanted me to tell you that you are my favorite sin."

His chuckle was low, deep. It made me ache for him all the more. "Am I?"

"At the moment, yes."

"You didn't confess it then."

I heard the question even though he hadn't phrased it that way.

"No." My eyes fluttered shut before I opened them again. "You started touching me and I could think of nothing else."

He nuzzled the back of my neck before reaching around to cup my breasts. Heat shot through me. His fingers traced the outer curves, circling closer to the peaks in the center. When he brushed across them, they hardened. My breath caught as I sunk my teeth into my lower lip. I inched back, craving more of his heat, and noticed how affected he was.

"Tell me what I did in your illusion that made you call for me."

I flushed. There was no way I'd tell him about *that* part. I closed my eyes and gathered my resolve, forcing myself to not be embarrassed. With renewed confidence I allowed myself the freedom of letting go. "You were gently pulling me against your arousal and your hand slipped under my skirts. You touched me. There. With your fingers."

"Did it feel as it did in the Crescent Shallows?"

"Almost. It felt incredible, for a mere moment. Then I awoke."

"Before you climaxed?"

"I...believe so."

"Allow me the honor of making that up to you now."

He didn't move right away, and I realized he was waiting for my consent. Wrath would never take without permission. "Please."

"With pleasure."

He slipped one hand beneath the silk gown and his light touch slid over my calf, against my inner thigh, then slowly traced circular patterns there, roving a bit higher with each daring stroke, until I could no longer stand it. I stopped pressing my knees together and he dragged a finger across the apex of my body. It felt better than the Sin Corridor and Crescent Shallows combined.

Wrath pressed me forward until I was nearly bent over him, then trailed kisses down my spine. My skin tingled with each pass of his lips. All the while his fingers teased and danced across my body, driving me into a frenzy.

Once I was convinced I'd perish from the pleasure, he slipped them inside me. I stilled, getting accustomed to the feel of it as he slowly began moving them.

Unable to handle how good each sensation was, I sat up and pushed against him, his arousal hard and welcome against my backside. He paused his kisses and gently bit my neck.

My breathing quickened. I was chasing a feeling, almost familiar and not quite. It was magnificent. Ecstasy unlike any other. Sensing my growing need, Wrath's fingers moved faster and that ache turned into the most glorious tidal wave of euphoria.

I stopped being self-conscious and shut out thoughts of everything except that incredible feeling. I moved against him, chasing the rapture, realizing Wrath was now letting me take my own pleasure. I was setting the pace and moving as fast or slow as I wished. That I was in command of my own body, my own desires, that no mortal rules would bind me...

...I came undone.

I cried out as pleasure broke through my body, in one marvelous tingling wave after another, then finally slumped against his chest, breathing as if I'd just run for my life.

Once I stopped trembling from the release, Wrath slowly removed his hand from beneath my skirts and righted the top of my gown. A long beat of silence stretched between us as I adjusted the straps with more care and attention than was necessary.

I shifted in his lap, noticing his arousal hadn't abated. My heartbeat sped up. We could complete one of the next steps of accepting our marriage bond in moments.

Right here. In the weapons room. Only his trousers and my gown lay between us. And they could be removed easily enough. Perhaps it was the euphoria still running through my veins, clouding my senses, but it didn't seem like such a terrible idea.

If a ceremony was needed as the final step, we didn't have to perform it. We could indulge in carnal pleasure and remain free from any bond that would tether us for eternity. I shifted in such a way that our bodies intimately rubbed together. The sensation it created, especially after the pleasure he'd just wrought from me, was a new level of rapture.

Wrath didn't move. He was giving me leave to choose.

I grabbed the hem of my skirts and slowly brought them up, over my thighs, my ass. Now all Wrath had to do was release himself from his trousers. I sat back, and the friction of his arousal against my body had me swallowing a moan. His hands tightened on my hips.

A bolt of alarm shot through me, stealing my breath. I no longer knew if sleeping together was a good idea, or if my judgment was impaired from what we'd just done. It was probably nerves. I steeled myself, refusing to succumb to second-guessing anything.

"Our training for this evening is done."

In one swift motion Wrath stood, bringing us both to our feet. I spun around, staring at him. He was wholly unreadable. *"Training?* That's how you'd describe what just happened?"

"You asked for seduction. I obliged." He bent at the waist, offering a polite bow. "Now that you know what you enjoy, you may find the same pleasure at your own hand. Good night."

TWENTY-FOUR

"**He said what?**" Fauna's eyes were as big as saucers. She looped her arm through mine and escorted us out onto a covered pathway. "Maybe you misheard him. Or misinterpreted his meaning. That's possible. Isn't it?"

"Of all the things he could have said after that moment." I exhaled, my breath clouding in the frosty morning air. I was too annoyed to be embarrassed. After the incident in the weapons room, I hadn't seen Wrath for the rest of the night. "I well and truly loathe that demon."

My friend snorted but held her tongue. We strolled across one of the long stretches of covered parapets that surrounded the castle. Guards nodded from their stations on the wall as we passed. Once we were far enough away, Fauna leaned in. "Perhaps he only said it because he'll be envisioning you doing that from now on."

"Doubtful. He couldn't remove himself from the room fast enough."

"I bet all of House Greed that he took himself in hand last night and thought of you while he spilled his seed."

Even with my newfound confidence in owning my desires and feeling no shame, my face heated from the openness with which Fauna discussed such private matters.

She'd called on me first thing in the morning and managed to wrangle what had been troubling me before I'd donned my velvet cloak. Fauna hadn't blushed or batted an eye at the topic, one that would have caused shock and scandal back home. She'd simply asked if I'd returned the favor with either my hand or my mouth, then giggled wildly when I'd asked for clarification on the latter.

"Maybe he didn't want to take you in the weapons room where anyone could walk in. You are to be his wife. It's not out of the question that he'd protect you from prying eyes."

"Please." I nearly snorted. "Half this realm is content to fornicate in public. I doubt he'd let someone walking in on us deter him."

He certainly hadn't minded an audience when we'd ended up in the corridor outside our rooms. I gritted my teeth at the memory. Facing him after that encounter hadn't been awkward. The same could not be said for when I saw him next. I had no idea how to act.

"Actually, public rendezvous are not as common outside of House Lust and House Gluttony. Sure, other princes show off debauchery on occasion, like Greed and his gaming hell, but not to the extent as those particular Houses. His highness may want you to be certain you're choosing him with a clear head. Perhaps he wasn't sure that's what *you* wanted and he left before he did something he thought you'd regret."

Frustration built in my chest. "Lifting my skirts was a clear indication of my wants. If he wishes to secure the marriage bond, he's not convincing me that's something *he* wants."

"From what you described, my lady, it sounds like physical attraction is not the issue."

I halted in my tracks. I had no idea why this was this getting under my skin. Regardless of what transpired the night before, *I* still did not want to secure our bond. The thought that he felt the same shouldn't consume my thoughts. Especially when I had a hundred other things to be concerned with. Like the fast-approaching Feast of the Wolf.

I shook off the annoyance and proceeded toward the tower with my friend. "Enough talk of princes for now. I don't want the matron to overhear us and report back to Wrath."

Fauna laughed. "That, I can promise, will likely never happen."

"I take it their animosity isn't new."

"Not at all." Fauna pulled us to a stop, then glanced around. "Rumor claims it's centuries old. Some say her daughter was cursed and the prince did nothing to save her."

"Is her daughter in the castle?"

"That's just it... no one knows. There is speculation that his highness banished her from this circle. For a time, at least. It's possible the matron retrieved her and has her hidden somewhere."

For some reason goose bumps rose along my skin. I thought of the wailing that floated up from below the statue of the woman and the serpent. I couldn't imagine Wrath punishing someone by sending them deep underground. Perhaps that was because *he* hadn't done it.

Even though I hardly knew her, I didn't doubt the matron could have done something like that. Especially if it wasn't to punish, but to protect.

Maybe the wailing, miserable creature I'd heard was her missing daughter. And if the matron brought her daughter back and kept her locked away, I was even more curious to know why. Wrath knew everything that went on in his circle, and I doubted the matron would keep this secret from him for long. Which indicated she was hiding her daughter from another prince.

A new suspicion entered my thoughts. This story was similar to another I'd heard. One that involved La Prima Strega and her daughter. The First Witch was rumored to have cursed the devil because her daughter fell in love with him and they refused to give each other up.

Was the Matron of Curses and Poisons actually the First Witch?

If she was and she'd cursed the devil, I wanted to know why she was currently in Wrath's castle, claiming to be someone else. He must know her true identity. Which meant he also knew what she'd done to his brother, and would explain their hatred and history. So why, then, would he be willing to keep her secret, unless she knew one of his? And if that was the case, it had to be a secret so wicked he'd be willing to strike a bargain with a sworn enemy.

Given what he'd done to save me, that didn't seem so unbelievable.

"Daughter of the Moon. Lady Fauna." Celestia opened her door before I finished knocking. I hid my smile. Wrath would be furious she'd answered so quickly. "How may I be of service to you?"

"I have a few questions. About curses."

Her delight appeared genuine. "By all means. You've come to the right place. Come in."

I walked into the tower chamber and was immediately hit with the pleasing aroma of herbs and oils. I swallowed the pang of homesickness, the sudden reminder of Nonna Maria making spell candles in our small family kitchen. *My family was safe.* And I would finish what I set out to do and get back to make more happy memories with them. Soon.

I wrenched myself into the present. Celestia moved across the chamber and pulled books and pots off of stools, making room for us to sit around her prep table. While she did that, my attention shifted to items I'd missed during my first visit.

The matron had even more strange and curious things in her collection. From corked jars filled with blinking eyes, to baskets of bird beaks, one overflowing with claws, and another bin stuffed with feathers. Pots of salves and ointments and lotions of all kinds.

A bird skull with runes carved into it was placed on top of a pile of leather-bound books.

She noticed what caught my attention and nodded to it. "Ravens symbolize many things. Death, healing, fertility. Wisdom."

"And the runes?" I drifted closer but did not touch the carvings or the remains. If she was the First Witch, she might have enchanted the skulls and sent them to me. I was unsure if she was trying to help, or if my theory was wildly wrong. She might be exactly who she claimed, and I was forcing together puzzle pieces that didn't fit. "Do they animate the skull?"

"No." Celestia eyed me with what appeared to be suspicion. If she *was* the First Witch, she was directly birthed from a goddess. I wasn't sure if she could sense emotions like Wrath could, but I did my best to keep calm. "They come to me when I meditate over the skull. I etch what the raven wishes me to see. Arcane symbols can be a powerful ally to those with magic in their blood."

Fauna shifted uncomfortably, her attention riveted to the jars tapping with unseen forces on the far side of the chamber. I glanced back to the matron and lowered my voice. "Can they be used to enhance Source?"

"For witches, yes. For those who *are* Source, no. Arcane symbols originate from their essence."

"Those who . . . you mean the goddesses."

Celestia nodded, her gaze sharp as she studied my face.

According to Nonna's legends, the goddesses were the original source of our power, diluted over time through the First Witch's descendants.

I looked the silver-and-lavender-haired woman over carefully. Her face was lightly lined, but there was no clear indication of her age. Fauna had mentioned that her animosity with Wrath was centuries old, which meant she was likely immortal. The shade of purple in her hair also did not escape my notice. It was the same color of my tattoo with Wrath, and also when I saw *luccicare*, the faint aura surrounding humans.

I couldn't tell if it was excitement or fear pumping through my veins.

"So if a witch uses arcane symbols with their spells, it increases the potency of that spell."

"Correct."

I slid my focus to Fauna, who was squinting into a cauldron now. "Is it possible for anyone to enchant a skull and send a message? Perhaps a prince of Hell, or a witch."

"All is possible; whether it's probable is another story. Those with knowledge of arcane symbols might be able to do such a thing." Celestia motioned for me to sit. "Were there any symbols carved onto the bone?" I shook my head. "Then I doubt a demon prince or witch was responsible. It was likely someone much closer to Source."

Someone like the First Witch. I kept my breathing even, unwilling to alert anyone to my heightened emotions. If Celestia was the First Witch and her daughter was cursed, that meant the devil's first wife wasn't dead after all. And if she truly lived, then I was definitely right about the witches on my island being murdered for a different reason.

One that had nothing to do with the devil seeking a bride.

And everything to do with revenge.

"Lady Emilia?" Fauna broke into my spiraling thoughts. "Shall we go back to the main palace?"

"Yes." I stood, then spun around to face the matron. "One last question. The Curse Tree. I've been told it grants more than wishes, that it offers knowledge. How would one go about obtaining information instead of a wish or a hex?"

Fauna's attention shot to me like an arrow, but I ignored it. Celestia narrowed her eyes.

"Carve the true name of the one you seek information about into the trunk. Then take one leaf from the tree. Careful when you do—the leaves are as fragile as glass. When you desire the truth, break the leaf in the presence of the one whose name you carved."

I thought about the First Witch, of legends and fables we'd been told. None had ever used her name. "What if I'm unsure of the person's true name? Will their title work?"

"Names *have* power. Titles are a *show* of power. One can be taken or given on a whim, the other cannot." Celestia smiled in a way that set my nerves on edge. "Was there anything else, *my lady*?"

The way she said "my lady" drove home her point. It was a courtesy title, something given that held little meaning outside of this realm. My name was different. Aside from my first name, I would only be a princess or lady here. On my island I would forever remain Emilia Maria di Carlo unless I married. And only my surname would change, never my first.

"No, thank you. You've been most . . . informative."

TWENTY-FIVE

I gently placed another book on the floor. Haven, the heavenly counterpart to Wrath's personal Hell below, appeared as if a storm had raged through its rainbow-colored shelves. I snagged another ancient tome and flipped through it, mindful of the delicate pages.

The books in this library were all written in Latin, so I understood most of what was in them. Not that it helped my situation.

"Blood and bones."

Another grimoire, another disappointment. There were no records of the First Witch, though that could have been due to the fact I didn't know her true name. In Palermo, Wrath had said something along the lines of "the First Witch, as you call her," which meant that was not the name the demon princes knew her by. If I couldn't find something soon, I'd have to ask him. Which I'd prefer to avoid for several reasons. The first being if he knew La Prima was here and was harboring her, I wasn't sure if he would thwart my efforts at uncovering that mystery.

I'd searched for records of Celestia, but there was no mention of the Matron of Curses and Poisons, either. If she was a royal healer as well as a poisoner, I would have thought there would be court records of her. Either mentions of her saving lives or taking them.

There was nothing.

It was as if she did not exist outside of that tower chamber. Further proof she might not be who she claimed.

I dropped to the ground, my skirts pooling around me. I was in a lovely navy and gold gown today with flowers embroidered across my bodice, elegant enough for a lady of the Royal Demon Court, and comfortable enough to spend hours on my knees in a darkened corner of the library, searching for answers.

I flipped through a rather thin journal filled with notes and sketches. It spoke of demons that had been made through unnatural sources. Not quite lesser demons, but close. These creatures ranged from human-passing in appearance to a mix between the natural world and mortals. I paused on one illustration. It was humanoid in shape, but its skin was tree bark, its beard moss, and its fingers and limbs were branches of varying lengths and widths.

The next image was of a young man with an enormous set of elk antlers. Another showed a woman with pointed ears and ram horns that curled down to her shoulders.

Notes spoke of spells and hexes that went wrong, turning mortals into nightmares. Shunned and cursed from their world, they ended up here, where they could roam the underworld without fear of persecution.

According to the book, most had scattered across the realm, ending up in the Undying Lands to the northwest, and an eastern mountain range called Merciless Reach.

One note caught my attention.

KINGDOM OF THE CURSED

Creatures made through primordial fear often crave blood. They seek life and there is no greater symbol of life than the heart.

"Lovely." They were this realm's version of a vampire.

I set that illustrated journal aside and scanned the next grimoire, one ear turned toward the entrance. There were just pages of notes on spells, charms, and hexes. I dropped the book onto the towering pile beside me. Then I pulled up my knees and leaned against the shelves.

No matter how hard I tried to stop imagining creatures feasting on hearts, I couldn't shove my sister's mutilated body from my mind.

One night in Palermo Wrath had said that Pride's wife had had her heart torn from her, too. He'd also mentioned that the First Witch had used the darkest of magic to remove her daughter's power and it had unforeseen consequences.

What if her missing heart wasn't part of the murder ritual? What if it was one of the consequences brought about by La Prima? It might have also been a way to set her free from any mortal constraints. I vaguely recalled Nonna saying something like that in passing.

If La Prima's daughter was cursed and not dead, *she* might be the monster who ran around ripping out witch hearts and devouring them.

Perhaps she was motivated by revenge against her mother, at whatever humanity might have been stolen when her powers were wrenched from her. If the devil was her eternal love, maybe she was driven mad and killed any potential brides who would take her place.

Or maybe it was as simple as the illustrated journal claimed—
if she was no longer in possession of her humanity, maybe she
craved hearts for everything she no longer had.

"Perhaps there are too many maybes and not enough defini-
tive answers."

I stood and pulled my shoulders back. Now that I was alone, I
would go back to the matron and directly confront her about my
suspicions. If she *was* the First Witch, I didn't think she'd harm
me. There was a reason she'd been sending the enchanted skulls,
and it wasn't to frighten. Maybe she could tell me more about the
Triple Moon Mirror and offer any ideas on where I might find it,
or the Temptation Key.

I brushed my hand against the hidden sheath at my thigh.
And if she *did* try to hurt me, I would not go without a fight.

Anticipation had me standing outside the matron's tower
chamber in what felt like mere moments. Disappointment had my
jaw clenching as I tore off the note tacked to the door and read the
hastily scratched message.

Gone for a spell.

It was impossible to determine if she meant it literally or
figuratively. The matron would either return in a few minutes,
or she'd gone in search of a spell. There was no telling how long

the latter might take, but, on the off chance she'd be back soon, I milled around outside her tower until snow began falling and chased me away.

I'd taken all of two steps into the corridor of my bedroom suite when a prickle of awareness slid over my skin. Wrath leaned against the door to my chambers, his attention fixed on my face. I swallowed the surge of . . . whatever that feeling was and arched a brow the way he'd done countless times before. I still hadn't seen or spoken to him after our last *training* session. And this visit was most unwelcome.

I paused a decent distance away. "May I help you?"

"I was here to ask the same."

He didn't elaborate, and I was not in the mood to play the game of *ask Wrath a thousand questions and receive frustrating answers*. I moved toward my door, expecting him to step aside, and inhaled deeply when he didn't budge. I crossed my arms and waited.

Sensing my resolve, or attempting to re-strategize his battle plan, Wrath changed tactics. "The library is in shambles."

"That's a bit dramatic. There are a few piles of books scattered in one section. I will clean everything up this evening."

"You're looking for information on the First Witch."

"I'm interested in my history. She is part of that."

His expression darkened. It was not quite thunderous, but certainly stormy. "Lie."

"What I may be searching for is none of your concern."

"Everything in this castle is my concern. You, especially."

"I do not press or pry into your plans. I expect the same courtesy."

"Even if I've come to offer assistance?"

"After our last 'lesson,' I was under the impression you wished for me to take matters into my own hands from now on. Quite literally."

Wrath's attention drifted along my silhouette. He looked as if he were mentally replaying our weapons room tryst, dragging my gown up my thighs, touching and caressing me as if my pleasure was his own. When he brought his gaze back to mine, there was no heat or hint of the emotion that had just claimed him. He was remote, unfeeling. A wall was slowly being built between us. I couldn't tell if it was relief gnawing at the pit of my stomach, or something else.

"We leave for Gluttony's royal House in three nights. Send word to me if you'd like to train before then."

He turned to leave and, devil curse me, I called out, "Fine. Meet me in the weapons room at midnight. We'll have one final lesson before the real games begin."

I arrived in the weapons room nearly a half an hour ahead of schedule. I wanted to set the tone of our lesson and with each strike of the ticking clock, my pulse raced faster. I glanced at my reflection in a particularly shiny shield hung on the wall, relieved that I still looked impeccable on the outside, no matter the chaotic state of my insides.

I shook my jitters out and moved to the center of the room.

At precisely midnight, Wrath stepped into the chamber and halted near the door. It closed with a snick that reminded me of a blade sliding free of its sheath. A fitting sound, given the battle that was about to be launched between us.

Wrath took in my gown—a black off-the-shoulder bodice covered in pale beaded flowers and vines with frothy dark champagne skirts that split on one side a little past my knee.

His focus paused on my footwear. I'd had the shoes specially designed for this dress and was fairly confident the demon prince liked them almost as much as I did.

They were heeled shoes that had a glittering black snake that wound from my ankle to my thigh. The serpent's tongue flicked out but was semi-covered by my dress.

If Wrath wanted a full visual, he would need to push my skirts out of the way. The shoes were inspired in part by the statue in the gardens.

"Tonight we'll—"

"—we'll work on pride." I smiled, noting that my deep berry lip stain captured his attention. I slowly spun in place. "I had this designed for our lesson and I'm quite happy with the results. It's the first time I've created something entirely from my imagination."

"It's beautiful."

"I know." I winked and Wrath actually chuckled. "It's perfection."

"I see your pride is already primed and ready for the lesson." His eyes flashed with something dark and dangerous. "So let's begin."

"Do your worst, your highness. I'm ready."

This time the magic was like a tiny bead rolling between my shoulders, slipping down my spine, pleasant and enticing. I almost arched into it, remembering at the last moment to shove it away, to focus on creating a barrier between the demonic influence and me.

I inhaled deeply, my chest swelling with elation. I was

resisting Wrath's influence, and I was hardly breaking a sweat. Battling away pride was by far the easiest thing I'd done yet.

I gave him a cocky grin from where he stood half in the shadows. He hadn't taken another step into the room; he remained by the door, looking ready to bolt. It was about time he felt unsteady. Whenever he was near lately I felt as if my world had tilted wildly off its axis.

"You'll have to try harder. I've gotten quite good at resisting you."

"Have you?" Amusement glinted in his eyes. "Sounds as if you're a little prideful."

I lifted a shoulder and dropped it casually. "Not prideful. Only honest. You've been a decent enough teacher, but this student has surpassed the lessons. I accept my desires. I welcome any challenge. I have little fear of losing. I think your brothers ought to be worried."

"Oh?"

"Of course. There is nothing more dangerous than a woman who owns who she is and apologizes to no one." I gave him a slow once-over. "I believe I am powerful, therefore I am. Isn't that the principle you live by? Well, I *know* I'm powerful. I know power comes from many sources and I now have many weapons in my arsenal, your highness. In fact, I can own *you* right now if I chose to. And you would be powerless for a change."

"Cocksure. Boastful. An inflated sense of self-image." Wrath checked each one off on his fingers. "You're right. It doesn't sound as if you're under any prideful influence at all."

"You know what else I believe? I believe you'd secretly *like* me to own you. At least in certain...areas."

I moved with deliberate, even strides across the room, allowing my hips to sway. My skirt fluttered to the sides, showing off the snake winding up my leg.

If Wrath wanted a lesson, I'd give him one he'd not soon forget.

I backed him against the wall, my lips curving upward as I dragged a finger across his chest, then followed the line of buttons down to his trousers. Twisted demon. He was already aroused. I flicked my gaze up to his, watching intently as I slid my palm over the bulge. Air hissed through his teeth. I followed the hard outline over his pants and his breathing quickened.

The demonic magic he'd been wielding snapped and fell away. Just as I suspected it would. Wrath's personal set of morals had revealed themselves during each of our lessons, and I'd been watching carefully, learning anything I could even when I'd been unable to block his influence. He *never* used magic when things turned romantic.

"Emilia."

It was more plea than warning. Now that his influence was gone, our lesson was only just beginning. I leaned into him, pressing my chest against his, enjoying the way his focus shifted to my décolletage. I knew precisely how tight my corset was and how our new position showed off my assets best from his vantage point. He seemed torn between looking his fill and maintaining gentlemanly manners. Which wouldn't do. I wanted him completely undone.

Suddenly, an image so vivid and real slipped into my senses, confusing reality with illusion. For a startling moment, I was in two places at once.

There was a low hum of music filtering in, strings and pianos, the sound dulled and haunting through the walls. We'd snuck off together, far from the boisterous sounds of a party taking place down the corridor. Shadows hid him from view, but he found me quickly enough. His hand cupped my breast over my bodice, his kisses plundering and possessive. My passion burned as intensely as his. I nipped at his lip, daring him to do the same. He did one better. He tugged the top of my gown down, replacing his daring hand with his mouth.

I slipped inside his trousers, finding him hard and wanting, then smiled as he cursed at the first stroke I made. I brought my mouth to his ear. "Shhh. They'll hear us."

I took him in hand as if it had been something I'd done hundreds of times. I knew exactly what he liked and how to elicit the most pleasure. His body, his heart; I knew them as well as my own. I used that knowledge to my advantage now.

He did not seem to mind.

Several moments later, he shuddered against me, his breathing ragged and hard. Once his trembling ceased, I rolled up onto my toes and kissed him, long and deep. "Meet me in the garden at the witching hour tonight. You know where."

He'd barely managed to refasten his trousers when I ran off, glancing over my shoulder one last time before I slipped from the darkened room.

Wrath called my name, drawing me back into the present. I'd never had a vision like that and had no idea what to make of it. Something about it didn't feel like the realm's magic.

It felt like a memory.

Wrath traced the curve of my cheek, his voice quiet. "Emilia—"

"I..."

I stepped away from him, giving us both much-needed distance and considered my next words with care. I felt as if I were losing my grip on reality. Concern slipped into his features, so I did my best to pull in that prideful feeling again. To wield it to my advantage.

I purposely dropped my focus to his trousers; there was no longer any sign of attraction or lust. Apparently, my distraction hadn't gone unnoticed.

I offered him a cutting smile. "It seems our lesson is over."

Before my mask slipped, I spun on my heel and headed out the door. Something strange was occurring. And it seemed to happen whenever Wrath and I were in passionate situations.

If they were memories and not illusions created from this realm...then I might have discovered another one of Wrath's secrets. Except I had no idea how any of it could be possible.

But I was damn well going to find out.

TWENTY-SIX

Snowflakes danced wickedly outside my window.

Frost crept up the panes like wintery vines. I sat on the wide sill, staring out at a world blanketed in a fresh layer of snow. Night was quickly falling, tinging everything deep shades of blue. Two days had come and gone since I last saw the prince of this circle. I'd been avoiding him after the vision, still unsure if it was memory or fantasy. It had to be something the realm conjured, but it *felt* so real it was difficult to shake off.

The Matron of Curses and Poisons hadn't yet returned, and I did not want to confide in anyone what I'd seen or experienced. I'd been hoping she could create a tonic or might know of any magic that would unlock the truth hidden inside me.

If it *had* been a memory, then I'd been to this realm before. And Wrath and I...I couldn't fathom how he'd pretended to not know me back in Palermo. There were times there, though, I wondered how he knew details I hadn't shared. Like where I lived. My name. I'd comforted myself by thinking it had something to do with what I'd thought was his rebirth spell—that night I'd been attacked by the Viperidae, we'd been inside each other's minds for brief seconds.

Was that what was happening now? It was possible I was seeing into *his* memories, witnessing him with someone else. Maybe I was experiencing the world through *her* eyes, reliving *her* memories. I knew demons could possess people, but I'd never heard of a witch doing the same. At this point, nothing would surprise me.

I'd spent the better part of the last two days trying to decipher all possible meanings. No theory was too silly. I wrote everything down. From thinking Wrath might be Pride, to considering if *I* was the First Witch, cursed to forget as punishment for what I'd done.

After a while, details started to blur, confusing me more. I couldn't recall if I'd seen Wrath's face, or if it was just an impression I'd had of him.

I remembered the room being dark in the vision, the sounds of a distant party, but couldn't remember the sound of my lover's voice. If he'd sworn loudly when he found his release, or if it had been a murmur. And if it wasn't Wrath with me in the vision…

I exhaled, my breath creating clouds on the windowpane. That complicated matters even more. When I arrived at the feast tonight, I might recognize the lover from that memory. If we danced together, would that unlock other memories that had been secreted away?

I slipped from the window's edge and leafed through the notes I'd made from the enchanted skulls. *Past, present, future, find.* I'd thought it was referencing the Triple Moon Mirror Envy was after. Now I wondered if it encompassed more than that.

Were those visions part of my past, or my future? If they were images of the future, perhaps it related to the prophecy. The part where I could set right a terrible wrong.

When I'd been under Lust's influence, I'd had that impression of choice, balance. That I could damn everyone, or make something right. But *what*?

I kept circling back to the devil's slain bride. Could falling in love be the key to breaking the curse? On the surface it seemed simple. But it wasn't. I'd need to fall madly in love with Pride. And to accomplish that, I'd have to end my betrothal to Wrath for good.

"Goddess help me, this is a disaster."

Pride would be at the feast. If he'd been the mysterious lover in my vision, and if it was part of the past and not the future, it was entirely possible neither one of us would be able to deny the sizzling connection in person. Which frightened me.

If it *was* the past I saw...then that would mean I was already Pride's wife. Maybe to break the curse I had to fall in love with him all over again, without any memories of us.

A theory so outlandish, it just might be true. Which could be the real reason Pride hadn't invited me to his circle. Maybe it went deeper than my accidental betrothal to Wrath.

Without knowing what I'd done, maybe I'd broken Pride's heart and damned them all by choosing the wrong brother. It would also explain Wrath's hatred when I first summoned him and he demanded I reverse the spell before it was too late.

A knock on my outer door drew me from my reverie. "Come in."

Harlow bobbed a quick curtsy, then held a dress bag aloft. "The cobbler will have your shoes ready shortly. Did you want me to lay out the gown for you?"

"Please."

Through all of my worries, I'd completely lost track of time. We'd be traveling to House Gluttony within the hour. This evening marked the first of three nights dedicated to the Feast of the Wolf, an event I'd rather avoid if not for the potential information I could gather. Thinking about having my greatest fear ripped from me caused my heart rate to triple, though.

At first I'd been worried my greatest fear was my secret mission of vengeance being revealed. Now it could be my fear about the creature wailing below the statue, my family dying at the hands of our enemies, my magic never returning, or the possibility that my memories had been stolen and the life I'd been living was all a lie.

The biggest fear of all kept circling like a portent of death and doom.

I couldn't stop thinking that *I* was the devil's bride and I hadn't been murdered—I'd been cursed to forget. My palms dampened. There was no possible way that was true.

Still, the thought haunted me the entire time I prepared for tonight's opening event. True or not, if I couldn't shove the fear aside; it would be revealed to each of my enemies and their subjects. Not only would it be humiliating, it would indicate I had not left the past behind when I'd sold my soul and was actively working to destroy one of them.

If the demon princes were suspicious of my motivations for coming here before, they'd have those thoughts confirmed. And I didn't want to know what they'd do for retribution.

I descended the stairs, shoulders back, head held high. I'd been expecting to see Fauna and Anir. Instead the Prince of Wrath waited, dressed to devastate, his attention riveted to mine. I hadn't chosen to wear one of his signature House colors. Not that he seemed put off by the crushed red velvet gown, or the way it clung to my curves before pooling around my feet.

In fact, I almost missed a step when I noticed the color of his shirt. A deep, enticing cranberry peeked out from the layers of black waistcoat and swallowtail suit jacket. Either Harlow or the seamstress must have given him information on my attire.

I reached the bottom step and slowly pivoted in place. My shoes were the same snake design from a few nights before, but these were deep gold instead of black. It was the one tribute I made to my current House of Sin. Regardless of if any of my theories were correct, in this reality, in this version of myself, this was where I felt comfortable. There was no use denying that I aligned with the sin of wrath more than any other.

"Well?" I prompted. "How do I look?"

Wrath's gaze darkened into a shadow of sinful promise. "I suspect you know."

"Indulge me, then."

"Trouble incarnate."

"Mighty praise coming from one of the Wicked." I glanced around the empty foyer. Silence stretched between us, which didn't help to soothe my growing nerves. The more I tried not to focus on my theories, the more they haunted me. "Where are Fauna and Anir?"

"By now they're nearly at Gluttony's already."

"Who else will be joining us?"

"No one." He held out his arm for me. I wondered if he knew

he also looked like trouble. And temptation. But if Pride was the man from my vision, Wrath might also look like a fond memory before the night was through. Something pinched in my center at the thought. "Tonight we'll use my carriage. It's considered rude to arrive at the Feast by *transvenio* magic."

I accepted his arm and we made our way out of the looming set of double doors.

Outside, our conveyance sat waiting, bits of snow sticking to the roof like powdered sugar. Wrath's carriage was darker than the night with flecks of gold in the lacquered finish. There was no driver waiting, only horses.

"Will you be driving the carriage?"

"No. My power will guide it."

"*Transvenio* magic is rude, but steering a carriage with magic is not?" I shook my head. "I may live a thousand years and will never understand these ridiculous demon rules."

The four ebony steeds snuffed the air, their red eyes the only mark that they were not quite the same as horses in the mortal world. Wrath set about checking their bridles, tsking a little when one of the hell horses nibbled at him.

I drew in a quick breath. I'd been wrong. Their eyes weren't the only thing that marked them as different. Their gleaming, metal teeth indicated they were more predator than simple equine. The hell horse nipped again, more insistently.

"Gentle, Death."

"Goddess give me strength." I eyed the three other beasts. "Famine, Pestilence, and War, I presume." Wrath's grin was confirmation enough as he glanced over his shoulder. "I cannot believe you named them after the four horsemen, and yet I'm not terribly surprised."

He strolled over to where I waited, then handed me up into the carriage. "Perhaps they aren't merely named after them."

Wrath settled onto the plush velvet bench seat across from me, his expression smug as I let that information sink in. With a quick rap on the ceiling, we were off.

The wheels clattered across the stone, but the sound and jarring feeling was muffled by the well-stuffed seating and plush, layered carpets. I'd never ridden inside such an opulent conveyance. I'd never ridden in a shabby one, either. Before my ride with the emissary, the closest I'd ever come to traveling via carriage was a horse-drawn buggy.

I drew my brows together. That couldn't be correct...after disembarking from a ship, we had to travel by carriage to visit Nonna's friend in northern Italy. Except I couldn't quite remember how we'd gotten there.

Wrath studied me. "You appear as if you're in the midst of a vexing riddle."

I lifted a shoulder. "I suppose it's mostly nerves."

"About the fear portion of the festival?"

"The fear, the whole ordeal. Meeting the rest of your brothers. Dancing."

He was silent for a while. I doubted he'd expected such honesty and was unsure of how to proceed. Finally, he shifted forward. "No harm will befall you. I will not allow it."

"Perhaps it's your brothers you should be concerned for."

"If they are stupid enough to ignite your fury, they deserve to feel the burn."

I smiled at him. "And yet you still toss matches onto the kerosene all the time."

"Wrath and fury are my sins of choice. I *like* your temper."

After an indeterminate amount of time of descending and ascending a few mountain peaks, our carriage abruptly came to a halt. Wrath peered outside, his expression once again carefully set into that cold, unforgiving mask.

"We're here." He reached for the handle, then paused. His muscles were tense beneath his well-tailored suit. He shook his head once, then looked at me. "Should you find yourself in need of a partner, I will dance with you."

Before I could react, he shoved the door open and exited the carriage. His hand appeared from the shadows, waiting for mine. I gave myself a moment to gather my emotions. I hadn't lied to Wrath about the cause of my nerves, but I hadn't expressed *all* of the reasons behind my pounding heart. I would now have an opportunity to speak with every demon prince of Hell. And one of them, quite possibly, had orchestrated my sister's murder.

Much would either be gained or lost over the next few days. And, if my sister's murderer was here, there was no telling if he'd try to rip my heart from my chest, too.

If I was about to enter into a battle for my life, at least I had Wrath at my side.

His fingers tightened on mine as I stepped from the carriage and took in House Gluttony. It was massive, if unusual in design. A cross between open Roman terraces with tall arched windows and medieval towers. It was built into the side of a steep mountaintop and looked like something out of a gothic fairy tale.

"Prepare yourself." Wrath escorted me up a small flight of stairs and stopped just outside the castle's grand entrance. "My brother's debauchery knows no limits."

Words failed me as we walked inside House Gluttony. The prince of this circle did not hide his namesake sin or vices.

Immediately upon entering the palatial receiving foyer, we were greeted by the most scandalous scene I'd ever borne witness to.

A table the size of four oversized mattresses was prominently on display, forcing guests to squeeze around it if they were to enter the castle beyond. The table was not covered in food or wine. It was covered in lovers. Some were engaged in acts I'd never dreamed of.

On one end, a woman lay naked, her legs spread wide as a man poured a trail of chocolate sauce over her breasts, down her stomach, and across the apex of her body. He tossed the jug aside, dropped to his knees and began feasting. There was no romance, no seduction. Only pure, animalistic hunger. Not that the woman seemed to mind.

My attention darted to the opposite end of the table, where a young man lay with an arm bent behind his head, watching as his partner sucked whipped cream from his arousal, and another lover entered her from where she was bent over. My face flamed at the erotic scene.

Before I'd learned that Pride wasn't my intended, Wrath had mentioned his brother inviting lovers into our bed. I now understood what he meant. I also knew with vivid clarity what Fauna had been asking when she'd inquired about taking my mouth to Wrath.

"My brother enjoys shocking guests upon their arrival." Wrath's low voice at my ear sent a shiver skittering along my spine. "His subjects are all too happy to participate in his favorite vices. The lovers here want to be seen. They desire for us to over-indulge in their pleasure. Our attention feeds them as their trysts feed us. It will not be this way throughout the entire House."

Wrath's hand on my back did not uproot my feet from where I'd planted them. "Will Gluttony's influence make me do that? In front of everyone?"

Wrath followed my gaze, his own expression inscrutable. "No."

I subtly studied the demon at my side. He was completely unaffected by all of the naked bodies and grunts and groans. He might be gazing upon furniture, noting it was there to sit upon, but worth no more than a cursory glance. The same could not be said for me. I tore my attention from where the man was licking and sucking with fevered abandon.

"How can you be sure? Lust managed to influence me. As did Envy. I'm sure your brother can make me do whatever he pleases with whomever he pleases I do it. Maybe our lessons weren't enough. Maybe—"

"Breathe. No one will touch you while we're here, Emilia. It would be an act of war and we're all gathered with the understanding of temporary peace. You belong to House Wrath. If they forget, I will take pleasure in reminding them."

One look into his harsh features drove his promise home. I had little doubt this prince would tear someone limb from limb if they laid a finger on me without my consent. I wanted that power. I wanted to know safety at my own hand and almost swore I had once upon a time. Perhaps that was why I'd felt so envious when I'd first met Envy and he'd used his influence on me. I longed for the power to defend myself and my loved ones.

My focus drifted back to where the man knelt between the woman's thighs. He worked her now with mouth and hand. A female lover moved to her chest, adding more whipped cream and licking her skin clean before adding another dollop.

Gluttony wished to shock his guests, to unnerve them. Except most were from this realm and had likely witnessed much more debauchery. No, this tableau was not for *all* of his guests. This was for me. To unsettle the mortal guest of honor long before I entered his ballroom.

And he'd almost succeeded.

Nakedness, people seeking sexual pleasure, no matter how much I kept trying to move past it, the mortal way of thinking of them as wrong and shameful kept creeping back in. They kept shocking and embarrassing me because deep down, I still worried about being ruined by human notions of scandal. Most of all, I kept worrying about what others would think.

Enough. I'd had enough of falling back into old fears. I strode over to the table and dipped my finger into a bowl of whipped cream, then slowly turned to Wrath as I licked it off. There wasn't anything in his expression now that spoke of boredom or disinterest. He tracked each movement as if committing it to memory.

A waiter appeared, holding a tray of champagne flutes.

I gave Wrath a small, devious smile and snagged a glass of sparkling demonberry wine. "Cheers to being scandalized."

Without waiting for his response, I rotated and walked past the table of lovers.

When I entered the Feast of the Wolf and the herald called out my name, I'd convinced myself I was the most fearsome one in the room.

TWENTY-SEVEN

The Prince of Gluttony was not at all what I expected. He wasn't perched on a throne, or giving off the appearance of cool boredom, or exuding royal arrogance. There wasn't anything particularly dangerous looking about him, either. Except for the threat he posed to hearts.

He stood, arms full of buxom ladies, near a fountain of spirits, a secret smile pulling at the corners of a luscious mouth. The prince leaned in to whisper something in each of his companions' ears, their laughter sultry and filled with wicked promises.

I arched a brow as he took turns nibbling at their necks. He was a rake through and through. And he seemed adored for it.

He was not quite as tall as Wrath, but his shoulders were broad, his hips narrow, and the width of his thighs suggested a fit body hidden beneath his blackberry-colored suit.

His slightly ruffled brown hair had strands of gold and red in certain light, though the darkness never relinquished its hold for long. He wore a bronze crown, fitted with multicolored gemstones. Gluttony's hazel eyes were a mixture of brilliant shades of green and gold and brown. All vying for dominance, all indulging in their own beauty.

And they were now trained on where Wrath and I stood. One brow quirked up.

"Brother! Come meet my newest friends, Drusilla and Lucinda. They were just telling me the most interesting story."

"I don't doubt that." Wrath's lack of decorum didn't seem to surprise anyone but me. He placed a hand at the small of my back. "My wife, Emilia di Carlo."

Gluttony's attention shifted to me. His nose looked as if it had been broken once or twice, but that imperfection only succeeded in making him more interesting. His gaze raked over me and a spark of mischief flared. "Soon-to-be wife, from what I understand."

"Actually," I cut in, "I haven't decided to accept the bond."

"Hear that, brother?" Gluttony stepped away from his companions and tossed an arm around Wrath's shoulders. "There's hope for me yet."

"Breathe in her direction without her expressed permission, and she will disembowel you." Wrath swiped a glass of demonberry wine from a passing tray and sipped it, the picture of casual elegance. "I've already requested that she refrain from violence for our visit, but if I were you, I wouldn't tempt her fury."

The brothers exchanged a long look. Wrath had basically come in and set his own rules at his brother's royal court. Just as he'd done in Envy's House of Sin. It was a wonder that Gluttony didn't so much as lift a brow at Wrath's impertinence. "You're a violent little vixen, then?"

"I have my moments, your highness."

His laugh was full and rich.

"Explains how you've captured this one's attention." He

leaned in and spoke in a mock whisper, his tone serious, as if sharing a grave secret. "Wrath has an unquenchable taste for fury. Though he never overindulges in it. Much to everyone's dismay." Wrath did not return his brother's smile, which only succeeded in delighting the prince of this circle more. "Perhaps you will surprise us all, dear brother. This may be the year you let loose after all. Live down to our expectations. Gorge yourself on some fun for once."

"Be grateful I limit my idea of fun, brother."

"Well, the hunt begins at dawn, so you can saddle up a hell horse and unleash your warrior spirit then." He glanced to me, troublesome smirk in place. "You, too, Lady Emilia. Let us see if you're equally inspired by bloodlust."

"I don't ride."

"No?" His eyes twinkled with amusement. "Then I shall stay and keep you company. While they're getting into trouble, I'm sure we can find some of our own."

Whatever levity Gluttony had been feeling was gone in an instant, replaced by an icy glare. I followed the direction of his gaze, surprised to find the object of his loathing was a beautiful, prim noblewoman. Her pale blue hair was coiffed in the style of proper English ladies and her elegant dress buttoned up to her neck.

She wore kidskin gloves that ended past her elbows and an expression of revulsion as she spied the host, her gaze cutting from across the room. She leaned next to her companion and whispered something that sent the other noblewoman tittering.

"If you'll excuse me." Gluttony's mood darkened further. "There's a party crasher in our midst."

Without uttering another word, Gluttony strode off toward the giggling ladies.

I turned to Wrath. "What was that about?"

"She's a journalist from the Shifting Isles. And she rarely has anything flattering to say about the royals in this realm. She's been particularly vicious with Gluttony."

I thought back to the lovers on the table. "She doesn't enjoy his displays of overindulgence, I take it."

"On the contrary." Wrath's mouth edged up on one side. "She called his last gathering 'perfectly ordinary and utterly contrived. A predictable, uninspired evening.'"

"I cannot believe you memorized that."

"My brother quoted it so often, it stuck. Gluttony was furious. He has since thrown the most lavish, over-the-top, debauched parties he can."

"He wants her to eat her words."

"Amongst other things, no doubt."

I couldn't help but smile. "Hate is a powerful aphrodisiac for some."

"Indeed. It is." Wrath's attention briefly fell to my lips. "Would you like to tour the pleasure gardens or settle into your rooms?"

I recalled what Fauna had said about the twilight gardens and my stomach did a nervous flip. If Wrath and I snuck off now, I would miss the opportunity to meet the rest of his family.

Not to mention, I wasn't sure being alone with him where seduction was being served for public consumption was a wise idea.

As if he'd plucked the thought from my mind, he added quietly, "Pride will make his grand entrance at the masked ball tomorrow. Sloth will slip in right before the fear ceremony. Greed and Envy will arrive fashionably late this evening."

"And Lust?"

"I imagine he's here and is indulging. While he tends to siphon feelings of happiness to enhance his power, he does participate in carnal temptations when they're offered to him. These parties tend to feed his sin on multiple levels."

I glanced toward the veranda, where a set of doors were thrown open and a cold breeze blew snowflakes in from the patio beyond. Tiny flickering silver orbs floated in the darkness.

Going to my bedchamber was the best decision, yet I found myself saying, "Let's take a quick stroll through the garden."

Unsurprisingly, Gluttony's idea of a pleasure garden was quite literal. We walked past lovers barely hidden in the shadows, the sounds of their bare skin slapping against each other and breathy moans created a strangely haunting symphony. I did my best to keep my attention fixed on the torchlit path in front of us, not daring to seek out writhing shadows near the hedges.

Wrath, as always, seemed unaffected.

"Have you toured the gardens before?" I immediately wished I hadn't asked.

"Yes." He gave me a sidelong glance. "I always survey the grounds to ensure there's no hidden threat."

Almost on command, a woman screamed her lover's name.

"Of course." I rolled my eyes. "It certainly sounds as if there's *danger* here."

"Hidden armies, unwelcome guests, clandestine meetings between scheming Houses." Wrath leaned close and dropped his voice. "A lot can happen in the dark, my lady."

"He's not wrong." The Prince of Lust's grin bordered on feline as he stepped into our path and stretched his arms above his head, exposing a sliver of golden skin above his trousers. His charcoal eyes drank me in, then spit me out with disinterest. "Hello again, little darling."

"Lust." Despite the inner voice urging me to run, I held my ground. All of my senses heightened as I waited for that first lick of his soul-crushing influence. "I would say it's nice to see you again, but..."

I lifted a shoulder, letting the rest go unsaid.

"I will have to remedy that. Later." He turned to his brother. There was no anger or glint of retribution in his expression. As far as I was aware, the last time they saw each other, Wrath had stuck a dagger in his chest. "I need a word. Privately."

Wrath hesitated before nodding once. He turned to me. "I'll stop by your chamber later. Unless you'd like me to escort you there now."

"No." I shook my head, grateful for the excuse to leave Lust and his troublesome influence. "I'm sure I'll find my own way back."

Wrath nodded, but didn't move to follow his brother. I felt his gaze on me until I turned the corner. Halfway down the next path, a servant appeared. Wrath, no doubt, had managed to arrange our meeting. "Lady Emilia, if you'll follow me. I can show you to your chambers."

After settling into my well-appointed room—all cobalt blue, silver, and dripping in an overabundance of luxury—I waited, perched on the edge of my bed, for what felt like hours. Straining to hear Wrath's light knock at my door.

It never came.

At first I worried Lust had struck him, vengeance for what had occurred between them in Palermo. Then a new worry slipped in. We were staying in a House filled with debauchery. If Wrath hadn't made it to his bed, I wondered if that meant he'd tumbled into someone else's.

SilverFrost Garden,
southeast tower, dawn.
Wear something to die for.
And come masked.

I stared down at the note that arrived well past midnight. Cobalt blue paper inked with platinum—the parchment thick and luxurious.

There was no indication who the sender was, what I'd find if I accepted the invitation, or what manner of mischief I might be inviting into my already complicated world. The handwriting didn't belong to Wrath, who still hadn't shown up.

Given the rich indulgence of the paper and ink, I imagined it was penned by Gluttony, but there was always a chance one of the other princes in attendance had sent it along.

Wearing something "to die for" might not be a demonic euphemism.

I carefully considered my options. I could ignore it. That was certainly the safest route. After the assassination attempt at House Wrath, it wasn't a stretch to believe it was a trap.

With everyone meeting at dawn to start the hunt, I'd be alone and vulnerable. Whoever sent it must know I'd chosen not to ride out with the group.

And the only person who knew that—aside from Wrath—was Gluttony.

If my attire mattered, it might indicate a clandestine party. One where masks were required to keep anonymity of the attendees. A mysterious event hosted in the underworld, by an unknown source, was not the typical gathering I'd ever considered.

But now...I exhaled. Now I couldn't decline something that might present an opportunity for me to interrogate a prince of Hell without Wrath chaperoning.

I flipped the card over, end by end, thinking. Just because I'd been asked to meet at the SilverFrost Garden did not mean that's where I had to show up. At least not initially.

A plan slowly came together in my mind. There was an expansive veranda outside the southeast tower ballroom with a grand staircase that led to the gardens. I'd arrive early and wait in one of the darkened corners there. I swung myself out of bed and quickly dressed in a gown made of shadows.

Gluttony strolled onto the empty veranda, a knuckle's worth of liquor poured into a crystal glass. A decanter was tucked beneath his other arm. I would claim it was too early to drink, but he didn't appear to have made it to bed. There was a mussed quality to his hair, a slight wrinkle in his suit. As if his bedmate had kept him occupied all night and well into the morning. He played the role of a debauched rake to perfection.

He took a healthy swig from his glass. All princes seemed to enjoy their alcohol the same, though the quantities in which they indulged differed.

I pressed myself deeper into the shadows and watched his approach through lowered lashes, holding my breath to avoid detection. As if the slightest inhalation would give me away.

"I can't decide if I'm amused or insulted."

My entire body tensed at having been discovered so quickly. I reached for my dagger, relaxing once I felt its familiar weight in my grip. I stepped into the watery predawn light.

There was no use hiding now.

I waited in silence for him to continue. Clearly he desired this meeting alone. He might as well dazzle me with whatever speech he'd prepared.

He leaned over the stone railing, surveying the decadent garden below. Silver flowers coated in frost glistened like diamonds. "Perhaps your strategy will work famously."

"What strategy?"

"Winning the hunt. In five minutes, the whole of the castle will come charging out of the stables." He set his drink on the wide railing before him, then motioned to the dark roof in the distance. Snow-covered hills rolled into an evergreen forest. "People rarely notice what's in front of them, especially when they expect to find something else."

"I'm not sure I follow your meaning."

He slowly twisted to look at me, his expression a study of false chagrin. "I may have left out a few important details in the note. Like the prize for winning the hunt."

I kept the trepidation off my face. I didn't think it was anything more than typical country sport. "I was unaware that there was a prize."

"Prize. Prey. Some might argue they are one and the same." His grin was carved of wicked intent. "The host chooses the prey each Blood Season. Participants only learn what they're looking for in the stables, right before the hunt begins."

My blood turned cold. "Wrath said there was no sacrifice involved during any portion of the three-day event."

"I never said anything about a sacrifice. I just said someone or some*thing* will be hunted." He studied me closer than I would have thought possible, considering how much he'd had to drink. "No one kills the chosen prey." He winked. "We're not total monsters."

"Why did you want me masked?"

"To see if you'd indulge me." He lifted a shoulder and dropped it. As if that were all the reason anyone needed. I was glad I'd decided against wearing a mask. "Has anyone told you why it's called a Blood Season?"

"No, but I'm sure it will be a delightful story."

"If a lesser demon or noble wins the hunt, they have the option to drink the elixir of life."

"Blood."

My stomach flipped as Gluttony nodded. Nonna used to tell us the Wicked drank blood. Now I knew where that rumor had come from. "What if a royal wins?"

"We have the option to claim our own prize, if at least four of us vote in favor of it. But drinking the elixir of life is not the only reason we call it a Blood Season. The winner of the hunt is decided by whoever draws first blood. Participants choose how much to spill, and how they spill it. Claws, blades, arrows, teeth." His gaze turned back to the stables. A gunshot rent the air, startling me. "Ah, yes. They've found the ice rifles. If I were you, I'd consider joining the hunt now."

"I told you, I don't ride."

"A shame. This year they're hunting an ice dragon. Majestic, violent, creatures." He tore his attention away from the building in the distance and looked at me again. "And as for riding, I'd reconsider. I've found that sometimes our bodies recall what our minds do not."

Gluttony inclined his head, then strode back into his castle, leaving me to contemplate his parting words. A second shot cracked like thunder and the sound of a stampede followed, the ground rumbling beneath my feet. Something stirred in my blood.

Before I could talk myself out of it, I hiked up my skirts and raced toward the stables.

TWENTY-EIGHT

Outside the stables, a pale violet mare toed the snow with spiked metal hoofs before turning quicksilver eyes on me. Intelligence gleamed out from those liquid eyes as I slowly approached the massive hell horse. A silver crescent moon glimmered on its forehead and a handful of stars spread over its rear end like a constellation.

"Aren't you divine, girl?" I stepped close. "I'm not sure what your name is, but I need to call you something. How about Tanzie? Short for Tanzanite."

I smiled as the horse inclined her head in approval.

The moment of tranquility was short-lived. In the distance, shouts rang out, followed by an earthshaking roar. I imagined it belonged to the ice dragon Gluttony mentioned.

The hunt was clearly in full swing, but I was less concerned with it than I was with the growing need to ride as hard as I could over the frosted grounds.

My heart pounded like a war drum. Riding fast across this terrain would be dangerous, if it weren't for the claw-tipped horseshoes. I petted Tanzie's flank with confidence, somehow knowing she would tolerate nothing less from the person she allowed the honor of taking her saddle. And what a beautiful saddle it was—dark and oiled so it appeared like frozen ink.

A small pouch hung on its side. Gluttony must have had it readied.

Placing one foot in the stirrup, I swung myself up and over, grateful I'd decided to wear thick stockings under my dress. Choosing to sit astride was hardly an appropriate position, but I doubted anyone in the underworld viewed it the same way as mortals.

My thighs tightened around the horse as I readied myself. I clucked my tongue and lifted the reins. I didn't have to urge the great beast further. Tanzie trotted away from the stable and made her way down a sloping hill, gaining speed on the decline instead of slowing.

Judging from the muffled sounds of hooves beating snow, the hunting party was behind us, either in the forest or just at its edge. There were no rules that stated I had to participate in the hunt, but I didn't want to get caught out here and be encouraged to join them.

My breath clouded in front of me as I leaned forward in my seat, heart thumping in time with each beat of the steed's hooves. We careened around Gluttony's castle, the gentle slope turning into a sharp drop-off. My unbound hair flew back as the biting winds stole nips of my flesh. Tears stung my eyes, but I couldn't blink, couldn't help myself as I stood higher in the saddle while the horse plunged down the mountain. A memory was stirring... I felt as if I'd been here before, racing the wind and riding like a warrior into battle.

I forgot about the hunt, the Feast of the Wolf, and all of the demons riding close by. I had no idea where I was going, but something called to me, deep in my blood. It screamed at me to remember, to let go of thoughts and simply *feel*.

Tanzie neighed as if confirming those feelings. As if she'd wanted me to recall this was what we'd been created for. This feeling of ultimate freedom and shucking restraints away. All that mattered was the ground we hurtled over and the blood pumping in our veins.

As we crested a massive hill, a field of black rose like an ink stain across the snow. I drew us to a slow trot and led Tanzie closer to the shimmering hill. Up close, I saw that the dark mass wasn't solid. It was millions of tiny black flowers growing through the ice. I brought Tanzie to a stop and jumped down. The ebony petals had silver dots on them.

Intrigued, I plucked one, surprised when the whole root slipped out easily. The odd silver roots glimmered brightly, then dried up before my eyes. Magic or some peculiar hell plant. I wanted to study them later and see what else they could do. I grabbed a handful of flowers and tucked them into a small leather pouch fastened on the saddle.

Tanzie neighed, stomping imperiously, signaling her boredom with our diversion of flower picking. Without looking back at the undulating field, I hopped back onto the horse, and we rode even harder than before. I was so caught up in the sensory aspect of the ride, of the exaltation of the icy air nipping at my skin and stealing my breath, that I didn't notice the castle towering before us. Nor was I aware that we'd crossed some invisible boundary line.

It was only when the first round of guards circled us, swords aimed and ready, shouting for me to halt, that I realized my error. I'd invaded another demon prince's domain without invitation. Tanzie reared back, then dropped to the ground, stamping her feet as one guard silenced the others and called out a clear command to me.

"Dismount and drop to your knees."

"There seems to be a misunderstanding." I held tight to the reins. "I was riding at House Gluttony and didn't realize I'd come so far."

"I said, dismount and drop to your knees."

The guard who'd spoken stepped from the formation. His open-faced iron helmet had deadly-looking wings on either side. Across the top band, where the helmet molded over his forehead, a set of gold claw marks were etched onto the metal.

I noted none of the other guards shared that design, making him the obvious leader of their group. Another line of guards appeared from the castle, arrows nocked in their bows.

I paid them little mind, focusing instead on the biggest threat.

My gaze slid over the lead guard's features, committing them to memory should things go wrong and I needed to recall details upon my escape. Burnished gold hair peeked out from the upper portion of his helmet. His sun-kissed skin was free from all but one imperfection: a pale silver scar that diagonally cut across a pair of arrogant lips.

I couldn't make out the color of his eyes from where I sat, but the hardness in them would never be forgotten. Tanzie snuffed the air, dancing back as the other guards took another step forward, closing their ranks. If I dismounted now, I would certainly regret it.

I sat taller, donning my most commanding tone. "I demand to speak with the prince of this House. There has been a mistake."

"Dismount before my sword finds its way into your gut."

"Touch me, and I promise you will feel more than my wrath."

The smile that tugged at my lips was as vicious as his weapon. "It might be worth the pain just to watch the Prince of Wrath carve you apart. I doubt he'll go easy on anyone who harms his princess."

Surprise flickered in his gaze before he schooled his features.

"Forgive me, but I do not recall receiving word that you were invited onto our lands." He stepped closer, lining his blade up with my heart. "Which grants me permission to remove the threat to our territory as I see fit. Now get off the fucking horse, *princess.*"

If I were to focus on the positive in a very bad situation, I was not chained and escorted into a cell. I was brought to a lavish parlor and promptly locked inside with a handful of armed guards stationed at the doors and windows. I ignored their icy stares and scanned the room.

White marble floors and walls shined cheerfully in the flickering candlelight. Silk furniture—gilded and ornate enough to rival the Sun King's famed palace in France—surrounded me. I sat on the edge of a pearl-colored brocade settee, fingers itching to clasp my hidden dagger. No one spoke. There were no royal crests on their uniforms, nothing to indicate which royal House of Sin I'd accidentally invaded.

Not that I could identify anything other than Greed's crowned frog insignia if I did spy a crest. I knew with certainty I wasn't in House Wrath, Envy, or Gluttony. As far as I could recall, almost all of the seven demon princes should be at the Feast of the Wolf by now. Which was the likely complication behind the guards not knowing the proper protocol for dealing with a trespasser. One bright note in this dismal situation was I'd found the perfect hiding place to avoid the hunt.

An imperial rococo clock above the mantel ticked the seconds away. The lead guard had dropped me off here and left, murmuring orders to the two guards standing on either side of the door. Their attention had slid to me before they jerked their chins in acknowledgment of whatever he'd said. A quarter of an hour passed. Surely, as the guest of honor, someone from House Gluttony would notice my absence. Wrath most assuredly would come looking.

A full hour crawled by. No one came. Another hour passed in what had to be the slowest shift of time in history. Still, no prince arrived, dagger in hand, to free me.

It was time to become my own hero and save myself.

I cleared my throat. "Which royal House is this?"

Silence.

No one shifted, or even blinked. It was as if I hadn't spoken at all. I settled back onto my seat, getting comfortable. Another hour slipped by and just when I was about to go mad, the door cracked open. One of the guards blocked my view, and the voices were too quiet to make out any part of the conversation. The guard nodded, then closed the door.

He pivoted in my direction, his expression cold. "Get up."

My knees locked. "Where are we going?"

"His highness is releasing you."

"I don't understand . . . doesn't he wish to speak with me?"

The guard's face split into a cruel grin. "Best to not inquire about his wishes. I suspect they would give you nightmares."

The ride back to House Gluttony was cold and miserable.

I couldn't shake the sense of foreboding that trailed me like a shadow. Tanzie seemed just as disturbed; she rode hard and fast, her hooves brutally digging into the snow and ice as if she couldn't get us away from the cursed demon House fast enough. We crested the mountain and ran full force to the south side of the castle. Gluttony leaned against the railing outside the stables, a cobalt capelet fluttering in the breeze. He watched our approach, one brow quirked.

"Anything interesting happen?"

I dismounted and patted Tanzie's flank. "What game are you playing at?"

"Currently?" He checked a pocket watch. "The sort where I escort you to your chambers. The masquerade ball begins in a few hours. Your little jaunt almost put us behind schedule."

My little jaunt into being a prisoner. Before I could quip back at him, he was in front of me, blade flashing as he cut the small leather pouch from Tanzie's saddle.

"This"—he plucked a flower out and held it up, the silver roots sparkling as they twisted in the light breeze—"is slumber root. Capable of knocking out even the most powerful royal. What sort of nefarious plans do you have for this evening?"

"None."

"Really?" He sounded disappointed. "You have in your possession a plant most princes fear, and you have no cunning designs on using them against us?" He tossed the pouch of slumber root to me. "Scheme bigger, my friend. Let your inner deviant free."

"Now that I know what it does," I said sweetly, "I'll be sure to put it to use."

"Good. Now let's get ready for some debauchery."

TWENTY-NINE

My beaded gown was extravagant. And heavy. Goddess above, I swore it almost weighed a quarter of my full body weight. A corset was built into the fitted top, and it was tight enough through the hips that I felt as if I'd been dipped in liquid gold. Metal sequins sewn in a series of geometric designs accentuated my curves. Hips, waist, bust. Each section boasted a mix of beads, sequins, and patterns designed to draw the eye.

I twisted in the mirror, admiring the hard work that went into making such a garment.

Champagne-colored silk whispered across my skin. The skirts split in the center, a few inches above my knees, and the beaded portion ruffled over pure, untouched silk. A shiny gold belt with vines and thorns brought an edge of danger to the beauty.

My mask...that was all House Wrath. I'd been informed that the princes could only wear wolf masks, and the rest of the assembly were free to wear whatever they'd like.

The half-mask I'd had made was tasteful. Dark gold with delicate lines of spun glitter, offering the barest hint of snakeskin.

I'd left my hair loose and wild, adding a few gold clips to pull it back from my face. I'd just finished the final touches when Wrath walked into the room and halted.

I couldn't stop the coy smile from lifting my lips as I tossed the needle and thread I'd been holding back into my sewing kit. "It will do, I think."

His intense gaze strayed to the mask. "Where did you find that?"

I reached up, brushing my fingers against the cool metal. "A proper gentleman comments on his date's beauty. Not where she found a mask."

"Are you my date tonight?"

His tone held a note of teasing. Underneath I sensed a thread of tension, though. I tried not to think about where he was last night, why he never came to my room when he promised he would. I had no idea what Lust wanted but could guess the sort of entertainment he might seek and goad his brother into. The sudden tightening in my chest felt too much like hurt.

"You're escorting me there." I lifted a shoulder. "I'm not sure what else to call you. If you'd like me to try, I can probably come up with a few choice descriptions."

"Of that I have little doubt."

I openly admired his suit. Ebony and gold—his waistcoat also featured snakeskin, except his was made entirely of metal, like chain-mail armor. "Expecting a battle?"

"Only if you ask me to fight off suitors."

"Where's your mask?"

He held out an arm. "Enjoy the mystery of it."

"I am about to be subjected to the *honor* of having my biggest fear or a secret of my heart torn from me. Enjoying anything about this evening doesn't feel realistic. I'd like to know what exactly to expect from each portion of the evening."

"Dinner is next. And I'm certain you will find it pleasing."

Without offering any more hints, Wrath escorted me down a stunning set of stairs and into a foyer filled with masked attendees sipping from champagne flutes and chatting in hushed tones. The atmosphere tonight was more subdued, but no less enchanting.

Gluttony noted our arrival and clapped his hands once, smoothly drawing the assembled partygoers' attention. "Everyone, please, go into the dining room and take your seats. The feast is about to begin."

Wrath led me to our places, and I was happy to see Fauna had been assigned the seat next to mine. Anir was across from her, and that was where my good fortune ended. Lady Sundra glided in, radiant like sunshine, her expression turning stormy when she spied me.

"Lady Sundra."

Her jaw tightened, and I immediately realized the unintentional trap I'd set for her. With Wrath present, I'd forced her into using my title. "Lady Emilia."

Envy swept into the room and sank into the chair opposite Wrath—and beside a still-glowering Lady Sundra—with a knowing grin tugging at the corners of his mouth.

Before he could taunt me with whatever was brewing in his gaze, a chef strode into the room. "Good evening, lords, ladies, and princes of the underworld. Tonight's menu theme is Fire and Ice. Each mortal land's dish will represent the chosen elements in some form or another. Our first course is a frisée salad that features ice. You'll see why shortly."

An army of servants carried out individual plates and set them before each guest at the same time. Worries over Lady Sundra vanished. I could not tear my attention from the dish. Greens were placed in a circle on a wooden slab, resembling a bird's nest plucked from a tree.

Sprinkled around the greens were bits of cheese and crushed pecans. In the center was a ruby-colored egg-shaped form filled partially with liquid. It was not simply a salad—it was a work of art, of passion. Creative genius on a level I'd never encountered.

I was happy to see I wasn't the only one who hadn't picked up a utensil yet, not quite ready to disturb the edible sculpture.

"A frozen strawberry vinaigrette." The Prince of Gluttony tapped the faux egg, cracking it and spilling the dressing. He tossed the bits of cheese and crushed nuts into the leafy greens, mixing it all with the dressing. Everyone followed suit, their excited chatter filling the large dining chamber.

Wrath watched me, the corners of his mouth twitching as I cracked my vinaigrette egg and marveled at the dish. "You're having a terrible time, I see."

"Dreadful." Despite the intrusive attention I felt coming from the opposite side of the table, I returned his grin. "It's almost too pretty to eat."

Finely cut bits of mint, shaved red onion, and fennel paired exquisitely with the bitter greens. Once our plates were cleaned, the waitstaff quickly disposed of them, making way for our next culinary delight. As if he were a maestro and the food the orchestra he was conducting, the chef reappeared, proudly announcing his next dish.

"Our second course for you this evening features fire. The 'candle' is made from bacon fat. As it slowly burns it will create a sauce for you to dip your scallops and shaved, charred parmesan brussels sprouts in."

Waiters leaned in, lighting the bacon candles in unison. Gluttony encouraged everyone to sip from their wine and watch the candles melt. Bored with the theatrics, Envy turned to the male demon seated beside him. "Any word on the Stars of Seven?"

"Nothing new, your highness. All indications lead to the forest."

Wrath's attention slid to his brother. He carefully sipped his wine. "Chasing fairy tales again?"

"I wonder, dear brother, when I become the most powerful, will you still taunt me?" Envy's smile was vicious. "Or will you bow down to your new king?"

Lady Sundra subtly glanced at the prince next to her, her gaze calculating.

I pressed my lips together, trying to keep the questions from spilling out. Anir leaned across the table, a twinkle of mischief in his eyes. "Power is currency here. Mortals accumulate wealth; our royals do the same with magic."

"Can the princes of Hell be dethroned by lesser demons?"

"No. They always rule their circles. It's basically a test of who holds the most power amongst them. Sibling rivalry, if you will."

"So the devil is a title that can be passed to different rulers."

The princes near us stiffened, but Anir paid them little attention. "Not always. It more or less influences different eras on Earth. You can see through the ages which of the seven princes held the most power and influence based on the mortal world. Wars, greed, sexual awakenings. And yet," his whisper was anything but soft, "I cannot seem to recall an era of envy."

Envy slammed his wineglass onto the table. "Mind your tongue, mortal."

"Or else..."

Before they came to blows, the chef reappeared, his voice carrying over the chamber. "The third course is our most interactive. I ask that you place the slices of raw, marinated beef over the coals and quickly sear them on each side. Once the meat comes off the coals, sprinkle the frozen bleu cheese crumble across the strips."

Wrath shifted on my right, drawing my attention. He was focused on the door, where Greed had just walked in and bowed politely. He was in a bronze suit, his hair and eyes matching the exact shade of the metal he seemed born of. There was still that sense of wrongness in his sharp gaze, as if he were not quite as accustomed to the pageantry as his brothers were.

He gave Wrath a small nod before taking a seat at the opposite end of the table. "Apologies for tardiness. Do not stop the feast on my account."

"Fucking sit, already," Gluttony muttered. "Chef! Bring out another dish."

Taking advantage of family dramatics that diverted Wrath's attention, I leaned over to whisper in Fauna's ear. "Have you ever heard of the Stars of Seven?"

"Oh, you mean the Seven Sisters. Of course. Everyone here has. In old legends, they appeared to travelers in need, their forms no more substantial than shadows. Some say encountering them is a blessing, but most here believe it's a curse."

"Why?"

"If you interrupt their celestial spinning, there's a chance they may pluck and weave the wrong thread of fate. Sometimes the results of such interferences are immediate, and others take decades."

"How...intriguing. If they weave threads of fate, they must be able to recall the past. See the threads they've already spun." Fauna gave me a wary look but nodded. "So if anyone would know where lost objects are, it's the Seven Sisters."

"Emilia..." Fauna warned. "You cannot seek them out. Asking about a living being can cause damage to both the past and future."

"I wasn't planning on asking about a being. Only an object."

"Whatever you're scheming, stop. It's too dangerous."

Dangerous or not, I would find the mysterious spinners of fate. One of the enchanted skulls had mentioned "Seven Stars" and "Seven Sins." I'd immediately guessed the demon princes, but hadn't known what the seven stars meant. Now I was fairly confident I did. And the demon who Envy asked at the start of dinner had mentioned a forest.

Excitement thrummed through me. When I'd visited House Envy, he'd made it a point to tell me about Bloodwood Forest. I never did piece together why he wanted me to learn about the Curse Tree fable. I was beginning to suspect he'd also been hinting at something else.

His choice of topic this evening also was no accident. Envy wanted me looking for the Seven Sisters. And I'd wager it definitely had to do with the magical objects he was after; the Temptation Key and Triple Moon Mirror. For whatever reason, he must believe I'd have a better chance at gathering the information from them. Regardless of his motives, this information played into my own quite well.

I tried to recall the map I'd seen in House Envy. I could see the forest but couldn't remember where House Gluttony sat in relation to it.

"Where is Bloodwood Forest from here? The Prince of Envy mentioned it's not part of any royal land, but you have to pass through a territory to get there."

"From here?" Fauna contemplated. "The fastest route would be through Pride's circle."

I glanced around the long table. Wrath, Greed, Envy, Gluttony. I didn't see Sloth but recalled what Wrath had said about him slipping in before the fear ceremony. I sipped my wine and let my gaze travel around the other side of the room. Lust smirked at me from the far end of our side of the table, crooking his finger in a mocking wave.

Ignoring him, I asked quietly, "Has the devil arrived yet?"

Conversation ceased. Hands holding utensils and glasses paused mid-mouth. I might as well have cast a spell to freeze time. Apparently asking about the devil was a taboo subject.

"For our final course," the chef's voice cut through the silent room, "we have a combination of fire and ice together. Crème brûlée, fired right at your seat, topped with a garnish of frozen raspberry pearls and shattered mint leaves."

Once the chef left us to our dessert, warm fingers brushed against my wrist. I glanced up into Wrath's face. "Dance with me tonight."

He stood, as did the rest of the princes in attendance. Servants rushed to pull out their chairs before disappearing back into the shadows. "Where are you going?"

"It's time for us to don our masks."

"And shed our civility," Gluttony teased. "See you at the masquerade."

THIRTY

This prince of Hell certainly knew how to host an unforgettable event.

Despite what negativity the columnist would undoubtedly print about the party, it was entertaining. And spectacular. The ballroom that Fauna and I stepped into dripped decadence from every square inch. In the mortal world Gluttony's sin was thought to be food-centered, but here, in the Seven Circles, it was pure indulgence.

Last night's opening event was a mere glimpse into how far Gluttony could push his sin of choice. Glasses made of diamonds spilled sparkling demonberry wine over tables and trays encrusted with gemstones. More than a dozen crystal chandeliers hung from curved poles set up in even intervals around the dance floor.

Garlands of flowers with clear crystals sewn onto petals were twined around the poles. It looked as if we'd walked into a winter fairy tale. If ice was made of diamonds instead of water. When the candlelight caught the crystals and precious stones, it seemed as if the flames were caught inside ice. Gluttony's theme carried through from our meal in a grand fashion.

"This is—"

"Look!" Fauna nearly squealed. "Over there."

Desserts—glittered with edible gold and fashioned into life-like fantastical beasts—stood as tall as the guests. Winged ice dragons, beautiful pastel unicorns, three-headed hellhounds. It was as intriguing as it was almost unappetizing. Masqueraders did not seem to find it off-putting, carving into the flank of a unicorn, indulging in the berry-stuffed cake that resembled blood a little too closely for my tastes. My attention drifted to a platter of chocolate-covered fruits, piled as high as the night Wrath had tested me for this sin.

I swept my gaze around the room, searching for him and the other princes. None of them had arrived at this portion of the party yet. I glanced back at the ice dragon dessert sculpture. "Who won the hunt earlier?"

"I believe his highness did. He seemed intent to win at all costs."

"Wrath did?"

"Hmm? Oh, yes." She grabbed my elbow as if to keep herself from taking off. "Look over there. The rumors were true." Fauna's tone filled with awe. "He has tryst chambers."

As if we were moths drawn to the flame of debauchery, we drifted closer. The infamous glass rooms lined the west side of the ballroom. Low candlelight flickered from within them, and the drapery was neatly tied back, ensuring all who passed could look their fill at the romantic displays happening in those not-so-private chambers.

Fauna clutched my arm in a viselike grip, her gaze widening

behind her iridescent mask with each room and couple we strode by. The scenes were becoming more uninhibited, more daring. Thank the goddess we were masked. No matter how often I saw such public displays of sexuality, I could not stop my initial flash of embarrassment.

I felt the heat of my blush and knew my face must be close to scarlet.

Fauna was not having the same reaction; she studied the couples, as if committing certain positions to memory. If she had pulled out a notebook, I wouldn't have been surprised.

"Did you see that?" Fauna's voice held a hint of appreciation. "I had no idea so many people could fit into such a small chamber, let alone do what they were all doing and maintain their rhythm. That takes tremendous skill."

"And stamina. *That* is the real feat on display."

She giggled and swatted at my arm. "To think...these are the tamer tableaus. I've heard the twilight garden is much more risqué than I'd originally been told."

Unbidden, I thought of Wrath. I tried not to let suspicion claw its way back in.

What he did, and whoever he might have seen last night, was none of my concern. I internally scolded myself. If Wrath were here he'd smirk and call me on the blatant lie.

Before I could examine my feelings further, a strange hush descended like a regiment of soldiers surrounding the masquerade. I scanned the ballroom, searching for the cause of such a reaction. My breath caught. Six imposing figures wearing wolf masks emerged from the corners of the ballroom. Tall, silent, deadly.

There was something about them all standing together—their inner battles and schemes forgotten as they became a fearsome unit—that turned a prickle of unease into a fight-or-flight response. Even lords and ladies of Hell seemed ready to bolt.

Tension rolled through the crowd.

My focus landed on the biggest as he prowled forward. Even with a mask covering his face, I'd recognize that confident gait anywhere. Wrath didn't simply walk into a room, he strode in and dominated it. And he wasn't even trying to. Everyone else could fade away and he'd be left burning brightly. A constant source of power and vitality.

The princes slowly circled the crowd, as if herding everyone. Fauna and I shuffle-stepped along with everyone else, the space between us growing smaller with each step we took. Then, once everyone was near the dance floor, the princes turned and watched the stairs.

I dragged my attention from Wrath and waited. In a well-choreographed move, a lone prince made his way down the grand staircase, his hands tucked into his pockets, shoes shining like gemstones in the flickering candlelight. Even from across the massive space, I could hear the faint clap of his steps as the leather soles smacked the marble floor.

Fauna leaned close. "That's the Prince of Pride."

I watched the striking figure stroll through the crowd. Like the other princes, he wore a wolf mask that covered all but his bottom lip and chin. His was silver and gold. Ornate yet retaining elegance. He did not glance at anyone, nor did he acknowledge those who curtsied or bowed as he passed. His hair was a chestnut brown with threads of gold spun in. It was cut close on the sides and stylishly longer on top. Not a strand was out of place.

Not a crinkle to be found in his swallowtail suit.

Dressed in dark navy and silver, he did not blend into the

shadows. He stood slightly apart, as if he wished for them to remember who owned them.

I hadn't realized I'd been holding my breath, openly staring at him behind the safety of my mask, until I exhaled. *The devil* stood only a few feet away. A figure reviled and loathed by almost all. If the stories were true, here was a rebellious angel, cast from Heaven.

Now the king of demons. So corrupted by sin, so monstrous, that he ruled over the worst denizens of each realm. His silver gaze collided with mine, flashing like a star streaking across the sky. A chill rolled down my spine. If I hadn't accidentally betrothed myself to Wrath, and if he hadn't accepted the bond, I'd be staring at my husband now.

Pride scanned me from mask to toe, his head tilted to one side. I had an awful feeling he was sizing me up, debating how to best show off his skills as he took down his prey. If Wrath reminded me of a caged panther at times, Pride was a golden-maned lion.

Both princes ferocious. Both deadly. But only one could blend into the night, strike hard and fast under the cover of darkness, then slip away, undetected. I tore my attention from the devil and searched for Wrath. He'd disappeared.

"Hello, Lady Vengeance."

The low, slightly gravelly voice was at my ear. It took all of my effort to not show surprise or tension. I hoped he didn't sense the item I'd smuggled on my person. I slowly brought my attention to the prince at my side and offered a slight incline of my head. He was not my king. And I'd never been instructed to bow. "Your highness."

"Would you honor me with a dance?"

Fauna sunk her teeth into her lower lip, practically dancing on the balls of her feet as she nodded vigorously in encouragement.

"I . . ."

"You?" He swept his attention around the room, a knowing gleam entering his eyes. The crowd surged back, as if terrified of his attention settling on them. The dance floor cleared. "Is there someone else you were hoping to dance with first? If so, let's make him regret not asking before I did."

"I will dance with you, but there's no ulterior motive in it."

"Of course."

His amusement remained as he whisked me onto the dance floor and the orchestra immediately began playing a waltz. For a few beats, we didn't speak. He simply whirled us around the room, my nerves over dancing in public a forgotten memory as he easily led us through the steps. He was lovely. A shining diamond encapsulated in pure platinum.

Or maybe that was what he wanted me to believe. Maybe he was really a blade. Forged in hellfire and deadly as sin. As we waltzed closer together, I waited for some spark of memory to catch and ignite hidden flames of desire. If he *was* the lover from my vision, my body didn't seem to recognize him.

He leaned scandalously close. "If you're this intrigued by my mask, wait until I take it off."

"I assure you I am not looking at your mask, your majesty. Honestly, I'm trying to find a new set of horns or fangs."

Pride's eyes glittered. "I can be terrifying. When I want to be."

"I'm sure you can, but not like someone I know."

"Wrath?" His mouth turned down at the edges as my gaze searched the dance floor, hoping his name would be enough to summon him. "I'm unused to such beautiful dance partners thinking of my brother while in *my* arms."

I couldn't help myself. I laughed in the devil's face. "You're exceedingly conceited."

"One of our most prominent family traits. Though I assure you my ego is well justified."

"I'll have to take your word for it, your highness."

We waltzed across the floor, between other couples who'd joined us, his steps steady and smooth as he led me around and around. Even after Wrath's impromptu lesson, I'd been worried I'd miss steps or stomp on his feet, but his skill was enough to overcome any of my mistakes. Part of me was disappointed. If this had gone terribly, it might have been my current largest fear.

"The Prince of Wrath is quite serious compared to the rest of you."

"That's what he does—he excels at war and justice. Both serious matters. And it's why none of us have to bother with the messy bits of ruling." I drew my brows together. "This realm would have ripped itself apart if he didn't terrify it into submission."

"I'm not sure I understand."

Pride swung us around until I could see Wrath leaning against the marble column. His mask was tugged back and his gaze followed each step, each glide around the ballroom.

He looked neither pleased nor angered, but there was something about his expression that made me think he was...jealous. Pride lowered his hand, skimming my spine, no doubt purposefully stoking Wrath's annoyance. I stepped on his foot and internally smiled as he winced.

"He, dearest darling, is the balance. And is usually the only thing standing between us and total destruction. Wrath is impartial justice made flesh. He is feared because he does not hesitate to carry out a sentence, to mete out justice on those deserving punishment. If he must send someone to the Prison of Damnation, what mortals consider their version of 'Hell,' it is no light matter."

Thus far, no one had spoken of the mortal souls sent here. "Where is that located?"

"It's adorable you think I'd tell you. Have you asked Wrath?"

I had and I was fairly confident he'd said something about an isle off the western shore. "I was under the impression that was what your role is supposed to be."

"Rules are more fun when they're broken." He lifted a shoulder. "Delegating is also part of ruling, is it not?"

Before I could answer, he swept us across the room once again, his motions fluid and graceful and commanding. Understanding he was no longer interested in speaking of power, I changed tactics. I waited until we were far enough away from other couples, then said quietly, "I know it's private, but I wanted to offer my condolences."

Pride tensed beneath my touch. I doubted I would have noticed if we hadn't been dancing, which was exactly why I wanted to broach this subject on the dance floor.

"Losing someone you love," I continued when he didn't speak, "is a horrible kind of pain. I would not wish that on my worst enemy."

"As I'm sure my brothers and I are counted amongst those you consider foes, it pleases me to hear that."

It was only partially true, but I didn't correct him. With the next rotation around the dance floor, his mask slipped back, revealing his mouth. A small diagonal scar carved through his upper lip and ended just below the lower one. I'd seen it before and hoped the rapid beating of my heart was mistaken for the increased tempo he used as we continued dancing.

We were gliding closer to the edge of the dance floor, nearing an alcove hidden by a series of large potted ferns. Just as we stepped close to it, I swung us around and pulled him into the shadowy spot, far from prying eyes. I couldn't see his full expression, but I heard his sharp intake of breath as I pressed him against the wall and brought my lips to his ear.

Needing no further encouragement, he tugged off his mask, and dropped it to the floor, then went to work removing mine, mistaking our current position for something it was not.

A reaction I'd been hoping for.

"Your brother thinks you're debauched. Too drunk on wine and lovers to bother with anything of importance." I pulled back enough to study him. Wariness entered his features. "Yet you were leading your guards around the grounds of House Pride this morning, looking anything but intoxicated."

"I beg your pardon?" He feigned confusion like a skilled actor. I noticed he didn't directly address my question, giving him a way to avoid speaking a lie. "I'm here for kissing, not an inquisition. If you're interested in talking, I can find more scintillating topics."

He brought his mouth close to mine and I stalled him with a palm to the chest.

"Allow me to speak more clearly, your majesty. Do not stand here, pretending as if I do not recall that you were the one who made me dismount from my horse. Why did you hold me hostage at your House for so long? Was it to hide how many guards you have patrolling your grounds?"

"You cannot expect me to share information with another House."

"Fine. Answer this for me. Why are you hiding the fact you aren't nearly as drunk and prideful as you'd like others to believe?"

"As a matter of principle, I rarely show my true face to anyone. You would be wise to do the same."

371

My gaze strayed to his scar. I doubted that was the only rea-son he chose to hide. "You didn't show up to the monastery that night; you possessed Antonio. To maintain anonymity?"

"Shouldn't you be asking about the curse?"

A familiar demon deflection tactic; answering one question with another. "I know my birth signaled the end of your curse. Therefore you must have had other reasons to hide."

His temper flared. My hit to his pride had reached its mark. "I was not *hiding*. I was otherwise occupied."

"Well, while I'm sure we could talk in circles for eternity, I didn't pull you aside for a frustrating chat."

"Then let's get to the fun part." Pride dragged his hand down my silhouette and slowly drew it back up, pausing near my thigh. His brows quirked. "What do we have here?"

"My dagger." I grinned as he abruptly unhanded me. "The fun part is this. I will cross your lands, twice, on a time and date of my choosing, without any interference from you, your guards, or anyone who calls House Pride or that circle their home."

"Why should I agree to such a bargain?"

"Because I know one of your secrets."

"My bedroom talents are already widely known."

His teasing was another attempt to deflect. I had him cornered and he was showing his teeth by smiling as if he was unbothered. I understood where the term *devil-may-care* originated. Pride exuded a carefree attitude perfectly. Suspiciously so.

"I won't tell your brother about the slumber root. You've cer-tainly got enough to knock out an entire army. And that, your highness, sounds like information you'd be desperate to keep to yourself. Unlike the *bedroom* talents you boast about."

His gaze was hard, calculating. A muscle in his jaw twitched as he jerked his head in agreement. "Fine."

"You'll need to be more specific."

"You may cross my lands, twice, without any issue from anyone who calls my circle their own. In exchange, you will not tell my brother about my slumber root. There." He glared down his nose at me. "Satisfied?"

"More than you can possibly imagine, your highness."

Suspicion crept into his features. Rightly so. He'd just made a grievous error.

I turned and strode out of our little alcove, but didn't make it far before I was intercepted by another prince. Envy's mask was off now, too, and his green eyes practically glowed as he glanced behind me. "Well played, Shadow Witch. One stone, two princes."

"Are you drunk already?"

"Not on spirits." He flashed the smile that showed his dimple. "I've come to collect you, guest of honor. It's time for you to feed us your biggest fear. And I cannot tell you how hungry I suddenly am."

THIRTY-ONE

I caught sight of Fauna in the crowd; her brown skin had paled considerably beneath her mask. My friend looked around, as if trying to find a way she could distract the assembly and stop this nightmare before it began. Anir stood beside her, his expression radiating enough anger to be worthy of his adopted House of Sin.

He seemed poised to grab the blade I knew was hidden under his evening attire and fight his way to my side. His hard gaze promised anyone who tried stopping him would suffer his fury. He and Fauna both knew there was no getting out of this, but they did not have to like it, or make it easy on the royals. Despite the abundance of worry coursing through me, their show of friendship bolstered my spirits.

I pushed away from Envy's proffered arm and glanced around, searching for Wrath. I needed his familiar scowl to calm my nerves. I rolled up onto my tiptoes, looking past shoulders and heads for the demon prince's imposing figure. Of course, he went missing again.

I didn't see Lust or Greed in the crowd, either. And Sloth must be in attendance—there had been seven princes in wolf masks earlier—but he was also noticeably absent. Or lounging some-where. Perhaps there was a gaming room that they'd retired to. Part of me wanted to dash around the castle until I located them. Which was only stalling the inevitable. Maybe it was a blessing that all seven princes would not be privy to my greatest fear.

Pride slipped out from the alcove where we'd struck our bar-gain and sauntered over to a column, leaving me to face this trial on my own. Not that I was surprised.

"Come." Envy didn't bother controlling the excitement in his voice. "Allow me to introduce you to the master of ceremonies."

I followed him through the parting crowd, pulse pounding with each step we took closer to a dais that had been brought in. A blue-skinned demon with red eyes waited, wicked dagger in hand. It was a miracle my heart hadn't thrashed out of my body. I held each side of my beaded skirts as I walked up the stairs to stand beside the demon. He nodded once, then lifted the blade above his head, showing off the runes carved into it, the crowd going uproarious at the sight.

"Without further ado, if there are no objections, we will release the biggest fear from our guest." The master of ceremonies held out a hand to me. "Lady Emilia. If you will be so kind as to offer your wrist. I must take a bit of blood for the magic to work."

Panic thrummed in each of my cells. I could barely see past the little white spots floating across my vision as I slowly lifted my arm. All our lives Nonna Maria wanted us to keep our blood from our enemies. And here I stood, offering it freely. To a blade etched with magical runes that would steal my secrets.

I held my arm steady, fighting the urge to yank it back and flee.

To his credit, the master of ceremonies did not radiate joy or triumph. He offered a sympathetic look and whispered, "One tiny pinch and it will be over shortly."

The blade felt like ice against my skin. Panic seized me. This was really happening. I squeezed my eyes shut, silently praying to the goddesses for this to—

"Stop." The deep voice echoed. "I will be the one to sacrifice a secret of the heart."

The metal disappeared from my skin at once. I opened my eyes, looking from the master of ceremonies to the crowd. As one, the audience turned, staring with open shock at the demon who'd spoken. I followed their stares until I found him.

Wrath stood with his arms crossed, his attention fixed on me.

"With all due respect, your majesty, you cannot substitute yourself..."

"I won the hunt. I am claiming it as my prize."

The master of ceremonies shook his head as if carefully considering his phrasing. "I...I do not believe it can be completed without great cost to you."

"I am well aware of the price."

I watched in disbelief as Wrath made his way down the aisle and up the stairs of the dais. Was he afraid my biggest fear would have worse repercussions than revealing his truth? Wrath trained me to withstand demonic influence, but he'd never seemed concerned about this portion of the feast. Had he always known he'd stand in for me?

He was scheming, but I had no clue what his goal was.

Without taking his gaze from mine, he slipped out of his suit jacket and rolled back the sleeve of his left arm. At the sight of our matching tattoos, a murmur went up in the crowd. Apparently not everyone knew our betrothal had been forced.

For them, it was one thing to woo a prince, and apparently another to magically bind him into matrimony. Perhaps they worried his unexpected show of heroics was brought on by a magic spell. The master of ceremonies stared openmouthed at the demon prince. I doubted this prince had ever offered something like this before. Even I couldn't believe it. Wrath, the demon who valued his secrets more than anyone I knew, was offering one up.

For me. In front of every enemy court. It was not a declaration of love, but it was close.

Wrath finally tore his attention from me. "Get the dagger."

"I..." The master of ceremonies fumbled for the blade, clearly uncomfortable with carving into one of the rulers of Hell. "Before we begin, there is still the matter of needing your brothers to vote on this being your prize."

"Oh, for shit's sake. Enough." Pride shot up from where he'd been slumped against a column, his silver eyes narrowing in warning. "This is incredibly dull. Surely there is some other more diverting prize to be claimed? I find secrets tiresome." He stared at his brother in challenge. "Perhaps this year's sacrifice will come in the form of a forbidden tryst. I'm sure we can find a volunteer willing to bed the guest of honor. Then my brother may pick a different prize."

The assembled demons subtly looked from Wrath to their king, their breath held.

"No."

Wrath's tone was cold enough to rival ice. He glanced to me, probably to see if I'd been intrigued by the idea and he'd spoken too quickly. I imagined if I said yes, he'd stand back and not utter a word of protest if I chose to bed Pride. No matter how much he'd hate it.

And hate it he would. Wrath's mask of indifference had slipped and he hadn't put it back.

"There seems to be a misunderstanding." The devil's smile was sinful as Wrath cast a wary glance his way. Pride was practically preening, pleased he'd laid the perfect bait and Wrath had fallen into his true trap. "I did not mean to suggest *I* would be offering services. As Lady Emilia is your intended, I believe *you* ought to be the one to bed her, brother."

I stiffened. If Wrath and I shared a bed...

...we'd be that much closer to completing our marriage bond. And Pride knew it. He looked undisturbed by the idea; if anything, he seemed eager for me to marry his brother. Which indicated he never cared about the contract I signed and I'd never been his intended. So what in the seven hells was really going on? If the devil's curse had been broken by Vittoria's and my birth, I still couldn't understand why the demons had lied about the brides.

Envy, who'd been glowering at the interruption, suddenly perked up.

Wrath looked to me then, his expression blank except for the slight tightness around his mouth. It was the only indication he wasn't happy with the turn of events.

Whatever he saw in my face had his tone going hard when he addressed his brother again. "Pick another option or stand back and let's vote to complete the ceremony."

"I told you," Pride drawled, "I've grown quite bored of secrets. It's time for a new tradition. I'm sure our host is willing to oblige."

Pride nodded to Gluttony. The prince of this circle rubbed his hands together. "Indeed. I do love breaking the rules. You have two choices. Either bed each other in one of the glass chambers here." He stood aside and with a grand flourish, yanked a gold cord that held draperies back. Inside, an unoccupied candlelit bed-room softly glowed. "Or—"

"Your royal suite," I offered, stunning everyone, myself most of all.

"My suite?" Wrath stared at me as I nodded. "We do not have to change the rules, Emilia. If I want to claim the fear as my prize, I will."

"Only if you gain enough votes." Gluttony's grin widened as Wrath's temper rumbled through the ballroom. "You may have won the hunt, but this is no longer your prize to claim. We're sub-stituting the guest of honor's sacrifice. And she's made her deci-sion. You may choose the royal suite, the glass room, or, best yet, you may stay right here. Take her over the dais, or against the column. Then we can be sure you complete the task."

"Unless you'd like to stand aside and have someone else vol-unteer," Envy offered, his too-innocent smile indicating he was using the sin he ruled over to taunt his brother. "My vote would be on Gluttony. He is the host."

"No."

Wrath's tone indicated there was no chance in this circle of Hell that he would turn this into a spectator sport and would go to war if his brothers tried any maneuvering.

Gluttony took it all in stride and I wondered if his mood ever soured or if he was permanently happy. "A tryst in your royal suite it is." He clapped twice. "Master of ceremonies. Complete the ritual."

Wrath paced around the quiet royal suite, a mighty predator caged. It did not matter that his cage was a well-appointed bedroom suite with chilled champagne, chocolate-covered fruits, crystal chandeliers, and silk sheets. And a fiancée who craved his touch.

Even if he hadn't offered one of his secrets to allow me to keep mine, I would want him. It was time to stop lying to myself. To stop pretending that it was only the seductive magic of this world and our bond creating this attraction. I wanted him. It was his imposing figure I looked for in each crowded room. His protection I welcomed and his sin I aligned best with.

Regardless of our past and the circumstances that brought us here, to this moment, together, I wanted this night of passion with him.

The prince did not appear to feel the same. He prowled over to the fireplace and leaned against the mantel, watching as the flames turned silver and writhed before him. He did not speak on our walk here, nor did he look at me once we'd entered his suite.

Without turning to meet my stare, he said, "It's not too late for me to give up a secret instead. We do not have to do this. I vowed you would have a choice. I stand by my word. My brothers will not vote against me, no matter what they said earlier."

"I *did* choose."

He finally turned, his expression thunderous. "Choosing between two less-than-ideal options is not a choice."

My lips curved upward. "Will bedding you be less than ideal?"

"Do not make light of the situation."

"I'm not." My voice lost the teasing edge. "I've never wanted to give up a fear or secret. I cannot say the same about desiring you."

His focus slid from my eyes to my mouth. "This is not the same."

"Is it the most romantic proposition? There's no denying it

isn't. However, I cannot say I'm displeased. As you're an expert at sensing emotions and lies, I should think you know that. Therefore, I'm left to believe you're upset because you feel as if *your* choice has been stolen." A different thought occurred. "Or perhaps you don't want to bed me."

"Is that what you believe?"

"If you visited someone else last night and do not want to be with me, I understand. We can go back downstairs and I'll complete the fear ceremony. You do not owe me anything."

Wrath stalked across the room, and I held my ground. He gently set his hands on my hips and pulled me against him. A little thrill shot through me where our bodies connected. Even through his trousers and my beaded gown, I could feel his truth pressed against me.

"You see?" His voice was rough, deep. It scraped against some inner part of me, making me want to lean into him more. "It is not a matter of wanting you, Emilia."

"Then what is it?"

"Call it selfish. But I do not want there to be any outside forces driving you into my arms." He tilted my face up, his lips hovering above mine. "When you decide to come to my bedchamber, I want you to know whose sheets you're climbing between. I want you to call out my name."

"I know who you are."

"Do you?" His lips lightly trailed across my skin, almost touching the sensitive area of my neck, but not quite, as he brought his mouth to my ear. "I should like to hear you say it."

"Your brothers only said 'tryst.' " I abruptly changed the subject. "They did not specify that we needed to..."

"To?" He leaned back, his mouth twisting up on one side as

he waited. The devil knew exactly what I meant. And he'd feign confusion until I said it.

"Fuck. Or fornicate. Though I've only heard the first word in this circle, repeated like a wicked prayer when I left the pleasure garden last night."

His laughter was loud and lovely. I wished I could stuff the crass word back into my stupid mouth as my cheeks pinked and I silently cursed them and the demon.

He brushed his knuckles across my jaw, his expression filled with warmth.

"No, I suppose they did not specify whether we had to fornicate." His eyes darkened to a molten gold. "What would you have me do instead, my lady? This?"

I didn't have time to answer. He trailed little love bites along the column of my throat. I didn't even attempt to rein in the sigh that escaped me as his tongue flicked over my pulse point.

"Tell me what you desire and it will be yours."

I closed my eyes and leaned into his caress. An image of the lovers spread out on the table in the entryway during our arrival crossed my mind. Wrath's mouth moved along my shoulder, his kisses hot and distracting the closer they drew to my décolletage.

"I want..."

He stopped long enough to draw back and look into my eyes. "Yes?"

"...you to take off my gown."

Nimble fingers began undoing the buttons along the side of my dress. Unlike his assistance during our trek through the Sin Corridor, he did not move swiftly. He took his time, as if he knew precisely how each button coming undone was driving me wild with want. Each accidental graze of his fingers on my skin, each hitch of my breath...I was already close to combusting and my clothes hadn't even come off.

He slipped the straps from one shoulder, trailing open-mouthed kisses as he went. Then the other strap slid off, his tongue and teeth following the path. He carefully tugged the top down, halting only when he'd freed my breasts.

"You are so godsdamn beautiful." He looked like a man who'd been offered the finest meal money could purchase after nearly starving. But instead of feasting, he planned to enjoy every bite, savoring it. One thumb slowly passed over my nipple, causing it to tighten with pleasure. Heat pooled low in my belly. "What else would you like, my lady?"

"Pleasure. Seduction." I gathered up my courage. "I want you to stay. All night. With me. And if you even *think* of bowing afterward and leaving like you did last time you touched me, I will hunt you down and make you regret it."

"Threaten me again."

His raw tone indicated he liked it very much. "Twisted heathen."

"Only the best for you."

He took possession of my mouth with his. His kiss dominated, owned. I was only too happy to submit. For a moment. I ran my tongue over his bottom lip, sighing as he took advantage and swept his into my mouth. Conquering, seducing. Just as I'd requested.

I pulled him in closer, tighter, nearer. I missed this. Missed *him*. The way he felt, the sound of his breath catching as he touched me, unleashing his desires and giving in to our connection. His clever fingers cupped my breasts, fondling with maddeningly light caresses that left me desiring more. My gown remained wrapped around my waist. I wanted it off. I wanted his bare skin on mine, his hands free to explore every inch of my body.

I tugged him through the little sitting chamber toward the bedroom, wanting to feel the weight of him pressing me into the mattress. In this, he allowed me to lead, never breaking from his slow exploration of my mouth. He followed me down onto the bed, slowly pulling my gown the rest of the way off. I lifted my hips, helping to shimmy it over them as he tossed it aside.

His jacket and shirt hit the ground next. The only thing left between us were my scandalously thin undergarments and his trousers.

Wrath eyed the ribbons at my sides, looking eager to unwrap the present they offered. And, goddess curse me, I wanted him to tear them to shreds. A slow, triumphant smile spread across his face as he probably sensed my arousal.

He fitted himself between my thighs and bent forward, tugging the ribbons with his teeth. I squirmed beneath him, unsure exactly what it was I wanted him to do next, but knowing his current position was very tantalizing.

He halted his movements. "Is this all right?"

"Yes." I cupped his face and caressed his cheek. "Please, don't stop."

It was the permission he'd been waiting for. Without delay, he finished the task he'd started. Once my undergarments were gone, he admired me for a long moment, his focus searing with its intensity. I fought the urge to close my legs or cover myself.

As if he'd plucked that fear from my head, he glanced at me sharply. "Don't ever hide yourself from me. Unless you want me to stop, or I'm not pleasuring you the way you like. You are beautiful. And I want nothing more than to do this," he dragged a finger down the center of my body and I almost saw stars. "With my tongue."

He gazed deep into my eyes, making sure I saw the truth in his, then he brought his mouth to me. The first stroke of his tongue was a shock of pleasure, electrifying my whole system. I arched up from the bed, body tingling with anticipation of the next touch.

Wrath hooked his arms around my legs and lowered his mouth once more. This time he held me in place, angling my hips up to allow for the most pleasure. Blood rushed through my head. Oh, goddess, every touch was sweet torture. Just when I thought it couldn't feel any better, he plunged a finger inside me, his mouth moving harder against me.

I writhed beneath him, hands searching for something to grasp, desperate to ground myself in the swirling storm of pleasure lifting me up and away. I gripped the sheets as his openmouthed kisses continued in that intimate place, his fingers pumping in time with each beat of my heart. I was coming undone, chasing that line of fire streaking through me.

My fingers dove into his soft hair, my breath coming in shallow bursts, my pulse pounding through every glorious inch of my body. I was so close.

Wrath's strokes turned demanding, the demon of war commanding my body to obey his wish and shatter against his mouth. Because he willed it. Desired it.

I rolled my hips forward and he growled in approval, the sound and vibration of it nearly unleashing me. Before I could call out his name, he moved up my body, pressing his own arousal against me, his mouth crashing into mine. He rocked his hips, the force gloriously rough as our bodies slammed together. He withdrew and moved against me again. And again.

I dug my nails into his shoulders and greedily met his movements with my own.

Each thrust pushed me closer to that edge. The hard length of him sliding against me created friction that heightened my pleasure. His cursed trousers were still on, still preventing us from fully connecting, but it did not stop me from finally shattering beneath his massive body.

With a groan so powerful it damn near shook the bed, Wrath followed me over the edge.

THIRTY-TWO

I laid within the circle of Wrath's arms, my back snug against his chest, as we both caught our breath. He traced the outline of my tattoo with his fingertips, his idle touch stirring a new set of emotions. There was something more intimate about the gentle action than any sexual act or physical expression of love. I wasn't sure Wrath was fully aware he was doing it. Which complicated things more.

I nestled against him, trying to push my worries aside and enjoy the moment.

He pressed his lips to my temple. "Please refrain from wiggling like that. At least for a few minutes."

"Is it painful?"

He smiled against my skin. "Quite the contrary."

Intrigued, and not very good at following commands, I did it again. Wrath's body hardened against me. Goddess above. His thirst for seduction was unquenchable.

I rolled over to face him. "Take off your pants."

He arched a brow. I swept an arm to indicate my naked body.

"I refuse to be the only one completely nude."

"If I remove my trousers, I cannot guarantee there will be much sleeping."

I mimicked his arched brow and waited. I'd never said anything about sleeping. Bold of him to assume he'd figured out my plans. With a sigh, his pants vanished. He tucked me against him and I grinned as I shimmied closer and heard his sharp intake of breath.

"Emilia."

"Yes?" My tone was innocence sprinkled with sugar. "Is there a problem?"

I should have known better than to taunt the general of war. Wrath did not play fairly; he played to win. From behind, he situated himself right at the entrance of my body, causing my breath to hitch. I went tight and loose at once, ready for him to press himself deeper.

"Tell me, fiancée. Are you certain you want me as your husband?" He gripped my hip in one hand and slid the other under me, pulling me closer. The tenuous hold on my self-control was slipping. I arched into him. "You're ready and willing to spend eternity here, with me?"

My mind was still deciding but my body was slick and willing. This time when he rocked his hips, his strokes were deliberately slow, tantalizing. Without his trousers on, his velvet skin slid over mine, the sensation pure bliss. I would give up almost anything to experience all of him right now. Except my mission.

With great effort I slipped out from beneath his arms and stood. He put up no resistance or fight. To soften the blow of my rejection, I leaned over the bed and gave him a chaste kiss.

"How about a drink before bed?"

Wrath watched me carefully, but there was no disappointment or hurt in his expression. Only victory. He knew I would not go through with bedding him. "Would you like me to get it?"

"I'm already up. You stay there." He rolled up onto an elbow and gave me a bemused look as I pointed at him. "No moving. No bowing. You promised."

"I am a demon bound by my word."

"Good."

I picked up my gown and strode over to the sitting room where the chilled champagne waited. Heart thumping wildly, I glanced over my shoulder, ensuring he'd remained in bed, then said a quick prayer to the goddess of lies and deception to guide my hand.

I'd made a vow to someone I loved well before I knew Wrath. And this opportunity was too good to pass on. No matter how much my heart roared in pain, anticipating the break.

I grabbed the item I'd sewn into my skirts, my movements sure and quick. Before I talked myself out of it, I sprinkled a pinch of the mixture into Wrath's glass, then poured the champagne over it. I dropped a piece of chocolate-covered fruit into each glass. Bubbles fizzed around the unwelcome intrusion, doing a fine job of covering my treachery.

I sauntered back into the bedroom, pleased to see Wrath—as respectful as he was—distracted by the sway of my hips. I hadn't bothered to put on my night clothing yet. Not that he had, either. His muscled upper body was bare, though he'd pulled the sheets up around his waist. He patted the spot next to him, a lazy grin curving those wicked lips.

In a different life, I could happily kiss him for eternity.

"To new beginnings." I offered the prince his drink then raised my own glass. *"Iucundissima somnia."*

Wrath's brow crinkled at the last part of the toast. If he recalled he'd once said it to me, he didn't comment. He clinked his glass against mine, then downed the champagne in one go.

I sipped mine and silently counted. His glass hit the floor before I finished my first sip.

"Emilia." He turned a sluggish gaze on me, eyes flashing with fury. And betrayal. The temperature plummeted around us, then returned to normal as he battled an invisible foe fiercely before slowly slumping back.

The mighty demon of war was no longer a threat.

I set my glass on the bedside table, then reached over to brush the hair from his forehead. Whatever peace we'd made would be gone when he awoke. It was a sacrifice I'd been willing to make, but it didn't make it easy. I kissed his brow, savoring the moment before I straightened.

"Sweetest dreams, your highness."

Tonight I was a thief of a different sort as I stole through the corridor between Wrath's suite and mine, slipping in and out of shadows like a pickpocket swiping purses. I crept into my room and raced to the trunk. I yanked out the fur-lined leather pants, thick sweater, and socks I'd brought, tugged on boots, and swung my ebony cloak around my shoulders in record time. I fastened my dagger in my thigh holster and tugged it to make sure it was secure.

In moments I was back in the hallway, rushing down the servants' stairs. With the party still underway, no one was near this end of the castle. I hoped.

Heart thundering in warning, I peered around the corner. A door was propped open in the back of the kitchen—just as I'd suspected—to let out the heat created by oven fires.

With a quick prayer to the goddess of lies and deception, I darted across the corridor, then slowed once I entered the kitchen. I had no idea how long the slumber root would keep Wrath unconscious; given his immense power, I didn't think I had long. I needed to be far enough away that he couldn't catch me before I crossed into Pride's territory. I rushed across the wide expanse connecting the back of the castle to the stables, not halting until I reached the entrance.

My gaze swept along the outside of the building, landing on every nook and cranny, searching for any sign of movement in the near dark. The grooms must be abed, having tended to the horses after the morning's hunt. I cracked the door just enough to slip inside and rushed along the stalls until I found Tanzie. She snuffed in greeting, her silver-clawed hooves shredding the hay.

"We're going on an adventure, sweet girl."

I quickly saddled the horse, impressed and thankful I recalled the proper steps needed to do so after seeing it done back home on a few occasions. I led her out by the reins, and, bless her, the horse moved swiftly and silently out of the main door, as if she knew stealth was required.

"Take me to House Pride." I swung up onto her and with a quick pat on her flank, we were off. "We're visiting Bloodwood Forest."

Tanzie shot off through the night, snow kicking up behind us as we practically flew over the slopes of House Gluttony. I gripped on with my knees, leaning into the wind.

Each thunderous step made me want to glance over my shoulder, convinced castle guards had been alerted and were in pursuit. We rode through the hills of slumber root, and on our right, where I hadn't noticed it before, was the upper edge of the Lake of Fire.

Sulfur blew in on a cold breeze, lifting strands of my hair and coaxing a shudder. I kept my attention on the castle looming in the distance, tensed for Pride's guards. As if she refused to be taken by any army again, Tanzie pushed herself faster, hooves greedily eating the frozen earth. We skirted the edge of House Pride and blew past it, never stopping or being stopped.

I let out a whoop of joy. One small victory down.

If memory served correctly, I'd pass from Pride's circle into Envy's. I'd already been invited onto Envy's land and he hadn't revoked that permission. With any luck, I would pass through and make it to Bloodwood Forest unscathed.

As we rode like the devil was chasing us, my mind raced with all the thoughts I'd tried hiding during the feast. Envy was after the Seven Sisters. And he'd pointed out the Curse Tree when I'd strolled through his gallery. I might not know specifics about the forest, but I could find that unusual tree thanks to the fable that had indicated it was "deep in the heart" of the forest.

And hopefully the mystical beings who might help me find the Temptation Key or Triple Moon Mirror would be nearby the fearsome tree. At this point, any information they could offer on either magical object would be useful.

We passed through House Envy without incident. Since the

prince of that House was dropping subtle clues in my presence, I didn't think he'd stop my pursuit through his lands. Too soon we came to the smaller tributary of the Black River that bisected Envy's territory and opened on Bloodwood Forest. Tanzie slowed to a near stop and toed the ground, considering the jump. I was considering the sight before us. Bloodwood Forest was aptly named. Even under the blanket of a night sky, I saw that the bark was a dark crimson.

Deep into the woods, puffs of smoke floated along like ghostly fog. I had the worst suspicion it was not created by fires, but was the breath of large beasts prowling through the crimson wood. Or maybe it was from some of the demons I'd seen in the journals. The ones who craved hearts and blood. I inhaled and slowly exhaled.

"Ready to find the Curse Tree next, girl?"

Tanzie jerked her head, then charged the ebony river. I forced my eyes to remain open as we were momentarily airborne, my stomach dropping. We touched down and Tanzie didn't pause to catch her breath; she darted through the woods, careening around trees and underbrush.

I'd expected unnerving silence. In reality a chorus of bugs chirped so loudly, it was disorienting. If any predator was near, it would be impossible to hear the attack until it was too late. Tanzie seemed to know that. My mighty hell horse tucked her chin and wove in and around any obstacle that came up. Determined to bring her rider to our destination unscathed.

We rushed through a clearing, and at the edge I caught sight of an Aper demon. It tossed its giant head in the air, and that was all I saw; we left it drooling behind us. Crimson trees flashed by, the colors streaking across my peripheral vision like hundreds of shooting stars dripping blood. I gripped tighter to the reins, counting each beat of my heart. We had to be nearing the center of the forest by now.

A few minutes of hard riding later, Tanzie abruptly stopped.

There, amongst a thick outcropping of crimson wood, was an oversized silver tree. We'd actually found it. I stared a moment, taking it in. The Curse Tree was unmistakable; taller, wider, and different in color from all other trees in the forest. In the moonlight, its silver bark gleamed like an enormous sword thrust deep into the earth. It was beautiful and frightening.

I dismounted and patted Tanzie. "Stay here and stay alert."

She nuzzled my shoulder as if telling me the same.

I inched toward the tree, dagger now in hand. The bugs had gone silent. An ominous mist drifted above the frozen soil, hiding any sign of recent tracks. Roots jutted up like the rotting fingers of slain giants. I moved closer to better inspect the leaves. They were similar to a common birch, but were ebony with silver veins. According to the legends I'd read, they were both sharp as blades and as fragile as glass.

"Have you come to request a blood wish?"

I spun around, the hood of my cloak falling back. A lone figure leaned on a walking stick, too far away and hidden behind the mist to make out clearly. Tanzie was nowhere to be found.

I gripped the hilt of my dagger and subtly moved into the fighting stance Anir had taught me. "Who are you?"

"The better question is, who are you, child?"

"I am someone in need of information."

I couldn't see her face in the mist, but had the impression she was smiling. "How exceptional. You see, I am someone who has information. And expects payment."

I paused at that, tamping down my initial response to offer her whatever she wanted. That would be dangerous in any realm, let alone this sinful one. "I will pay you in one secret."

"No." The figure moved closer. The hood of her cloak was pulled low, covering her face. "I know your secrets. Better than you, I imagine. I want a favor. Collected in the future at my discretion."

Goddess curse me. It was a terrible bargain. "I will not commit murder."

"You either accept the favor, or you don't. It will all depend, I suppose, on how badly you are in need of information. Consider this a test of courage. Which will it be? Bravery or fear?"

Bravery might be the absence of fear in most cases, but it also seemed a little like acting foolishly for a good cause. I was not worried about being brave. I was interested in watching out for myself, making the best decision I could. If the mystery woman did indeed know me better than I did, then the best choice was to agree. Consequences be as damned as my soul.

"I accept."

Before the words had completely left my lips, the figure lashed out. It happened so quickly I barely registered the sting in my arm. She'd cut me. I glanced up, ready to defend against any other attack, and halted as she carved her palm and placed it to my wound.

She whispered a word, and a blinding flash of light cracked the night sky.

"Go on, then, child. Ask your questions."

"I want to find the Seven Sisters. Are they here?"

"No. They dwell where no sin rules above all."

"That's not an answer."

"When the time is right, you will understand."

I gritted my teeth. Fine. "I want to know about my twin. She was murdered and I need to know which demon house is behind it. If any."

"You cannot expect to find answers to anyone else's mystery, when you do not yet understand the mystery of yourself."

"Isn't that the purpose of our little conversation? I didn't agree to your bargain simply to have you toss more questions my way. You cannot tell me where Seven Sisters are, you cannot tell me about my twin. What exactly can you help me with?"

"If you hope to find what you're looking for, you must pass my test of courage."

"That was not part of our bargain."

"Oh, but it is. You, my child, find yourself in the center of your own mystery. Until you discover the secrets of yourself, you will not know the answers to your sister's mystery. And that is something I cannot tell you. Some truths you must find on your own. What else troubles you?"

I swallowed hard. "My magic. I cannot access it."

"I may know a way for you to gain it back. And find an answer your heart yearns for. Regarding your prince." The figure suddenly stood before the tree. "You want to know his truth, then carve his name into the tree and take one leaf."

I thought back to the fable I'd read, a sick feeling twisting like a knife inside. This robed figure had to be the Crone. The goddess of the underworld. And she was something to be feared. "If I do that and guess wrong, there will be a price."

"A true act of courage does not come without the risk of a great cost." Her sharp smile was the only thing I could see and did little to alleviate my nerves. "After you carve his true name and take the leaf, you must shatter it in his presence. If you are correct, you'll know. If not..."

I swallowed the rising bout of terror. If I was correct and she was the goddess of the underworld, her price would be death. A small detail both Envy and Celestia had left out of my education. "I don't know for certain."

"You do know who he is, but you choose to remain in the shadows, comfortable in the dark. Maybe it's not his truth you fear, but your own. Perhaps you refuse to look too closely at him because of what it reveals about you. He is your mirror. And rarely do we appreciate what stares back at us. That, my child, is where the true test comes in. Are you brave enough to confront your demons? Not many are."

I glanced down at my magical tattoo—the one that told our story. "This wasn't the question I came here for."

"No. But it is the one you're too frightened to ask. Therefore I inquire again, Daughter of the Moon, not who he is, but who are you?"

"I...I don't know."

"Wrong." She stomped her foot, displacing the mist with her sudden movement. "Tell me. Who are you?"

"I don't remember. But I'm damn well going to find out!"

"Good. It's a start." She gave me a small, knowing nod. "What are you going to do?"

I glanced over my shoulder. Tanzie was back from wherever the Crone had hidden her, those liquid eyes solemn. This choice could cost me my life.

I lifted my dagger and pressed it against the Curse Tree. I was going to carve Wrath's true name into the wood and do as the Crone suggested: confront the truth I'd been running from.

And if I was wrong... I'd have to pray to the goddesses I wasn't, or I'd be joining Vittoria in our family's tomb before the night was through.

THIRTY-THREE

Wrath wasn't in his chambers, nor his library. I checked his balcony and was about to march down into the Crescent Shallows when I decided to pass through the kitchens.

It was one of the last places I expected to find the demon of war, but there he stood, back to me, knife in hand, carving a chunk of hard cheese and adding the perfect cubes to a tray he'd already filled with various fruits.

"You do not need an invitation to join me, Emilia." He hadn't turned to face me. "Unless, of course, you don't want to be in my company."

"I sought you out. I should think that indicates I want your company."

"After you drugged me to get out of my bedchamber, I wondered if that changed."

"That . . . it had nothing to do with you."

He continued chopping, the knife thwacking the cutting board. "It felt pretty personal, given what had transpired between us."

"I—"

"You do not need to explain yourself."

"I wasn't going to. I was going to apologize that you were a casualty of what I needed to do." Silence stretched between us. "How long were you knocked out?"

"You cannot expect me to share that information."

"No, I suppose I don't."

I strode over to where he worked, admiring his knife skills. The way he'd laid out the fruits and presented them was also impressive. Figs were cut neatly in quarters, berries and grapes laid in appealing heaps. He'd even found a pomegranate.

"I didn't think you enjoyed spending time in a kitchen."

"Neither did I." He lifted a shoulder, his gaze focused solely on his task. "I don't care much for baking or mixing, but butchering, cutting, and slicing are oddly relaxing."

I grinned. Of course that part of the kitchen would appeal to him. Instead of commenting or breaking the moment, I plucked a slice of apple from the platter and popped it into my mouth. I was stalling and well knew it. So much for my test of bravery.

"In some mortal religions, apples are said to be the forbidden fruit."

Wrath paused for less than a heartbeat, but I'd been paying close attention. He did not lift his attention from his mission. "For someone who was raised with witches, I'm surprised you spent so much time with human beliefs."

I chose another piece of fruit. "I've also heard that figs, grapes, and pomegranates are contenders for the forbidden fruit."

"You've put a great amount of thought into forbidden foods."

"I visited the Curse Tree." He kept carefully cutting the hunk of cheddar on his board. I moved around the other side of the table so I could face him. "I made a bargain with the Crone. And something she said made me think of forbidden fruit and trees of knowledge."

Wrath's knuckles were white as he gripped the knife tighter. "And?"

"I wanted to know about my sister, but she insisted I needed to discover *my* truth first. To face my fears. She said part of my truth can be found if I acknowledge who you are." His gaze collided with mine. "She told me to carve your true name into the tree."

"Please tell me you refused to do so. The Crone is worse than my brothers."

I slowly shook my head and set the ebony and silver-veined leaf down. Wrath stared at it, looking as if I'd brought a viper into the room. I raised my fist to smash it and his hand shot out, covering mine. He tugged me close, holding my hand against his heart. It was pounding fiercely.

"We will go back and strike another deal with the Crone."

I drew back enough to look him in the eye. "You're nervous."

"You carved a name into a tree that demands blood in exchange for truth." He blew out a frustrated breath. "Of course I'm wary."

I moved my free hand to cup his face. That wasn't the full truth behind his nerves and we both knew it. "I know who you are."

"I highly doubt that."

His tone indicated if I knew his truth, I would not be standing so near, embracing him as I was. His secret terrified me, but I would never get past it if I didn't bring it into the light. I would never discover who I was, what happened to my twin, if I remained afraid of the truth. The Crone was right. I'd grown accustomed to the dark, I'd been kept in it for so long. First from Nonna, and now by my own design. It was time to set aside my fears and step into the light.

Before he could register what I was doing, I kicked the table as hard as I could, sending it tumbling over, the fruit and cheese and Cursed leaf shattering in the rubble.

He wrapped his arms around me, as if he could shield me from the Curse Tree collecting its price. But I did not feel any sudden onslaught of pain. Nor did I weaken or lose consciousness. I did not die. Did not even bleed.

Wrath held me tighter, his breathing coming hard and fast.

Tears suddenly pricked my eyes, but I refused to let them fall. Standing there, safe in the circle of Wrath's arms, meant I was right. And the Crone was correct once more.

Now that I possessed the truth, I didn't know what to do with it. I thought I'd been prepared, thought I could handle his secret being out in the open. I'd been wrong.

And I hated myself.

I exhaled a shaky breath, needing a moment to fully digest what I'd discovered. Wrath sensed me tunneling inward and reluctantly dropped his arms and stepped away, putting much-needed space between us. He said nothing, only waited patiently for me speak.

Blood and bones. This was hard. But I'd been through worse, and I'd survived.

No matter what happened next, I'd survive that, too.

"When you brushed off the name I'd called you in the monastery, I'd wondered if there was a reason why you didn't react more strongly." I swiped at my eyes, still not looking at him. "You acted as if it meant nothing, that I simply irked you." I smiled down at my hands. "Because, according to Nonna, a prince of Hell will never reveal their true name to their enemies."

I could feel his attention boring into me, but I still could not meet his gaze.

"I know witches and demons are enemies. But there's more to our story, isn't there?"

"Emilia..."

"You are temptation. Seduction." I finally dragged my focus to his arm, nodded at the intricate snake tattoo. "The serpent in the garden. The one who'd encouraged mortals to sin."

I pulled my attention higher, finally settling it on his eyes. I took him in, *really* looked at him objectively. His face, his body, his entire presence and how he carried himself screamed authority. Domination. And was designed to seduce. He was temptation made flesh.

His expression shuttered as he waited. Now, more than ever, I desperately wished I could sense his emotions. Though I suspected he was sensing mine, and that was why he'd grown so distant. His armor was firmly back in place. And he was shielding himself from me.

"I don't know how you've fooled humanity for so long, but it's as Envy said. You are the most skilled liar of all. *Samael.*"

His true name seemed to unsettle him. It didn't look as if he'd taken a breath since our conversation began. He exhaled now. "Prince of Darkness. King of the Wicked. I have been called many things, but I am no liar."

I searched his face. I'd been right. I knew it the moment the tree did not collect its due, but the truth was hard to digest. Wrath was the devil. The evil feared the world over.

And I'd stupidly fallen for his seduction. For his smoldering gold eyes and keen wit. His pride in his appearance. The way he protected those under his care and chose justice over revenge. No wonder the mortal world confused the two princes so easily— Pride and Wrath certainly shared a lot of similarities.

"You had plenty of opportunities to tell me you were the devil. *You* were the one cursed by La Prima. Did Pride's wife even die, or was it your consort?"

"I have not directly lied to you."

"Stop omitting things."

"Unlike Pride, I've never had a consort. But yes, I was cursed by the First Witch. As were all of my brothers. My penalty for not aiding her was steeper—she stole something very important to me. Something I will do nearly anything to get back."

"The Horn of Hades," I guessed, thinking of the devil horn amulets.

I hadn't missed them. If anything, I felt...relief at my charm's absence over the last few weeks. It was completely at odds with how I'd felt when he'd first taken them back. Though I suspected it had to do with my painful experience in the Crescent Shallows.

I recalled my worry over the devil being mad at Wrath for letting me borrow the *cornicello* that night. How foolish I must have seemed to him.

"You were the only one who didn't seem to want them. Which I suppose indicates you wanted them more than the others, and didn't want to appear too eager and raise suspicion."

"They are my wings, not horns. Your first witch cursed them into a mockery of mortal lore, then hid them from me." He seemed to be lost in a memory. One that had his hands fisting at his sides. When he looked at me again, a cold fury burned in his eyes. "In order to restore them, I need a spell found in her grimoire."

"You have wings." Because he was an angel. Goddess above. It was one thing to suspect it, and another to have that suspicion confirmed.

"Had."

There was a world of anger and pain wrapped in his voice. Part of me wanted to go to him, soothe the emotional wound that was still raw. Instead I remained where I was, reeling.

His wings were a connection to the angelic world. The realm he'd left behind. It was hard to believe the devil mourned something that tied him to the place he'd hated enough to be thrown out of for eternity.

Or maybe none of that was true. Maybe those were just more mortal tales, twisted and slightly wrong through the passage of time. Wrath didn't seem like evil incarnate. Or some grand seducer. Except... he had slowly worked himself into my life. And my heart. Was that not proof of seduction? Of a slow scheme unfolding?

"Emilia." He reached for me and I flinched. His hand dropped away. "I can sense your basic emotions, but I want to know how you really feel."

"You're the devil."

"So you've reminded me."

"But Lucifer... Pride... I don't understand."

He heaved a great sigh. "My brother's sin of choice makes it nearly impossible for him to deny being the king of demons. Mortals assume that's who he is, and his pride keeps him from admitting the truth. He's only too pleased to feed his ego. I harbor no emotions one way or the other about my true title. It is a duty to me. An obligation thrust upon me. Nothing more. If anything, with Pride soaking up the prestige, it allows me to complete my job without posturing."

"Has anything been real between us, or has it been a careful seduction? A bit of truth sprinkled in with the lies."

"Tell me." His eyes narrowed. "When you agreed to marry Pride, thinking he was the devil, did it matter then?"

Unbidden, a memory came back to me. "In the Crescent Shallows, the night we...you called me your queen."

"You came here, believing you'd be Queen of the Wicked. That is all true. If you choose to complete our marriage bond, you will be not simply my queen, but *the* queen." He searched my face, his expression turning remote. "The only change is which brother you will be marrying. Everyone in this realm knows who I am. My true title. It's only mortals who assume otherwise. So, I ask once more, does it truly matter now that *you* know who I am?"

"I'm honestly not sure. It's a lot to absorb. You are the devil. Evil incarnate."

"Is that who you know me to be?"

"Outside of this realm, it's what the whole world thinks of you."

"I am not interested in what others think. Only you." He stepped back and inclined his head. His movements stiff. "Thank you for your honesty. That is all I needed to hear, my lady."

"Wrath, wait. I—"

He vanished in a glittering cloud of smoke.

THIRTY-FOUR

"I'm sorry," I whispered to the empty room. Smoke hung in the air several long moments after Wrath left. I stared at it, eyes burning, wishing I could cast a spell to reverse time. It would be so much easier to simply forget what had happened. Or, better yet, forget the truth of his name. His title. And the way my heart ached at the thought of any or everything between us being part of some larger game.

I leaned a hip against a table, surveying the mess on the floor. It seemed a fitting metaphor of my life. Each time I thought I was closing in on the truth surrounding my twin's murder, something new got added to the heap, distracting me with more trash to pick through.

Thanks to the curse being sentient and having an active role in keeping its secrets, it was nearly impossible to fit the puzzle pieces together.

An old worry crept back in. I'd started to think I'd been experiencing forgotten memories, usually after or during some romantic encounters with Wrath.

If I wasn't the consort, was I the First Witch? I'd been almost convinced the Matron of Curses and Poisons was the First Witch, but now that seemed less likely. I couldn't imagine Wrath keeping her around, knowing that she'd stolen his wings.

Was locating the First Witch the true reason behind the murders? It would make sense for someone to try and find her and make her pay for all she'd stolen. And if every prince of Hell lost their wings, or something as precious, then it could be any one of them.

If I was the First Witch, it would also make sense why Wrath had hated me the night I'd summoned him. He'd called me a creature then, swearing he'd never be tempted by me when I'd mistakenly believed demon bargains were sealed with addictive kisses.

"Congratulations, Emilia," I scoffed. "You have fully given into madness. And paranoia."

Speaking out loud to myself wasn't helping to soothe worries of growing madness. I almost cackled at the thought. Maybe I *was* losing all sense of reality.

Perhaps there was a tonic I could take to rid all memories and foolish thoughts from my mind. Wipe the slate clean and begin anew.

I snorted. It was preposterous and...and entirely possible. There was someone in this castle who was gifted with creating tonics and tinctures. Someone who just might possess the skills needed to break any curse placed on me. First Witch or not, I could use her help.

I hurried to visit the Matron of Curses and Poisons, praying to every goddess I could think of that she would be in her tower.

"Daughter of the Moon." Celestia gave me a bemused look as I rushed past her and motioned for her to close the door. "What brings you here?"

"Do you know who I am?"

It was hard to tell if her hesitation was out of concern for my well-being, or if she was treading carefully around the truth. "Yes, my lady."

"Not my courtesy title. Have we met before?"

Now her perusal was sharper. "Have you ingested something peculiar?"

"No." I walked in an agitated circle. "I experienced some memories that didn't seem to belong to me at first. Now I'm not so sure. Is there a tonic you can give me? Something to detect a curse or break it?"

"Sit." She glided over to the little table and stools she used to work. I followed and perched on the edge, knee bouncing. "Give me your hands." I leaned over the table and did as she asked. "Sometimes forgetting can be a gift."

I wrapped my hands around hers, thumbs resting on her wrists. "Do you speak from experience?"

"I speak as one who wishes for such a present."

"Am I the First Witch?"

Celestia's expression softened. "No, child."

"Are you?"

"No."

I released her hands and sat back. Her pulse hadn't ticked faster for either of my questions. "I admit I'm only marginally relieved. The more I learn of her, the more she doesn't sound like the hero of our fables."

"Every villain thinks themselves the hero. And vice versa. In truth, there's a little villain and hero in each of us. Depending on the circumstances."

I glanced around the circular chamber, my attention pausing on the carved skull. "I've been trying to solve a riddle. About a key that doesn't necessarily open a lock. And seven stars and sins, and the angel of death."

"You seek the Temptation Key." Celestia heaved a great sigh. "I can tell you this, Daughter of the Moon, you have already found it." I whipped my attention back to her. "If I were you, I would reconsider. Once you march down this path, there is no returning from it."

"Whoever killed my twin should have thought of that." I stood. "Is the Temptation Key here, in House Wrath?"

"It is dangerous. Divine objects...they are not to be taken lightly."

"But it *is* here."

Celestia pressed her lips together. It was enough confirmation for me. I thought back to my conversation with Envy, when I'd mistaken his ramblings for drunkenness the night we'd had truth wine. He'd mentioned not all keys appeared the way one typically thought they did.

Blood was the key to unlocking demon magic, for example. So with that in mind, there were no limits to what might actually unlock the Triple Moon Mirror. The Temptation Key might be an elixir, for all I knew. And yet...something toyed with the edges of my memory.

If Wrath had a divine object and wanted to keep it hidden, there was no safer place than in plain sight. Wrath made the obvious questionable, casting doubt. It was the same way he'd acted when I'd first called him Samael back in Palermo.

I doubted he'd keep the Temptation Key in his bedchambers. Which led me to believe the key was in one of two places. His personal library, or the weapons room.

I stood, ready to rush off and tear them both apart if I had to.

Celestia snagged the sleeve of my gown, halting my exit. "If you do this, prepare for consequences that will be out of your control."

"Very little is in my control now, matron. The only thing that will change is I will finally know the truth."

Celestia dropped my arm and stepped aside. I wasted no time racing to the weapons room. I'd half-feared Wrath would be there, working off excess emotions after our conversation. It was silent, empty. I hurried through each portion, running my hands over every gold design, searching for any secret compartment or object that might be a key.

I halted in the back of the room near the serpent mosaic. Like the first time I saw it, I swore there was something familiar about it . . . my mind raced, searching for a memory.

"Blood and bones." I gripped the roots of my hair and gently tugged. *"Think."*

I'd seen it before. I would bet whatever was left of my soul. If only I could—

"Devious demon. You're brilliant." I clapped a hand over my mouth to keep from screaming in glee. "I've got you now."

I stood over Wrath's desk and picked up the serpent paperweight.

Or what I'd originally mistaken for a paperweight. Turning it over, I studied the ridges and geometric design with a different eye. It could certainly be a key. Given the shape, it would fit on top of a hand mirror nicely. And it would explain why Envy had shared this information.

Without an invitation to House Wrath, he would not be able to search the castle himself. Showing up outside in the garden for a minute or two was one thing, but strolling through Wrath's personal library would be another. Though, knowing Wrath, he likely had the interior warded to keep his brothers out. None of that mattered.

I held the Temptation Key to my chest, feeling the first pangs of hope. I wasn't sure why Celestia worried so much about touching a divine object. Thus far it only gave me peace. Joy. After all of the starts and stops, this was a tangible lead. A true thread to tug on. Now all I had to do was locate the Triple Moon Mirror. And, armed with the key, I had a new plan forming.

Back in my personal suite, I pulled out my notes and a pen. If I could just figure out the enchanted skulls message, I would have a direction.

~ *Enchanted skulls* ~

Skull one: Angelus mortis lives. Fury. Almost free. Maiden. Mother. Crone. Past, present, future, find.
Skull two: Seven stars, seven sins. As above, so below.

I tapped a quill against my lips, staring at the notes, willing the answer to manifest itself. The first skull's message was a little clearer now. I was positive it related to the Triple Moon Mirror and its ability to see into the past, present, and future.

It was the second skull's message that I kept getting caught on. Knowing what I did now about the seven stars being another name given to the Seven Sisters, and the fact that Envy was interested in locating them, I wondered...

I sucked in a sharp breath, distracted by a new thought. If Wrath kept the Temptation Key in plain sight, then maybe he'd done the same thing with the Triple Moon Mirror. Maybe he couldn't *tell* me anything about the curse, but he'd tried to help in a subtler way.

The case Envy had would fit a hand mirror. One such mirror had been gifted to me before I'd left for House Envy. Hope had me clutching the key and racing into my bathing chamber, pulling out the gorgeous mirror from where I'd kept it in the vanity. I'd admired the etching on the back before, but hadn't considered it might be more than a pretty design.

Excitement filling my chest, I placed the Temptation Key on the back of the mirror and twisted. Or tried to. Finding the correct alignment was difficult. I shifted it a few more ways, tried several directions. I flipped the key over and studied the raised lines. Some of the excitement dissipated. They didn't look like a match, but I didn't want to give up just yet.

After trying every way I could to fit the two objects together, I finally accepted the fact that the pieces did not match.

I trudged back into my bedchamber and plopped back onto the bed, rereading the notes. What I needed to do next was find the Seven Sisters and ask if they knew where the Triple Moon Mirror was. The skulls had to be the key to figuring that out, if only I could solve their riddles.

Seven stars, seven sins. As above, so below.

I inhaled and exhaled, emptying frustration and previous theories from my mind. The Crone had said something I'd only partially paid attention to. I concentrated on that conversation, her words slowly coming back to me about the Seven Sisters. *They dwell where no sin rules above all.*

That was it. I stared at the message delivered by the second skull again.

Seven stars, seven sins. As above, so below.

I'd been so convinced the seven sins was the easiest part to decipher, but that might not be true at all. Perhaps it was the simplicity of that portion of the clue that was meant to stand out. I thought it referred to the seven princes of Hell. But what if it was a place within the Seven Circles? "As above, so below" typically was used to indicate balance.

The clue might point toward the place where all seven sins were used equally, where none ruled above the others. Just as the Crone had hinted at.

The Sin Corridor.

Heart thumping, I grinned down at my notes. That had to be it.

The Seven Sisters were somewhere in the Sin Corridor, and I had a feeling they were in possession of the mirror. It would explain why they kept moving through the realm, hiding from the princes. They were either magical thieves or keepers of the peace.

Regardless of the role they played for the demon princes, they were *my* salvation.

I hastily packed a satchel of supplies—the Temptation Key, the Crone's spell book I'd stolen from Envy, extra stockings, and dried fruit I'd pilfered from the kitchens—and changed into something warmer.

I stripped my dress off and replaced it with my fur-lined leather trousers, a lace-up tunic, and velvet cloak. I yanked on boots that went up to my thighs and snagged the strap of the bag as I rushed outside. I paused near the stables, the selfish part of me wanted to bring Tanzie for company, but I had no idea what I was looking for and didn't want to miss anything by riding too fast. This was something I needed to do alone.

Before I could talk myself out of it, or draw the attention of any nosy members of House Wrath, I set off toward the edge at the back of the property and slid down the steep mountain. In record time I was on semi-flat ground again. I glanced behind me—the mountain Wrath had opened with a whispered word was as tall and as imposing as I remembered it.

I hoped I'd see it again soon.

With an image of my twin in my mind and determination in my heart, I began my trek through the unforgiving mountain pass. This time I was prepared for the subtle prodding of emotions.

And I knew how to fight off demonic influence. I felt the first licks of power sliding along my skin, searching for a place to sink its teeth in. I bared *my* teeth at the realm. Even without the use of my magic, I was not helpless. I had a dagger and newfound grit.

"Do your worst."

I was certainly going to do mine. I trudged through snow that gradually reached the top of my knees, my steps slow and unsteady. I didn't think of the cold and ice. They were distractions. I kept my attention on my surroundings, looking for any hint of the Seven Sisters.

The first time we'd walked through here, I'd sworn I'd seen women using bones as knitting needles. I convinced myself it was my mind playing tricks, but I didn't think that was the case. If the Seven Sisters made themselves known to me then, I prayed they'd do so again, especially now that I was no longer walking with the enemy.

A third of the way up an enormous section of the mountain, an ice storm struck. I pulled the hood of my cloak up and continued on. Little pellets struck me, over and over. As if furious with my defiance. The realm was wrong there. It was not defiance that drove me forward, taking step after excruciating step through this hell. It was love.

This journey may have begun with vengeance and revenge, but below that, it had always been about the love I felt for my twin. Nonna had been right; love was the most powerful magic. And I would harness it and—goddess above. I stopped walking, my attention catching on something that didn't form naturally on any tree.

I squinted at the giant cedar and felt the blood drain from my face as I beheld a carving.

VII

"Hello?"

I reached for my dagger and glanced around. There were no sounds, no footprints, no otherworldly indications the Seven Sisters were near. But that seven carved into the trunk...I'd been taught to never overlook the signs. And that one was glaring.

I circled the tree, not finding anything else unusual about it. It was average sized, if not a bit more sparse than the surrounding cluster of cedars. I replaced my weapon in its sheath and dropped to my knees, digging through the snow. There *had* to be something here.

A few painful moments and frozen fingers later, my nails scraped against frozen earth. I tried scratching the surface and only succeeded in breaking several nails.

I stood, hands fisted at my sides, and tried to rein in my temper. The Sin Corridor sensed my momentary lapse in control and pounced. My favorite sin unleashed my fury, and I screamed, the sound muffled and smothered by the freshly falling snow.

I released all of my emotions, kicking at the snow, snapping branches off, and beating the ground. Sweat beaded my forehead and I couldn't stop. I brought my fist to the tree and punched it as hard as I could.

"Godsdamnit!"

Pain lashed up my arm. I winced at my bloody knuckles, the fight and fury immediately leaving me. Godsdamn fool's errand. Ridiculous riddles and...a thought occurred to me as blood dripped into the snow. On a hunch, I smeared a few drops on the tree, right across the Roman numeral seven. There was no moment of hesitation—the trunk clicked open, revealing a set of stairs hidden within it. I walked around the tree again. It didn't seem possible for such a large set of stairs to fit inside, but I was finished asking questions. Now was the time for answers.

I said a prayer to the goddesses and stepped inside. The hidden door closed behind me, and torches flared to life. I went to grab my dagger again, but some innate feeling warned me against it. I don't know how I knew with such certainty that I would not find a foe here. In fact, I feared any act of aggression might work against me. If I was about to locate a divine object, I needed to have faith that all would be well.

I inhaled deeply and pushed on. The stairs were wooden, semicircular, and curved around an enormous trunk. I took sure, confident steps, excitement and trepidation pumping through my veins the closer I got to the bottom. At the ground level a small stone chamber greeted me, a solitary pedestal in its center. And there it was. It *had* to be. I paused, taking in the sheer beauty of the mirror that was on display. Crafted from what appeared to be a combination of mother-of-pearl and raw moonstone, it was the most magnificent thing I'd ever seen.

It glowed from within. I stood before it, hardly noticing the tears spilling down my cheeks until the drops hit the mirror and sizzled. I set my satchel down and went to reach for it when candles suddenly lit around the chamber.

Seven ghostly shadows flickered in the light. They didn't speak. Did not make a move toward me. They waited. The Seven Sisters had arrived. It was not fear, but awe I felt, deep in my soul. And a sense of familiarity.

"Hello, I'm—"

"About to make a critical choice. What you set into motion here, cannot be undone." Celestia emerged from the opposite end of the chamber, her strange starlit eyes glowing. I should have been surprised by her appearance, but I wasn't. "I offer one last chance, child. Walk away."

"I cannot."

She gave me a long look, then smiled. It was one I'd seen before, half-hidden behind a cloak, deep in the Bloodwood Forest. *Now* I was surprised. I stared at her for another second, unable to believe the truth before me. "You're the Crone." She nodded and I took a quick breath to digest the information. "Does Wrath know?"

"We mustn't waste time speaking of him. I am calling in my favor, Daughter." She strode over to the Triple Moon Mirror and gazed at it lovingly. "Once you activate the mirror, I ask that you return my spell book."

"That's all?"

"No, child." She turned her attention back to me. "That's *everything.*"

Celestia waved her hand at me, and a strange tingle settled over my skin, feeling as if invisible threads were snipped and whipping across my body in rapid succession.

A wave of magic bubbled up inside me and I dove into my source, almost crying out in elation when I tunneled past the wall that had erupted.

She gave me a knowing look and motioned toward the shadows. They peeled away from the wall and moved beside her. "When you receive your answers, come find me. I'll expect my payment without delay."

THIRTY-FIVE

I sunk onto the floor inside the magic tree and flipped through the spell book, the paper rustling like dried leaves as my fingers trembled. A note that hadn't been there before fell out. I gingerly picked it up and read the carefully penned lines.

Some truths do not grant the freedom you seek. Once known you can't ever go back. Choose wisely.

—S.

Samael. *Wrath*. His note was eerily similar to the warning issued by the Crone, but for me, no matter what, there was no going back or moving forward until I granted my sister eternal rest and peace. I traced the *S* he'd signed the message with, his truth I could never again deny.

I wasn't surprised Wrath had found the stolen grimoire. He was, after all, searching for a spell to restore his cursed wings. However, I *was* surprised that he'd left the spell book alone, even after deducing that I'd take it from his House of Sin.

He knew firsthand how truth could cut as much as it had the power to heal. I'd shown him that. He had proven through his actions that he wasn't as evil as the world believed. He was a blade of justice and he cut down those who'd been condemned without emotion.

A soldier following orders, ruled by duty and honor.

And I'd been unable to tell him I saw that. Saw *him*. He was the balance of right and wrong. He was neither good nor evil; he simply existed, just as he'd once told me.

Candles flickered wildly, casting shadows around the darkened chamber. The Crone and Seven Sisters had disappeared, leaving me alone to my task.

I ignored the fear pressing in, stealing my breath. Maybe it was my brush with an actual goddess—something I hadn't quite wrapped my mind around—or maybe it was this subterranean chamber, but I'd never been one to get squeamish over small spaces or being in cellars. I refused to start now. I was so close. So close to the truth that had evaded me all these months.

If all went well, in minutes, I'd finally know what had happened to my sister.

I paused. The Triple Moon Mirror might show me the

421

moments leading up to my twin's death. Or worse, I might witness her murder firsthand. It was one thing to come upon her brutalized body after the fact, but to watch it happen...I shuddered.

"Be brave." I found the spell I'd marked a few nights before and exhaled. This was it. No matter what I saw now, I'd know who had taken Vittoria's life. "Past, present, future, find. Show me my biggest desire hidden deep within the universe's mind."

At first, like the summoning spell I'd used on Wrath, nothing happened. I stared at the hand mirror, willing the biggest desire of my heart to the forefront of my thoughts. I pictured my twin, and, for the first time in months, could imagine her crystal clear. I heard her carefree laughter, smelled her lavender and white sage scent, felt the strength of her love for me.

A bond so powerful death could not diminish it.

Light flickered in the mirror, followed by swirling dark clouds. It seemed as if a storm were brewing in the glass. Magic buzzed through the metal, startling me, but I held tight, unwilling to look away or drop the Triple Moon Mirror now that I had it.

The storm inside it persisted, but muffled voices now slipped in. My pulse pounded. I willed the storm blocking my view to subside, to grant me the chance to see my twin.

Slowly, as if the scene had been captured in a jar of honey and lazily tipped over, dripping into view, a room emerged. There were windows set inside a nook. Outside, snowcapped mountains towered above mist. It took a moment to place, but it looked like the chamber where Wrath held Antonio prisoner.

The mirror's vantage point shifted farther back, allowing more of the space to be seen.

I blinked as the oversized leather chair was plainly visible. Along with the human who'd murdered my twin. He was in the middle of a conversation, but whoever he spoke to was just out of view. Then I heard the other voice. And my heart stuttered.

"...my bidding well."

Vittoria. Unshed tears stung my eyes when I realized it must be an illusion. Antonio hadn't been speaking to a person—someone probably sent an enchanted skull to him. I had no idea how this one sounded so close to the real thing, especially when mine had sounded slightly wrong, but I desperately wanted it to speak again. No matter that the voice was clipped and edged in steel, it was the closest I'd come to hearing my twin in months.

I silently begged the voice to speak again.

Prayers answered, a woman strode over to Antonio and perched on the arm of his chair. She wore lavender gauze that seemed to blow on some magical breeze. Dark hair cascaded in loose curls down her back, and her bronze skin practically glowed. She looked like a painting of a Roman deity sprung to life. And yet there was something so familiar about her casual pose.

"Holy goddesses above. It cannot be."

The woman looked strikingly like my twin. At least in profile. She turned as if sensing a magical presence in the room that didn't belong. Lavender eyes, not rich brown, glared at me. Or whatever she sensed about the mirror. Her face was familiar and foreign at once.

It was Vittoria, but not.

I could barely process what I was seeing. My mind churned slowly through my emotions as I sorted through the image being shown to me. Vittoria was in House Wrath. With Antonio. She must have come here before she was killed. But Wrath swore he didn't know her...and I would not doubt him again. Which meant it was not an image from the past. It was either the present or the future. And somehow, someway, my sister was alive. At least in this realm.

Tears threatened again, but I held them back, unwilling to miss a single second of the image playing out in the magical glass. The Vittoria in the mirror cocked her head, still staring toward whatever magic my presence created. I thought of her diary, of how she'd claimed she could hear magical objects speaking to her. Perhaps the Triple Moon Mirror was chatting now.

"Vittoria!" I shouted, waving my hands. "Can you hear me?"

"It's time." She tore her gaze from my direction and fixed her attention on Antonio. "Are you ready?"

"Yes." I couldn't see Antonio's face, but he sounded breathless. As if he knew he was in the presence of something awe-inspiring. "I vow my life to your cause, my angel."

Vittoria patted his head, then stood. "Give me one moment, then we'll be off."

"No!" I screamed. If this was the present, I could not lose my twin again. I almost dropped the mirror in my haste to get to the tower dungeon. I managed to place it in my satchel and dashed up the stairs, racing around and around until I reached the tree trunk door.

I darted into the night, racing through the Sin Corridor, tripping over the roots and rocks I hadn't noticed the first time. Bloodied and bruised, I pushed harder and faster. I had to get to House Wrath. In far less time than should have been possible, I burst through the doors, doubling over as I caught my breath. Anir's dagger was at my throat.

"Devil's blood, Emilia. I thought..." He sheathed his blade and offered a hand. "Are you hurt? Wrath couldn't detect you anywhere."

"Where is he?"

"You're bleeding."

I could not care less. *"Where is he?"*

"He just left for the Sin Corridor. It's the only place he can't sense you."

"I need to get to the dungeon tower. Get Wrath. Now."

Anir shouted something, perhaps a curse, or a plea, but I didn't dare stop. I had no way of knowing if the scene I'd been shown was the present or future. But one way or another, my sister was here or would be here, and I didn't know whether to laugh or scream or collapse in tears.

I raced up the stairs, up and up as I climbed with energy and strength that seemed to be endless. Without stopping to collect myself, I wrenched the door open. Wrath said he had magicked it to my hand, and he hadn't lied.

"Antonio?" I called out, fully stepping into the room. A taper smoked from the chairside table, as if it had just been blown out or had been snuffed by fast movement. My hand moved to my dagger. The room was not large, only big enough to house his bed, the small reading nook, and a curtained screen to offer privacy as he washed and used a chamber pot. I stared at the screen. There was no sound coming from behind it. "Hello?"

A prickle of unease slid down my spine as I slowly made my way to the screen and whatever lay hidden beyond. I yanked the curtain back and blew out a frustrated breath.

There, set next to a pitcher and washbasin, was another enchanted skull. My heartbeat quickened as I drew near, waiting, body tensed, to hear its message. It came to life just as I closed the distance with my final step.

"Come to the Shifting Isles, sister. We have much to discuss

about breaking the remainder of our curse. Answers await your arrival. Until then. Stand back."

I didn't think, I leapt aside and the skull exploded into glittering dust, leaving nothing but the chilling message ringing in my ears. I stood there, chest heaving as the impossible became real. My sister was alive.

Vittoria *lived.*

I choked on a mad giggle that bubbled up from my throat. Vittoria could come home. We could go back to Nonna, and our parents. We could cook and laugh and teach our own daughters how to cook in Sea & Vine. Life would resume. We could still have the future we'd dreamed of. Together. And if somehow she couldn't return to the mortal world, I would stay here. No matter what, we would be reunited soon. She'd been here. I'd missed her by minutes, seconds.

Lighthearted relief slowly descended into something darker as my shock wore off. Vittoria had been here, so close, and yet she'd taken Antonio and vanished without seeing me.

She left an enchanted skull with a message. As if she'd been too busy to bother with a simple visit to my chambers. Or wait until I arrived here. Tonight. She had to have sensed me. And she'd still left. As if I didn't matter at all and my shattered heart meant even less.

I'd spent *months* lost in rage and vengeance.

Months of sorrow and fury.

Of mourning.

All the while, my twin was alive. Well. Better than well if her new, powerful magic was any indication. My twin had been enchanting skulls. Leaving them like morbid clues. When all she had to do was sneak into my room. Instead she toyed with me. Tried breaking me.

And she'd almost turned me into a monster.

I inhaled deeply and exhaled. The air like fire in my lungs. Wrath's lessons on controlling my emotions incinerated in the face of my fury. My twin was alive. She'd come for Antonio. And it hadn't been to attack him or make him pay for what he'd done.

On the contrary, he looked as if he'd received a blessing. He called her his *angel*. As in, the angel of death he'd mentioned the night in the monastery. I thought he'd been referencing Wrath or another prince of Hell. If he never killed Vittoria, then that meant he'd never been influenced by a demon prince. I had no proof yet, but I had new suspicions.

Deception. Lies. Betrayal.

All the words I'd associated with the Wicked now belonged to Vittoria. She'd orchestrated everything—a playwright crafting her own twisted tale, doling out roles for unsuspecting players, myself included. And I was through with being a pawn in her game.

No matter that her end goal was to break the curse, she had no right to lie to me. To keep me in the dark. I was no longer cloaked in shadows. I was burning with rage.

My hands stung. I glanced down, noticing the tiny cuts in my palms where my nails dug in so hard I'd broken the skin. I exhaled, banking the fires of anger at last.

I had a new plan, a new direction. I would gladly pay my beloved sister a visit. And I could not help it if she soon regretted extending her invitation. It was high time Vittoria met the furious, unforgiving witch she'd helped to create.

I turned on my heel and headed for the door. The Shifting Isles beckoned. But there was one final thing that needed to be done before I left House Wrath.

I strode through the corridors, mind whirling with strategies and plans. I no longer cared who had started playing these games. Witches. The Wicked. My twin. And all the cursed and feared creatures in between. If my sister was alive that threw into question the murders that came before and after hers. Were any of the witches *actually* dead, or was it part of some larger conspiracy to accumulate more power or transfer it? I had no idea what else the true "killers" would gain by committing fake murders, unless they were hoping to incite a war between realms, and not simply break the curse.

And a war was something I refused to let happen. Regardless of my twin's scheme, I would protect my family and the mortal world at all costs.

Each step closer to Wrath's chambers brought a greater sense of clarity. My choice was made. And the only regret I had was how long it took me to arrive here.

I kicked in his door and glanced around. The receiving room was empty, the fire banked. Wrath hadn't seen his suite all night. He must have started searching for me shortly after I'd left. Even after I doubted him, doubted the goodness in his heart. His soul. He'd searched for me.

Removing my cloak, I walked toward his bedchamber, grabbed a bottle of demonberry wine from a rack, and continued onto his balcony. He could sense my general whereabouts here through our tattoo. I had little doubt he'd find me soon enough. I popped the cork and sipped the wine directly from the bottle, staring out at the lake. At this hour the crimson waters looked like a pool of spilled blood. It was an omen of sorts. And for once, I welcomed it.

Glittering black smoke wafted toward me on a breeze as the king of demons prowled closer, his voice a low rumble of thunder at my ear.

"Emilia."

I turned slowly and took him in. Danger lurked in his gaze, along with his namesake sin. He wasn't the only one who was angry, but my wrath was not directed at him; he was the only one who grounded me. I dove into the source of my magic, releasing all of the rage and fury I'd been bottling up since I saw my twin. My power answered my call immediately.

I held up my hands, attention riveted to Wrath's face as a burning flower appeared in each of my palms. There was no flash of surprise. No widening of his eyes or tightening of his mouth. I released my grip on my power, allowing it to burn out. The flowers charred to black, the tiny dying rose-gold embers the only specks of color before the breeze carried the ashes away.

Wrath knew I possessed this talent. This power. And he'd never let on. I wanted to know what else he knew about me, what other secrets I'd yet to uncover about my past.

The Crone told me to solve the mystery of myself. And I intended to do just that.

Perhaps, no matter what Celestia had said in her tower chamber, I really was the First Witch, and this block on my memories was the price I'd paid for using dark magic. That would certainly explain why Nonna warned me away from certain spells.

I gritted my teeth, recalling the way she'd make us bless our amulets during each full moon. Did she know the truth of who I was? She had to. And her betrayal carved deep.

Maybe—unlike what Nonna claimed about our amulets hiding us from the devil—my *cornicello*, his wings, had actually been used to keep *my* power in check, not his. And if that were true, then perhaps Wrath took my amulet not only for his benefit but for mine. My power had definitely shifted since its removal.

I exhaled, focusing on the question I wanted an answer to first.

"How long have you known I can summon fire?" He pressed his lips together. I shook my head, laughing bitterly. "My twin is alive. Though I suspect you already know that, too."

Emotion finally flickered in his eyes, but he remained silent, watchful. On guard. As if I was something to be feared. He wasn't wrong.

"I want answers."

I would not wait for my twin to give me *her* version of the truth when I saw her in the morning. I wanted to gather it myself. Starting now. I looked Wrath over. Once, he'd told me to study my enemies closely. To look for any sign of the truth in their mannerisms. He wasn't speaking. And it was unusual.

"Judging by your silence I imagine this is the curse at play again. We're skirting around things it does not want me to learn." A gleam of approval entered his gaze. Gone in the next instant. "If I accept the marriage bond, I have the strangest feeling some of that will change. The curse may not fully break that way, but I believe there are some bonds more powerful than dark magic. And there is nothing more dangerous than love, is there? People fight for it. They die for it. They commit acts of war and treason and all manner of sin in its name."

I would know. I'd been willing to do dreadful things to avenge my twin.

Something resembling worry flashed in his eyes. "Feelings are not facts."

"Interesting."

My mouth curved seductively. Wrath had just lied. In the closest way he could.

Curse be damned, he still wanted me to wield my power of choice. To accept our bond without outside forces interfering in my free will. The prince of bargains was forfeiting a winning hand. And he was doing it for me. Always for me.

"Tell me about our amulets, your wings. I want to know why Vittoria and I really wore them. Was it to keep our power on a leash, or was it as my family claimed: a way to hide them from you?"

"I have no proof, but I believe both are true. I've also been looking into the possibility that they may have been spelled to ensure you forget certain things."

"You had me wear them in the Crescent Shallows to test that." I inhaled as he nodded in confirmation. At least his expression was one of guilt.

"I'd hoped the truth properties of the shallows would remove any blocks on your mind. I did not anticipate the extreme reaction it caused."

"Do they really lock the gates of Hell?"

"Yes."

Internally I breathed a sigh of relief. At least not *everything* I'd been told was a lie.

"I have one final question for now, your highness." I placed my hand on his chest, feeling the steady thumping beneath my touch. His attention dropped to that tiny connection before he dragged it back to mine. "Pretend there's no curse. No magical betrothal. Or romantic urges created by our bond. Would you choose me? To reign beside you. To be your queen. Your friend. Your confidant. Your lover."

"Emilia..."

"You tricked me into a blood bargain with you before I crossed into the underworld. Do you recall what you said?" I swore his heart stuttered a beat before furiously picking up its pace. "You told me to never make a bargain with the devil. 'What's his is his.'"

"It was a figure of speech. A blood bargain does not equate possession."

"Perhaps not technically." My hand fell away and I stepped back. "You did it as another means of protecting me. In case I didn't want to accept our bond. You claimed no other prince of Hell would be stupid enough to challenge you. It was your secret way of offering me a way out of any contract with another demon House. The blood pact I made with Pride included. Am I wrong?"

"No."

"Don't answer now, but I want to know if what you said then stands."

"You'll have to be more specific. I said a great many things."

"If I am still yours."

He stilled. My words hung between us, heavy and lingering. Like his gaze.

"If I am, I would tell you that you are mine. That I am choosing you as my husband. There is no one I'd rather confront my demons with, no soul I'd travel through Hell with. And no one else I want standing beside me when I go to the Shifting Isles tomorrow."

He was quiet for a long moment, seeming to gauge my sincerity and weigh it against his own feelings. "And if I don't require time to think it over?"

Thank the goddess.

I exhaled quietly and moved from the balcony into his bedchamber, tugging the strings of my tunic loose as I passed by him. I glanced over my shoulder, noting with satisfaction the desire darkening his gaze as I slipped the shirt from my body and let it drop to the floor.

"Then I suggest coming to bed, your majesty."

ACKNOWLEDGMENTS

Writing a book during a global pandemic was quite a challenge, and I am immensely thankful for the following people who cheered me (and this story!) on.

Stephanie Garber—I am forever grateful to the hours of brainstorming and talking through scenes. But even more than that, I am so thankful for our friendship outside of publishing.

Anissa de Gomery—our friendship and love of books and food and all things romance is the best, just like YOU.

Isabel Ibañez—I am so happy I get to call you a dear friend. Thank you for reading early and giving stellar notes and for literally driving the extra mile(s) to come visit me with everyone. (Shout out to our lunch crew: Kristin Dwyer, Adrienne Young, Stephanie Garber, and my sister Kelli!)

To my family—I love and appreciate you beyond measure. Special thanks to my sister Kelli (Dogwood Lane Boutique) for reading early and whose store continues to inspire so many details in my books.

Barbara Poelle, my agent, friend, and forever champion, cheers to a DECADE of being partners in publishing crime.

To my teams at IGLA, Baror International, and Grandview—Maggie Kane, Irene Goodman, Heather Baror-Shapiro, and Sean Berard, thank you a million times over for all that you do.

To my new team at Little Brown Books for Young Readers and the NOVL, you took over this series with excitement and enthusiasm and your love of the characters shines brighter than Wrath's metallic tattoo. From my publishers, to the editorial team, marketing, library and publicity, the amazing production crew, the art department, and our sales and sub-rights departments, I am forever thankful for all of the hard work you do behind the scenes.

Special thanks to my editor Liz Kossnar for fully embracing the romance in this book, Virgina Allyn for creating the stunning map, Alvina Ling, Siena Koncsol, Savannah Kennelly, Stefanie Hoffman, Emilie Polster, Victoria Stapleton, Marisa Finkelstein, Scott Bryan Wilson, Tracy Shaw, Virginia Lawther, Danielle Cantarella, Shawn Foster, Claire Gamble, Karen Torres, Barbara Blasucci, Carol Meadows, Katharine Tucker, Anna Herling, Celeste Gordon, Leah Collins Lipsett, Janelle DeLuise, Elece Green, Michelle Figueroa, audiobook narrator Marisa Calin, and my publishers Megan Tingley and Jackie Engel. Publishing a book is no small feat, and you all made magic happen during a pandemic.

JIMMY Patterson Books—I'll always remain grateful for all this team and James Patterson has done to help launch my books into the world.

My UK family at Hodder & Stoughton—Molly Powell, Kate Keehan, Maddy Marshall, Laura Bartholomew, Callie Robertson, Sarah Clay, Iman Khabl, Claudette Morris, and the whole team, you are such rock stars and I am so happy I get to work with each of you.

To booksellers, librarians, indies, bloggers, Instagrammers, the Bookish Box, FairyLoot, the Librarian Box, and beloved, enthusiastic BookTok fans—you are the true magic makers. Thank you for talking about this series, for handselling it, and for all of the positive word of mouth. Each and every one of your efforts is appreciated more than you will ever know. I hope the magic you help create comes back your way tenfold.

ABOUT THE AUTHOR

Kerri Maniscalco grew up in a semi-haunted house outside New York City, where her fascination with gothic settings began. In her spare time she reads everything she can get her hands on, cooks all kinds of food with her family and friends, and drinks entirely too much tea while discussing life's finer points with her cats. She is the #1 *New York Times* and *USA Today* bestselling author of the Stalking Jack the Ripper quartet and *Kingdom of the Wicked*. She's always excited to share early snippets and teasers on Instagram @KerriManiscalco. For news and updates check out kerrimaniscalco.com.